A Petal in the Wind
Book 4

Lala

Smetana

OTHER BOOKS BY MIKO JOHNSTON

A Petal in the Wind

A Petal in the Wind, Book 1

Lala Hafstein, Book 2

The Great War, Book 3

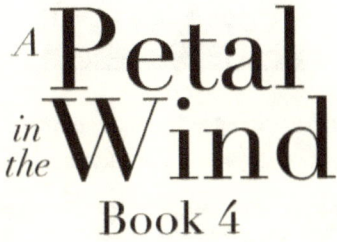

A Petal in the Wind

Book 4

Lala

Smetana

Whidbey Writers Group Press

Cover Design by Audrey Mackaman
Edited by Kitty Kladstrup

This is a work of fiction. Names, characters, places, brands, media, and incidents are either the product of the author's imagination or are used fictitiously. Any resemblance to similarly named places or to persons living or deceased is unintentional.

Print ISBN 978-1-944215-19-4

EPUB ISBN 978-1-944215-20-0

First Edition

DISCOUNTS OR CUSTOMIZED EDITIONS MAY BE AVAILABLE FOR EDUCATIONAL AND OTHER GROUPS BASED ON BULK PURCHASE.

For further information please contact wwgpress@gmail.com

Whidbey Writers Group Press is a d/b/a of
Whidbey Writers Group

DEDICATION

To Rose, my most devoted and sweetest fan –
105 years was not enough.

PART ONE

A FACTORY TOWN
NORTH OF PRAGUE
April 7, 1917

CHAPTER ONE

Lala Hafstein climbed the hill that led to her family's home alongside Josef Smetana, holding hands. A natural gesture, walking with the man she loved, fingers entwined, palms touching in a manner that was at once polite and intimate.

Hard to believe that twenty-four hours ago they'd been estranged, until she found him living in a dingy apartment in Prague. Even harder to believe that after seeing him again for the first time in over two years, she'd closed her heart and walked out the door, perceiving him as the man who'd led her to love but would not take her over the threshold. That is, not until she'd deduced how he had loved and protected her, very privately during her childhood, and more personally through the years, and even steadfastly amidst the unremitting hardships brought on by the past three years of war...

"Josef, you knew!"

She'd hurried back to him and Josef had admitted it was true – he had loved her long before she even knew him. At that, all the devotion, the love, and the desire she'd once held for him came rushing back. After that, she had no doubt she'd never live without him by her side.

Last night he'd taken her to his bed and made love to her. Unprepared for the intensity of this, she still basked in the exquisite pleasure of it, the feel of his skin against hers, the smell, the taste of him, with every step.

As they approached the wooded area before the meadow beyond, Lala gave Josef's hand a gentle tug and with an open glance at him, stopped. Even in childhood she thought him to be the handsomest man she'd ever seen, tall and trim, though a bit too trim now, courtesy of food rationing. The years had turned his brown hair more silver, and creases enfolded his eyes...his dark, mesmerizing eyes.

He drew her into his arms and kissed her, gently at first, then with more passion. Her thoughts swirled as she responded, reviving memories of their very first kiss in Berlin, of the first time he made her swoon in his private quarters, of the sensations that charged through her like electricity last night. How for a brief moment, the sorrow, deprivation, and adversity that filled their lives could be set aside. How they could be together, right now, despite what kept them apart.

And what still might.

He broke off the kiss. She wanted more, but knew they had to fulfill their mission first. That kiss fortified her for what was to come – facing her family, for they might not welcome her news. With hands clasped, they walked on.

She lifted her face toward the sky, seeking warmth from the sun that winked between the trees. Its brightness radiated through her closed eyes, turning her vision white, evoking a childhood memory...of sunshine blazing across a cloudless sky, of riding in a horse-drawn carriage...

Lala peered out at a copse of trees ahead. As they passed under the shade of the leafy canopy, the temperature fell several degrees. A gust of wind rode alongside their carriage, lifting spirals of dirt from the road and rustling the leaves until it sounded like applause....

This recollection came as she passed through the same stretch of road she'd crossed with her adoptive parents eighteen years earlier, when she became Lala Hafstein. When excitement started to outweigh the constant feeling of terror as the three traveled to their new home.

History repeats itself, she thought as she turned her gaze to Josef, her beloved. The events that preceded both journeys were equally tragic and equally miraculous. Horror and sorrow could give way to contentment, even joy, through the gift of love. Through a new family, although this time she wouldn't be the daughter. She'd be the wife—

She quickly purged the thought, forbidden as long as Josef's wife Romy was still alive. Josef had banished Romy from his life, with good reason, but now Romy was dying.

As the couple strode up the walkway to Lala's home, she spied her mother Sarah trudging away from her, carrying an armload of kindling branches toward the front door. With the war into its third year, Sabbath had ceased to be a day of rest as the need to survive became paramount.

Lala's two-year-old nephew Jacub sat on his heels, next to his mother Paulina alongside the vegetable garden. His face filled with wonder as she showed him how many of the seeds they'd planted two weeks ago had sprung up, yielding tiny shoots of green that would soon grow into peas and beans, beets and potatoes.

Lala tightened her grip on Josef's hand as she called out, "Mother?"

Turning, Sarah exclaimed, "Lala, you're home!" Relief washed over her. Then she noticed Josef standing by Lala, their hands clasped.

Lala could see it in her mother's face – she knew.

Paulina looked up and squinted into the sun until she focused on Lala and Josef. A glance at Sarah stopped her from approaching. Paulina attempted an impassive look but could not repress a smile at the sight of them together.

The toddler, however, ran to Lala, arms extended.

"Antila, Antila, you home!"

Lala knelt as he reached her. Laughing, she scooped him into her arms and hugged him. When he was little he couldn't pronounce "Auntie Lala," so he called her "Antila."

The little one turned his attention to Joseph. "Hello, I Jacub. Are you Papa?"

"No, Jacub. I'm not."

"He's your uncle Josef," Lala explained. "Papa is still fighting in the war."

Awe filled the toddler's face as he stared at Josef. "You big."

Josef chuckled. "I suppose I am. Would you like to be bigger than me?"

Jacub nodded, and Josef swooped him up, lifted him over his head and sat the boy on his shoulders. "Now what do you think?"

The boy giggled in delight as Josef carried him to his mother.

Paulina wiped her dirt-covered hand with a rag before offering it in greeting to Josef. "How lovely to see you again, Mr. Smetana."

"Josef, please."

"Then you must call me Paulina."

Lala waited behind as Josef stepped away with the boy perched on his shoulders. She watched her mother's gaze follow Josef, the tightening of her face.

Sarah turned back to Lala, standing alone on the pathway. Sarah's eyes began to ask questions, more than Lala could read from her face, let alone answer.

Lala took a deep breath for courage and said, "Why don't we go into the house."

CHAPTER TWO

News of Romy's death came on May fourth, four weeks after Lala had visited her in Bohnice Hospital where she'd been institutionalized. Romy's suffering had ended.

Josef took the news stoically, but by day's end Lala noticed how much his spirit had relaxed and his mind calmed. One chapter of their lives had been laid to rest. Time to start a new chapter.

After some discussion, Lala and Josef decided a simple wedding ceremony, to be held ten days later, would be appropriate. Sarah agreed with their decision to marry as soon as possible. Then she surprised them with a white crocheted bedspread she'd made, which they could use at their wedding for a traditional bridal canopy, the chuppah.

They set the date.

On the morning of May fourteenth, shortly after dawn, Lala sprang awake. She sat up and gazed around the room until she saw blonde curls splayed across a pillow; Paulina asleep in the adjacent bed. It struck Lala that this would be the last time she would sleep in her own bed, in the room she'd shared with Paulina since her father's death. After today, her life would be different. From this day forward, she would awaken next to Josef. Her beloved. Her husband.

A pleasant tingling coursed through her.

She left her bed and tiptoed to the closet.

"You're awake," murmured Paulina.

"Yes." She turned to her friend. "For the last time here, with you." Her eyes welled and she blinked back tears. "I will miss this."

Paulina laughed. "No, you won't. You'll be too happy waking up with your husband by your side to think about me."

Lala sat beside Paulina on her bed. "You once told me we were like sisters, but that no longer describes us. You are my sister, as much my sister as if we'd shared the same parents."

Tears filled Paulina's eyes. "I've felt that way for some time."

"I doubt anyone else could understand this, but despite what we've been through the last three years, living together in this house, sharing this room with you and then Jacub, have been some of the happiest times of my life."

They clung together and cried until Paulina swept away tears with her finger.

"I've been working on a surprise for you since you returned from Prague with Josef." She reached under her bed and pulled out a large white box tied with red ribbon, one of many remaining from the dress shop she'd been forced to close during the war.

"May I open it now?" Lala asked.

"Please do."

Inside was a chic wool jacket and skirt in dark blue, Josef's favorite color on her. She lifted the jacket out and held it against her. "Paulina, it's so beautiful."

"You should have something stylish to wear when you leave for your honeymoon. The belted jacket will flatter your figure, and longer, narrower skirts are in fashion. I borrowed a trick from Jeanne Paquin and added a few pleats to allow easier movement." The Parisian couturier had long inspired Paulina with her designs and her professional success.

Lala ran her hand over the soft fabric. "Something new. And it's something blue, so that's two out of four."

Paulina nudged Lala off her bed. "Josef will arrive at noon with the Rabbi. I'm taking my dress and Jacub's outfit into your mother's room. We'll get dressed there, and when you're ready I'll come help you put up your hair."

After Paulina left, Lala massaged a few drops of olive oil into her walnut hair and pinned it up, then donned her robe and ran a bath. As she undressed she caught her reflection in the mirror. Although very slender, more so than before the war, she no longer looked skeletal as she had months earlier. A wet autumn had destroyed much of the potato crop, followed by a bitter winter that left little food. She and her family had nearly starved; many others did.

With spring approaching, food had become more available, at least through foraging, an advantage they had over city dwellers. Her greatest hope remained a swift end to the war, but it continued on despite the arrival of American troops. With casualties, discontentment and hunger mounting, the home front had become almost as treacherous as the battlefield. She shut off the water flow and willed herself to do the same with bleak thoughts.

Lala luxuriated in the tub, letting the warm water soothe her body and spirit. When it turned tepid she stepped out and toweled herself dry. She glanced at the window. Hours ago she'd stood there, staring at the night sky filled with stars and a sliver of moon, reliving the moment Josef first took her in his arms and kissed her.

The tingling sensation returned.

From this day forward....

She returned to her room to dress. The silk crepe de chine bridal gown Paulina had made three years earlier, after Lala's engagement to Josef's son Armin, hung from the closet door. Designed to hug the body before flaring out from the knees to the hem, embroidered tulle ran along the shoulders and sleeves. Her finger traced the edge of a single appliquéd flower placed off-center on three crisp pleats that accented the waist.

Lala laid the dress across her bed and began to unbutton the back when she heard soft rapping at the door. She opened it to let her mother in.

"Oh Mother, you look absolutely stunning."

Sarah wore an antique gold high-waisted dress, with black velvet trim around the neckline as well as the pleated panel that resembled a half-opened fan, which wrapped across her belly and fastened along her left side. Paulina had pinned up Sarah's hair into a flattering chignon accented with a gold bow.

"Paulina made this for me. She said the higher neckline and empire waist would flatter and elongate my figure. That and these high heeled boots I saved from before the war." She peeked at her reflection in Lala's mirror and gave the bodice a tug over her full bosom. Sarah had lost several kilos since the war began. Out of habit she reacted as though she were still stout, though her elfin height hadn't changed.

She patted her gray hair into place and turned to Lala. "Before you get dressed, dear, I have one more secret to reveal."

On her wedding day? Lala tensed. "I thought we were through with secrets."

"This one is different." She reached into the pocket of her dress for a small box. "Back in 1914, when you became engaged to Armin, your father bought a gift which he intended to present to you on your wedding day." Sarah's eyes reddened. "As he can't be present, I..."

Lala hugged her mother. "I wish more than anything that he could be here. The hardest part of today will be walking down the aisle without him by my side."

"I know, dear, but he'll be here in spirit, as will Armin, and I'll be at your side every step of the way."

"For which I'm so grateful." Lala opened the box to find a silver brooch with multicolored cabochon stones. Signed by a jewelry artist named Josef Hoffmann, the design resembled an art deco gate.

"Your father said it reminded him of the modern furniture you admired."

"It's magnificent. I'll wear it today."

"It's forbidden to wear jewelry under the chuppah. I'll hold it for you until after the ceremony." Sarah reached into her pocket again. "I don't want the pin to spoil your dress. There's a small loop in the back to wear it as a pendant. You can hang it on my silver chain."

Lala strung the brooch on the chain. "That's something old and something borrowed."

"Let's get you into that dress." Sarah finished unbuttoning the back as Lala stepped into her ivory satin boots and laced them up. She slid the dress over her head and slipped her arms into the sleeves. "Would you please button me up?" she asked.

After Sarah had stretched up to close the last button, Lala turned around.

Overwhelmed with emotion, Sarah's hands fluttered and her face brimmed with joy although she looked ready to cry.

"Oh my, look at you. Never a more beautiful bride have I seen."

Lala kissed her mother's cheek. "Or happier."

Sarah's smile faded.

"What is it, Mother?"

Sarah turned away and paced. "As your mother, I'm supposed to explain to you what you should expect from marriage and prepare you for what will happen...tonight."

Lala waited and said nothing. Neither did her mother. Judging by the trepidation on her face Sarah seemed to be searching for the right words without success.

"What is it you want to tell me?" Lala asked.

Sarah stopped pacing and took a deep, audible breath. "We still have Jacub's cradle."

Lala coughed back a laugh. "Not to worry, Mother, I won't need that anytime soon."

Tension drained from Sarah's carriage and her face registered relief.

Lala told her, "Although I'm not concerned about tonight, I am about tomorrow, and every day thereafter. You and Father had a wonderful marriage, and I wish nothing more than to have that with Josef. Any advice?"

"There's no magic answer, dear," Sarah told her. "It's something you both will have to work out for yourselves. I sense you truly love him, and that he loves you. I also know you're both level-headed people and are not entering into marriage with starry eyes, which is good. Because no matter how much you love each other, dawn comes, the stars fall away and you're left with clear daylight." Her gaze swept across the room she once shared with her husband. "I wish your father was here to talk to you."

"He already did." Lala sat on the edge of her bed. "When I ended my engagement to Armin, I asked Father about the sort of man I should marry. He told me my future husband should share in common whatever is most important to me. When I asked him, 'How will I be sure,' he said, 'When the time comes, you'll know.' It's the same advice Mama and Papa gave me in my vision, when I was trying to decide whether to love you and Father, so I took Father's advice to heart.

"Josef is everything Father wanted for me. Our love may have begun as a head-in-the-clouds romance, but my feet have been firmly planted on the ground for some time. Josef loves our family. He honored his commitment and took care of Romy, even after everything she'd done, so he'll always be protective of me. And when I see him with Jacub, I know he will be a devoted father to any children we have. Josef has a loving heart and a strong character."

Her mother sat down next to Lala. "Then all I'll say is don't expect too much from him. You tend to idolize the men you love. But remember, Josef is a human being with flaws and faults like everyone else. Often the one quality that draws you to a husband becomes what will eventually drive you crazy. And you aren't perfect, either. You have a temper that flares when it's provoked. So learn to keep your heart open and your ears, and eyes, half closed."

"I'll remember what you've told me."

Sarah gave Lala's hand a pat. "Good. I'm not trying to

scare you."

"You're not. And I understand this is not what you hoped for or expected from me."

Sarah stood up and smoothed the creases from her dress. "I admit that when I first learned you were in love with Josef, it took me by surprise. He's much older than you, and for a time I worried I'd pushed you into it, when I urged you to marry into the family. Of course, at the time I meant his son, before we knew Armin's inclinations. But once I became accustomed to the idea, I realized if I were to choose a husband for you, I couldn't find anyone more ideal than Josef. I'm very happy for you, dear, and I'm sure your father is as well." Sarah turned to the door as footsteps echoed in the hallway. "That will be Paulina coming to fix your hair."

The Rabbi performed the ceremony in the two-story stone house where Lala grew up, with her mother, Paulina, and Jacub in attendance. Sarah had asked the Rabbi to bring his wife, two teenage sons and father-in-law to join in the family's celebration and hold the four poles of the chuppah. At Lala's insistence, they set out two empty chairs to symbolize Armin and her father Jakob's presence, placing a wildflower boutonniere on each seat. Paulina stood as Lala's matron of honor, her yellow dress complementing her flaxen hair. Josef had asked Jacub to be his best man, which thrilled the boy. He made a point of showing everyone the gold bands he'd been entrusted to carry for the couple.

At the appointed hour, Paulina and Jacub stood in the entryway alongside Josef as Sarah escorted Lala down the staircase, where a chair had been placed at the foot of the landing. When Lala sat, Josef lifted the veil that draped behind her head and covered her face with it. When she stood, Sarah stepped aside and Josef took Lala's arm in his. He escorted her into the parlor, followed by Paulina, Jacub and Sarah, where the Rabbi and his family waited. The couple stood together under the chuppah before the Rabbi. Lala handed her bouquet of tulips picked from an abandoned farmhouse to Paulina as the ceremony began.

The Rabbi's words echoed in her ears, but they barely registered until he instructed her to circle the groom seven times. At each pass, glances at her mother and Paulina caught them smiling and dabbing their eyes. Jacub stood very straight, with the two rings clutched in his little hands. He looked so serious she almost laughed. And Josef kept smiling although his eyes reddened, which brought forth tears to Lala. She'd seen him cry before but never in joy. When the seven circles were completed, she stood at Josef's right as the ceremony continued.

They drank wine from a shared cup as the Rabbi recited the blessing over the betrothal. They exchanged rings, signed the ketubah – the Jewish marriage contract – and received the seven blessings over a second cup of wine.

The Rabbi set a glass wrapped in a napkin on the floor in front of Josef and said, "Marriage is a covenant, which we make by breaking or cutting something, as the Ten Commandment tablets were broken. The tradition of breaking the glass has more than one meaning in our faith. It is said that even on a joyous occasion, we must recall the sorrow of the destruction of the Temple in Jerusalem. Then there are some who say this is the last time the groom gets to put his foot down."

The Rabbi's wife chuckled at that.

Josef shattered the glass with his foot, which Sarah and

the Rabbi's family acknowledged with a cry of "Mazel Tov!" and a round of applause, joined by the others, as Josef and Lala kissed.

When the ceremony ended, the adults celebrated with a cognac toast. At one o'clock the photographer arrived and took pictures of the bride and groom. Afterward, the family and guests sat down to the best lunch Josef's cook Mrs. Havlik could manage.

After lunch, the Rabbi's wife volunteered to clear the table while Lala went upstairs to change. She fetched her suitcase for Josef to bring to the car and prepared to leave with him for the train station.

Josef bent to kiss Sarah's cheek. He picked up Lala's suitcase. "I'll wait for you in the automobile," he told Lala before leaving.

Lala hugged Jacub. "I'll bring you a present from Prague when I return next week," she promised, then turned to Paulina.

"Well, my friend, here we are. Two married women," Lala said, and hugged her.

Paulina blinked back tears. "I wish you every happiness, my friend."

Lala kissed Paulina's cheek, then wiped the lipstick off with her finger. "You as well." She approached her mother, arms out, and they embraced tightly.

When it ended, her mother asked, "Aren't you forgetting something?" as she gestured to Lala's bouquet. "You're supposed to throw it."

"And who's to catch the bouquet, you or Jacub?" she laughed.

"It's too pretty to waste. What would you like to do with it?"

She handed it to her mother. "Lay them on Father's grave."

Sarah had teared up often during the marriage ceremony, but she wept openly at those words.

CHAPTER THREE

The newlyweds' pace quickened as they climbed the stairs to Josef's apartment on U Luzichkeho Seminaire in the Mala Strana, Prague's "little quarter" along the west bank of the Vltava River. They wanted to spend their honeymoon in the flat where they renewed their courtship and first made love.

Josef lifted her in his arms and carried her over the threshold.

"Put me down, Josef, save your strength," she teased.

He set her down on the sofa and stood before her, arms crossed. "Already casting aspersions on my virility, are you?"

She could tell by his mischievous grin he was teasing her back. She reached up to stroke his chest. "Do you remember our first tryst in your private quarters at the factory?"

He eyed her warily. "I recall our amorous activities ended rather abruptly...where is this going?"

"Afterward, when I expressed my concern about what might result, you implied there were ways to avoid that complication."

His body went rigid. "Are you telling me that you don't want to have children?"

"No, my love, only...not yet. I want to wait until the war

29

ends. I watched how Jacub suffered. He's still small for his age and I worry he'll never catch up. I don't want our children to endure deprivation, so if you have ways of preventing that..."

"There are ways."

She stood and moved close to him and asked, "Then will you show me?" before drawing him in for a kiss.

They spent the afternoons wandering the streets, in part to seek out areas where they could spend weekends and holidays, then live full time once Josef retired from the factory. Lala accepted Josef's decision to not move into his mansion. She hoped in time the memories of that harrowing day that forced him out would diminish, and eventually, after they'd had children of their own, their new family would use the house as their retreat from city life.

As they strolled they saw firsthand how the war had taken its toll. Although far from the battlefield, critical shortages fueled demonstrations that rocked the city. Looting left shops damaged; several storefronts and buildings had boarded up windows.

Lala turned to Josef. "Are we wrong to be enjoying ourselves like this, with the war still going and everyone suffering so?"

"We fought, too, for this bit of happiness. Let us enjoy it while we can."

One day she and Josef played tourist, counting the statues along the Charles Bridge as they crossed into Stare Mesto, the historic old town. From there they meandered along the streets to the Old Town Square. They waited in front of the Gothic tower of Old Town Hall for the hour to strike and watched with amusement as the tower clock's two trap doors opened, followed by a procession of the Twelve Apostles.

Lala pointed out to Josef two others who watched with them; young children staring at the spectacle, utterly enchanted, while their mothers stood behind them complaining about how much prices had gone up in the market. Their voices grew louder and soon other mothers with their children began to gather, echoing their disgust with shortages in the market. She felt Josef grasp her arm.

"We should leave now before a demonstration starts."

"But I agree with them."

"Do you want to spend the rest of our honeymoon in jail, or worse?"

They escaped the gathering crowd and hurried away toward the Jewish quarter.

"I don't recall seeing this much damage across the river," Lala observed along one street near the synagogue, strewn with litter and broken glass.

They forewent their planned dinner in a local restaurant and returned to their apartment. Tinned fish, leftover bread and jam would have to do, though Josef scrounged up a nice Chablis. They finished the bottle and decided to turn in early.

Lala peeled back the covers and climbed into bed. "Tomorrow, let's stay on this side of the river."

Josef closed the draperies before joining her. "A good plan. I have always preferred the Mala Strana to the old town."

"I do as well."

***

31

The following morning, after walking to Pražský hrad, Prague's castle, for a glimpse, they strolled the neighborhood. Lala spotted an unusual two story house at the tip of Tržiště Street. She stood for a moment and admired the splendid Renaissance-style mansion before continuing north along the street toward Malostranské Square.

As they approached Letenská Street, Josef took her hand. "My agent Cerveny's office is on the next block. I want to stop in and speak with him."

Lala remembered Emil Cerveny, the silver-haired gentleman who had surreptitiously arranged for Josef to purchase Lala's Monet painting when she needed money. Cerveny also paid Romy's hospital bills, which was how Lala found Josef living in Prague.

They entered an arcaded building and climbed two flights of stairs to the office. Cerveny's assistant, a young man wearing a prosthetic mask of tin where his left eye and nose should have been, looked up from his paperwork as they entered. Although Lala had seen a few disfigured war veterans in Prague, she had to force herself not to stare.

He rose from his seat. "Good afternoon, Mr. Smetana."

"Good afternoon, Tomas. May I present my wife."

Tomas froze.

Josef explained, "I have recently remarried, which is why I'm here."

Tomas bowed in recognition. "May I offer my congratulations, Mr. Smetana, Mrs. Smetana. I will inform Mr. Cerveny of your arrival."

Before he could, Cerveny stepped out of his office. His poised carriage bespoke of good breeding, but the surprise on his face upon seeing her was apparent.

"Mr. Smetana. Miss Hafstein. You're here. How did

you...?" To Tomas he said, "Had you already sent them telegrams?"

"No, Mr. Cerveny." Tomas turned to Lala. "Are you, that is, were you Miss Lala Hafstein before your marriage?"

"I was."

Cerveny apparently understood. "Then I'm glad you're both here. If you have time, we can see to our business."

"What business is that, Mr. Cerveny?" she asked.

"The last will and testament of Romy Smetana. Please, come into my office."

They entered a cozy room filled with bookcases. Tomas brought coffee for all as Cerveny took a seat behind his desk. "First, allow me to offer my congratulations on your marriage. I must say this simplifies matters." He almost smiled.

"How so?" asked Josef.

"The only names mentioned in the will are Josef Smetana and Lala Hafstein, who is now Mrs. Smetana. Shall we settle this today?"

Lala's head spun. The cool air did nothing to quell her shock as she and Josef walked back to his apartment.

"You can't be surprised that Romy remembered you in her will," Josef said as they crossed the street.

"I expected she might have left me a piece of jewelry, but not the bulk of her estate. I had no idea you didn't own the house."

"Unlike me, Romy came from a wealthy family. Her father owned the factory and I worked for him. That is how we met. Her parents gave Romy the house as a wedding present, and I received the factory. She inherited a great deal of jewelry from her mother, some real estate holdings and a few collectables from her parents, but as you know, I purchased most of the furniture and art over the years."

He sounded defensive, but she accepted this. It would be natural, a part of his complicated relationship with his former wife. She asked, "What does it matter whether I inherited her estate or you? We're married now. It's ours."

"Then I won't have to pack up my possessions and cart them away, unless you insist."

Horrified, Lala hissed, "That isn't funny, Josef." She shook her head. "What will people think?"

"That Romy was very fond of you, which is true."

"Still, leaving you nothing but a reimbursement for her expenses while in Bohnice Hospital and a few antiques doesn't seem fair," Lala said. "It's hard to believe she had a period of lucidity before she passed away. Changing her will like that at the last minute will seem suspicious."

They turned onto U Luzichkeho Seminaire. Josef started to chuckle. "You may be wealthier than I am now."

"And you find that funny?"

"At least no one can say you married me for my money."

She laughed with him at that.

They returned to his flat. As they entered Lala recalled the first time she came here, just months ago. How shabby it looked. Josef was far from poor....

Then why had he been living so austerely in Prague when she found him?

CHAPTER FOUR

Lala still hadn't shaken her feeling about Josef's apartment, but curiosity failed to prod her into asking him why he chose to live there. Following her mother's advice to... *"keep your heart open and your ears and eyes half-closed,"* sounded better than admitting cowardice.

When the week ended, Lala and Josef left the apartment and moved into Paulina's house, which allowed Josef to return to work at his factory. Her mother and Paulina had prepared the long vacant house for the newlyweds in her absence. Lala spent the first day familiarizing herself with their new home while Josef went to the factory to meet with the managers.

At four o'clock she began cooking dinner and set the table. It brought back warm memories. Every evening, upon hearing her husband's approaching footsteps outside, Sarah would check her appearance in the entryway mirror before greeting Jakob with a peck on the cheek and a glass of Scotch. Then she'd leave him to relax in the parlor as she returned to the kitchen to finish dinner. During the time Lala co-managed the factory, her mother did the same for her. Lala came to treasure that half hour before dinner, when she

35

could sit back and forget about the troubles and travails of work. It became a lovely respite, a moment of peace and tranquility in a challenging time. Josef would enjoy it as much as she had.

Dinner simmered on the stove when Josef returned home. Lala offered him a glass of cognac, which he declined in favor of sherry. He selected a bottle that he'd brought from his apartment and opened it while she got two glasses from the cupboard.

Josef sniffed the cork and laid it down. He handed her the bottle. "Something smells...interesting. What are we having for dinner?"

"Tinned fish, with potatoes and some early peas from my – that is, Mother's garden. It's almost ready." She poured them both a glass.

"Then come sit with me in the parlor," he said.

She followed him out of the kitchen, bringing the sherry glasses with her. "What was it like to be back in your factory after all this time?" she asked as she handed him a glass.

He took a sip. "Very strange. I hadn't seen the ambulatory equipment and prosthetic limbs we're producing before today. Hajek and Strahov have done a superb job of running the factory. The production lines are operating so smoothly I almost feel as though I'm not needed."

"You will be, more so, when the war ends and they switch back to making furniture. Remember, they became co-managers after the conversion to wartime production had been completed." She stopped herself from adding that she oversaw the conversion.

Lala cuddled up with him on the sofa as they drank their sherry. The room had a decidedly masculine feel, which had been deliberate. At the beginning of the war, Lala had converted Paulina's home into a boarding house for three men who worked at the factory. Dear, sweet Elia had traveled to Italy to visit his family, but couldn't return when the country switched allegiance to the Allies. Lew was drafted when he turned eighteen, and Gershom Kindemann, her factory co-manager who'd briefly courted her, had to flee after he killed a man to protect her.

All had left the country, and her life.

She pushed the thought from her mind and returned her focus to the parlor. She could change some of the décor. Lala didn't expect Josef to be ready to return to the mansion yet, but she had full access to the mansion's contents. She could transform the rooms into a home more suitable for a married couple, which she explained to Josef.

"I'll leave the decorating to you, love," he said.

"I won't do too much, as we'll only be here temporarily."

"What do you mean?" His eyes narrowed, and his tone sounded more accusatory than curious.

Caught off-guard by his reaction, she answered, "The house belongs to Paulina. When Ivo comes home, and even if God forbid he doesn't, she'll want to return here. We'd have to find new housing and I don't think you want to move in with my mother."

Josef set his empty glass on the table. "I thought Paulina said Ivo wanted to live in Prague. "

"That's likely as he intended to teach at Charles University, but they couldn't afford two houses. I suppose Paulina could sell it to us, if you wanted to live here."

"Who knows if we'll even want to stay here."

His dark mood puzzled Lala. "When you said you wanted a *pied à terre* in Prague, I assumed that meant our primary residence would be somewhere here, near your factory."

"And by here you mean over the next hill," he said, gesturing in the direction of the mansion. "You surprise me, Lala. Do you really want to live in that overly grand home? Does that lifestyle appeal to you?"

"Not particularly, but it was your home—"

"Not anymore."

"Love, we're married. It's our home."

"No, Lala. It will never be mine again."

So that was it. "If Romy leaving it to me bothers you that much, I'll sign it over to you right now. I don't want this – her – ruining our marriage."

Josef leaned over to kiss her. "I love you very much, but that won't change anything."

"... *It will never be mine again...*"

Whether out of anger or hurt, Josef still couldn't separate the mansion from the atrocities that forced him out. She'd expected the bad memories to eventually fade once a sense of normalcy returned; he would reassume ownership of his former home as he currently was of his factory. How foolish of her not to consider that his misgivings might be permanent.

Lala gathered the empty sherry glasses and said, "Dinner should be ready now."

She tried to engage Josef into talking about the factory as they ate, wondering who still worked there and how production was going, but he didn't want to discuss it in any detail. Honoring her mother's rule of avoiding stressful talk at the dinner table, she changed the subject to their living quarters, which he found more agreeable.

Later, as they prepared for bed, Josef said, "You should hire a maid to do the housework."

"Perhaps Mrs. Havlik could recommend someone. I'll speak with her tomorrow."

Mrs. Havlik knew of no one qualified and available. She suggested Lala speak to the women who lined up at the market. Lala could then train the woman to keep house in a manner that suited her. She also advised Lala of a fair salary for an inexperienced housekeeper. Lala thanked her and left. As she walked out of the Smetana mansion, she looked back at the house she'd visited so many times, as a child, as a teenager, as a young woman. The house that now belonged to her, but where she couldn't reside, not with Josef.

Lala asked around on market day and found a war widow with two preteen children who was willing to take the job. The next day, Mrs. Klima arrived at the appointed time. Lala invited her in and observed how large the woman's eyes became as she stepped inside the house. Extensive repairs to the exterior and upgrading to the interior, courtesy of the former boarders, gave the home an elegance that belied its original state. The improvements complemented Lala's skill at decorating. She'd furnished the rooms with several fine pieces from her parents' house, including a few made by her late father, as well as expensive objets d'art sent as gifts by her Aunt Naomi. As she escorted the woman into the parlor she suddenly felt self-conscious and blurted, "It's not a very big house...."

Mrs. Klima's eyes grew impossibly larger. "Why, my whole house could practically fit inside this room," she blurted, and pressed her lips together.

Lala cleared her throat. "Shall we start upstairs?"

Lala walked Mrs. Klima through the house, explaining her

duties, which the woman responded to with nodding and very little comment. She seemed surprised when Lala asked to have the bed linens changed twice a week at the behest of Josef.

"How often must I do laundry then?" she asked.

"Once a week will suffice," explained Lala. The notion of owning more than one set of bed linens appeared to stun the woman. Lala pulled back the bed covers to reveal spotless sheets with frayed edges.

Lala did not include food preparation in Mrs. Klima's duties. She remembered the difficulty her mother's maid-in-training had learning about the special requirements of a Kosher kitchen. Without the daily responsibility for cleaning and laundry, cooking would be a simpler chore. She would have more time to work in her garden, perhaps raise chickens again like she did at her mother's house. She'd have time for other endeavors as well.

Leaving Mrs. Klima to her duties, Lala fetched her drawing paper, intending to make detailed sketches of each room she wanted to revamp. Since their home was temporary, better to leave the furnishings as is and refresh the rooms with art, pieces that had meaning to Josef and her. She would save her design skills for another time. Another place.

Lala and Josef pooled their resources with her mother and Paulina. Lala restocked her mother's henhouse with half a dozen chicks and through Josef's connections they procured one egg layer. Lala's garden couldn't provide enough food for them all, but the steady business at his factory enabled its managers to purchase food on the black market to supplement the employees' rations. Josef took advantage of his share. Although Lala still objected to the idea morally, she couldn't bear to see her family suffer as they did the previous winter. The lesser of two evils, she decided.

By midsummer, with adequate food on the table, a roof over their heads and, thanks to her housekeeper, time to focus on other things, Lala sensed there was one more project she needed to tackle. The question was whether Josef was ready.

CHAPTER FIVE

It took days of gentle prodding from Lala to convince Josef the time had come for them to visit his former home. She wanted a complete inventory so they could decide what to keep and what should be sold, including perhaps the mansion itself. He agreed, albeit reluctantly.

Josef had not stepped foot into the house since the end of the mourning period, shiva, for his son and the institutionalizing of his first wife, Romy. To the world, she went mad after Armin's death in Berlin. What no one outside their small circle knew was that Romy had paid a henchman to violently threaten Armin's male lover, Karel, to leave her son. Severely beaten, Karel had secretly fled to America. Unbeknownst to anyone, before Karel had left, he and Armin had switched identities. Armin had announced he'd joined the military, so Romy assumed it was Karel who'd returned to the men's apartment when she instructed the henchman to "go back and finish it once and for all."

That command led to Armin's murder; his body dumped like garbage into Lake Wannsee outside of Berlin. Learning she was responsible for Armin's contract killing drove Romy insane. Years of ingesting a complexion tonic laced with arsenic led to her early death.

Josef arranged for Smolak, his former chauffeur and now house steward, to pick them up. Josef had kept on a skeletal staff to oversee his mansion, primarily to ensure their employment, which Lala had embraced and continued. Smolak, a tall, stocky man with kind eyes and a fleshy nose anchored by a handlebar moustache, radiated good cheer in seeing his employer once again, his gratitude apparent.

Lala had ridden in the back seat of the Rolls Royce many times when she co-ran the factory in Josef's absence, but being here with Josef felt pleasurable. She sat back, leaned against Josef and closed her eyes.

The last time Smolak drove her to the mansion was to pay a shiva call to Josef after Armin's death…

Ten men stood in a circle, prayer shawls draped across their shoulders, bowing back and forth as they recited Kaddish, the mourners' prayer. She spotted Josef among them. Upon the mantle, two candles burned side by side. One for a dead son, one for the woman who was now dead to her husband….

She pushed the painful memory from her thoughts as Smolak parked the vehicle in the mansion's driveway.

Smolak opened the rear door and offered his hand to Lala. Once she stepped out, he went around to open the door for Josef. "Shall I have Mrs. Havlik prepare lunch for you and Madame?" he asked.

"Please call me Mrs. Smetana, Smolak."

"As you wish…Mrs. Smetana."

She saw the hint of a smile when he addressed her by her new name.

***

Mrs. Havlik, the cook Josef had promoted to head housekeeper, met them at the door, her hair now as white as her apron. As Lala stepped inside she caught her breath. The once magnificently appointed house now seemed bereft, thanks to Romy's drinking. Much of the fine furnishing and paintings had disappeared, used to buy cognac on the black market. The antique Aubusson rug that covered the grand hall's marble floor had gone to Romy's henchman. It had purchased Armin's death.

Lala perceived Josef tense up as they entered. He stopped, glanced around the great hall, and his eyes filled with tears. She expected this to be difficult, but the depth of his reaction startled her. The sorrow that filled his last days in the house had erased all the happy moments from the quarter century before. She touched his arm and said, "Go into the kitchen, where you have no memories. I had Smolak stack some of your books there. Sort through them and leave the inventory of the house to me."

Lala went from room to room with Smolak, writing down everything she found—all manner of furniture, lighting, draperies and rugs. Paintings and statues. Shortly after noon Lala joined Josef in the kitchen for lunch.

Mrs. Havlik set out two bowls of soup with bread for them. Josef seemed uncomfortable. After a few bites he put his soup spoon down.

"I cannot spend another minute here." His face looked as if he hadn't slept in days.

"Have Smolak drive you home. I will take care of this for us."

He brought her hand to his lips and kissed it. With a ragged breath, he got up and left.

Lala resigned herself to the fact that they might never live here. So be it. She would keep all of Josef's prized possessions, then put the house with the remaining contents on the market. When it sold, she'd allocate the money toward someplace new, someplace without tragic memories for Josef. Someplace where they could make their own memories.

Mrs. Havlik accompanied Lala as she went through the kitchen and pantry. Missing were the gold rimmed Bavarian china, the French crystal, and the English sterling, pieces she remembered so well from the many formal dinners at Armin's invitation. Lala trusted Mrs. Havlik enough to believe Romy sold it all on the black market.

Lala entered the dining room and turned on the lights. The trio of Murano glass chandeliers reminded her of the last time she had dined here, on the night of her engagement to Armin. He'd presented her with the ring she now wore on her right hand, a lovely pearl surrounded by small diamonds. The ring had belonged to Josef's mother. After she and Josef shared their first kiss in Berlin, it became a symbol of her love for him.

Once she surveyed the room, Lala switched off the lights before continuing.

She excused Mrs. Havlik to return to her duties when Smolak returned. Lala stepped into the parlor, still resplendent in its Venetian décor, including a Canaletto painting of Venice upon the wall. Scenes from the past played in her mind as she glanced around. This room was where she first met the Smetana family on her seventh birthday and where she celebrated her next ten birthdays.

The parlor was where, as a child, she became captivated by the Monet painting that had hung on the wall, the painting

Josef gave her years later. Where she'd convinced Armin to marry her. Where she'd tried to bolster Romy's spirits to keep her from drinking. Where she'd learned of Armin's fate. Some painful memories, she thought, but many more good ones.

Several crates had been stacked against the wall between the windows and fireplace. She called Smolak into the room and asked, "What are these?"

"Some of the household items retrieved by the police," he explained.

She riffled through the contents. The Corot painting that used to hang in the great hall was among the items, as was the Aubusson rug. She pushed away the dark memories and continued her inventory.

Dusk had fallen by the time they reached the second floor. She asked Smolak to wait downstairs while she finished the day in Josef's bedroom. The memory of that dreadful night when she last walked into his room sent a shiver down her back.

She entered and caught her breath. In the darkness, the bedroom looked as it had the only other time she'd been here, when she sought to comfort Josef in the depths of his grief after learning of Armin's murder. But it was she who left the room in grief when he told her they could no longer be together...

"I have no choice. Whether Romy is declared insane or tried for murder, I cannot divorce her because neither insanity nor imprisonment are legal grounds. And where would that leave us?"

Lala jotted the contents of the room on her list and hurried out, dazed. She walked down the long corridor, ignored the stairway and continued to the three rooms at the end of the hall. Memories from childhood flowed through her with every step....

"Which is your room, Armin?"

"All three." He pointed to the door on the left. *"This is where I have my classes. Opposite it is my bedroom, and in between is my playroom. Would you like to see it?"*

She opened the door to Armin's playroom and peered inside. It was still a wondrous place, lined with colorful hand-painted shelves once filled with toys, stuffed animals, and books. Now most lay empty. In one corner of the room the fanciful wooden horse with rocking chair legs sat idle, awaiting a rider. She walked over to stroke the painted wood. Her fingernail caught on the ragged edge of an ear, where the paint had chipped off. Still, she thought, what child wouldn't treasure this?

In the opposite corner was a table and chair and in between, a row of chests, low enough for a child to sit upon, along the wall with a bay window in its center...

"I have something for you." Armin went to a chest and lifted the top. *"My father had told me it was your birthday today, so I made you a present...a drawing of your house."*

Standing in the room where her friendship with Armin was born brought back warm memories of it all. This house was where she grew to love him, grew to love art. How could she let go of that? Eventually, Josef would get past the tragic events that befell him and fall in love with his former home again, wouldn't he?

She left the room, frozen in time, and closed the door behind her before going downstairs. "Smolak, I'm ready to return home."

***

After her visit to the mansion, Lala wrote a letter to the staff addressing their concerns about changes that would occur. She commended them for their ongoing care of the property. She thanked them for preserving the orchard trees from felling, converting sections of the lush grounds to vegetable gardens, and raising chickens for eggs. She assured them that whatever produce they raised that her family didn't need, the staff could keep. Combined with their other resources, none of them would starve as long as the weather cooperated.

Lala asked Mrs. Klima if she would also clean Sarah's house for double her salary. The woman accepted the offer. Lala's new role as Mrs. Josef Smetana was falling into place.

CHAPTER SIX

Of all Lala's chores, none pleased her more than restocking the food pantry. Although bare spots remained on the shelves, Josef's share of factory rations and what she could buy in the market kept an adequate supply in the cupboards. Between the mansion and her mother's garden, they'd reaped a decent harvest throughout summer and fall. Relief came knowing she and her extended family wouldn't starve this winter.

No longer forced to scrape by day to day, and with Mrs. Klima tending to the house, Lala had more time to pursue other activities. She attempted painting again but was disappointed in the results and decided her time could be better spent while Josef was at work.

On days when Josef went to the factory she had Smolak bring her to the mansion. Accepting the futility of keeping it when Josef couldn't bring himself to return didn't deter her from inventing reasons to visit. At present, only a war profiteer could afford to buy the house, something she could not abide. That, and her desire to keep loyal employees like Smolak and Mrs. Havlik working delayed her from seeking a

51

buyer.

Completing the inventory and preparing lists of what to keep and what to sell kept her busy for several weeks. She tried to get Josef involved with the decisions, but other than his personal assets he refused to participate. With that task finished she sought a new one.

She brought out her old portfolio and found sketches she'd made of the splendid rooms in the Hotel Grande in Berlin. They no longer brought back memories of those heady days before the war began, when the undercurrents of rage and fear charged the city like static in the air before a thunderstorm. Instead they reminded her of her passion, abandoned long ago – decorating the interiors of homes, businesses, public spaces and especially hotels and inns. She had a knack for creating rooms as comfortable as they were beautiful. That skill proved invaluable when the war began; she rearranged the furnishings in her home to accommodate Paulina moving in, as well as Paulina's home to create an income-earning boarding house.

Once peace was declared, Josef would take charge of the factory's conversion back to making furniture, returning it to the business he loved. Lala had already told Josef she'd like to work there again, creating a showroom that would display furniture arranged as it would be in an interior space like a parlor or bedroom. Josef had promised she could advise on styles, finishes, fabrics, and colors in the design process as well. That plan had to wait, but she could prepare for that day.

Lala studied the set of blueprints of the mansion included in the documents of Romy's estate. It showed the room dimensions as well as the placement of doorways, windows and fireplaces. She fetched her sketchbook, a ruler and pencil, and began to draw.

After clearing away the breakfast dishes, Lala poured coffee for Josef and herself before sitting beside him in the kitchen. Weak winter sun reflected on the bare trees in the yard. Josef looked pensive, which made Lala wonder what he was thinking about.

"Have you plans today?" he asked.

"Nothing important. Why?"

"Would you consider coming with me to the factory? I've decided to sell some of the objets d'art I keep in the office and would like your opinion."

Lala leaned over to kiss him. "My love, nothing would make me happier than helping you. What made you decide to sell some of your collection now?"

"I'm curious to see if there's a market for it. Besides, it will be more constructive than anything else I can do at the factory."

Lala forced a smile. Josef still hadn't gotten used to the change in the product line. Although most of his duties had involved running the factory, the pleasure came from creating the furniture they once produced. Wheelchairs and prosthetics did not have the same appeal as tables and bureaus. He rarely stayed at work all day and on more than one occasion he had returned home before she'd begun dinner.

She gulped down her coffee. "I'll change my clothes quick as wings and be ready by the time Smolak arrives."

***

Miko Johnston

Lala, wearing the honeymoon outfit Paulina had made for her, followed Josef into the building. Upon entering the factory for the first time in three years, she was struck by how little it had changed, including most of the faces who acknowledged her. Several of the executive staff came to greet her. Many addressed her by her maiden name before Josef corrected them.

Mr. Hajek, one of the factory's co-managers, bounded from his office. "Welcome back, Miss, that is, Mrs. Smetana. And may I offer you my belated congratulations on your nuptials in person." He shook her hand and offered a smile as broad as it was genuine. She and Hajek had clashed early on, but they earned each other's respect during the factory conversion. He'd always expressed gratitude to Lala for recommending him for the position he now held.

"I have something to show you," he said in a mischievous tone before darting back to his office. Moments later he emerged, pushing a boxy wheelchair which he parked beside her. "Do you remember this?"

"Oh my," she laughed out of embarrassment. An error in measurement resulted in the awkward looking device before her. Several dozen units were manufactured before anyone realized the blunder. Fortunately, she and Gershom, who'd designed the wheelchair, came up with a clever way to surmount the problem. "My great mistake."

Hajek shook his finger. "No mistake, Miss. This has been one of our best-selling devices. No one else had the foresight to design a wheelchair with this type of shelf before. But now several companies have copied our model and sales have fallen."

"What have you done to upgrade this unit?" she asked.

"We discussed offering a free commode or a blanket."

54

"That would raise the price too much to be competitive. What about something simpler, like extra padding?"

Hajek patted the seat cushion. "They're already padded."

"Can you pad the arm rests?" She felt Josef grab her wrist and give it a gentle squeeze.

"Mr. Hajek, my wife has other duties to see to."

"Of course, I apologize. It's just that she...." He fell silent.

Josef's grip became firmer. She removed his hand from hers.

"Excuse us, Mr. Hajek. I must help my husband sort his figurines."

Together they walked toward Josef's office in silence. She understood his displeasure in her taking the lead in a business discussion, but not his hostility. They passed Josef's private sitting room, where she'd enjoyed her first tryst with him. She would never forget a moment of it, not a caress, not a kiss. She knew that for certain, as sure as she knew that a repeat performance was out of the question today.

The war dragged on into the new year. Once a week Lala would accompany Josef in the automobile and after Smolak brought Josef to the factory, he would drive her to the mansion. She had the staff help her move the furnishings to be sold into the ballroom and whatever she wanted to keep for herself and Josef into the parlor. That still left a great deal of furnishings in place, their future undetermined.

Lala went upstairs and meandered through the bedrooms. Each looked beautiful, pleasing to the eye, but they left her indifferent. Was it due to bad memories of what happened here? It couldn't be; she'd never been in most of these rooms.

Picturing her future job creating displays for the factory, she pondered how she could make each room more inviting, more of a living space than an arrangement of beds, tables and chests, something that would appeal to buyers. She repositioned some furniture and varied the décor, but it didn't change her feeling that something was missing.

Mrs. Havlik entered the room with a maid in training, who carried a stack of fresh linens. "Pardon me, Mrs. Smetana," she said. "We'll come back later." She directed the trainee to the next room, and began to leave when Lala called her back.

"Mrs. Havlik, what do you think this room lacks?"

The woman thought for a moment. "I would have to say it's what all the rooms in this house lack. People. A room is just a place to store things unless it's occupied."

Lala gazed through the room with fresh eyes, imagining it filled with guests, perhaps artists or antiques dealers from the city, here to spend a quiet weekend in the country. Friends. Family. Children.

"Would you come with me, Mrs. Havlik?" Lala led the housekeeper to Armin's former quarters. She opened the center door to the playroom and pictured it filled, not only with playthings but with little ones at play...bobbing to and fro on the rocking horse, cuddling stuffed animals, or building castles out of wooden blocks carved with numbers and letters. She could envision them curling up on the window seat with a picture book, or being read a story, or mounting the drawing they'd just made on the easel.

She turned to Mrs. Havlik. "Do you know if any of Armin's old toys and books have been kept?"

"I believe some were stored in the attic, Mrs. Smetana. Would you like me to have the staff bring them down?"

"Please. Tell them to stack everything in this room and I'll sort through them."

"Very well, Mrs. Smetana."

Mrs. Havlik's observation became clear to Lala. Rooms weren't meant to be looked at, but lived in. The house needed people. She breathed in with excitement. *Then it comes alive.*

She envisioned the mansion as a luxurious country getaway. To tackle the design of each room, she pictured a guest or family staying there, considering not only what they'd like, but what they'd need to be comfortable in an unfamiliar place. Practical concerns became as important as the room's appearance. She wanted to keep the feeling of luxury without the formality, so she chose less ornate furnishings and added fabrics with tactile appeal. All this would translate well when she assumed charge of the factory's showcase department, creating a living environment within four walls that people could picture themselves in, with the comfort and charm that would let them slip into the space and feel at home.

She tackled the playroom first, setting it up so nannies could bring their young charges there to have fun. Then one by one she redesigned the guestrooms, saving the three formerly occupied bedrooms for last. She'd instructed Smolak and staff to strip Romy's room bare on her first visit. Neither she nor Josef wanted any of Romy's possessions, so they were set aside for sale.

Lala cherished the view of the gardens afforded by French doors and balcony. The placement of furniture needed to take full advantage of it. A platform upon which Romy's hand-painted and gilded four poster bed once stood cried out for something comparably striking. Lala made a few preliminary drawings before walking to the other end of the hallway to Josef's former bedroom.

Of all the rooms, his felt the most comfortable. Elegant and lavish with fine furnishings, but not teeming with décor or overly embellished. A decidedly masculine feel infused the space. Lala sensed no one but Josef had ever spent time here. A few feminine touches would change it from a man's abode to a room suitable for a couple. A dressing table to balance the writing desk. A place to store her rings and bracelets as well as one for his cufflinks and shirt studs. A well-dressed bed designed not only for sleeping, but for passion.

She fetched her inventory list of furnishings in the home and with a renewed purpose, began to sketch.

CHAPTER SEVEN

With her sketches completed and spring approaching, Lala turned her attention to gardening. She decided to use the plot she'd developed at her former home as an excuse to visit her mother, Paulina, and Jacub. Gardening had taught her forbearance, unlike Josef.

His impatience with the factory grew worse. She tried to get him interested in helping in the garden, but he wasn't keen on working in the dirt. He spent another day at home, restless, moving from room to room as Mrs. Klima cleaned.

"Why don't you go to work if you're bored?" Lala asked him.

"I have nothing to do there."

"Nonsense. Not a day went by when I didn't have to...." She fell quiet. Reminding him of when she had to take over the operations would lead to an argument. "There must be something that needs your attention."

He scoffed at that. "The management team has everything in place. They're producing the same products they produced three years ago."

"Because they lost their design department. Can you help

with that, perhaps come up with better or more up-to-date designs?"

"What do I know about wooden legs, unless they're on tables or chairs."

"Sitting home and sulking will solve nothing. Why don't you go to Prague for a few days?"

"I don't relish going there by myself anymore. Will you come with me?"

With only Lala's small travel satchel to carry, the couple spent a few hours strolling through the streets of Prague before returning to Josef's apartment. Sunrays poked through scattered clouds and the merest hint of a breeze made for a pleasant March afternoon.

Their walk took them past the National Theater and to the Legion Bridge, where they crossed the Vtlava River to Strelecky Island for a picnic of bread and pickles. Nearby a trio of preteen boys lobbed crude fishing lines into the river, pails at their feet empty of catch. One boy whipped around as Josef bit into a pickle. The boy elbowed his two companions to turn. Lala felt their eyes bear down on them with longing. Her appetite vanished. She pushed the sack containing her lunch in their direction and urged Josef to leave as the boys descended on the food like wild boars on a felled deer.

She and Josef continued across the bridge to the Mala Strana and wended their way north. After nearly four years of fighting, hardly a day went by without protesters marching and chanting. Rumors circulated that Prague came close to having a major workers demonstration. The mood of the city seemed somber. Sullen faces appeared everywhere she looked. Sullen, almost angry. Her mood soured as well, which made her feel more tired than had the journey.

"Josef, let's go directly to your apartment. We'll eat whatever you have there." Josef kept his place stocked with tinned food, clothing and linens for his occasional trips into the city.

"Wouldn't you rather have something fresh tonight? I'll check my contact."

"I certainly wouldn't mind, but I'm exhausted."

"Then go upstairs and rest." He handed over her satchel before reaching into his pocket for the apartment key. "I shouldn't take more than a half hour."

She patted his arm. "All right. I'll put up my feet for a few minutes and then set out everything I'll need to cook whatever you find, or if that fails, I'll make dumplings." She kissed him before entering the building.

Each flight of stairs seemed longer than the one before. She took off her shoes for the final flight to the top floor. As she jiggled the key in the lock she heard a door behind her open and a throaty voice say, "I didn't expect you back this week, Josef."

Lala turned to find a woman in her mid-forties dressed in a silk robe with a matching turban wrapped around her salt and pepper hair. She looked as shocked at seeing Lala standing there as Lala felt, but it passed quickly — too quickly. The woman sprawled against the doorframe and raised a cigarette to her rouged lips for a puff.

"You must be the new Mrs. Smetana." Cigarette smoke curled in the air, along with the words leaving her mouth.

"And you must be the old neighbor."

Lala shut the door behind her. *Is that why Josef was living in this austere apartment when we reunited?* If so, it didn't explain why he kept it after they wed. Memories flooded back, rumors whispered long ago between Armin and his friends about Josef's private life.

She stepped into the bedroom, her eyes drawn to the bed. Did he make love to that woman here? She turned away, toward the window. Next to it, "She", Armin's masterful portrait of her, still leaned against the wall. Did he stare at it when...?

The apartment door opened, startling Lala.

"Sorry, no meat tonight." Josef entered the bedroom and leaned in for a kiss. "You seem upset."

"I met your neighbor."

"Which one?"

She glared at him.

"Oh, Xenie. What did she say?"

Lala repeated their conversation word for word. Josef chuckled. "What a sharp retort. My my, I never knew you had a bit of cat in you." His amusement passed. "I haven't said more than 'good evening' to her since the day you walked through my door."

Lala refrained from saying, "And before that?" aloud. She stared at the bed.

Josef took her in his arms. "Look at me." When she did, he said, "I moved here during the darkest days of my life, in exile from my home, ousted from my factory, about to turn fifty, and then..."

His breath shuddered. "Armin's death left me inconsolable, even more so when I had to sever my relationship with you. Xenie kept me sane in the early days. She's the only reason I didn't climb to the roof and throw myself off. I will always be grateful to her for the comfort she provided to me, but that's all in the past."

Lala considered what he'd said, the emotions his words

invoked. Stories abounded about mistresses during his marriage to Romy, but she wasn't Romy, nor had she any reason to believe he would be unfaithful to her. She chose to believe him. As she surrendered to his embrace, she recalled her mother's advice...*"Don't expect too much from him...Josef has flaws and faults like everyone else...."* and broke off the hug.

"I should start dinner," she said. "I hid four eggs in my satchel when I packed. If you have flour and jam I can make syrove knedlíky."

She set about to make the dumpling dough, which now rivaled her mother's version for delicacy, and waited for the pot of water to come to a boil. Josef opened a bottle of wine.

"Will you pour me a glass?" she asked.

"This wine needs to breathe first before we drink it."

"Much like me after our conversation."

He exhaled audibly. "That woman has never stepped foot into this apartment as long as I've lived here."

She didn't respond.

"Lala, are you going to be unhappy staying here?"

"Not if you explain why you wanted this apartment after we married."

"I've kept it as insurance. It's not ideal but you didn't seem to mind it until now."

"The issue has nothing to do with snobbery." She dropped balls of jam-filled dough into the boiling water. The steam rising from the pot mirrored her mood.

"We could move or give it up, but why?" Josef asked. "We have use of Paulina's house until Ivo returns. Where would we go then?"

Lala knew he wouldn't consider the mansion and neither of them would be comfortable living with her mother.

He poured them each a glass of wine before continuing.

"We can move elsewhere if you insist, but to what end? We don't know what the future will hold. We've got Czechoslovak Legions siding with the Allies while our K.u.K. soldiers fight alongside Germany. Communists agitating in our factories while their Russian brethren battle our armies. Even here, loyalists to the Empire clash with the Czech National Council over independence." He swirled the wine in his glass. "Once the war ends we'll have a better sense of where and how we want to live."

"All right, I'll agree. We'll keep this apartment for now."

She wasn't happy with the situation but it made sense, and in wartime that had its advantages. Since their present housing situation would only last until the war ended, or when Ivo returned, Lala hoped the arrangement would be temporary. Very temporary.

CHAPTER EIGHT

Lala closed the front door after Mrs. Klima left to clean Sarah's house. Josef would be picking up his share of extra rations from the factory today, so she held off starting dinner until he arrived. He might have fresh meat. Even a little could flavor a soup or stew.

She felt a chill in the parlor and added another log to the fire. She spotted Josef's good pen in the stack of wood. It must have fallen out of his pocket that morning. She brought it to his office and laid it on his desk. His calendar stared up at her; 15 October, 1918. She recalled on that day four years earlier, the monthlong period of mourning for her father ended. Her dear father Jakob. Last month, on the anniversary of his death, she'd been so bereft it took all of Josef's skills as a lover to comfort her, turning sorrow into life-affirming pleasure.

As she headed back to the parlor with a small smile playing on her lips, Josef suddenly rushed in, looking elated. He grabbed Lala around the waist and kissed her with zeal. "Where's the bottle of cognac you've been hiding for a special occasion?"

"In the pantry. Why, what are we celebrating?"

He disappeared into the pantry and emerged with the bottle in hand and two glasses. "Then you haven't heard. The Emperor has 'renounced participation' in the Empire. He's issued a manifesto declaring free sovereignty to all the nations within the monarchy. The Allies have officially recognized Tomas Maseryk and his provisional government for Bohemia."

"We're finally an independent nation?"

"Yes." Josef poured a finger of cognac in each glass. "The Empire has collapsed and with it the K.u.K. army." He gave a glass to Lala.

"Then the war has ended."

"It has for Bohemia, though I doubt it will continue much longer for the other nations."

They clinked glasses and forwent dinner in favor of an early bedtime.

Standing in line at the market, Lala heard a sound, off in the distance, rhythmic and insistent. Soon it was echoed by other similar sounds.

The other women queued heard it as well. They all turned in unison toward the south, in the direction of Prague. The sounds grew louder and closer, until the source was clear. Church bells.

Church bells ringing out before noon on a Monday. Lala put her marketing basket on the pavement and listened as the bells clanged near and far, in town as well as far away. It brought a smile to her lips and relief to her soul. The war was finally over. At long last, the hostilities between nations would cease, and the surviving soldiers would return home to their families. Home to their lives.

The queued women hugged and cried out in excitement, but none left the line. A declaration of peace would not put food on their table anytime soon.

Excited, she wanted to find Josef, see the look on his face when she told him the good news. It would have to wait, though.

Tonight. She'd tell him tonight.

She found her mother, Jacub and Paulina waiting outside her door. Ecstatic, the women embraced Lala; they laughed and cried and danced in a circle as Jacub jumped up and down.

"Will Papa come home now?" he asked.

"Yes, my love, Papa will come back to us," his mother told him.

"When, Mama?"

"Soon, very soon."

"Come to the house to celebrate," insisted Sarah. "Josef, too when he returns from the factory. Oh, come with us now and put a note on the door for him."

"All right," said Lala. "But first, let me get the bottle of champagne we've been saving for this day."

She entered the house and went to the pantry, placing the cheese she'd bought at the market on the window sill to stay cold. Josef stored his wine in there as well. She added a bottle of Bordeaux and the champagne to her marketing basket along with the bread, eggs, potatoes and onions she'd bought, the beginning of a celebratory meal on a day with much to celebrate.

She rejoined her family outside and together they walked

back to her mother's home to prepare for the festivities. Lala relayed what she'd brought in her basket.

"Mama Sarah, do we have any cabbage left?" asked Paulina, nestling Jacub in her arms.

"At least a few heads. Why?"

Paulina shifted Jacub from her left hip to her right. "It would go well with Lala's onions and the plums we dried."

"If only we had a stewing hen," Lala said. Her mouth watered at the thought.

Sarah smiled. "That can be arranged. We've one hen that no longer lays eggs."

"What can I do, Grandmama?" asked Jacub.

"We'll think of something," she said.

Lala ruffled the boy's dark brown hair. "You can draw a picture to hang on the front door, so everyone will know the war ended today, November eleventh."

Jubilant, the boy clapped his hands.

The aroma of Sarah's hen stewing filled the kitchen. Lala left Paulina and Sarah to tend to dinner while she set the table and monitored Jacub. She marveled at how well he managed on his own, fortuitous as he had no playmates his age and rarely spent time around children.

He sat on the dining room floor with a piece of charcoal and a sheet of paper from one of Lala's old sketch pads.

"What are you drawing, Jacub?" She sat next to him and watched as he moved the charcoal across the paper in short, quick strokes, as he'd seen her do many times.

"A picture of the end of the war. See, there's Papa and the other soldiers coming home, and here's Mama and Grandmama and you and Uncle Josef and me waiting in front of the house."

"What's that?" she asked the boy, pointing to a tall spire with a round disk near the top.

"It's the clock tower in Prague, where Grandpa and Grandma Chytry live." He drew another circle at the top of the page, with lines radiating out from it. The sun, thought Lala.

Jacub pointed to the circle. "And this is heaven, where Armin and Grandpapa Jakob are. When they smile, it makes the sun shine."

"What a dear thought, Jacub. Let's hang your picture in the front hall, so Uncle Josef can see it when he arrives."

"Will you draw a picture of the end of the war, Antila?"

"I might."

He handed her the finished picture. "What will you draw?"

"I'll show you giving your papa a big hug when he comes home, and all the soldiers coming home to their families."

"In the sunshine?"

She cupped his chin. "Yes, in the sunshine."

The door opened and Josef came in, arms open, looking ebullient.

Before she could get to her feet, Jacub had run to Josef, assuming the waiting embrace was meant for him. Josef caught him, lifted the boy high over his head and spun him around. Lala couldn't tell whose laughter rang out more, Josef's or the boy's. It warmed her heart to see them together. Josef was kind, patient and loving with Jacub. How he missed being a father.

Nothing could ever fill the chasm left in his heart by the death of his son, but like Lala when she was adopted, his heart was big enough to make a place for a new family. Lala never doubted Josef would be a devoted father, as he'd been a devoted husband.

Josef put the boy down with a grunt. "You're getting too big for this, young man."

"The war is over, Uncle Josef."

"Yes, I heard."

"Papa will come home now."

"That is wonderful news."

The boy scampered off to the kitchen, leaving Josef and Lala alone. He held her in his arms and said, "At last. We can all get back to our lives."

Josef's joyous expression faded.

"Why are you sad, love?" she asked.

"I'll miss that little boy."

"When we move to Prague? We'll still see him, quite often."

"Ivo's his father. Once he returns, he will take up the boy's affections, and rightly so. I'll be an afterthought."

"Nonsense, Josef. You've been the only man in Jacub's life since he was born. He adores you and that won't change."

"Everything will change now."

Lala suppressed a grin. "Some changes are good, though."

Sarah came in from the kitchen. "Josef, you're finally here. Then shall we get this celebration started?"

The adults gathered in the parlor for a champagne toast. Afterward they feasted on Sarah's hen stewed with prunes and cabbage, accompanied with potato dumplings and Josef's Chateau Margaux. They ate and drank heartily, their good spirits rising with every bite and glass. As happy as Lala was to sit at the table and celebrate with her family, she counted the minutes until she could be alone with Josef.

"I can't remember when I've had such a fine meal, Sarah," said Josef. "Probably before the war."

"Yes, Mama Sarah, excellent dinner," added Paulina as Jacub began to fuss. She picked him up. "Time for bed, young man." To the others she said, "I'll be down shortly." She carried Jacub upstairs.

Sarah stood with difficulty after champagne and wine. "I should clear the table before I fall asleep."

"Let it be, Mother. This is a special occasion. It can wait."

Sarah sat down without an argument.

Lala stroked Josef's arm. "Josef, let's go into the kitchen."

Her mother teased, "Someone wants to celebrate in private," and giggled.

Lala led him to the back of the room and took his hands in hers. "My love, I've wanted to share some wonderful news with you all day, before you learned about it elsewhere."

"I felt the same way, but when the church bells rang out—"

She put her finger to his lips. "Not that." Her palm stroked his cheek as she gazed into his eyes. "I wanted to tell you first, before I tell my mother and Paulina."

She didn't have to say another word. By the way his face blossomed into elation, he knew.

CHAPTER NINE

While finishing the breakfast dishes, a wave of nausea swept over Lala. She grabbed the pail she kept handy for such purposes and held it before her mouth as she retched. The last few days had been particularly difficult, lasting well beyond morning and affecting her ability to keep down food.

She heard Mrs. Klima at the front door and let her in, along with a blast of cold air. "I'm going out for a few hours," Lala told her.

"Yes, Mrs. Smetana." Mrs. Klima sounded as glacial as the blasting air as she eyed the bucket. "Anything special you need from me today?"

"No, I'll clean this." Lala wiped her mouth. "Mrs. Klima, you have two children. Have you any advice for me?"

"I never had this problem. I used to eat offal sausages, pork dumplings and sauerkraut...."

At the mention of food, Lala winced and grabbed the pail again just in time.

***

After fetching a basket for eggs, she left Mrs. Klima to her work and walked to her mother's house. A chill in the early December air and the steady pace seemed to have a settling effect on her stomach. She turned off the thoroughfare leading to town and onto the road that led to her childhood home.

As she passed the wooded area she stopped to breathe in the frosty air. All was quiet save for birds foraging around tree roots, clouded from view by mist rising from the forest floor. She heard no gunshots as hunting had nearly ceased; much of the forest game had been killed. Another casualty of war.

The road cut through the meadow and continued to the house. For an instant, Lala thought of having been here several years before, during the spring when Gershom courted her. She rarely thought of him anymore.

The chicken coop Gershom and his apprentices had built for her still stood, once again filled with laying hens thanks to Josef's black market connections. Replacing them proved invaluable – the eight healthy birds laid enough eggs to help feed not only Paulina, Jacub and Sarah, but Lala and Josef.

Her mother opened the front door as Lala neared. "Come in, dear. It's turned cold and I don't want you to get sick."

Sarah took her coat from her and hung it in the front hall closet as Lala sat in the parlor by the fireplace.

"I was just about to go out to gather firewood. Shall I make some tea first to warm you up?" asked Sarah.

"No thank you." Lala would have loved some but doubted she could keep it down.

Jacub emerged from the kitchen, taking a bite out of one of Sarah's cinnamon cookies. Lala pinched her lips together and took deep breaths as she refocused on the boy, now three and a half. He looked taller, a good sign considering how little he'd grown when food had become scarce.

"No eating in the parlor, Jacub," Sarah admonished.

"Yes, Grandmama." As the boy gobbled the rest of his cookie, he noticed Lala and broke into a wide grin. "Antila, you're here." He ran to her and snuggled next to her on the sofa. "Antila, when will you bring me my new cousin?"

Lala chuckled. "Not until mid-June, when spring ends, Jacub."

"Why can't he come sooner?"

"Because it takes a long time to make a cousin. Besides, 'he' may be a 'she.'"

"I would rather have a boy cousin. Will he be Check…Checko…or Bohemian?"

"Czechoslovakian," Lala said slowly. "Yes, the baby will be Czechoslovakian, like everyone living in our new nation."

Lala heard footsteps coming down the stairs.

"I thought I heard you," said Paulina as she entered the parlor. Thanks to adequate nutrition, her face had regained a healthy glow.

"Have you any more news about when Ivo is due home?"

"Any day now." Paulina's expression grew concerned. "Lala, you don't look well."

Another wave of nausea rolled through Lala and she stood, clutching her stomach. "I don't think I can make it to the toilette."

"Then hurry to the laundry sink!" Paulina took her arm and helped her. Lala barely made it in time before she spit up a little water, all she had left in her stomach.

"You poor dear," lamented Paulina.

Lala cleaned and rinsed the sink, then splashed water on her face. She held fast to the sink ledge to steady herself while she took a few deep breaths until the queasiness passed. "I don't remember you having it this bad."

"You forget I went through this before we lived together. I used to have this trouble most mornings, but you weren't there to witness it. Come, sit down."

The two went to the kitchen and sat at the table.

"How long will this continue?" Lala asked.

"It settled down for me after my third month."

"I'm nearly there. Unless...."

Paulina crossed her arms. "I know what you're thinking. Don't."

"What?"

"That crazy curse you believe hangs over you. It's all nonsense, but whenever you consider it you drive yourself into a state much worse than anything you could have been afflicted with by someone else."

"You're right. It's perfectly normal to experience nausea when with child. Did anything help you?"

"A few women suggested dry bread but I found mint more helpful. Steep it like a tea and sip it slowly." Paulina rummaged through a cabinet and brought out a jar. "I found some. I'll make you a cup and we'll see if it works."

"Thanks, Paulina. What would I do without you?"

Paulina put the kettle on to boil. "Hopefully we'll never find out."

Lala returned home an hour before sunset. She could see Mrs. Klima cleaning the window in the front hall as she approached and assumed the woman saw her as well, but the housekeeper flinched when Lala opened the door.

"I didn't mean to startle you," said Lala.

A Petal in the Wind IV — Lala Smetana

Mrs. Klima threw her rag in her bucket and announced, "I'm done for today."

The housekeeper's attitude puzzled Lala. The woman had always been reserved, but deferential. Lala hung up her coat and waited for Mrs. Klima to return from the kitchen.

Mrs. Klima hadn't taken off her apron or her head scarf but put on her coat and buttoned it up. Lala opened her purse and took out several koruny.

"Since Christmas is two weeks away, I wanted to give you something extra to buy presents for your children." She handed the money to the woman.

Mrs. Klima stuffed it in her coat pocket. "I will, missus," she said before leaving.

Lala shook her head. Not even a thank you. What had she done to offend Mrs. Klima? She'd always been generous with her, paid her a good salary, gave her time off to tend to her children when they were sick, provided lunch and even food to take home.

It suddenly occurred to her that if Mrs. Klima felt slighted, the woman might have done something to punish her. Was her housekeeper stealing from her? She hurried to the kitchen to check on the silverware, dishes, and pantry, then went upstairs to examine the linen closet and her jewelry box. A careful check showed nothing absent.

Perhaps she misread the situation. It might have nothing to do with her. But the woman's sudden coldness made Lala doubt that.

77

CHAPTER TEN

Lala waited until after dinner to broach the problem with Mrs. Klima to Josef, following her mother's rule of never discussing troubling news at the dinner table. She sensed Josef held back distressing news himself and hoped he would be willing to unburden himself after they finished eating.

She cleared the table and washed up in a hurry while Josef relaxed in the parlor with his after-dinner tea. He hadn't yet taken a sip when she joined him with her cup. He smiled at her as she sat but then turned away, looking pensive. *Something at work must be concerning him.*

Feeling chilly, she got up to place another log on the fire. "With Christmas approaching, I gave Mrs. Klima some extra money today."

"Good idea." His full attention remained elsewhere.

"She didn't seem to appreciate it; she never even thanked me."

Josef turned to her. "How ungrateful. You should let her go. Tell her I insisted, to protect you after the latest outbreak of influenza."

"I'd rather not, at least without a better reason. She does a fine job keeping house and hasn't stolen from us. Whatever is troubling her may have nothing to do with us or the job."

Josef's eyes darkened. "Don't be too sure."

"Why do you say that?"

He hesitated before answering. "Attitudes have changed since the war. I've noticed an undercurrent of disrespect, even hostility, toward me at the factory. I presumed it was because many of the newer workers didn't know who I was and considered me an interloper, taking food and money when I did nothing to earn it."

"Nothing? It's your factory. You spent years establishing it into one of the finest in Europe." She stood, arms crossed. "During the war, you kept it open and provided employment. This town would have died without it." She thought that would have improved his spirits, but he seemed to be fuming.

He'd said, "presumed." She was about to ask him what he'd meant when they heard knocking on the door. Worry rippled through her.

Josef put his arm out to block Lala from going to answer it. "Wait here."

She looked on, fighting the urge to bite her lip as Josef opened the door.

There stood Sarah, holding a small satchel in one hand and Jacub's hand in the other, an apologetic half-smile on her face. "Guess who came home today?"

"It was Papa!" shouted Jacub before darting into the house. Josef took Sarah's bag and escorted her in.

"We had a little welcome home party and then thought we'd give them some privacy. May we stay tonight?"

"Of course, Mother," Lala said as she ushered them into the parlor. "We have a bed in Josef's office. You two can stay there."

Josef took her satchel to his office and returned. "I trust Ivo is well, Sarah?"

"Thankfully, yes. He admitted to a few scars on his legs from shrapnel, but nothing more. He'd been quarantined to ensure he didn't have influenza. Many soldiers have come down with it." She sat in the slipper chair that had once been hers, where she used to sit every evening next to Jakob. Lala smiled. Time seemed to have tempered the sad memories for her mother. Time and reupholstering.

Lala offered her mother her untouched tea. She heard Jacub giggling when she fetched the sugar bowl. Josef had picked the boy up and swung him around in a circle.

"That's what Papa did to Mama when he came home."

"Tell us all about it, Jacub." Josef said, and set the boy down on the sofa next to Lala.

His eyes grew wide as he gathered his thoughts. "When Papa came to the door, Mama yelled very loud and then she cried, and then they kissed a long time." He took a breath. "Then he gave me a present." He showed them a small rectangular cloth with a banner of white above a banner of red from his pocket. "It's the flag of our new country. Then Grandmama said we should come here tonight because Mama and Papa have a lot to talk about."

Sarah nodded as she stirred a lump of sugar in her tea.

Lala recalled how much her mother struggled under sugar rationing; Sarah's sweet tooth was legendary. "Take another lump, Mother. We have plenty now."

But Sarah declined. "I've grown to prefer it this way. So has my figure."

Lala pulled the boy onto her lap. "It's wonderful that your Papa is finally home, Jacub. Uncle Josef and I are happy you're going to stay here tonight, but it's nearly your bedtime.

Go wash up now so we can spend some time together before you go to sleep."

"Why can't we talk all night like Mama and Papa?"

Sarah spit out her tea and coughed. Josef couldn't refrain from chuckling.

Josef selected a book of fairy tales and offered to read one to Jacub. The boy kissed Lala and Sarah goodnight and went to the guest quarters with his uncle.

From her purse Sarah removed a small cloth bag that smelled like licorice. "I found anise seed in the cupboard. It's supposed to help with morning sickness." She gave the bag to Lala.

"I wish Paulina hadn't told you about that. I don't want you to worry."

Sarah reassured Lala with a pat on the hand. "Paulina didn't say one word. I know most women in your condition have this problem, so I asked Mrs. Havlik as well as some of the women at the market for advice."

A daughter of a servant herself, Sarah had developed friendships with both the gentry and servants over the years. Lala always admired her mother's egalitarian nature and tried to emulate it. Growing up she'd had a cordial relationship with her mother's young housekeeper, but breaking through Mrs. Klima's reserve posed a challenge.

Lala set the bag on the side table. "Mother, what's your opinion of Mrs. Klima?"

"Why are you asking?"

"I'm getting the feeling she's not happy working for me."

Sarah picked up her tea cup and took a few sips to delay responding. "Since you asked, I'll be honest. There's something about her I don't trust. I'm not saying she steals, but she's too aloof, almost as if she thinks she's better than us. But she does a good job and nothing's missing from the house. I check all the time."

Lala nodded. "Me too. I do feel sorry for her. Being alone with two young children can't be easy."

"There are too many lonely widows now, thanks to the war." Sarah finished the tea and brought the cup to the kitchen, with Lala following. Sarah washed the cup and handed it to Lala to dry while she washed the saucer. "Is this a general feeling or did something happen to bring it on?"

Lala dried the saucer. "Both, really. She's always been reserved, but today it seemed more so. I gave her extra money in advance of Christmas and she didn't even thank me."

Sarah wagged her finger. "That was a mistake. Not for giving her money, but for telling her that reason. Never give money to Gentiles for Christmas and especially not for Easter."

"Why?"

"Dear, don't you know they blame us for their savior's death? And now they're blaming us for losing the war."

It took a moment to grasp what her mother meant. "She's given me no reason to believe she's anti-Semitic."

"And I hope you're right. In the meantime, keep your eyes and ears open at all times around her, and I'll do the same."

When Josef returned to the parlor, Sarah sent them off to bed, insisting she could entertain herself with her embroidery work until she felt sleepy.

Lala kissed her mother goodnight, as did Josef, and left her to cross-stitch while they went to their bedroom. A sense of contentment brought a smile to Lala. She enjoyed having her mother around once again, if only for an evening. Then it occurred to her — it might be longer. With Ivo back, he'd want to move his family into Paulina's house. Lala and Josef would have to go elsewhere, but it would take time to find appropriate living quarters. Josef still had his apartment, but with a baby coming it would be too small, and she felt less comfortable there after learning about Xenie. Josef would never consent to returning to the mansion, and as much as she loved her mother, returning to her childhood home felt like a step backward.

Josef undressed and got into bed; Lala did as well. She snuggled against him.

Josef enfolded her in his arms. "Our guests have raised your spirits."

"I do miss being with my family sometimes." She rubbed her belly." Especially now."

"I'm pleased that you're feeling better."

"You should have seen me this morning, though on second thought, it's just as well you didn't."

"I heard you in the toilette." He kissed her forehead. "It will pass soon, I promise."

"At least someone in this house is an expert on the subject," she teased, then waited to see if Josef would turn out the lamp by his bedside. He didn't, so she relayed her conversation with her mother about Mrs. Klima, including Sarah's conclusion.

Josef sat up, his arms crossed over his chest. "I agree with your mother."

She propped herself up on her elbow. "Is that what you

implied earlier?"

He nodded. "Anti-Semitism has gotten worse since the war began, but in my situation, there may be more to it. I'm out of my element now. Hajek and Strahov resent having to run everything by me. I'm beginning to think they're right."

"Nonsense," exclaimed Lala. "They never would have taken over the factory if I hadn't stepped away and recommended their promotions. Why, I should march right into their office and—"

Josef took her hand and gave it a firm squeeze. "You'll do nothing of the kind. I don't want you there."

"I understand. I won't confront them, but—"

"No, I don't want you there at all."

She sat up and turned to face him. "But Josef, you told me years ago you wanted us to work together, be partners in the factory."

"When it was the only way we could be together, but now it's different. We're married. There's no reason for you to be working there, or anywhere else."

"What about the showrooms and consulting with major purchasers? Aren't I going to be running that operation?"

"Lala, I doubt either of us will be connected with the factory for very long. No one wants me around, and frankly, running a major company no longer appeals to me. I'd rather sell the business while it's still profitable, take the money and do something else."

"Sell part of your art and antique collections?"

"For a start, then use the profits to reinvest in more art and antiques, the finest I can obtain."

"Where does that leave me?"

"As my wife and mother of our child. Isn't that enough?" He kissed her as though to prove his point.

85

Josef turned off his lamp and within minutes she could hear his breath deepen; he'd fallen asleep. She rolled over and turned out her lamp.

"Where does that leave me?"

"As my wife and mother of our child. Isn't that enough?"

Was it enough?

CHAPTER ELEVEN

Lala slept late that morning, awakening to an empty bed and a sizzling sound from the kitchen. Was Josef preparing breakfast? He hadn't cooked for them since she showed up at his apartment in Prague almost two years ago. Then she remembered her mother had stayed overnight.

Her stomach felt settled for the first time in days. No morning sickness, for which she was grateful. She dressed and headed toward the kitchen. She passed Josef in the parlor, Jacub on his lap, as he read a story from his volume of fairy tales to the entranced boy.

"You're not going to work?" she asked.

"Not today." He smiled and ruffled Jacub's hair.

"Read me one more story, Uncle Josef," the boy pleaded, and Josef reopened the book.

Lala left them and went to the kitchen where her mother stood before the stove, basting fried eggs with melted butter.

"This will be ready shortly. Sit down, dear, and eat something. You look too thin."

"I haven't been able to keep anything down for days," Lala said. "But that looks tempting."

"You've always enjoyed my cooking." Sarah slid a few

eggs from the frying pan into a plate and placed it in front of Lala. "Eat, dear."

Josef carried Jacub into the kitchen and sat him at the table. Sarah put plates with eggs before them both, then poured coffee for the adults. They hadn't finished eating when Lala heard knocking at the door.

Sarah took off her apron. "That must be your parents, Jacub." She hurried out and returned with Paulina and Ivo.

He looked leaner than before, and older than a man in his mid-twenties, with creases in his face and a touch of gray along his temples. Lala noticed he walked with a slight limp and suspected he'd downplayed his leg injury. Still, she leapt from her seat to embrace him. "Welcome home, Ivo."

Josef rose and shook Ivo's hand. "So good to see you back in one piece."

"Thank you, Mr. Smetana."

"Josef, please. We're all family here."

Ivo scooped Jacub up and sat the boy on his shoulders. "I can hardly believe I'm back. So much has changed."

Sarah took hold of Jacub's leg, the only part of him she could reach, and planted a loud kiss on his shin. "Hopefully for the better."

"Yes. I have a beautiful wife and son, whom I'm taking on a picnic this afternoon."

"In this cold weather?" Sarah blurted.

"Cold?" he scoffed. "You've never been to the Eastern front. This is balmy to me." He lifted Jacub off his shoulders and set him down. "Besides, cold air stimulates the appetite and I have to fatten us all up. Look how thin we are."

Paulina's smile paled and she cast her eyes downward.

Josef spoke up. "Why don't we all have dinner here tonight to celebrate your homecoming. Afterward we can discuss our living arrangements," Josef suggested.

"Dinner would be lovely," said Paulina. "Ivo, tell them of our plans."

Ivo wrapped his arm around Paulina. "The three of us will be staying with my parents until New Year's Day. They want to spend time with us all and I need to find work. I'm hoping for a position at the University, where my father works. Then we'll sell Paulina's house and move to Prague."

"How exciting," Sarah said.

Lala saw through her mother's words. Sarah's forced smile couldn't fool anyone.

With Jacub gone for the day, Josef returned to the factory. Lala suggested to her mother to spend another night with her and let the Chytrys have more time to prepare for their extended trip to Prague.

"We have everything backward now," Sarah observed. "You, me and Josef in Paulina's house and them in ours. I'll miss them, but naturally they'll want to spend time with his family. At least I don't have to share you with anyone." She misted. "I can't expect you two to move in with me once Paulina sells her house."

"No, Josef wants to find a new apartment in Prague, somewhere where we can raise our family."

"Won't that be too far from the factory?"

"He doesn't want to work there anymore."

"Why? Does it remind him too much of the war?" Sarah asked.

"That may be part of it. I think he wants everything that went before purged from his life. The factory, the mansion."

"He's never recovered from Armin's murder or Romy's

betrayal. How could he?"

A complete break with the past. A new life to go with a new family. That seemed to be what Josef wanted. But she wasn't ready to let go entirely, not yet. Maybe never.

CHAPTER TWELVE

Lala stopped going to the mansion. What would have been the point of practicing her showroom designs when there would be no showroom? Instead she stayed home, wrote to Paulina in Prague, and tried to avoid interrupting Mrs. Klima's routine. The woman's coolness toward her persisted and she finally gave up.

"I'm going upstairs for a nap," Lala told her. "Please don't disturb me."

She awoke an hour later. Mrs. Klima had already left. She went to the pantry to select food for dinner when she heard the front door open. Josef had arrived home early again.

He greeted Lala with an absentminded peck on the cheek and then tried to settle himself on the sofa without succeeding. She heard the newspaper rattling and him grumbling but couldn't make out what he said. Lala debated whether she should offer him a drink to calm him or ask him what happened at the factory, but as soon as she touched his shoulder to ask, a tirade burst forth like water from a shattered dam.

"I met with Hajek and Strahov to discuss selling the factory to them. I made a very fair offer, but they turned me down. They both said I'm asking for too much. Too much!" His hands shook in frustration. "After all these months of marginalizing me, acting as if I had no place running my own factory."

He leapt up and paced. "All the years I put into the business, investing in the most modern equipment, securing the best designers and craftsmen in Europe, keeping half the men in this town working." His hands flicked and waved at every slight.

He stopped pacing at the bar cart and poured himself a finger of cognac. "Wasn't I the one who ordered the conversion of the factory to wartime production? Didn't I put you and Kindemann in charge of overseeing it in my absence? They didn't take over until the hard work had been completed, and at your recommendation as I recall." His voice grew louder. "And yet, they have the audacity to expect they deserve a discounted rate based on their contributions!" He put his drink down on the table so hard Lala feared the glass would break. "I'd sooner sell to one of our competitors, or shut the factory rather than sell it for half its worth!"

She knew he didn't mean that. "Are they open to bargaining?"

"I suspect so, but they insist they can't afford the price I want."

"Is that true?" she asked.

Josef picked up the glass and drained it with one swallow. It was true.

A thought occurred to Lala. "When you sell your factory, does it include everything? The building and all of its contents?"

"In this case, yes. Everything except my personal effects and...oh." He bent over and kissed her. "You, my dear, are a genius."

Mrs. Klima sent an elderly neighbor to tell Lala she wasn't feeling well and needed the day off. Lala worried aloud it might be the Spanish flu, a virulent strain of influenza which had spread rapidly for months; many had died from it.

The woman took offense at Lala's suggestion and implied Lala posed a greater risk than Mrs. Klima. Lala apologized to the matron and offered her a cup of tea for her trouble, but she declined and stormed off. Lala could understand if the woman was inconvenienced or concerned for her health, but the animus felt personal. Regardless of the reason, afterward Lala began to relish the idea of being alone for a while.

After washing her lunch dish, Lala checked the day's mail and opened a letter from Paulina. She and Ivo had not found housing in Prague yet, but they'd talked with an agent about selling her home. She also saw the storefront she'd tried to obtain years ago on Jinrisská Street; a "For Lease" sign still hung in the window.

Lala was about to write back when she heard a commotion outside. A delivery truck had backed up to the front entrance. Josef burst through the door and announced, "I have a surprise for you."

She couldn't help but laugh. "I can see that. Will I like it?"

His smile grew broader as he called out, "Bring it in, men."

The front door swung open wide as two delivery men brought in a bureau-sized piece of furniture covered in a drop cloth. They set it down in the parlor. Josef removed the cloth

93

to reveal a drop leaf desk with an inlaid top, made by Lala's father as part of a two piece set.

She ran her hand over the desk's top. Josef had kept it outside the workroom where her father used to make custom pieces for the factory's top clients. She'd called the inlay "patchwork" as a child, when she'd seen the companion piece in the home of her Aunt Naomi.

"Put it in my office," Josef instructed as he gestured to the room. The men lifted the desk and moved it away.

"I wanted to bring this here straightaway," he told Lala. "There will be more, but we have no place to store them yet."

"I presume you've made a deal with Hajek and Strahov."

"The factory is now theirs. I have enough money to start my new business and fulfill my promise to Paulina to be her silent partner. The deal includes my office furnishings, and every unsold piece of furniture. However, this means we must find housing with a shop and storeroom in Prague without delay, for there's no place to store the rest."

"What about the mansion? There's ample room there."

His joy shifted to sternness. "I don't want anything poisoned by that house. Why do you insist on keeping that place, knowing we'll never live there?"

"Let's be practical, Josef. You needn't step foot inside, merely consider it safe storage. There must be some paintings and furnishing you'll want once we have a home that can accommodate the pieces, and others to add to your business inventory. All you need to do is decide what you want to keep and what you want to sell, and I'll do the rest."

Sullen and silent, he nonetheless nodded his agreement.

***

The following Tuesday Mrs. Klima arrived early and seemed in a hurry to finish. While dusting the sofa table she knocked over a figurine, which fell to the floor, nearly breaking it.

Lala scooped it up and placed it back on the table. "Why are you rushing so, to the point of carelessness?"

Mrs. Klima nearly shouted back, "Just how long do you expect me to work today?"

"Why should today be any different—"

"It's Christmas Eve."

"Why didn't you mention it straightaway?"

"Because everybody should know that!"

Exasperated, Lala said, "Then why don't you leave now. In fact, take the rest of the week off. Maybe you'll be in better spirits when you return next Monday."

The housekeeper gave her a defiant glare. She gathered her things and left.

Lala suspected the woman's mood would not improve in a week, nor did she care why Mrs. Klima had become so bad-tempered. As sorry as she felt for the woman, she had to find another housekeeper.

The day after Christmas Mrs. Havlik paid a visit to Lala. The disturbing story she relayed had the mansion's housekeeper in nervous tears and Lala quaking with anger. She gathered her wits as she bade goodbye to the woman, adding her assurance that with so many townspeople attending Christmas mass, no one could ascertain the informant.

Lala barely felt the frigid air as she hurried into town. The malicious gossip, as cruel as it was untrue, rang in her ears:

Lies about how her "affair" with Josef drove his first wife insane. How she and her mother had "poisoned" the mind of Paulina, a good Christian woman, and her little boy. How the cowardice and disloyalty of "those people" caused the carnage of the war and led to defeat.

Thursday mornings were always busy at the market. Lala anticipated her nemesis would be there, waiting in line. She was, near the head of the queue, chatting and laughing with the women standing alongside her.

A surge of anger swept over Lala and she had to compose herself enough to retain a level of civility. Finally, she spat out, "Mrs. Klima!" and waited until the housekeeper turned to face her.

The surprise on the woman's face faded quickly, replaced with a smug look as she exclaimed, "It's my lucky day. Now I won't have to waste my time going to your home to tell you I quit!"

The women surrounding her drew in closer, offering support and murmuring their agreement. Other women standing in line stared at the spectacle, including a well-dressed middle aged woman, her arm around the shoulder of a teenage girl, who gazed at Lala with curiosity.

Lala summoned her voice. "Quit? You're fired. And don't expect me to give you a good reference after hearing of your vile gossip."

Mrs. Klima issued a derisive laugh. "Gossip? Everyone knows your kind don't belong here. And I don't need your references, Mrs. Smetana. I've a new position with a good family."

The well-dressed woman unexpectedly stepped out of line and approached Lala, her back to Mrs. Klima. "Are you Mrs. Josef Smetana?"

Lala sensed this woman's motives were sympathetic to her, and answered, "I am." Over the woman's shoulder Lala could see Mrs. Klima stiffen.

"What a pleasure to finally meet you. I'm Mrs. Hajek. That's my daughter Marie." She gestured to the young lady, who curtsied. "Please forgive me, this is long overdue, but I wanted to thank you. My husband wouldn't co-own the factory now if you hadn't recommended him for the management position. In fact, everyone here owes you and Mr. Smetana a debt of thanks. If not for the two of you, the war would have devastated this town."

Temper now in check, Lala shook the woman's proffered hand. "My congratulations to you both, Mrs. Hajek. I wish you every success with the factory." Lala glanced at Mrs. Klima and saw fear.

"I couldn't help overhearing your exchange with Mrs. Klima." Mrs. Hajek raised her hand to keep Lala from responding. "I found her comments rather ironic, as the only reason I hired her was that she'd mentioned working for you, which as you can probably imagine after my speech, spurred my good will enough to take her on. My husband had urged against it, given that he remembered firing a factory worker named Klima for stealing."

"I had no idea," said Lala.

Mrs. Hajek turned to address Mrs. Klima. "You may have denied Mrs. Smetana the satisfaction of firing you before you quit, but not me." She took a step forward. "Find yourself another job, and if you don't apologize to Mrs. Smetana right now, I'll see to it that no one in town will hire you."

Mrs. Klima proffered a feeble, "Sorry, missus," but Mrs. Hajek replied, "That is not a sincere apology."

Lala approached Mrs. Hajek to say, "Please don't," but the woman's stance, rigid as a soldier at attention, and her pitiless expression made it obvious she would not settle for anything less than a full apology from the housekeeper.

Mrs. Klima still quaked, though now more in humiliated fury than fear, as her friends averted their scowls and burning gazes from the two women responsible for the chastising. She raised her chin and sputtered, "I'm sorry for what I said behind your back."

Before Mrs. Hajek could demand more, Lala said, "That will do."

Lala thanked Mrs. Hajek again before leaving, though she wished the woman hadn't insisted on the apology. Lala knew it would solve nothing, and as she just witnessed, might cause more resentment.

Despite honorable people like Mrs. Hajek, enough of the townsfolk who'd suffered through the war needed someone to blame and, as so often happened, chose a perennial target. Lala had heard enough snippets around town to understand that while most did not hold the extreme views of Mrs. Klima, sentiments had been creeping in that direction. The question of whether Josef would ever return to the mansion no longer mattered. She would no longer consider living there.

Her hand rested on her swelling middle as she walked toward home, thinking how much of the town's good will toward Josef stemmed from the Smetana Furniture Company, which provided employment for so many. As he no longer owned the factory, that would not continue.

Prague beckoned. They needed to seek housing as soon as possible.

CHAPTER THIRTEEN

The realtor shivered as he waited in the unheated storefront while Josef and Lala inspected the premises. He kept his hands in his coat pockets and his shoulders hunched to cover his neck. "What sort of business were you planning for this location, Mr. Smetana?"

"A dress shop," Josef answered.

Lala stood before the windows facing Jinrisská Street, a busy Prague thoroughfare. A steady stream of foot traffic passed by the shop, undeterred by the sprinkle of snowflakes. She turned back to see Josef facing the realtor.

"Our proximity to Wenceslas Square would make this a prime location," the man offered.

"I would agree if it weren't three blocks from the Square." Josef glanced around. "This storefront has been vacant since before the War began. If I decide to lease the space, I would expect that to be reflected in the price."

The realtor shivered again.

Josef thanked him and escorted Lala from the vacant shop.

"Put your face mask on," Josef urged Lala. "The risk of

catching influenza is higher in the city, especially in winter. I don't want you to get sick."

"Then you ought to as well, love, to protect the baby and me."

Josef turned back and waited until the realtor had locked the door and walked away. He tied his mask on before the couple continued toward the Charles Bridge.

"It's certainly priced well," Josef said when they had walked out of earshot. "We can keep looking, but if Paulina's happy with the location I will sign the papers. Then we can focus on what Cerveny has found for us."

Josef had asked his agent to scout out some potential buildings with storefronts in the Mala Strana.

Lala adjusted her gauze mask as they walked along the snow-dusted cobblestones. "She's always liked that shop's location, especially now. It's close to the University where Ivo will be teaching. Paulina wrote that they're looking for housing in the area if they can afford it."

"Can they?"

Lala shrugged.

"Are you hungry, or tired? " he asked. "Would you like to sit in a café and rest before we continue?"

She tucked her arm in his. "I'm fine, love. Let's go on and find our new home."

They looked at two more buildings in the old town before returning to Josef's apartment. As she climbed each step she wondered if her husband's neighbor Xenie would make an appearance. If so, Lala would unbutton her coat and let the small but noticeable bulge in her middle speak for itself. When they reached the landing, Lala heard music and laughter drifting from the woman's apartment. Good. She'd found a new companion.

Josef unlocked the door and they entered the dusty apartment. Lala went to find a rag to clean up, but Josef insisted she rest. After taking her coat, he guided her to the settee and urged her to sit. He hung her coat on the coat rack next to his and sat beside her.

"What time is our dinner with Ivo and Paulina?" she asked.

"His mother invited us to come at half past seven."

After dinner, they returned to the apartment shortly before ten. Lala tore off her mask and threw her coat on the settee before stamping into the bedroom. Josef followed her inside as she sat on the edge of their bed in a huff and struggled to remove her shoes.

Josef helped her. "You shouldn't be angry at Ivo for urging Paulina to eat more."

She glared at him. "Urge? He practically force-fed her at the table."

He sat beside her and untied the laces on his shoes. "You can't take it personally and neither should Paulina. Remember how he suffered during the war—"

"And we didn't?" she heard herself shout. She paused and took a breath to quiet down. "We starved, too."

"Which is why he's so concerned that Paulina and Jacub get enough to eat, as much as I'm concerned about you, especially now." He leaned over to kiss her forehead.

She folded her arms. "But you don't nag me about it."

He chuckled. "No, I leave that to your mother."

She couldn't argue with that. Still, Ivo fell in love with a voluptuous woman and Lala worried he'd lost interest in Paulina now that she was slender. The couple only knew each other for a few months before Ivo went off to war, leaving Paulina behind carrying his child. A forty-eight hour pass allowed Ivo to return home long enough to meet his infant son and marry Paulina. Their long separation served to increase their ardor, though the hardship of wartime washed away romantic notions, as did the reality of married life, something Lala knew all too well.

"He's only been home for three months," Josef said. "Give him some time to get over his obsession."

My sensible husband, she thought as she got into bed. Josef laid down next to her, his hand lightly stroking her belly. It felt pleasurable. His hand then wandered lower, stirring up her passion for the first time in months. She turned and curled against his body. "The doctor assured me it's safe to make love now."

His hand traveled from her inner thigh to her breast. "Welcome news."

Bundled up against the frigid January morning, they walked the streets of Mala Strana to look at potential housing, armed with the list prepared by Cerveny. The first house, located along the Vltava, had an apartment available with lovely views of the old town across the river, but the building wasn't for sale. The second house needed too much repair work. Two others had potential, but Lala disliked the location of one, and Josef vetoed the other due to insufficient space for his shop. Dejected, they decided to find an uncrowded restaurant near Malostranské Square for lunch.

As they left the restaurant Lala said, "I do like this area.

It's lively and has a feel similar to Wenceslas Square without being as bustling. Shall we wander around?"

Josef checked Cerveny's list. "There is one building for sale nearby, on Zámecká." He indicated toward a narrow street north of St. Nicholas Church.

She nodded. "Let's go see it."

They walked up the slight incline of the street. The slope would allow water to drain away, but not make walking treacherous if icy. They found the building near the end of the block. Lala liked the rounded Renaissance archways over the front door and the two ground floor windows, and the understated trim on the upper floor balustrades, less florid than the Baroque architecture that dominated the area. The adjacent buildings looked well-kept.

Josef rang the bell, and as they waited Lala observed, "I do like the location. Being close to the Square, the shops and markets. Would it be suitable for your business?"

"Possibly."

They explained their interest to the building manager who answered the door. He gave them a tour of the building, which included two retail spaces on the ground floor. Upstairs were four vacant apartments on two higher floors, and an attic room above. The building faced west. Rooms on the upper floors facing the street would get good afternoon light while the buildings across the street would block sunlight for the shops downstairs. The interior felt warm even on a freezing winter day, suggesting an adequate furnace. While the apartments were small and far from luxurious, she liked their layout. The condition of the walls, floors, windows and fireplaces was much better than in Josef's apartment.

They climbed to the attic, the size of servant's quarters,

and saw no evidence of leakage from the roof. Josef had her wait downstairs while he went to the basement and checked the heating and the plumbing systems.

Afterward she and Josef stepped outside to inspect the exterior while the building manager waited inside. Josef noted no evidence of water damage, even from the devastating flood of 1890, and only slight wear on the two granite steps that led to the entry.

Lala began to tire, so they made their apologies and bade the manager goodbye.

"Shall I call for a taxi to take us back to the apartment?" Josef asked her.

"If I sit and rest awhile I'll be fine. I recall a café near the square that had some tasty looking strudel in the window." She'd been craving sweets of late.

"We'll dine in if there aren't many patrons," he said through his mask. "Otherwise I'll buy whatever you want and bring it back to the apartment."

Taking her arm, Josef escorted Lala to the café, where a lone couple dallied over coffee. They took a table at the other end of the café, ordered tea, and Lala asked for a piece of strudel. When the waiter brought the apple and raisin-filled pastry, her eyes welled up.

"This reminds me of being with my parents before the war. Father used to take us out for coffee and pastries. He called it 'having a treat.'" She began to weep and couldn't stop. Josef reached across the table and took her hand.

"I don't know why I'm crying," she bawled. "During the war I was a rock that stood firm against anything, and now a piece of pastry brings me to tears. What's wrong with me?"

"It's normal to be emotional in your situation." He offered her his handkerchief.

"Is my condition why I'm being so foolish?" she sputtered as she dabbed her eyes. "I don't understand. There's so much going on now in our lives, what with starting a family and moving to Prague, all happy things. Yet here I am crying for no good reason."

"Not so," he said. "It's been taxing with so many changes and challenges in our lives. It would be difficult even without...." His fingers brushed across her belly. "Is there anything I can do to bring you comfort?"

She blinked away tears as she met his gaze. In a low voice she said, "As I recall, that's precisely what put me in my present state."

It took a moment for that to register with Josef. When it did, he rewarded her with a lecherous grin that tempered her sad memories.

Snow began to fall as they walked arm in arm back to his apartment. Lala asked, "How many houses from Cerveny's list are left to be seen?"

He scanned the paper. "Six, though four are out of the area we wanted."

"I liked that apartment overlooking the river."

Josef shook his head. "I'd rather deal with tenants than a landlord."

"Good point. What about that last place we saw?"

"It has possibilities. Did you like it?"

"It had...potential."

"Yes, potential," he repeated. "The price was reasonable for the size, location and condition."

"Neither of us sound very enthusiastic about the house, although I can't think of anything I didn't like about it, other than we'd have to make great deal of changes to the building's interior before it would be right for us."

They turned onto U Luzichkeho Seminaire shortly before four, the sky already darkened by thick snow clouds. Street lights illuminated their way. Lala sighed with contentment. The glow of the gas lamps bestowed a fairy tale atmosphere to the beautiful city.

She smoothed the lapels of Josef's coat. "Love, why don't you check the two nearby properties on the list while I go upstairs and rest. If you think either of them has promise, we'll go back tomorrow."

"I should be home no later than seven." He blew her a kiss through his mask before leaving.

Lala had the table set and dinner ready when Josef came home. He seemed pleased. "Did you find anything worth considering?" she asked.

"Not the last two, but I've been thinking we're going about this the wrong way." He hung up his coat and hat. "We've been approaching this as though whatever we buy will be where we'll always live." He sat at the table. "Who's to say this has to be our final home?"

She ladled out stew into a dish and placed it before him.

Josef continued, "As I walked here, I kept thinking about what you said regarding the Zámecká Street house."

"You mean how it wasn't quite right?"

"And how it could be changed to make it closer to right. It's a good investment, so why don't we look at it like that? Ivo and Paulina want to sell her house, which means we need to find a place fairly soon. We can afford to remodel it before we move in, and if we decide we don't like it or want something different, we can sell it at a profit."

"I suppose that's one way to look at it." She set her meal on the table.

"Good, because I bought the house."

Lala dropped the silverware, which hit the tabletop with a clatter. "You did what? How could you buy a house for us without asking me?"

"Because it's my surprise for you. I realized by selling the factory I denied you the chance to design the showrooms, which you dearly wanted to do. Smolak mentioned you've been doing the same in the mansion, fixing up all the rooms and such. Now you have a new canvas on which to work, except we get to enjoy it when you're done."

She tried to think of something to say, but failed to come up with the right words. She couldn't even decide whether she felt angry at him for buying the building without consulting her, or thrilled that he had.

"I didn't mean it to sound as if you had no input into the decision," said Josef. "You mentioned you had no objections to the house, and with the price falling below our expectations, we can afford to take over the entire building without renting out any of the space. I thought you'd find this a satisfying project to fill the next few months, building a nest for us while we await the birth of our child. If you're pleased with the results we can make that house our home. If not, we can sell it and move elsewhere."

"But Josef, I—"

He offered her a pained smile. "All I want is for you to be safe and happy."

She had every right to be angry with him, but what good would that do? He'd already bought the house. Josef may have been presumptuous but his intentions were good.

Miko Johnston

It would give her a chance to continue designing interiors – more than designing. It would involve reconstruction and remodeling, a chance to gain valuable experience....

Once the shock wore off, Lala saw the potential in this project.

"Josef, once we settle on the budget, will you give me free rein in designing our new home?"

"I'll be busy preparing to launch my new business. I won't have time to interfere, if that's what you're asking."

The more she thought about it the more she liked the idea.

CHAPTER FOURTEEN

"That bureau should be centered on the far wall of the parlor," Lala instructed the workmen who were moving furniture into the larger of the two first floor apartments. She and Josef would stay there until their new living quarters on the second floor were finished. The adjacent apartment, currently a storeroom, would become Josef's office.

"You heard the lady," barked the foreman to his assistant.

While she dealt with their living quarters, she also helped Josef prepare for his gallery opening. At her suggestion he had separated the artwork from the antiques to create two shops, each entered through the ground floor lobby. She scouted the neighborhood and found nineteen-year-old Ludovik and his seventeen-year-old brother Hanus to assist with bringing pieces out of storage.

Judging by the care they took and their polite demeanor, she urged Josef to hire them on a permanent basis. Ludovik, tall and wiry with a strong jaw and sand colored curls, bore a slight resemblance to a young Karel. Lala found him thoughtful, deliberate and precise, qualities that would be suitable for Josef's chauffeur. His darker haired brother's

109

personality seemed more curious and intuitive. Josef asked him to assist in the shops.

Working with a construction foreman, plumbing contractor and an electrician, she arranged to combine the two upper floor apartments into a single unit, updating it with two bathrooms, an enlarged kitchen, formal dining room, library, parlor, and three bedrooms. The estimated completion fell around her due date. Once her family moved into the apartment upstairs, Josef would store overstock in the current apartment.

The two ground-floor spaces were in the midst of a good cleaning and a fresh coat of paint. The smell made Lala queasy. Hammering from above added to her discomfort. After reviewing furniture placement with the workmen, Lala excused herself and left to take a walk. The air did her good. After the chill of January, when temperatures hovered around freezing, an eight degree March day felt almost temperate.

Remembering that her nephew's fourth birthday was two weeks away, she thought it a good time to pay his mother a visit in her new shop on Jinrisská Street, on the other side of the river. She hadn't had time to stop in yet. Lala needed something else from Paulina as well – a few dresses to accommodate her growing belly.

A toy store near the Charles Bridge caught her eye and she went in to browse. There she found an adorable wooden paddle with painted chickens standing in a circle. Strings attached to the chickens' heads threaded down through a hole in the paddle's center and tied around a ball. Swinging the paddle made the ball revolve and the chickens noisily peck. Jacub would adore it.

After purchasing the toy, she stopped at a bakery next door and bought a few pastries to bring with her. As she approached Paulina's shop she felt flattered to see Paulina had used the same layout Lala had designed for her original shop.

Paulina gazed up and beamed as Lala entered. "How wonderful to see you."

She rushed to Lala and embraced her. Lala handed her the pastries.

"Ooh, a treat," cooed Paulina. "Thank you. I'll be able to enjoy this without comments."

Ivo must still be needling Paulina about her weight. "No ulterior motives, my friend," Lala said. "How is business?"

"Slow, but steady. So many people are home, ill or caring for their sick relatives. This awful influenza." She shook her head. "I've been open five days and I've sold eight dresses. Unfortunately, two in black, for mourners." Paulina took a bite of her honey cake. "Mmm, this medovnik is as good as mine." She brushed crumbs from her face and clothing .

A fashionably dressed woman stopped at the window to peer in. Paulina tucked her cake under the counter and greeted the woman as she entered the shop.

Lala pretended to be a customer perusing the merchandise. "It's wonderful to see pretty colors and longer skirts again," she said before selecting from the rack a rose beige dress she thought would look splendid on the other woman. Lala held it against her body as she stood by a mirror. "This one is exquisite, and so affordable. I wish it were in my size."

The customer, who'd been watching Lala, snapped, "It looks like it would fit me." To Paulina she said, "I want to try it on."

"Let me bring it to you." Paulina said. She suppressed a grin as she took the dress from Lala and carried it into the fitting room. Lala refrained from laughing as Paulina's customer marched behind. If the woman's nose were held any higher she'd scrape it on the ceiling.

Lala continued to "browse" until the woman emerged, declaring, "It fits perfectly," and asked to purchase the dress. Paulina wrapped it for her in one of her signature white boxes and thanked her customer. "Please come again."

"I most certainly will," she said as she left.

They waited until the woman had walked away before bursting into laughter.

"That reminded me of the time we had to buy food on the black market during the war, how we outfoxed that rogue of a man with a little blackmail," Paulina said. "You were brilliant back then, as you were just now."

Lala shrugged. "Maybe so, but I'm glad those days are past, and very glad to see how well you're doing." Paulina looked better than she had in a while. Reopening her shop, and likely time away from Ivo, had worked wonders.

"Ivo and I found a buyer for my house, which will help us afford housing in Prague. My in-laws have been very kind and patient with us staying there. Jacub's grown very fond of them, though he still asks for his Grandmama and Antila."

"Which reminds me, I have his birthday present." Lala gave it to Paulina. "Could you hold it here until his party? There's no room in Josef's apartment and I'm afraid if I bring it home it will get lost in the mess."

"That's the first time I've heard you refer to your new house as 'home.'" Paulina stowed the gift under her counter. "You needn't have come here just for that."

"I wanted to see you. And, I need a few new dresses." She

unbuttoned her coat. "Mine have grown tight around the waist."

"I expected you would and I'm all prepared. Come with me," Paulina beckoned. She took Lala to an armoire in a back corner. "This is where I store special orders." She brought out three dresses and held them up one by one. "These should fit you now and for at least the next month or so. I'm working on a few more to accommodate you later on."

The first was a blue cotton housedress with an undefined waist. The second, a wool coatdress for daywear in dark coral, featured a touch of embroidery on the edges of the collar.

Lala took hold of the third dress, a yellow chiffon evening gown. Paulina had sewn crystal beading along the hem as well as the shoulders and neckline, a clever way to detract the eye from a growing belly. "These are stunning, Paulina, especially this one." Lala rarely wore yellow, Paulina's favorite color. "I'll feel very special in it."

Paulina flashed an enigmatic smile.

Lala tried them on. They both agreed no alterations were needed.

"I'll take all three." Lala opened her purse. "How much will that be?"

Paulina waved her hand. "No charge." The smile lingered.

"I can't take them without paying."

"Yes, you can, just promise to take very good care of them. And one other thing..."

"What's that?"

"Return them to me to wear when you've outgrown them." Paulina patted her belly.

The reason for Paulina's bliss and radiance suddenly dawned on Lala and she gasped. "You, too?"

Paulina nodded.

"When?"

"End of summer."

Lala teared up with joy and hugged her friend. "Oh Paulina, I'm so happy for you and Ivo. I'm happy for us. Imagine, having our babies months apart. They'll grow up together as best friends as well as family."

"Like us." Paulina sighed.

"Ivo must be very pleased."

"He is. At least now his prodding me to eat makes sense. He's convinced fattening me up did the trick." She rolled her eyes.

"Perhaps it did." Lala handed Paulina the gown. "When can you have these delivered?"

"I'll send my girl around tomorrow. Now you go home and put your feet up."

Lala buttoned her coat before kissing Paulina on both cheeks. "I'm thrilled for you, my friend. For this," she gestured to Paulina's midsection, "As well as for all this." Lala's hand swept along the racks of clothing. "If you need any help, especially now," she patted Paulina's belly, "Josef and I are a short walk away."

"You and Josef have done more than your share. I'm training my girl and I've hired a spinster with dress shop experience who will help when I can't be here. I'll manage it all," she said with an emphatic nod. "Do let Josef know how pleased I am to have my shop open again."

Dusk approached when Lala stepped out of the shop. She felt a chill in the air and so walked at a brisk pace toward her home, where construction would soon stop for the day.

Thoughts of babies filled her mind. She pictured Paulina and her walking side by side pushing carriages, doting on their infants. Watching them frolic together along the river walk, playing in the gardens on Petřín Hill. Sharing clothing, books and toys; everything, as she and Paulina had done for years. She noticed people grinning at her and couldn't understand why until she caught her reflection in a shop window; her smile was so broad she appeared on the verge of laughing.

Lala felt so proud of Paulina, and inspired by her, running a business and caring for her family. She also felt proud of Josef, who honored Romy's lapsed commitment to Paulina and made it possible for her to reopen her shop. She could imagine a day when women would brag about their wardrobe, designed by Paulina. When collectors would boast about their latest acquisition from Josef's gallery.

And perhaps, when couples would announce to their guests that their vision of the perfect home was interpreted and created by Lala Smetana. But first, she had to return to the construction site and create a home that would make Josef proud, to show her appreciation of how he honored his commitment to her dream as well.

CHAPTER FIFTEEN

Lala sorted through the mail and to her surprise found a letter from Gershom, forwarded from her old address. She debated whether to open it, then chuckled at her silliness as she unsealed the envelope. As she read, the pleasant memories soured with news of his former apprentice, Elia. Gershom's adorable Italian cousin had been confronted by a band of Fascist thugs who strong armed him into joining their Action Squad, When he refused, they beat him to a pulp.

When the war ended, all the old hatred that had been submerged beneath the need to survive had resurfaced, conjoined with a new hatred bred out of the chaos that followed. Lala was fortunate with Ludovik and Hanus, but she couldn't afford to bring someone into their home who posed a danger to her family. Any future hires would have to be carefully vetted.

After relaying her problem with Mrs. Klima, Lala asked for Cerveny's help in finding a Jewish housekeeper. He sent over Ruth Barash, a robust spinster with a cheery disposition. Impressed by her manner as well as her resumé, Lala hired her.

A week later, the furniture had been moved in and set up in their temporary apartment. Once the curtains were in the windows, pictures hung on the wall, and decorative items arranged, Lala went downstairs to fetch Josef. She found him in the entry hall between his two shops.

Josef held a ladder steady as Hanus climbed up to insert light bulbs into the ceiling fixture.

"Love, when you're done here, come upstairs and see our new home."

As she waited, she thought about the time, as a girl, she'd redecorated Aunt Naomi's parlor, how nervous and excited she felt waiting for her aunt's reaction. After revamping her mother's house to accommodate three women and converting Paulina's home into a temporary boarding house for three men, she felt confident in what she'd accomplished.

Josef walked through the living and dining areas, complimenting her work. She escorted him to the bedroom, with a bed, two nightstands and a cabinet for storage.

"Where is the cradle?" he asked.

"It's still packed. We won't need it until we move upstairs."

"Are you sure? The new apartment won't be finished until at least July."

"No, love. They assured me it would be completed by early June."

"That's not what the foreman told me."

She'd been pleased with the quality of the work, other than finding the foreman to be patronizing at times. She'd tolerated that, but if he'd lied to her about the schedule... "I'm going upstairs right now to find out why he hasn't been honest with me."

Josef stopped her. "You'll do nothing of the sort. Wait

118

here and I'll speak to him, and I won't stop until I get the answer you want."

"Josef, I'm responsible for the work. I should be the one—"

"He will tell you whatever you want to hear."

"Because I'm married to the man paying his invoices. But he'll be honest with you."

Josef shrugged. "I'm also not in a delicate condition." After peeking into the new bathroom he smiled and said, "I expected something marvelous, but this exceeds my expectations. It's superb."

"Thank you for that, it's cheered me."

"This will cheer you even more. We should move in as soon as possible, which means you at last get to hear me say it's time to vacate my apartment."

Lala opened the door for Ludovik, an empty trunk balanced on his broad shoulders. He entered Josef's apartment ahead of Hanus, who brought in drop cloths and cord to wrap up the paintings. Josef met with the building manager downstairs to terminate his lease.

Lala folded the few items of clothing and linens she and Josef wanted to keep and offered the rest of Josef's garments, as well as the food in the cupboard, to the young men, which they accepted with thanks. With the trunk packed, she supervised the wrapping of the paintings. Ludovik moved with swift efficiency while his brother seemed to study each painting before covering it.

"Is this one of you?" asked Hanus, pointing to Armin's painting.

She nodded. "The artist was Mr. Smetana's son."

"Was?"

She swallowed hard. "He was killed...during the war."

The young man removed his cap and nodded. Lala preferred phrasing it that way so no further explanation would be sought.

Josef passed the youths carrying the trunk and artwork downstairs as he entered the apartment. He gave it a cursory glance. "I won't miss this place, other than a few memorable nights."

"I hope they included me." She smiled so he'd know she was teasing.

His hand brushed down her back. "What shall we do with the rest of the furnishings?"

An idea occurred to her. "Leave it to me. Go downstairs and supervise the loading of the artwork, and I'll join you shortly."

He eyed her warily. "What are you going to do?"

"Nothing that either of us will regret."

He hesitated, but went downstairs.

She put on her hat and coat, checked her appearance in the hallway mirror, and marched to the front door of Xenie's apartment. Lala knocked twice before the woman answered, wearing a frumpy housedress and no make-up, her hair tied up in a kerchief. She appeared much older than Lala had remembered, even older than Josef.

Xenie appeared startled to see Lala standing in her doorway.

Lala took a deep breath for courage and announced, "Josef and I are moving out of his apartment. We've decided not to take the furniture with us, so if you would like any of the items, they're yours."

The woman plucked a cigarette from her pocket and lit it,

taking a long drag before exhaling smoke back into her apartment. "And to what do I owe your generous offer?"

"It's my way of thanking you."

"So you're giving me your husband's old furniture?" She took another puff.

Lala waited until she released the smoke before answering, "You're entitled to a part of his past, but not any part of his future."

Lala asked her mother if they could spend the week of Passover with her, to which Sarah responded with a resounding yes. Lala told Josef that evening over dinner. "The timing couldn't be better with the accelerated construction schedule. They're painting the storeroom and all the hallways that week."

"Yes," Josef said. "I remember how unwell you felt when they painted the gallery last month."

"We ought to bring something to Mother."

"I have the perfect gift." Josef went to his desk and brought a deed. "I leased the apartment we saw, overlooking the river. With two grandchildren on the way, I thought your mother would like to live there or have a place in town when she wants to visit."

She hugged him. "Oh love, how thoughtful." She longed to have her mother nearby again, especially with the baby coming. Her mother would be thrilled as well.

Sarah invited Paulina and her family to join them for the Seder, but Ivo's teaching position at the University forced him to bow out. Paulina offered a compromise; she and Jacub would come for the first Seder and return home on the last train to Prague.

***

Josef arranged for Smolak to meet the four of them at the train station and drive them to Sarah's. Jacub, who'd never ridden in the vehicle before, asked if he could sit in "the best seat", up front next to Smolak. Laughing, and with Smolak's permission, his mother consented.

Lala asked Paulina, "Have you shared your good news with Mother yet?"

"I wrote to her the day after I told you."

"Then I needn't worry about ruining a surprise." She gave her sister's hand a squeeze.

Smolak parked the automobile in front of the house. Sarah came rushing out, her arms extended in anticipation of hugging whoever came near. Jacub dashed out of the car and ran to her, and Sarah smothered him with kisses. Lala heard squeals of delight from them both until Jacub wriggled away.

"My girls, my mamas-to-be," she cried with joy as Lala and Paulina entered her embrace while Smolak brought the luggage into the house. As Josef passed Sarah, arms still locked around her girls, she called out to him, "You're next."

Lala and Paulina followed Jacub into the house, with Sarah and Josef behind. Lala caught a strong whiff of menthol, definitely not a Passover tradition.

"What's that I smell, Mother?"

"It's camphor leaves. They say it wards off influenza."

"And you believe that?"

Sarah shrugged. "It can't hurt. I'd mark my doorposts with lamb's blood if it made a difference. Come in and sit, dear."

Lala settled into the armchair. She smiled when she saw lipstick marks covering Jacub's cheeks from her mother's kisses.

"I want to sit next to Grandmama," the boy announced, and Sarah eased herself on the sofa by his side.

"You look so handsome in your new clothes, Jacub," she cooed. "Did your mother make them for you?"

"No, they were a Christmas present from Dědeček and Babička."

"That's what Ivo's parents want to be called," Paulina explained. "It's Czech for 'grandma' and 'grandpa.'"

"I'm sorry Ivo couldn't join us, but I'm very glad to have you all back under my roof, if only for dinner."

"Me, too, Grandmama. I miss you so much. Nobody cooks as good as you."

"Oh my sweet boy, that's the most wonderful thing anyone could say to me. I miss you, too." She grabbed him and lavished him with kisses until he begged her to stop.

"You just want me to finish cooking so we can eat," she said to the boy. "The table is set, the food's prepared and all that's left to do is stir a few pots before we get started."

"We can help, Mama Sarah," said Paulina, but Sarah shooed her away. "No need, I've help now. Mrs. Havlik asked me to train a nice respectful girl for service." She emphasized "respectful." "Which reminds me – she brought a letter sent to the mansion addressed to Lala."

"Who would send mail to me there?" Lala wondered aloud.

"It's your house," Josef replied in a dry voice as Sarah fetched the letter.

Lala read it through. "Someone has made me an offer for the mansion and its entire contents. It seems a reasonable amount." Lala handed the letter to Josef. "Do you agree?"

His eyes widened as he read. "Quite."

She slipped the folded letter into the envelope. "I'll address this later. It's our first Passover since the war ended, since the founding of our nation. Let us celebrate our freedom."

With Josef's help, Lala drafted a letter offering to meet the prospective buyer, Mr. Zahradnik, three days later. She knew Josef would want to participate in the negotiations. The question was where. "Shall we have him meet us in the café near the train station?"

"This really should be handled in the house," he said.

"I agree, but would you be willing to go back to the house?"

"For this, yes."

Lala set up the meeting for Friday at ten o'clock in the morning.

At precisely ten o'clock a deluxe automobile stopped at the entrance to the mansion, where Lala and Josef waited. A chauffeur emerged from the driver's seat with a briefcase tucked under his arm. His uniform had more ostentatious trim than any general's. He sprinted around the vehicle to open the right rear passenger door.

Out stepped a squat man carrying a cane that seemed for effect rather than support, for he held it suspended more than he leaned on it. His dark eyes bulged from their sockets, punctuating a flat face with multiple rolls of fat under his chin that obliterated his neck. Although dressed in finery, he comported himself with the brusque gait of a workman.

The chauffeur handed the briefcase to his employer and

returned to the vehicle. The man approached Lala and Josef. "You're prompt. I like that." He offered his hand to Josef. "Otokar Zahradnik."

"Josef Smetana, and this is my wife, who owns the home."

Lala nodded to him. "Mr. Zahradnik. Please come in. Would you like to see the house?"

"I've already seen it. Shall we discuss the terms?"

She responded to his terseness with a truncated smile. "We'll talk in my husband's former office," she said before entering the house.

Without Josef's furnishings the room looked very different. A hunting scene, painted by a once popular artist Lala never liked, hung on the wall where Armin's portrait of her used to be. A suite of parlor furniture, secured as part of the factory sale, rounded out the scheme. Lala suggested they sit there.

Mr. Zahradnik settled into one of the chairs and rested his cane and briefcase alongside. "I've been looking for an estate to convert into a hunting lodge or inn, where Prague's society could retreat and enjoy the countryside in a manner befitting their station. One without ties to the royal family, that is. Your home would suit my criteria well, if it includes all contents, including that wonderful Rolls Royce, and staff. I've spoken to your housekeeper and steward and they have agreed to my terms should I take possession of the mansion." He reached for his briefcase. "I understand Mrs. Smetana organized all the rooms," he said to Josef as he removed a set of documents. "Were you planning to open a hotel, then?"

"Why would you think that, Mr. Zahradnik?" Josef asked.

"Because the entire house has been set up in that manner."

"I wanted it to be comfortable for visitors," said Lala. "I'm flattered if you think the rooms would be suitable for paying guests. In a sense that is what I was attempting."

"The house and setting are impressive, but seeing the bedrooms already set up for guests convinced me." Zahradnik attempted a smile. "I won't have much to do to prepare it for opening, which is why my offer is so generous."

Lala tried to think of a tactful way to find out how this man could afford to buy the house. If through the black market, she would refuse to sell to him.

"Have you always been in the hospitality business, Mr. Zahradnik?"

"I haven't as yet, Mrs. Smetana. However, I know how to run a business. I've done so for many years, successfully, I might add."

"I presume your success means you found a way to adapt to a war economy, like my husband."

He turned to Josef. "You owned the local furniture factory that began producing medical equipment during the war?"

"Yes, until recently. My wife and I have relocated to Prague, which is why I sold the factory and she's selling the house."

"Then you might say I had an easier time adjusting to the necessities of war than you did as I manufacture rifles. I did quite well during the war years, as you can imagine. It could be said you helped to patch up our wounded men and I helped to eliminate their foes." Zahradnik issued a dry chuckle. "Do we have a deal?"

She looked to Josef for advice. He sat rigid in his chair, lips pressed together, hands gripping the arms of his chair, knuckles white. She could hear his labored breath, as though he had to force himself to inhale and exhale. He couldn't bear being in this house, and likely never would again. The man's offer was fair, substantial in fact, and while he may have profited during the war, he earned his money honestly.

Lala took the papers from Zahradnik. "Where do I sign?"

CHAPTER SIXTEEN

Lala stood naked before the mirror and observed herself in profile. With her belly starting just below her bustline she looked like a capital P. Both belly and breasts seemed to have doubled in size in the last month and she still had eight weeks to go before her baby was due. She didn't know whether to laugh, fret, or cry, not that it mattered. Lately she'd been doing plenty of each.

With Josef's gallery opening in five days, she did not relish having to get dressed up for the formal reception. Fortunately, Paulina had offered to create a special gown for her to wear. Lala had teased her by saying she would have to host a formal gala in a few months so Paulina would have a chance to wear the same dress.

She donned a robe before opening a few windows to cross-ventilate the apartment. Despite the coolness of the early May morning, she felt steam rising within her. It may have been fifteen degrees outside but her body seemed to be making its own weather. It reminded her of the discomfort her mother had gone through a few years earlier when she'd reached her mid-forties. The flash of heat subsided. She put on her loosest day dress before her housekeeper arrived.

Lala gathered the three maternity dresses Paulina had given her and put them back in their boxes. Having outgrown them all, she'd fulfill her part of the bargain – return them to her sister who would now fit into them.

Ruth arrived and with a cheery greeting gathered her cleaning supplies. Lala went downstairs to the gallery where she found Josef supervising the installation of railings along the wall to hang paintings. On an adjacent antique chest she spotted a bronze statue mixed in with some pieces of crystal.

"That's the Degas ballerina you kept in your office. Why are you selling it?"

"It should fetch a good price."

"But I thought you liked it."

He gave a noncommittal shrug. "It was a gift."

Ah. Likely from Romy. She picked up the statue and before Josef could protest she placed it on a Demilune table, its cabriole legs as willowy as the ballerina's. Josef nodded his approval.

She rearranged the crystal pieces. "Dear, I must go to Paulina's shop today to exchange some dresses."

"I won't need the automobile today. Have Ludovik drive you."

Traffic and pedestrians clogged the bridge, forcing Ludovik to drive slower than a walking pace and stop frequently. Loud words outside drew Lala's attention. She saw a man confront a busker hawking postcards and placards from his stand near the statue of St. John the Baptist. From her seat she perused the art work, most of it propaganda celebrating the recent wave of Communist Party member assassinations in Germany. One placard resting askew against the statue's base illustrated a macabre street scene in Hungary, judging by the uniforms worn by a line of soldiers hanging from gallows. Wives and children wept at the dead men's feet while, standing in the middle of the road, a Bolshevik in uniform observed the carnage with a haughty air of satisfaction. The caption read, Erzet Harcoltunk? – "This is what we fought for?"

Political art thrived in the chaos that ensued after the war ended. Well-drawn, she allowed, despite the gory depiction. The artist had placed the smug-looking Bolshevik in the foreground, hands on hips, an unkempt uniform wrapped around his fat middle. Skinny legs stuffed into unpolished boots. Thin arms as well, implying physical weakness. A caricature she'd seen before. While she disagreed with Communists philosophically, and with their often volatile ways of expressing their views, she never thought of them as weaklings. Then she noticed the slight alteration on the Bolshevik's cap, a subtle nod to a trait he shared with many of the political assassination victims.

The gold star affixed right above the brim did not have five points, but six.

Traffic cleared and Ludovik exited the bridge. Lala took measured breaths to quell a wave of queasiness that washed over her, which had nothing to do with her condition.

Lala asked Ludovik to stop at her favorite pastry shop. Inside she ogled the selection, but the round fruit-filled kolace tempted her the most. She ordered a half dozen, two each with plum jam, a poppy seed filling, and cherry jam. As the clerk wrapped up her selections she considered whether the heartburn she would suffer after eating one would be worth it.

Ludovik parked the automobile in front of Paulina's shop. He gathered the dress boxes and brought them inside, where Paulina was supervising Elke, her new clerk, as the girl wrapped a customer's purchase. After tying the ribbon into a neat bow, Elke handed the box to the customer and thanked her, then glanced at Paulina for approval. Paulina smiled and the girl relaxed.

"Would you bring my other packages to my apartment this afternoon?" the customer asked as she handed the girl her calling card.

"Yes, Ma'am, I shall." She escorted the customer to the door and held it open for her.

"Excellent, Elke," praised Paulina.

"Thank you, Mrs. Chytry."

"Elke, I would like you to meet my sister, Mrs. Smetana."

Elke curtsied. "Very pleased to make your acquaintance, Ma'am."

"You may call me Mrs. Smetana."

Paulina remained behind her counter. "She has brought back some dresses. Would you take them from the boxes and hang them in the armoire?"

"Yes, Mrs. Chytry." Elke went to collect the boxes from Ludovik with a shy glance his way. The young man, eyes wide and mouth agape, didn't release them immediately. Lala suppressed a grin. He seemed captivated by the girl, which didn't surprise Lala. With blonde hair neatly braided around her crown, deep blue eyes stark against her pale complexion and nearly flawless features, Elke was blessed with natural beauty.

"Ludovik, you may either wait in the car or return to bring me home in an hour."

"As you wish." Ludovik bowed and with an open glance at Elke, left the shop.

Paulina took Lala's arm. "Come into the back room with me."

The two women passed through the door that separated the dress shop from Paulina's private quarters. Designed by Lala, it served as an office, a lounge for relaxing or entertaining special clients, and a sewing station where Paulina could make a quick alteration or repair.

Paulina held out a comfortable chair with arms for Lala to sit. Lala placed the pastries on the side table while Paulina fetched a platter and two plates from her cupboard. Lala noticed Paulina's belly had begun to show. The three dresses she'd returned would fit her sister well.

Paulina opened the package and arranged the pastries on the platter. "Shall I show you the gown before or after we eat?"

"Whatever you like. I probably won't indulge now."

"Heartburn?"

Lala nodded. "Everything I eat upsets my stomach."

"Try having small meals but more frequently. That helped me. And avoid lying down after eating."

"Look what you have to look forward to in a few months," Lala teased.

Paulina opened a cabinet beside her sewing machine and took out a sapphire blue gown of raw silk. She held it up for Lala to see. Copper beads embellished the sleeves and both sides of the gown, which detracted the eye from the belly, as did the flattering scoop neckline. A high waist and pleats below the bustline provided room for Lala's growing middle without swamping her in meters of fabric.

"Oh my, that is exquisite."

"It should be comfortable as well. And I contracted a fabulous milliner so I have the perfect accompaniment." Paulina brought out a hatbox tied with ribbon from her cabinet and placed it in front of Lala.

As Lala untied the ribbon Paulina said, "I know you favor simpler styles, but in your present condition I thought you'd want something dazzling to draw the eye away from your middle."

Inside was an evening hat, velvet with tulle and feather trim. Though more extravagant than anything she'd normally wear, she tried it on for Paulina. "What do you think?"

Paulina stepped around her. "It needs a bit of taming for you." She removed a piece of tulle and wound it around the base of the brim, flattening the feather trim. "Much better." She gave Lala a hand mirror to see for herself.

Lala agreed.

Paulina unbuttoned the back of the gown. "Try on the dress so I can make any necessary adjustments."

With Paulina's help, Lala undressed and stepped into the new gown. It fit perfectly to her mind, but Paulina grabbed her pin cushion and made some adjustments to the pleating. "I want to make sure you have enough room, as it's entirely possible you'll get bigger between now and the gallery opening."

Lala cast an admiring eye on the rose beige dress Paulina wore, with a drop waist that crossed the bottom of her belly. "You're carrying different this time," she observed.

"I think so as well," Paulina mumbled through the pins she held between her lips. "Much lower than with Jacub. Turn a little to your right."

Lala complied. "Perhaps you're having a girl."

Paulina pinned a final pleat in the dress and stepped back.

"A boy and a girl – oh! That was a little kick." She rubbed her belly and smiled. "This one's been very active."

"Mine has slowed down." Lala frowned. "I hope that doesn't mean—"

"That's normal in the last weeks, according to my midwife," Paulina assured her. "The baby's growing too big to have much room in there to move. Try not to worry."

"It's comforting to be able to talk to you about this."

"My friend, you'll have an easier time of it than I did with Jacub. And you'll be better at motherhood, having experience in raising him," said Paulina.

"But you had all the right instincts. You caught on straightaway. I learned from watching you."

"Then we'll both be the best mamas in the history of motherhood," Paulina exclaimed. "Now let's get you out of that gown so I can finish it and my dress on time."

"Aren't you going to wear the yellow gown I brought back for you?"

"I am, but I'll need to alter it for my figure." She drew her hand in a circle around her belly.

On the morning of the gallery's premiere, Lala checked every detail for Josef's reception twice. Together, she and Josef had chosen what items to display. She'd left enough space for guests to gather, sip champagne and nibble on tray-passed hors d'oeuvres. Hanus stopped by the caterer to confirm the final menu and time when the chef and his serving crew would arrive. Josef's storeroom had been cleaned and organized for private collectors to view additional pieces for sale. Josef's dress suit and a pair of silk shirts, cleaned and pressed, hung in his closet. Ruth polished his dress shoes until they gleamed. Josef had sent Ludovik to bring Sarah to help Lala, and Elke would deliver Lala's evening ensemble after lunch.

Lala bathed, slipped on her dressing gown, put up her hair, and waited.

The sound of Josef's automobile drew her to the window. She saw Ludovik get out but not her mother. Josef came outside to meet him. She couldn't hear the conversation as Ludovik spoke to Josef, but she saw Josef's reaction; his hands cupped his face and he bent his head.

Panic surged through Lala and she screamed Josef's name through the window.

He looked up at her, then ran into the building and up the stairs. Moments later he stood before her, gasping for breath.

"Josef, where is my mother?"

"She's fine, love. She had something to attend to and will be arriving late, that's all."

"Then what did Ludovik tell you that made you so upset?"

"A problem with one of the guests, nothing for you to worry about."

"I don't believe you. You wouldn't have reacted so strongly if that were true."

Josef took her in his arms. "Love, you must trust me on this. Please." He placed a soft kiss on her forehead. She nodded and walked with him to the dining room.

Ruth emerged from the kitchen holding a tray with a soup tureen and ladle. "Shall I serve lunch?"

***

After lunch Josef returned to his gallery. An hour later Elke arrived with boxes holding Lala's gown and hat. Lala observed the girl kept her head down and her gaze averted. Lala had her bring the boxes into the bedroom and place them on the bed.

"However did you manage carrying this all the way from the shop?"

"Your husband kindly sent his automobile to bring me here," she said shyly.

Despite her pale smile something was troubling her. Lala considered it might have something to do with Ludovik and hoped the young man did nothing untoward.

Elke removed the lid from the dress box. "Mrs. Chytry said I should assist you in any way needed. May I?"

With Lala's assent Elke lifted the gown from the box and inspected it carefully. "It doesn't appear to need pressing. Shall I open the buttons for you?"

Lala noticed a flicker of sadness in the girl's face. "Yes, thank you Elke."

The girl undid the back as Lala took off her dressing gown. Elke helped Lala slip the evening gown over her head.

"Elke, I don't want to pry, but you seem distressed. Has Ludovik said or done anything to upset you?"

"Oh, no Mrs. Smetana. He's been very nice to me, very respectful." Blushing at that, she finished buttoning the gown and after fetching her sewing kit, stood before Lala. She smoothed the hem and inspected the dress one more time. "I won't need to alter it at all. It fits you perfectly."

Lala gazed at herself in the mirror. The additional pleats Paulina added refined the fit around her belly, which as Paulina predicted had expanded since the dress was made. The gown looked stunning on her.

She turned to Elke and smiled. "Paulina's outdone herself. It's not only beautiful, but flattering and comfortable to wear. I can't wait to see it on her."

At that Elke burst into tears.

"Elke, what's wrong? Please tell me."

"I can't," she insisted between sobs. "I promised her I wouldn't until after the reception so as not to spoil it for you and Mr. Smetana." She took a handkerchief from her sleeve to soak up her tears.

Lala began to tremble. "You're frightening me."

Josef, who'd returned to the apartment to dress for the evening, burst into the room. Before he could say anything, Lala demanded, "Josef, do you know why she's crying? Is this what had you upset earlier?"

"Please, sit down," Josef urged.

"Only if you tell me right now!"

He nodded and she sat.

"Paulina had a…a mishap."

Lala leapt to her feet. "What happened? Is she hurt? How badly?"

"She's not hurt, exactly." Josef paused and let out a loud breath. "She lost the baby."

"She lost the baby?" She couldn't believe the words, even after repeating them several times. But Josef's reaction earlier on when Ludovik must have told him, her mother's absence, and Elke's outburst told Lala the dreadful news had to be true.

"I must go to her."

She tried to bolt but Josef held her back. "You can't now. It isn't safe. The doctor said the most likely cause this far along is illness or an infection. Your mother is with Paulina. They both insisted you stay away. They don't want you to risk our baby's health." Josef released her. "I know you want to be with her now, but you mustn't." He clasped his hands around hers. "She understands."

The reception proceeded as planned, except for three missing – and dearly missed – guests. Josef sold several pieces and cultivated a list of potential clients. Lala mingled with the guests, accepting compliments on the quality and variety of the collection for sale, on the fine champagne and delicious canapés, even several on her gown. Her smile remained steady if pasted on, her conversation stayed enthusiastic about the gallery and knowledgeable about its stock. All the while her heart and thoughts remained elsewhere, in a hospital room across the Vltava River where her sister lay in bed mourning a loss. The loss not only of her child, a girl who would have been named Jeanne Marie after Paulina's idol Madame Paquin, but of a dream. A dream of two sisters raising their children together, cousins as close as siblings.

Lala's hand circled her belly. She and Paulina would share this loss, as they had shared in raising Jacub. As they would in loving the child Lala now carried.

CHAPTER SEVENTEEN

Lala waddled back from the toilette and slipped into bed. After lying there for a minute in discomfort, she shifted from her side to her back. Not that it mattered. Whatever position she tried, she couldn't get comfortable with her swollen middle and the baby inside kicking more forcefully than ever. Sleep evaded her and she couldn't imagine how she'd get through the next month until the baby was due.

She struggled to sit up, which sapped her last bit of strength. Simple movements took great effort. Standing up or sitting down could fatigue her. As her belly grew, she'd begun experiencing pain in her back and lower abdomen. She didn't recall Paulina having so many problems when she carried Jacub. What if something was wrong?

Her thoughts began to drift into dangerous territory... *"They cursed his name and his family—"*

Stop! She knew it was nonsense. No one could put a curse on another person.

Pausing a moment to catch her breath, she shifted to let her legs dangle over the side of the bed. She contemplated getting up to open the window but sitting in that position aggravated her stomach cramps and she lay down again.

"What is it, love?" mumbled Josef, half asleep.

"I can't get comfortable."

He sat up. "What can I do for you?"

"Why don't you carry this baby for the rest of the month."

He'd learned to ignore her sarcasm. "Try laying on your left side instead of your back."

"Oh, advice from the maternity expert?"

"Lala, I want to help." He laid a pillow on the mattress beside her. "Turn onto your left side and rest your belly on this." He assisted her effort to turn, and once she was in position, he tucked another pillow behind her back for support. "Is that better?"

She sighed. "Yes, thank you." After he lay down again she asked, "Did you do this for Romy when she carried Armin?"

"I hired a lady's maid who also served as a midwife." He reached across and massaged her back.

"Mmmm, that feels wonderful." She felt some of the tension drain away as she closed her eyes.

"Is there anything else I can do?"

Her eyes opened. "Yes. Help me up. I need to use the toilette again."

He did as she asked. As she waddled out of the bedroom she muttered, "Fatigue, heartburn, cramping, back pains. I can hardly wait until it's time to have this baby."

She uttered that same complaint every day, often more than once, until labor began.

CHAPTER EIGHTEEEN

With a moan, Lala winced and gritted her teeth. The contraction felt like her insides were being squeezed like a dishrag and pulled out. She tensed from the pain, which made the pain worse. A few deep breaths for courage helped, so she continued to breathe deeply and push whenever the midwife told her to.

Between contractions Lala lay there panting, out of breath, her face drenched in sweat. She writhed as pain seared though her back, causing her to cry out. The midwife applied gentle pressure on Lala's lower spine until it subsided enough to be tolerable.

"It shouldn't be much longer," the midwife advised in a calm voice as another contraction hit.

Lala caught her breath as the midwife cleaned away the afterbirth before laying the newborn against Lala's breast. A wave of euphoria coursed through her as she gazed at her child's head, sparsely covered in dark hair, and tiny pink body. The baby let out a mewl. Her baby. Her perfect baby. With her fingers she stroked the infant's matted hair and caressed the soft skin. "Would you call my husband in?"

The midwife nodded and opened the door for Josef.

Lala cradled the baby in her arms. "Come meet your daughter."

His eyes filled with tears. "How are you?" He bent to kiss Lala softly on her lips.

"Tired, but happy now that she's here. Would you like to hold her?"

"More than anything." He picked up the infant and held her against his chest as he gazed at her with a tear-filled smile. "She is absolutely beautiful, like her mother. Welcome, little girl." He kissed his daughter's forehead. "What shall we call her?"

"I want to name her for Armin and my mother's sister Hannah. What do you think of Amalie Halette?"

"It's lovely, but don't you want to name her after your father?"

"Jacub is named for him, so I'd like to wait until we have a boy. Her Hebrew name will be Aharona Chana. I'll record it in the family bible."

"Amalie Halette, daughter of Josef and Lala Smetana, born on the evening of the 26th of June, 1919." He laid the baby next to Lala and kissed them both. "Amalie, would you like to meet your grandmother and aunt now?"

PART TWO

ZÁMECKÁ STREET, MALA STRANA, PRAGUE
June 26, 1921

CHAPTER ONE

Vilem Vesely poked his head into the Smetanas' parlor, where Lala chatted with his wife Zoe as she took photographs. "Josef said he needed a photographer straightaway and as luck would have it, the best one in Prague is here."

"I'm trying to work and you're interrupting," Zoe said as she lowered her Ica camera. "What would Josef like me to photograph?"

"Family and friends when they arrive for the birthday party." He added, "Josef said, 'I'm paying for this.'"

"Tell him I will get set up in the living room once I finish photographing his daughter."

Amalie and the Veselys' daughter Charis played amid a menagerie of stuffed animals on the Persian rug.

Zoe raised the camera to her eye and sat on her heels. Strands of black hair tumbled from her bun, held in place with a pencil. She swept them behind her ears, indifferent to her appearance. With her Mediterranean heritage, Lala thought Zoe could have leapt from a Greco-Roman frieze;

147

her sharp, angular features inspired several of Vilem's Cubist paintings.

Lala had grown to admire Charis's parents professionally and felt pleased the toddlers got along so well. Amalie, curious and outgoing, could be demanding and she bored easily.

Charis, a pretty child with her mother's olive complexion and dark curly hair like her father's, picked up a stuffed rabbit and made it dance, eliciting a marvelous reaction from Amalie.

"That should be darling," Lala observed as Zoe pointed the camera lens toward Amalie.

Zoe excelled at photographing children, capturing them in an unaffected way that never appeared posed. Their modern sensibility and lack of pretense, much like Zoe's subjects, appealed to Lala. She purchased one photograph of Charis being dazzled by an organ grinder's monkey, then convinced Josef to accept a few of Zoe's photographs on consignment, along with a painting by Vilem that sold within days.

"I truly appreciate your offer, Zoe," said Lala. "I can't think of a better gift than one of your photographs of my daughter. And do take some of the girls together."

"I've already something in mind I think you'll like," Zoe said as she focused the lens of her camera on the children. "But the photos are a gift for you and Josef, to thank you for all you've done to promote Vilem's work, and mine. We brought something more appealing to a two-year-old for Amalie. " Lala heard a click as Zoe took a picture. "Her dress is stunning. Did your sister make it?"

"She did," Lala said with pride.

"Amalie's a lucky girl. Someday I hope to be able to

afford one of Paulina's dresses." She choked back a chuckle. "If Vilem sells enough of his paintings."

"Or you your brilliant photographs."

She blossomed at hearing Lala's compliment. "I'm working hard for that day." She turned to focus her camera on the toddlers.

"You'll meet Paulina soon," Lala told her. "She'll be here with her family."

"Who else will be coming?"

"We've invited the Chermaks and their four children. You may know Klement, who manages the bank near St. Salvator Cathedral. He's an avid art and antiques collector, a fan of my late father's work for many years, which naturally endeared me to him straightaway. I don't know his wife. He recently remarried after the children's mother died in childbirth. And we asked the von Anhalts; little Pearl is darling, the same age as our daughters."

Zoe flinched. "The von Anhalts, as in...?"

Lala's broad smile kept her from rolling her eyes. "Yes, as in Leopold, our former Emperor's son-in-law. Moritz is his cousin, albeit a distant one, so no curtsying required. He's unpretentious and fun-loving. His wife's American, from a wealthy family, cowboys or something like that. Her name is Millicent Aimee, but she goes by Mamie."

"What's she like?" Zoe asked.

"We haven't met." Lala turned, hearing a commotion at the front door; more guests had arrived. "I'm told she speaks passable German, though some of her American expressions seem to defy translation," she explained as Josef entered the room.

Upon seeing him Amalie leapt to her feet and ran into his waiting arms. "Papa!"

He lifted her up and she threw her arms around his neck.

"Hello my sweet flower." He kissed her cheeks until she giggled. To Lala he said, "The Chermaks have arrived."

"Please meet them at the door. I'll be right out to greet them."

Zoe dusted her camera lens. "Amalie absolutely adores her father."

Lala took a deep breath and let it out slowly. "She certainly does, and it's mutual."

Klement Chermak kissed Lala's hand as he entered and greeted her. She thought him ruggedly handsome for a man of forty, with his strong nose and jawline accented by a cleft chin, and blue eyes sharp against his ruddy complexion and dark brown hair.

His wife Willete followed him inside, ushering his four children. With her rectangular face, strong jawline and broad, flat nose, she did not appear to be Czech. She wore her hair pinned up in a dated Edwardian pompadour, and her dress, while modern, seemed quite dowdy for such a young woman.

Willete carried her two younger stepchildren into the parlor as Lala escorted Klement to the living room. The entryway took on a raucous air when the adults momentarily left the nine and seven-year-old boys unchaperoned. They immediately launched into an argument over who would claim the window seat during the drive home.

Overhearing Klement III, as he insisted on being called, and Evzen quarrel reminded Lala of her cousin Saul and herself. Saul tragically lived up to his Biblical name. All four of his children died before their second birthday; the first two from the same disease that killed Saul's brothers, and the second two from the influenza epidemic that also claimed Lala's dear Uncle Hershel.

The caterer emerged from the kitchen. "Shall we begin serving the hors d'oeuvres now, Mrs. Smetana?"

Lala gestured for him to wait when she heard the downstairs door shut.

"Mr. and Mrs. Chytry," Ruth announced as Ivo and Paulina entered with six-year-old Jacub. Lala welcomed them in with hugs.

Paulina smoothed the collar of Jacub's shirt. "Would you like to see your cousin and give her your special birthday gift?"

He nodded.

"Tell Antila what you have for Amalie."

"A million million kisses."

"What a thoughtful present, Jacub. It's always been my favorite." Lala chuckled. Such a sweet-natured child. Jacub retained his gentle, loving personality. He adored his cousin and seemed totally captivated by her, something he shared with his Uncle Josef.

As the boy scampered away, Ivo admonished, "Be a good boy."

'I will, Papa."

"As if he could be anything else." Lala put the gift they brought on the entryway console.

Ivo handed Ruth his walking stick before kissing Lala's cheek. "Paulina told me your guest list. A banker helping to underwrite our government, a count related to the Hapsburgs, and a Communist artist." He rubbed his hands together in glee. "This should make for some interesting conversation." He bussed Paulina on the forehead. "And all you need to concern yourself with is gossip and fashion."

Paulina asked Lala, "Has Mother arrived yet?"

"She's taking a nap before the festivities. Join the others in the living room while I check in the kitchen."

Lala asked the caterer to begin serving hors d'oeuvres. His uniformed waiter immediately whisked a tray from the kitchen.

Zoe emerged from the parlor. "I took some photographs of your nephew with the girls. I'm ready to take more pictures."

Lala took her arm. "Then come with me to the living room. I'll introduce you to Paulina."

The gathered adults barely had time to sample the catering staff's food when the downstairs bell rang.

"That will be the von Anhalts," Lala announced. Ruth opened the door. Moritz waltzed in, baring a jolly grin and looking dapper in a slim fitting grey flannel suit. Handsome as a movie star and twice as charming, Lala thought. He shook hands with her before handing his hat and scarf to the housekeeper.

Then in stepped his wife.

Mamie stood taller than Josef and towered over her husband. Her broad face and even features gave her a regal bearing. Lala's recent issue of La Vie Parisienne carried an illustration of the couture dress the woman wore. Multiple layers of ruffles comprised the hoop skirt, forcing Mamie to hold her arms in a forty five degree angle from her body like a flamboyant shepherdess. Her shopping trips to Paris had become fodder for the society pages ever since her marriage.

The couple's entourage included their chauffeur, who presented an extravagantly wrapped package before leaving, and a cherubic nanny who carried the couple's toddler, Pearl, in her arms.

"Welcome. Josef and I are so pleased you could attend the party for Amalie."

"We postponed our trip to Italy for this." Mamie looked around. "What a cute little *pied à terre,* Mrs. Smetana," she exclaimed, mangling the French. "So modern."

Moritz being a valued client, Lala wanted to keep their relationship cordial. She affected a smile and said, "Thank you, and please call me Lala. Ruth was about to bring the children to the breakfast room for lunch. She'll show your nanny and little Pearl in as well."

Once Lala and Josef made introductions in the living room, Lala invited the women to gather in the parlor. Willete excused herself to check on the two older boys.

Lala noticed Mamie leveling a gaze at Paulina, who was sipping champagne, and asked, "May I bring you a glass, Mamie?"

Mamie dismissed the offer with a wave her hand. "Never touch the stuff." She leaned in as if to whisper, "At least not before five'," and snickered. "Oh well, it's legal here, so why not? It's five o'clock somewhere."

No one laughed.

Mamie resumed her appraisal of Paulina. "What a nice dress you've got on. Is it from your shop?"

Paulina issued a graceful smile and said, "It is. I design all my clothes, and Lala's."

"Really? I'd think sometimes you'd want to wear something...different. Like when you go to the same restaurant every night for dinner, after a while you want to eat something else."

Don't smile! Lala fought the urge to roll her eyes and groan. *Let it go.*

Paulina didn't rise to the bait either. "No, all my appetites are satisfied."

Willete knocked before entering the room. She began to curtsy in front of Mamie, who stopped her immediately. "None of that."

"Please forgive me, Countess. I don't know the proper etiquette for the wife of royalty in line to ascend the throne."

"The only throne my husband is ever going to ascend will be one that flushes, if you get my drift."

Lala bit her lip, a habit she'd fought to overcome, but it kept her from reacting to Mamie's crassness. She wondered if Americans were more tolerant of that sort of language.

Ruth entered the room and announced, "I believe it's—"

"Excuse me," snapped Willete, "You're interrupting a private conversation."

"I asked Ruth to remind me of the day's schedule, Willete." Lala glared at the woman as Ruth tiptoed out. "If you like, I'll have Josef escort you to his client room downstairs, where you may have all the privacy you need."

"No, Mrs. Smetana, that's not what I meant." She put her hand to her mouth as though it would stop the words from tumbling out. Her face flushed. "Please accept my apology for being so rude to your servant."

"Thank you, but it's Ruth who deserves the apology."

Mamie waved her hand. "Don't mistake servants for friends, Lala."

Angered, Lala was about to confront Mamie when Willete said, "Thank you, your highness." She sidled up to Mamie, but Mamie flared a look of disdain at her and stepped away from the woman as though she smelled like a rotting fish.

"I meant servants may not be our friends, but they are our employees and deserve respectful treatment," Mamie said before turning away from Lala to face Willete. "And don't try to butter me up. 'Your highness' indeed."

"I only meant we seem to think alike."

"Willete, you and I don't think alike and we're nothing alike. You have no class and some money, while I have a little class and lots of money."

Willete's attempt at a smile wilted. Lala couldn't see Mamie's face from behind but her aggressive stance looked intimidating.

"Ladies!" Lala's cry brought about a stand down. She gestured to the clock on the mantle and in a firm voice said, "I believe it's time for cake and opening presents."

As she escorted the women from the parlor Lala urged herself to remain calm. Gossip and fashion indeed.

CHAPTER TWO

After the birthday festivities, Josef suggested the ladies bring their children into the parlor for a group photograph. Klement, familiar with the camera, offered to take the picture so Zoe could be included.

Josef pushed a chair next to the sofa for Sarah. Lala sat in the middle of the sofa and placed Amalie on her lap, her daughter's little legs dangling over her knees. One arm encircled Amalie's waist, the other stilled her swinging legs from kicking Lala's shins.

Mamie sat next to Lala, who edged over to make room for the countess, or more accurately, her dress. Mamie took advantage and spread out each tier of ruffles before presenting her arms palm up as if preparing to accept a ceremonial sword.

"Give her to me," she instructed her daughter's nanny, who'd been holding the girl.

The woman placed Pearl in her mother's outstretched arms and there the toddler lay like a fishmonger's offering. The nanny flexed her fingertips slightly upward, a subtle gesture for Mamie to raise her arms a little more so the child

157

wouldn't tumble out. Mamie attempted a dignified pose but her discomfort shone through.

Paulina sat between Sarah and Lala, cuddling Jacub on her lap. She reached over to fan out Amalie's skirt. Lala thanked her sister with a quick smile.

Vilem carried Charis to her mother. "Do you want to hold her?" he asked.

"It would make a more interesting photograph if I stood behind the sofa and she sat up front," Zoe said.

"Where should I put her?"

She directed her husband to the spot, then arranged the child into a pose as though she were a piece of modeling clay. Zoe proposed the three oldest Chermak children sit on the floor near her daughter and Willete stand in back, holding the youngest. Willete insisted on posing with all four children. Zoe relented and set them together behind and beside Sarah's chair. Mindful of their father's presence, the two older boys curbed their frowns and stood with their step-mother. Charis remained frozen as a still life.

Lala turned to Paulina, who raised her eyebrows in acknowledgement of the oddity.

Klement snapped a few pictures before returning the camera to Zoe, who took more with the husbands included. Then Josef fetched the cognac decanter and escorted the men downstairs to his showroom to see his newest acquisitions. Lala suggested the ladies adjourn to the living room. Sarah volunteered to help Pearl's nanny watch the children in the parlor.

Ruth brought a tray with glasses of champagne for the ladies. She placed it on the sideboard and darted out, avoiding eye contact with Willete.

Zoe excused herself. "I'd like to take more pictures of the

children," she said. "The afternoon light reflecting from the building outside will put a glow on their faces." As she left, Klement III and Evzen burst into the room.

"I'm bored," exclaimed Klement, arms crossed over his chest, while his brother sulked beside him. "There's nothing to do here."

"Why don't you go into the parlor with your sister and brother?" Willete suggested. Her tone sounded more pleading than firm.

Klement's face twisted in disgust. "They're babies. We don't want to be around them."

"Where is our father?" demanded Evzen.

"He's downstairs with Mr. Smetana and the other men," Lala said.

The boy grabbed a bisque figurine from a tabletop like he was taking a hostage.

Willete blanched. "You really shouldn't touch things that don't belong to you, Evzen."

"You can't tell me what to do," he sneered. "You're not my real mother."

Before Lala could respond, Mamie leaned forward and leveled a gaze at the boys that might have set them on fire. "Neither am I, but that won't stop me from tanning your hide if you don't put that down."

His insolence dissipated faster than dandelion fluff. He put the figurine back on the table.

Willete flushed. "Such a lovely party, Lala, but I think we'd best be leaving." She ushered the boys out, then moved the figurine back to its original place before she left the room.

Mamie followed. "I'll watch these two while you get your young ones." Once more her eyes flashed warnings at them.

Lala nudged Paulina and whispered, "Did you see that?"

Paulina whispered back. "Something in particular?"

"That flaring look Mamie gives when she wants to make sure you're paying attention. Where her eyes turn large and her face edges slightly forward."

Paulina considered it and nodded. "Now that you mention it...she does show a bit of tooth as well."

"Aren't we lucky. We only have to contend with gossip and fashion."

They suppressed their amusement as Mamie strode back into the living room, her skirt swishing to and fro like a Sunday morning church bell.

Lala broke the silence before it became uncomfortable. "Your life must be very different living in Europe. Do you miss America?"

Mamie snorted, "Are you kidding? I love it here. Everyone treats me with respect. And I got me the pick of the litter with Moritz. Oh, I could've married higher, princes and dukes were begging me, but I'm old-fashioned. I wanted to marry someone I could love. Moritz may only be a count but he's a barrel of laughs and he treats me good. What more can a girl ask for?"

"He's certainly charming," Lala observed. "How fortunate you've found a pleasant life here."

"It's great, I tell you. We spend half the year traveling and the rest having a good time without all those puritans and snobs back home turning their noses up at me. It's a nice change after what we went through in the war, you know."

"Yes, I'm sure that was a difficult year for you back in America, with 'The War' and all."

Paulina coughed to mask her barely stifled laugh.

Mamie sat in Josef's favorite chair, which faced Lala's Monet on the far wall, and stared at the painting. "That picture's nice." Mamie's lips pursed, evincing disagreement with her words. "Did you know it's a copy? And not a very good one. I saw the real painting in that big art museum in Paris, and the colors were completely different."

"This painting is an original," Lala said, "as was the one you saw in the Louvre. Claude Monet painted thirty-one versions of the Cathedral of Rouen, each at different times of the day and in different light." If that embarrassed her guest, it failed to bother Lala after the woman's crudeness.

Mamie sniffed, "How about some more of that champagne, girls."

Lala brought glasses to Mamie and Paulina, then took one for herself. An uncomfortable hush commenced as they sipped their drinks until Mamie asked, "So what do you like to do for fun? Go dancing, see the picture shows?"

"Before Amalie was born, Josef took me to see The Cabinet of Dr. Caligari. Despite its interesting imagery, I found it too disturbing and we left."

They drank their champagne in silence, until Mamie asked, "What about when your husbands are at work?"

Puzzled, Paulina and Lala looked to each other for guidance.

Mamie turned to Paulina. "How about you, Mrs. Chytry?", she asked, mispronouncing Paulina's surname as "CHIT-tree" instead of "SHE-tray."

"Please, call me Paulina. And to answer your question, I'm usually working. Between my design business and my family, I keep quite busy."

Lala added, "And raising Amalie takes up most of my time, though I counsel Josef on purchases for his gallery."

"I was surprised to see you haven't hired nannies for your children." Mamie took another sip of champagne. "Funny, I thought you and Josef would be like the Knickerbockers."

"I don't know them. Are they your neighbors?"

Mamie issued a mirthless chuckle at that. It sounded sarcastic until she explained, "That's what they call New York's elite, old families with old money. My great-grandparents homesteaded out West. Their children bought up acres of forest, cleared some for ranchland. Made a fortune in lumber and cattle, all honestly earned. But as wealthy as we are, those East coast robber-barons wouldn't give people like us the time of day, not until I married my royal husband. Now you should see them fawn all over me, resenting every minute of it. But you know about that, don't you, Lala. I heard your husband used to be old money."

Lala bristled as her temper flared. "You obviously are misinformed about us, Mamie, and shouldn't make judgements about situations you can't begin to know about."

"Ladies, shall we switch to a more agreeable topic?" Paulina suggested. "Perhaps gossip or fashion?"

Lala put her hand over her mouth to keep from laughing. She heard the front door close; Josef and the husbands had returned to the apartment. She overheard Klement praising her father's desk, which Josef kept in his office.

Lala fixed her attention on Mamie. "Things may be different in America, but since the War, antiquated ideas about position and rank have been falling away. Opportunity abounds for anyone who works hard. No one here cares whether money is old or new. Money is money. What's the difference?"

Mamie flared a look at her. "You want to know the difference between old money and new? Old money takes everything for granted, but new money? We didn't start out rich. We never forget what it was like before, how hard it was to succeed. But I get it. You don't really want to talk to me because you don't care about who I am, only in what I've become through marriage. I know your husband sells antiques and paintings and that sort of thing. In other words, a glorified salesman who wants his wife to curry favor with me."

"A glorified salesman," Lala repeated. "In other words, the equivalent of an employee, with whom you advise to avoid friendships. Very well, Mamie. We don't have to be friends, but for the sake of our children let's remain civil. I'm the wife of a salesman and I, quote, 'deserve respectful treatment,' as you said."

Paulina stared into her champagne glass.

"Okay, I deserved that, and I agree about the children. God, what I wouldn't give for a bourbon and branch right about now." Mamie bolted down the rest of her champagne and set her empty glass on the tray. "At least you, Lala, I understand." She strode over to Paulina. "What about you? Are you afraid you'd lose your ritzy customers in that shop of yours if I showed up, dressed like this?"

Paulina smiled without a trace of irony in her eyes. "It's more likely your visit would make it an overnight success, especially after I've sold you a few ensembles you'll not only love, but that will flatter your figure which, like mine, doesn't conform to the silhouette currently in vogue."

Mamie ran her hands over her voluminous skirt. "You think this looks ridiculous on me."

"I don't like to criticize my competitors, but since you asked, that dress looks ridiculous, period."

"It didn't look good on the girl modeling it, either," Mamie confessed.

Paulina choked back a chuckle. "That dress would only

look good if it caught fire."

Mamie guffawed at that, which broke the tension. She patted Paulina's arm. "At least you're honest."

"Honesty has always been a central part of my business because it's a central part of me. You have a woman's figure, Mamie. You should dress to enhance it."

"I don't know how, that's why I buy whatever the sales ladies recommend. Do you know what a tomboy is?"

Lala had never heard the term before, but Paulina replied, "You preferred wearing trousers to skirts."

"Or denim coveralls," Mamie said. "I hated dresses. Never wore them except to church, until I turned eighteen. Then my parents forced me to dress like a woman and teeter around in these absurd high-heeled shoes, as though I need to be taller."

"So you went from one extreme to the other," said Paulina.

Mamie nodded and the harshness that had distorted her face mellowed. "I like you, Paulina. You remind me of me, except I tend to be quite blunt. My father calls me a bull in a china shop. I apologize to you both if I was rude."

Lala shook her head. "You were being straightforward, which we both can respect. My mother would call you a 'bold girl.'"

"I'll wager you gals are, too. There's something we all have in common."

Paulina took a business card from her purse. "If you like, I can arrange a private consultation for you to help you find a happy middle ground, with no obligation to purchase from me. I would never let you buy anything unless it looked spectacular on you and was appropriate for the occasion."

Mamie took the card. "So all is forgiven? Good. I can go

home now with a clear conscience. And I must admit you're both dressed startlingly well, so if I can find dresses as elegant as the ones you're wearing, and for a price you two can afford, maybe I will stop by Paulina's shop next week."

Mamie stepped into the hallway and hollered, "Moritz? Time to go. Tell the nanny to get Pearl ready." She returned and said to Lala, "Can somebody get my coat?"

CHAPTER THREE

Lala chased after her daughter as she scurried from the parlor to the front door. "Amalie, time for bed," Lala called out as Josef entered, the Tagblatt newspaper tucked under his arm.

"No," the child cried, her face in full pout as she reached out to him. "Papa home. I want Papa read me story." Her fingers opened and closed as though she were attempting to conjure him into doing her bidding. It was her way of pleading to be picked up, though she needn't have bothered with the gesture. She already had him at her command.

As he placed the newspaper on the entryway console, Lala observed how much Amalie looked like her father. Her hair had darkened to the same coffee brown as Josef's before his turned gray. She had his dark eyes and mouth but Lala's nose. Neither parent knew from whom she inherited her curled thumbs. Josef assumed it must have been Lala's original parents. Lala couldn't recall that detail. Nor could she tell whether Amalie's physical resemblance to Josef, Armin's death, or a lifelong desire to have more children gave their daughter ownership of Josef's heart.

He scooped Amalie up and she melted in his arms.

"Hello, my sweet flower. What would you like me to read?"

"Josef, it's after seven. She needs to go to bed and we need to eat dinner."

"And I need to spend some time with her. I haven't seen her since breakfast." He planted kisses on her cheeks. "Let's get you into your bed and Papa will read one story to you before you go to sleep."

Lala relented as she usually did when his request was reasonable. Josef had begun to spoil Amalie, who'd become more willful since her recent birthday. Mamie and Zoe assured her the behavior was normal for that age, although they spent so little time with their daughters, Lala didn't trust their judgement. Jacub hadn't acted out like that. Then again, with the War raging, when he was two his primary concerns were not freezing or starving to death.

While Josef read to Amalie, Lala checked on dinner preparations and set the table. She awaited his return to the dining room for some adult conversation. They often talked about the gallery – who came in, what had sold, or potential acquisitions. Josef occasionally sought her advice before procuring new merchandise. He trusted her judgement and taste, though he consulted with her less frequently since motherhood.

Ruth had dinner ready to serve when Josef rejoined Lala. "She fell right to sleep," he announced with pride.

They sat down to a meal of boiled beef, potatoes and carrots. Ruth placed the meat platter on the table and wiped her hands on her apron. "I've cleaned the kitchen. Would you like me to stay and wash up after dinner?"

"No, it's late. I'll finish cleaning up so you can get home. Shall I have Ludovik drive you?"

"Oh no, Missus. It won't be dark until eight and it's a

lovely evening for a walk. Besides, Ludovik needs to go home to his wife and new baby."

"That reminds me," said Josef as he fetched a notecard from his pocket. "I believe it's a note from Ludovik and Elke thanking us for the cradle."

Lala read the note. "That was sweet of them to name the child Tomas in memory of Elke's brother."

"Between the War and the Spanish flu we've lost too many good souls," Ruth observed. She bade them a good night and left.

Lala put an extra slice of beef on Josef's plate, knowing he'd ask for more as soon as she took the platter to the kitchen. She put the meat into the icebox and rejoined him. After several moments of quiet she asked, "Anything newsworthy happen in the shop today?"

"I have a lead on a painting by Charles-François Daubigny."

"The landscape of the Oise River, owned by Klement's friend?"

He looked surprised that she remembered. "The very one."

"How much does he want for it?"

Josef lifted his wine glass and took a good long swallow. "A fair price."

"Which is?"

"I don't want to talk business right now. Let's change the subject."

"Let's change the subject." Lala refrained from saying, "You brought it up, Josef."

He cut into his beef. "What did Amalie do today?"

Josef's interest in Amalie's exploits began in infancy. He delighted in every milestone, whether squeezing his finger or sitting up. How excited he became when he saw her pull herself up on a chair and take a few tentative steps, how he cried the first time she called him "Baba." The love in his eyes at every toothless grin. She filled him in on Amalie's day, which sounded boring to her, but Josef followed every detail with rapt interest. Lala sometimes wondered if she and Josef ought to trade places; she would run the gallery while he took on the responsibility for raising their daughter, though she would never dare mention it to him.

"Is she progressing in her training?" he asked.

"She can take her stockings off."

"Wonderful." He placed his napkin on his empty plate.

"Josef, it's not that special."

"Armin didn't do that until he was three."

"Armin had a household of servants to see to his every need," she reminded him. "Shall I make us some tea?"

"Not tonight, love. I'm going downstairs to my office to finish my month-end closing for an hour and then I'll come up to bed." At the end of every month Josef created profit and loss reports and reviewed his financial records to make sure they were balanced. It usually took a few days to finish. She escorted him to the front door. He kissed her before leaving.

Lala glanced at the newspaper he'd left on the console. In Germany, the far-right NSDAP Party had appointed a new leader, some fiery speaker who ranted about nullifying the Treaty of Versailles, reuniting German territories into a Greater Germany, and of course, barring Jews from citizenship.

She retreated to the library and searched through the shelves awhile for something more pleasant to read, finally selecting a book about *die Brücke* school of art, a birthday gift to Josef written by one of Ivo's colleagues. The artists' significance lay in being a bridge, linking the representative art of the past and the more contemporary styles. Armin, who'd sought to express art in a less figurative way, had been a proponent and it influenced much of his later works.

She settled into the high-backed leather club chair Josef favored and began to skim through the pages. Although well-written, it brought up memories she didn't want to revisit. As she shelved the book her hands tremored....

When you have nothing to do, you have nothing....

A single chime pealed from the mantle clock in the parlor. Nine-thirty. Josef would return soon. She took the newspaper he'd left on the console and brought it with her into the bedroom, turned on the bedside light and nestled on the bed to read. Several pages in, she spotted a photograph next to the Society column of Mamie, splendidly dressed, standing outside Paulina's shop. The opening paragraph of the column extolled the dress shop as "the place for fashionable women in Prague," thanks to Mamie's patronage.

Paulina will finally get the recognition she so rightfully deserves. Lala read further to see who else had been seen at the shop, when she caught an item:

The Excelsior Inn has become the most popular destination for the elite of Prague since it opened one year ago. Prized for the beauty of its surroundings as much as the relaxed atmosphere it provides, guests rave about the impeccable service and most especially the décor, which they say is not only exquisite, but comfortable. And now the world has taken notice. This reporter is sworn to secrecy, but I can say one of the Ambassadors to Czechoslovakia brought his

family to spend a weekend in the country. They
stayed in a special suite designed for couples with
young children and upon their departure showered
the owner, Mr. Otokar Zahradnik, with praise for
creating a most ideal retreat....

Lala heard Amalie crying in the next room. She dropped
the newspaper on the bed and went to check on her.

"What is it, love?" she asked as she picked up Amalie to
cradle her. But the toddler fussed in her arms.

"No, want Papa, want Papa."

"Mama's here." Lala nestled Amalie close to her body and
paced through the room, rocking her gently, whispering
words of reassurance. Her attempts to soothe her agitated
daughter failed, for the child's wails for her father only grew
louder.

Lala took a deep breath and let it out. Was there a single
soul who appreciated her?

CHAPTER FOUR

Lala had granted Ruth's request to take off the last Friday in August. That morning Lala dried the breakfast dishes and put them away. "Amalie, would you like to go to Petřín Hill today, or walk along the river?"

"Hill," she said.

Lala smiled her approval, for as much as she enjoyed Prague, sometimes she craved the pastoral setting of Petřín Hill. Filled with hectares of gardens and orchards, its panoramic views overlooked the city and the hills beyond. On a clear day Lala swore she could see the turret of the Excelsior Inn to the north. Amalie adored riding the funicular railway car that carried them to the hilltop, the highest point in the city.

The Nebozízek Garden, which rose from the base of the hill, would make a pleasant outing. Last May, Amalie took delight in scampering through the cherry orchard, picking up spent blossoms. Today the trees would provide relief from the sun and sweltering humidity.

After a brief squabble over what Amalie would wear, she finished dressing her daughter, then carried her to the stairs where they met Josef walking up.

"Where are my two girls off to today?" He gave Amalie an affectionate chuck under her chin.

"Hill," said Amalie. "Papa come?"

"Papa has to work," Lala explained to her, but Josef shook his head.

"My morning appointment has been cancelled and I've nothing scheduled until three this afternoon. Hanus can mind the shop for a few hours."

"Then join us. I can prepare a picnic lunch and we'll make a day of it." She let him take Amalie.

"What if Papa goes with Amalie, then Mama can have a little time to herself? " He leaned over to kiss Lala's cheek. "You'd like that. Why don't you go off on your own for a while? Get your hair done, or go shopping. Enjoy yourself and I'll take her to the hill."

Before she could respond he carried Amalie downstairs and left.

Crossing Charles Bridge to the Old Town, Lala spent the morning wandering through the city streets, stopping in every antiques store and gallery she passed. When she entered a shop she'd been in before, the owner greeted her as "Mrs. Josef Smetana." Polite but aloof, he presumed the purpose of her visit had more to do with her husband's business than with her personal interest in their merchandise, unlike her other stops where shopkeepers largely ignored her.

She tilted her hat's brim to deflect the sun as she walked aimlessly, until she found herself in Wenceslas Square, which separated the oldest part of the city from the newer section. The area pulsed with liveliness as people traversed the streets, shopping, dining in cafés, and people-watching. She considered a stop at the National Museum at the far end of the square, a splendid Neo-Renaissance building.

Suddenly a memory surfaced of being there on her eighteenth birthday. Armin and his friends had surprised her with the trip, taking her to Prague to see Armin's masterpiece, "She."

That was the day she resolved to study at the academy to pursue a career in the arts.

She remembered staring at that building...of Karel telling her it was completed on the day he was born..."*I've long believed that is why I was destined to work in the arts....*"

She turned away and fled the square. Her footsteps took her to Jinrisská Street within a block of Paulina's shop. As she approached she overheard men discussing the recent formation of the Czech Communist party. She spotted a familiar face amongst them.

Vilem sat outside a café across the street, nursing beers with three artists in paint-stained coveralls. He waved her over. The men stood when introduced. Each talked about his work as if making a sales pitch, which Lala supposed they were. One even inquired if he could bring some of his canvases for "Mr. Smetana" to see, which amused Lala as she pictured him chanting anti-capitalist slogans at the National House in Karlin. None of them asked her to join them, though Lala would have refused. After some polite chatter, she excused herself and retreated to Paulina's shop.

A woman carrying one of Paulina's white dress boxes left the store as Lala entered. She saw more boxes stacked waist-high on the floor near the counter, where a smartly dressed woman was tying another with ribbon. The woman greeted Lala as she entered. Paulina had hired the middle-aged spinster, who'd once run her own dress shop, after she lost her entire family during the Spanish flu epidemic. Petite and slight of build, she carried herself with a regal bearing.

"Mrs. Smetana, how nice to see you again. I trust you enjoyed your recent birthday celebration?"

"I did, Miss Horáčková. The dress Paulina created for me made it very special."

"It did look splendid on you."

"Is Paulina here today?" Lala asked.

The woman hesitated. "Madame is with a client right now, but I will inform her of your presence. If you will excuse me?" With a tip of her head, she retreated to the rear of the shop.

Lala browsed through the dresses on display, noticing how few remained on the racks of ready-to-wear merchandise. Business had been steadily climbing since the society page article, though many of Paulina's clients sought custom clothing. Her sister's salon rivaled the best that Paris had to offer. Lala predicted it would eventually achieve the stature it deserved as the finest couture house outside of France.

Miss Horáčková returned. "Madame Paulina requests that you join her. Countess von Anhalt is with her."

Lala followed her to Paulina's private quarters. After Lala turned down Miss Horáčková's offer of refreshments, the assistant bowed and closed the door behind the women.

Paulina kissed Lala hello. "You're just in time for the fashion show finale. Mamie's been trying on frocks." She whispered to Lala, "It's what Americans call daytime dresses."

From the dressing chamber Lala heard Mamie call out, "Lala, is that you? Good. I'd like your opinion." Her petite lady's maid opened the door and Mamie stepped out wearing a plaited gray dress, overlaid with a sheer organza tunic in a lighter gray. Her assistant tied the sash into a loose bow in back, tapering the fabric around Mamie's waist.

Mamie stepped over to the three-way mirror to appraise it from all angles. "I like this. It looks a lot classier than the one in the picture."

Paulina explained, "Mamie's mother mails her catalogs from a store in New York—"

"B. Altman and Company," Mamie added.

"Yes. Mamie saw a dress she liked and asked me if I could create something similar, but more in keeping with her current status."

"Or as you put it, less pedestrian." Mamie smoothed her hands over the sheer sleeves that ended above the wrist in a wide cuff of fabric. "I see what you meant when you advised against trimming the sleeves with ruffles. It would have been too much. This dress has many elements, but they're all subtle."

"It really flatters you," Lala said, noting how the dress flowed over Mamie's full bosom and wide rounded hips. "What a lovely figure you have."

"Doesn't she?" Paulina agreed.

"Hard to believe I used to be a corn stalk. I stood five foot eight by the time I was fourteen and kept on growing, but no chest, no hips until I turned eighteen. A late bloomer. After that I couldn't look like a boy no matter what I wore, so like Paulina says, why bother trying?"

Paulina nodded. "As dictatorial as fashion may seem, if a woman always wears what is appropriate for the season, occasion and her body, she will always be fashionable,"

"I'll take it, along with the rest of what you've got for me."

"Miss Horáčková is boxing up your purchases. Shall we deliver them to your home or would you rather we bring them out to the automobile for you to take now?"

Mamie chuckled. "You think they'll all fit in the motor car?" She checked her reflection in the mirror again. "I'll wear this one out. Bring out what's ready now and you can deliver the rest before we leave Prague."

"Are you traveling again?" asked Lala as Mamie ducked back into the dressing chamber.

"Moritz and I will spend a month in Munich, visiting his family. Then Vienna, where we're taking the Orient Express back to Paris."

"How fortunate Pearl is to see so much of the world at such a tender age."

"She's not going with us. Moritz and I want to relax and have fun, not be tethered to a toddler the whole time." She beckoned to her young maid. "Come, Veronique, toot sweet. We still have to pick up my hats from the millinery shop. What's the French word for hats again?"

"Les chapeaux."

"That's right. Let's go get my 'lay shapose.' So long, girls."

Mamie rushed out, Veronique running to keep up with her employer.

"Isn't she something?" Lala said after Mamie had left the shop.

"Yes she is," Paulina agreed. "I can't quite make out what that something is, though."

"Apparently a very good customer, according to the Tagblatt."

"And for that I'm grateful. That column brought in a great deal of new business."

"I noticed how empty the racks were." Lala checked her

wristwatch. "It's nearly two. I should be going. Josef has to be back before three o'clock, and suddenly I miss my little girl."

"Where is Amalie?"

"With Josef. He thought I needed some time on my own, to shop or get my hair done."

"At least your husband pays attention to you. Ivo's been so busy, staying late every night at the University doing research for his book, Jacub and I hardly ever see him."

Lala smiled. "You know what Mother would say," and in unison they said, "Don't complain."

She kissed Paulina's cheek and bade Mrs. Horáčková goodbye before leaving. Across the street, Vilem and his fellow painters were still talking over beer, though the subject had changed to the latest political assassination in Germany. Lala wove her way back to the bridge, where she spied Zoe taking photographs as passersby stared at her.

"Lala, what a nice surprise to see you. Please give me one moment to take this." She had her camera focused on the statue of St. Francis of Assisi. "My father is from Assisi, so this will be for him." She snapped the photo standing, then crouching.

"There, all finished." She closed down the lens. "I've been meaning to bring Charis around to see Amalie, but I've been busy trying to get enough photographs to submit for a juried exhibit next month. Do you know Paul Rosenberg?"

"By reputation only," Lala said. Rosenberg was a well-known art dealer in Paris.

"His brother Léonce, who's been a champion of Cubist artists, opened his own gallery."

"L'Effort Moderne?"

"Then you've heard of it. Léonce will display one of Vilem's paintings next month as part of a group exhibition.

179

And, if I can impress Paul with my work, Vilem and I will both be exhibited at the same time, in Paris." She smiled, revealing beautiful white teeth.

"Congratulations," Lala said. "What a coup that would be. You and Vilem must come over before you leave and tell us about it over dinner. And by all means bring Charis. Amalie would enjoy seeing her, as would we. Where is your daughter today?"

"With her father."

"No, Zoe, she's not. I just saw Vilem less than a half hour ago and Charis wasn't with him."

Lala's concern didn't get through to Zoe, for she merely shrugged. "That can't be. It was his turn to watch her today."

"He was at the café across from Paulina's shop. Oh dear." Panicked, she checked her watch. "I still have time before I must be back. I'll take you there."

The women crossed the bridge to Old Town and hurried down Husova until Zoe stopped at the corner of Karlova. Ahead they saw Vilem about to enter a building halfway down the block.

"That's where we live," Zoe told Lala. She called out to him. "Vilem, where is Charis?"

"Charis?" He looked puzzled. "Isn't she with you?"

"No, it was your turn to watch her today," she hollered back.

"I thought...?"

An elderly woman poked her head out of the second story window. "She's with me! I heard the child crying for over an hour and when I went to see why, I found the door to your apartment unlocked and her sitting on the floor, all alone."

Zoe looked relieved. "Thank you, Mrs. Mareková. My

husband will come upstairs right now to take her home."

"Me? Why me?"

"Because it's your turn, Vilem. I only have one day a week to work and I must make the most of the time."

Lala interrupted. "Thankfully, Charis is safe. Now I really must be going."

"Shall we still meet for dinner next week?" Zoe asked.

"Let's talk another time. I'm running late."

Lala walked home as quickly as she could, prepared to thank Josef for a day to herself. This should have been the respite she wanted from childcare. Now she couldn't wait to hold Amalie again.

CHAPTER FIVE

Upon waking every day, Lala vowed to devote herself to being a good wife and mother. She reminded herself how fortunate she was to have a home in a quality neighborhood near the heart of Prague. A maid to do the housework, cooking, shopping and laundry; Lala couldn't remember the last time she ironed. Her family could afford anything they needed and much of what they wanted, thanks to Josef. He deserved to have her make the effort for their family.

Amalie's behavior had settled down, which Lala attributed in part to her own more placid demeanor. It lasted a few days. Then the child's obstinance crept back, and after a few weeks of Amalie's escalating defiance, Lala, in meeting the challenge, found herself falling behind. She began chanting to herself, "She's only two, this phase will pass" over and over.

On a chilly October Saturday, Lala pushed the stroller holding her sleeping daughter along Janáckovo nábr, a quiet street alongside the Vltava River near the foot of Zidovsky ostrov, the little island. Josef had found the neighborhood in the recently formed Smichov district just south of Mala Strana while searching for housing, and leased a desirable apartment for Sarah. Lala had liked the mix of late 19th Century buildings, each in different architectural styles that somehow blended together harmoniously. Situated less than two kilometers from their house and three from Paulina's across the river, it kept the family near enough to each other. Like Josef, Sarah adored her granddaughter, so Lala tried to visit her mother, with Amalie along, at least once a week.

Fall foliage of olive gold, fiery orange, and red brightened the walkway. Mid-morning sun infused the street's tightly packed buildings, reflecting warmth from their stone facades. Hopefully that warmth would extend to her mother's mood when Lala spoke to her, one of the reasons she brought Amalie along.

Across, a tree-lined park created a pleasant greenbelt between the roadway and the water's edge. Lala passed two women crossing the street to join two others, sitting on benches in the park, as she wheeled the stroller to the front door of her mother's residence. An elderly man tipped his hat and held the wrought iron and glass door open for her as she maneuvered the stroller into the entryway. Lifting Amalie in her arms, she walked up two flights of stairs to her mother's apartment.

"Come in, your timing is perfect. I was about to pour some tea. Would you like some?"

Amalie blinked awake. She squealed, "Bubbie!" and practically flew into her grandmother's arms.

"And how is my precious little granddaughter today? Oh, you have a new tooth coming in. Would you like to test it with one of Bubbie's cookies?"

The child nodded with enthusiasm.

"Then let's take off your coat and—"

"Out," the child pleaded, pointing to the French doors leading to the terrace.

"Only if Mama says yes."

Lala smiled inwardly. Her mother, while very respectful of Lala's place as Amalie's mother, nevertheless managed to frame requests in a way so that Bubbie could always say yes and only Mama could say no. Fortunately, the balcony's ornately patterned wrought iron surround stood taller than Amalie.

"You may go out, Amalie, if you keep your coat on, but no cookies until you return to the kitchen."

"Cookie first," she insisted.

Sarah chuckled. "That's my granddaughter. Listen to your mama, dear."

Lala brought Amalie to the balcony. The child's little fingers slipped through two spiral bands of iron, clutching the cool metal as she peered through the lacy pattern of the barrier. She loved to watch the birds in the park across the street, the people walking along the footpath, and the river beyond. If she caught a glimpse of a boat gliding along the water, she'd squeal in delight. Lala left the door ajar and went to join her mother in the kitchen.

"Josef didn't come with you," her mother observed.

"He's working today."

Sarah placed two tea cups on saucers and filled them with tea. Lala helped her carry them into the living room, where they could keep an eye on Amalie.

Sarah left and returned with a plate of cookies. She passed it to Lala, who took one.

"Rosh Hashana begins tomorrow night," Sarah reminded her.

Miko Johnston

"Josef, Amalie and I will be here for dinner, Mother." She took a bite and changed the subject. "Cinnamon nut balls, my favorite. I still remember the first time you made these for me."

"Back in Russia, at my mother's house." Sarah had finally given up the pretense that she gave birth to Lala, at least in private. Lala and Josef had yet to decide what, when and how much they would tell Amalie about Lala's past, or Josef's.

Sarah rested her cup in its saucer. "Will you come to shul after dinner with me?"

"Yes, we'll attend services with you."

"By 'we' you mean you and Amalie, but not your husband."

Lala caught her mother's displeasure when Sarah referred to Josef as, "your husband." Josef had lost faith after Armin's death and refused to set foot in a synagogue ever since. He respected Lala's wish to observe traditions, maintain a Kosher kitchen, and raise their children as Jewish as long as they did not retreat from the world around them because of it. So many of their friends and associates were not Jewish that it would have strained their relationship if they couldn't socialize. That meant dining in homes and restaurants that weren't Kosher. At first Lala observed the dietary laws in spirit, having coffee and pastries in a café, or meatless meals when away from home, but she gradually succumbed to eating whatever was served. Lala continued to attend religious services on important holidays like the Jewish New Year and keep Kosher at home, partly to educate Amalie and partly to placate her mother.

"Cookie."

Lala blinked and saw Amalie standing beside her. "Let's take off your coat first and then we'll go into the kitchen."

"How many cookies may she have?" asked Sarah as Lala unbuttoned Amalie's coat.

"One."

"One two free four five," Amalie chanted as her fingers played out the count, which brought a gasp to Sarah.

"You already know your numbers, dear? Aren't you the smartest girl ever."

Lala slipped the coat off her daughter. "She has your sweet tooth, Mother. She'd have mastered algebra if it meant getting more cookies."

The three compromised on two cinnamon nut balls. Amalie sat at the little table and chair handed down from Jacub. The set had been a gift from Gershom and his two assistants. It lacked the finesse of her father's work, but brought back memories of old friendships. She hadn't corresponded with Gershom since writing of Amalie's birth. Gershom had begun courting a woman he seemed quite fond of, which pleased Lala. She always felt a tinge of guilt for upending his life, although Gershom insisted he was very happy living in New York. Never happier, in fact.

She wondered what the men were doing now, if they were building beautiful furniture like her father did. Functional works of art. In skilled hands, cabinetry was akin to sculpture; starting with raw unformed materials and shaping them into something practical and beautiful, in her mind, the highest degree of creativity.

"What's wrong, Lala? You keep sighing."

Her mother snapped her back to the present.

"I was thinking about old times."

"When you were her age?"

"More recent."

Sarah nodded knowingly. "When Amalie was born."

"Perhaps you don't remember that I had a life before I became a mother. Quite an accomplished life for a young woman, I might add. I ran a factory, managed a household and a victory garden. I designed the interiors for a comfortable boarding house, Paulina's shop and workspace, Josef's gallery and office quarters, not to mention one of the most successful hotels in all of Europe!"

Amalie began to cry. Sarah scooped her up. "Why are you yelling?" she scolded.

"I'm sorry, I didn't realize I was," Lala said, sighing again. She reached out to stroke Amalie's cheek. "I'm sorry, love. Mama didn't mean to upset you."

Sarah set the toddler down. "We'll have no more yelling in this house. Sit down and eat your cookies, Amalie." Then she put two more on the child's plate.

Lala knew better than to say anything.

Sarah took Lala's arm. "Let's step away from the c-h-i-l-d," she said as the two moved to the hallway outside the kitchen.

Lala threw up her hands. "I apologize, Mother. I'm feeling a bit out of sorts lately."

"What's wrong, dear?" Sarah's face suddenly brightened. "Have you any news on the family front?"

"No, not that. Josef doesn't want me to help him with the gallery anymore. He works long hours and when he's home he spends more time with Amalie than with me. Work or travel occupies my friends' time, Paulina's always busy—"

"And you're busy being a wife and mother."

"Which is constantly wearing. I don't know how you managed so well."

"You know it was different for me. I thought I'd never have children, and then I found you." She cupped Lala's face in her hand. "I loved every minute of being your mother, and it went by..." Sarah snapped her fingers " ...like that. In the blink of an eye your daughter will be grown and you'll wonder where the years went."

"Right now that seems like heaven. I know how important it is to raise Amalie, but being around a two-year-old all the time can get boring and yet exhausting...the constant questions, the attention she requires. Sometimes I wish I could have a break from it all, maybe attend a class at the Art Academy or take on clients who wants help with their décor."

"I'd be happy to watch Amalie if you wanted to take a class."

Lala frowned. "Josef doesn't approve of me furthering my art career at this time. He wants me to focus on Amalie. But sometimes I feel so tied down by my responsibilities to her... like during the War, when I felt obligated to take care of you and Paulina and Jacub. I had no choice back then, but it should be different now. I want to do something meaningful to me, something beyond being Josef's wife or Amalie's mother."

Sarah's gaze narrowed. "You would rather be like that photographer who treats her daughter like an object? Or that American woman who spends her days shopping and her evenings at parties with her bon vivant husband and doesn't even know how to hold her child in her arms?"

"That's not fair, Mother. Not every working woman is like that. I would never neglect Amalie to pursue a career any more than Paulina neglects Jacub."

"Paulina's been at this a lot longer than you. She began her business before she had Jacub and relied heavily on us to help raise him. Now Jacub is older. He's in school during the day and doesn't need constant supervision like Amalie does."

"Still, she manages to run her business and take care of her family. I don't see why I can't as well."

"I'm sorry, dear, but you can't have what you want and what you already have."

"Why not?"

"Because then you would have everything. No one can have everything."

Lala nodded. "I'd settle for a change of scenery, like a weekend at the Excelsior. Ever since I read that newspaper column I've been thinking about staying there, just to see what it's like now. I don't know if I'd enjoy it or if it would make me feel worse, not that it matters. Josef would never consent to going."

Sarah's brow furrowed. "Why should he? After all that went on in that house. And you? Why would you want to go there? To gloat over what you consider your big success?"

"Gloat? When Father framed the design award for that marquetry cabinet he built, did you say it was gloating? Or when Paulina publicizes she's sold a dress to Countess von Anhalt or some politician's wife?"

"It's not the same thing. They work for a living. If you want a change, take up knitting or embroidery, or better yet, have another baby."

Lala's temper, which began simmering at her mother's gloating comment, now threatened to boil over. She grabbed her coat. "I have to get out of here. If you would like to spend some time with Amalie, I'll come back for her in an hour. But right now I must leave."

"Why are you in such a state? Are you sure you're not in the family way?"

"You'd like that, wouldn't you, since my only value to you

now is giving you grandchildren. Lala, once the beloved daughter, now reduced to child bearer. If I didn't know any better I would swear you were a man." She fumbled with the buttons on her coat. "Should I take Amalie with me, or not?"

"Always with the temper." Sarah beckoned her closer. "Come here."

Lala reluctantly complied.

Sarah took Lala's hand and gave it a pat. "I know you think I'm ignoring you. I suppose I am. I'm sorry."

Lala gave her mother a hug. "I am as well. I shouldn't take my frustrations out on you."

"Shall I tell you what my biggest regret as a mother has always been?"

"What?"

"Not having known you earlier. Since your father and I didn't meet you until you were nearly eight, we missed out on so much. I suppose I'm trying to make that up with Amalie. She's at such a delightful age now, I want to share every moment I can with her without overstepping my bounds."

"I want that for you as well. You two should be as close as possible."

"And you need adult companionship that won't cross your husband or interfere with your family responsibilities. There's a group of mothers along the street who meet in the park most days for conversation and company. The ones with babies bring them along. They ask women like me to watch their older children awhile so they can have their break. You should ask to join them. It would do you a lot of good to be with other like-minded women to share your lives with, give you a little break from child-rearing and housekeeping."

Indifferent to the idea, Lala shrugged. "I'll think about it."

CHAPTER SIX

"It's half past four, Lala. Are you ready yet?" called Josef through the bedroom door.

"Almost. Take Amalie to the automobile and I'll be down shortly."

On Sunday at five o'clock, Ludovik parked the vehicle in front of the Chytrys' apartment on Melantrichova, a lively street linking Wenceslas Square and the old Town Square, for dinner with the family.

Paulina took the bouquet of gladioli and the bottle of La Romanée wine Josef brought and welcomed them all into the parlor, where Sarah was sitting.

"Amalie, Antila, Uncle Josef, you're here!" Jacub cried out, and ran to greet them, followed by Ivo, who shook Josef's hand.

"Good to see you, Ivo. It's been awhile."

Ivo explained, "I'm at a crucial point in my thesis, so I must return to the library right after dinner. I understand you have business to discuss with Paulina, so I won't be missed."

"That isn't true," Lala insisted as she put Amalie down. "You'll be missed."

"At least I'm here when it counts," he said, grinning.

Paulina started to say something, but refrained.

Josef took notice. "Then you must tell us about your topic at dinner."

Amalie had rushed over to Jacub as soon as her feet touched the floor.

Jacub hugged her. "We're having our dinner at the little table in the kitchen tonight," he said. "Let's play in my room until then." He took Amalie's hand and led her out.

Lala asked Paulina, "Do you think Amalie and Jacub should eat by themselves?"

Sarah barely suppressed a grin. "As long as you don't serve them chopped liver."

"Why is that?" asked Ivo.

"You haven't heard the story?"

"Mother," Lala admonished, but Sarah ignored her.

"This happened when Lala was rescued by her Aunt Naomi's family," Sarah explained. "They invited important guests for dinner and let their children and Lala dine by themselves. Lala hadn't learned her table manners yet."

Lala whispered, "Here I was, a poor child from the shtetl, sitting at a formally set table with three forks and two spoons. How was I to know which utensil to use for chopped liver?"

"What did you do?" asked Ivo.

"Go on, tell them," urged Sarah, giggling.

"I spread some on my tongue with a knife. My cousins thought it very funny, so they did it too, and soon we and the table were a mess, which naturally was when the adults decided to come in and check on us."

By now Sarah was laughing so hard tears ran down her cheeks.

"It wasn't very funny then, Mother. I feared I'd be

banished from their home and left to live on the streets."

"But it is now."

By the laughter that flowed through the parlor, everyone agreed it was.

Lala and Paulina settled the children at Jacub's little table and made up plates for them. As Lala cut up Amalie's food, she remarked to Paulina, "Your skin is positively glowing."

"Probably that new face cream Mamie's using. She gave me some to try."

"Whatever it is, it's working." Lala put the plate before Amalie. She and Paulina observed the children eat. Assured they could manage on their own, the women returned to the parlor.

"The children are having their dinner, so shall we go to the dining room and have ours?" suggested Paulina.

They sat down to a meal of roast duck and steamed dumplings with Josef's red Burgundy. Josef asked Ivo again about his thesis.

"I wanted to combine my art background with my interest in history." Ivo laid his napkin across his lap. "I finally decided to do a comparative study of Renaissance art in Florence against the political, social and religious history of the period."

"An interesting topic, and certainly one of the most glorious eras of art," observed Josef.

"And yet a tumultuous time," Ivo noted. "The Western Schism in the Roman Catholic Church, the rise of the merchant class and the rapid growth of cities as feudalism declined. You can see parallels with the present day. That's what I find so fascinating. The dean thinks my premise has potential, but after reading my synopsis he suggested expanding the scope beyond Florence. That will take a great deal more research." Ivo sighed. "A great deal."

Before Josef could intervene, Lala volunteered, "Could I help you?"

Ivo brightened. "That would be spectacular. I wouldn't impose much, just a few hours, maybe two, at most three times a week."

What an exciting proposition, a chance to further her studies, do something that wouldn't interfere with caring for Amalie. "I'd be more than happy. What can I do?"

"Could you meet Jacub at school on Mondays and Thursdays and watch him until Paulina comes home? Then I could stay at the library—"

Paulina put her hand on Ivo's. "I don't think that's what Lala was asking."

Extending his apologies for having to leave before dessert, Ivo fetched his briefcase and met the adults at the front door. He shook Josef's hand and bussed the ladies goodbye.

"Ivo, don't forget your scarf." Paulina unwound the gray muffler twisted around a hook on the coat rack. "It will be cold outside by the time you return."

Smiling, he gazed at her as she looped it around his neck. Then he kissed her again, on the lips.

Lala smiled as well, happy they could enjoy a few tender moments despite their busy schedules.

After Ivo left, Sarah went to the kitchen to check on the children and cut slices of her apple cake. She brought in pieces for Lala, Josef and Paulina.

"Aren't you having any cake, Mother?" asked Lala.

"You'll want to talk business so I'll have my dessert with

the children and after that I'll wash the dishes for you, Paulina."

"Mama Sarah, I can do that," Paulina said.

"Nonsense, you worked hard preparing this delicious meal, and you have to work tomorrow. It's the least I can do."

Paulina mouthed, "Thank you" to Sarah and ate a forkful of cake. She fetched her paperwork while Josef and Lala finished their desserts.

Josef set his empty cake plate aside. "What did you want to discuss with me, Paulina?"

"Happily it's good news. Business has been steadily building since the shop opened, and this past quarter was by far my best to date. I'm doing so well I can pay back your initial investment with interest."

Josef smiled. "You have something else in mind, though. What is it?"

"Would you be willing to reinvest that money into growing my business instead?"

"What are you proposing?"

"If you recall, originally, in addition to my couture designs, I sold semi-custom clothes modified from mass-produced garments. That idea is no longer practical. Mamie's patronage has brought attention to my shop and now women come seeking something designed by me. Everything in my shop should have my label, whether it's ready-to-wear or couture, and while I can originate both lines, I couldn't produce them both."

"You need to hire a few seamstresses."

"More than a few, Josef. I need a factory, something you have a great deal of experience in setting up."

"That many." The surprise in his voice was evident.

"I also need your advice on where to set this up." She removed a letter from her paperwork to show Josef. "The building that houses my shop is now for sale. I've checked comparable properties. The asking price is fair for the location and we've enough money to buy it. There would be ample room to set up a factory with an adjacent storeroom large enough to hold the materials I'd need and the overstock of finished garments. We could also look at less expensive quarters farther out before making a decision."

He read the letter. "We'd have to compare any savings against the advantage of having everything under one roof. The time and cost of transportation...."

Lala sat there listening and nodding. Silent. She loathed her envious thoughts stirred by Paulina's success. Granted, she also felt thrilled by her sister's achievements, as much as she marveled at how well Paulina juggled family and work, excelling at both. Lala had wanted the same for herself, but it had eluded her.

"Would either of you like some tea?" she asked.

"Yes, please," said Josef before turning back to Paulina.

Lala went to the kitchen and put the kettle on. The business discussion bothered her more than she wanted to admit. Not their success, but her lack of trying. She might succeed or not, but she hadn't done anything to make that happen, and that began to grate.

She heard her mother's voice drifting from Jacub's bedroom and went to see what she was reading to them. There she found Sarah sitting on the floor with an old book in her hands.

"...and the Ash Girl became a princess. She married the prince and lived happily ever after."

"Princess Ash Girl," said Amalie.

"No, dear. I don't think anyone dared call her 'Ash Girl' after she married the prince. Jacub, help your Grandmama up, please."

Lala went to give her a hand as well.

Sarah grunted as she rose to her feet. "You'd think it wouldn't be hard to stand considering I'm already so close to the ground." She patted Lala's hand in thanks. "Aren't you supposed to be talking business with your sister?"

"That's Josef. I've nothing to contribute except tea, and the water must be boiling by now." Lala hurried back to the kitchen with her mother following, and brewed a pot.

Sarah hummed as she set up the tea service on a tray.

"What has you so happy?" Lala asked, but her mother merely smiled.

Lala carried the tray into the parlor, where Josef and Paulina huddled over sales logs.

"Who wants tea?" Sarah sang out, which drew odd stares from the others.

"You're suddenly cheerful, Mama Sarah," Paulina observed.

"Yes I am," she beamed, then blew a kiss at Paulina. "So, anything new?"

"Josef has agreed to reinvest in my business."

Sarah waved her hand. "That's not what I'm talking about."

Paulina gave her a puzzled look. "What then?"

Sarah crossed her arms. "Your son told me you've been feeling ill every morning."

Paulina exhaled. "I didn't want to say anything this early, but yes. I'm expecting."

Her disclosure resulted in a near stampede to Paulina's side to congratulate her.

***

Josef and Lala settled into the back seat of the automobile with Amalie, asleep in her father's arms, as Ludovik closed the doors and drove toward home.

Lala asked Josef, "When will you go look at Paulina's building?"

"Tomorrow, if there's nothing pressing at the gallery."

Ludovik reached into his coat pocket for an envelope, which he held up for Josef to see. "Sir, the shipment you were expecting will arrive tomorrow afternoon. Three crates. Hanus and I will take them to the storeroom."

"Good. I'll look at the building in the morning. Leave the bill of lading on my desk."

Lala's curiosity piqued, she asked him, "What did you order?"

"Mainly paintings and drawings, and a few porcelain pieces."

"There must be quite a lot to fill three crates," she noted, trying to draw him out, but he didn't respond. He'd never made such a large purchase without seeking her advice. "Would you like me to inventory the shipment?"

"I'll need to do it, as I haven't seen any of the items yet."

"I can help with the design of Paulina's—"

"She wants to duplicate my layout in the upholstery department of the factory."

No need for my input. "I recall that was a very functional design."

As they crossed over the bridge she gazed at the sky and saw a nearly full moon poised between two clouds. A nearly full moon. A sign of change.

Everything had changed...

"...no Mama, want Papa..."

"...could you meet Jacub at school..."

"...she wants to duplicate my layout...."

... yet nothing had, and she knew whom to blame for that — herself.

CHAPTER SEVEN

Lala peered out her living room window, counting the seconds until the truck parked outside finally drove away. She wrapped a shawl around her shoulders. "Ruth, would you watch Amalie while I go downstairs to check on a delivery?"

Ruth looked up from her cleaning. "Sure, Missus. I'll keep an eye on her until you get back."

Lala went downstairs to Josef's storeroom and unlocked the door. Curiosity had burned within her all night.

Josef had called earlier to say he and Paulina were negotiating with the building's owner over a final price and would be delayed. He assured her Hanus and Ludovik could handle the delivery, and they did bring the crates up to the showroom. Lala thought it would be wise if someone checked the contents immediately in case of damage. Why not her?

She pried open the largest crate, marked "Fragile." Inside she found pieces of 18th Century Sèvres porcelain nestled in straw, a gold embossed footed vase as well as ten place settings in the Service de la Reine pattern. She lifted a plate, heavily banded in gold with medallions of roses and violets. Beautiful.

A second crate contained framed watercolors of Italy by German artist Jacob Alt and a painting of a peasant, an early work of Pieter de Hooch. The last crate, the smallest, contained one item – a battlefield print by Titian sandwiched between two panes of glass. *This should fetch a good price.* As she resealed the crates, Lala had to concede he'd chosen well.

In his "previous life," Josef collected art and antiques for pleasure. It came as no surprise that he could spot quality without her input.

No surprise at all, only disappointment.

Later that evening after they put Amalie to bed, Lala cornered Josef before he could duck into his office. Seeking a modulated tone, she took a calming breath. No sense letting the conversation plunge into an argument.

"Why have you shut me out of the business? You knew how much I enjoyed it, and I have a good eye for quality and a sense of what will sell."

He seemed puzzled by the question. "You wanted to be a wife and mother," he answered, as if that perfectly justified his reasoning.

"And I am. That doesn't explain why you think I can't handle acquiring pieces for the business, or a few clients."

"Because my clients are men, and they won't listen to a woman, particularly a 'bold girl' like yourself. At first they'll think you're a pushover and try to make a better deal until they find out you're not a pushover. Unfortunately, when they realize that, they won't fall in amazement. They'll walk away empty-handed rather than admit a woman out-negotiated them."

"You truly believe that."

"I've seen it happen time and again. The truth is, it's not fair, and I hate thinking of it, especially now that we have a daughter. But I can't change the world."

"Are you certain of that? For I always found you could. It's why I fell in love with you."

He fell silent, mulling that. "Come down to the storeroom and see my new acquisitions." Then he added, "I'd like your opinion."

They walked together in silence. He opened each crate, and as he brought pieces out for her inspection, she pretended to be surprised and complimented him on his selections.

"Where did you find such treasures?"

"Some came through sources I've cultivated, the rest from Moritz and his family."

"He's an outstanding resource," she acknowledged. "Have you a buyer in mind?"

"Klement expressed some interest in the Titian. Shall we invite him and his wife for dinner soon?"

Lala wasn't keen on seeing Willete again after what happened during Amalie's party. The woman lashed out at anyone she deemed beneath her station. Although she understood the reasons behind Willete's behavior, it failed to excuse any of it.

She forced a smile. "Exactly what I was thinking."

Lala and Josef welcomed the Chermaks a few weeks later. Willete arrived well along with child. Lala offered the couple her congratulations.

"I've ten weeks to go," Willete said, beaming. "It's been wonderful, every minute of it."

"I can attest to that," said Klement.

"Then you're very fortunate," Lala observed. "My sister is also expecting and having a difficult time."

"Is she? I saw her and her husband last Sunday at St. Nicholas Church, but she didn't mention it." Then Willete chattered on as she took off her coat, sharing her newly-gained expertise on maternity. Being with child lifted her spirits as well as her confidence, for she'd blossomed since their last time together. Lala had met women like Willete before, who derived their sense of worth through a prestigious marriage and having children.

She had Ruth take the Chermaks' coats and invited them into the living room. Willete behaved not only politely but cheerfully toward the housekeeper.

"Are you hoping for a boy or a girl?" asked Lala as they sat.

"It doesn't matter to Klement. Or to me," she added.

"As long as the baby is healthy," Lala noted. That was all she'd hoped for.

Willete's eyes grew large. "It has to be. Klement would be livid if he lost another child. His first wife had two miscarriages and a stillborn daughter between Evzen and Frieda, and she died giving birth to little Erich."

Lala changed the subject to the new baby's layette and nursery, which Willete effused about, as well as her stepchildren. Lala admired the woman for taking on Klement's brood. Willete had bonded with the two younger children and made progress with Klement III. Her limited observations about Evzen suggested she hadn't won him over yet, though not for lack of trying. Lala's respect for Willete grew.

After the men shared work-related banter over drinks and

canapes the four sat down to dinner. Josef had mentioned the Chermaks liked goose, which Lala prepared stuffed with bread, onions and dried fruit, and served it with potato dumplings.

Klement accepted Ruth's offer to refill his wine glass with more of Josef's Chateau Latour. "One of my clients told me an amusing story you would appreciate, Josef. As a teenager he'd been traveling with his family in the Netherlands, where his father met a fellow named Henk Bremmer."

Josef set down his wine goblet for Ruth to refill. "He's an art critic, yes?"

Klement nodded. "His father sought to buy Flemish art and asked Bremmer for advice, and he recommended some fellow named van Gogh. My client said, 'My father went to see some of the artist's work and, knowing nothing about him, pronounced him insane.'"

Josef laughed. "I happened to be in Paris the summer of ninety-four when I stopped in Ambroise Vollard's first gallery, the little one near Sacré Coeur. I purchased a Manet sketch from him and he asked me if I'd be interested in seeing his canvases by van Gogh. I'd heard about a mad Dutch artist by that name, but I found his work so unsettling I decided against purchasing any, a decision I regret to this day."

Art and travel dominated the conversation. Willete remained quiet except to occasionally agree with something her husband said. Josef had Ruth open another bottle of Bordeaux to accompany their meal.

"Wonderful dinner," Klement declared as he took a second helping from Ruth. "I don't think I've ever had goose prepared this way before."

"It's an old family recipe," Lala said.

"Would you be willing to share it with me?" asked Willete. "Klement rarely compliments a dish that much."

Lala promised to copy the recipe for her.

"Klement, when did you return from Berlin?" Josef asked.

"Last week."

"Business or pleasure?" asked Lala.

"Primarily business. My bank has been helping the German Republic stabilize after all the anti-government violence going on."

Lala noted, "The newspapers have dubbed it the 'White Terror.'"

"It's more than anti-government, though," Josef said. "These right-wing radicals want to foment revolution."

"Perhaps," said Klement. "While it's true they're disillusioned with the Weimar Republic, the groups are more concerned with the Russians and Polish Communists invading during this chaotic period."

"And killing anyone they consider enemies of the state," Lala added. "Matthias Erzberger wasn't a Communist, but last summer they assassinated him for signing the Armistice agreement on Germany's behalf."

Josef asked Klement, "Have you read Ernst Junger's book, Storm of Steel, based on his diary of the War? Terrifying. In it he predicts that the war was not an end, but a 'prelude to violence.'"

"I can't imagine why, after the horrors they endured, they would want more," Lala said.

Willete finished her wine. "They lost, Lala."

"So did we."

"But we won our independence," said Josef. "For Germany, all that violence was for naught." He used the moment of silence that followed to refill everyone's wine glass.

Klement took a sip. "I never finished answering your question. I did travel for business, but for me visiting Berlin is always a pleasure." He mentioned some of the pieces he purchased. "I'm looking for a larger house to hold everything."

Willete added, "Not only more art, but more children." She turned to him with a beatific gaze. "Many more."

"Did you leave any artwork for me this time?" asked Josef.

Klement issued a hearty laugh at that, which Willete echoed. "You should talk about hoarding," he said. "You have that extraordinary painting of your lovely wife, one of the best portraits I've ever seen, locked up in your office. You ought to proudly display it in your home so all can enjoy it." He raised his glass to toast Lala, who smiled at his flattery. "And speaking of hoarding, I understand the desk in your husband's office is one of your father's pieces."

"It is," she said with pride.

"Absolutely magnificent. Such graceful lines, and the woods he used in the marquetry, superb. I don't suppose there's another like it."

"My father made a similar piece as a wedding gift for his sister, a bureau with a small drop leaf, except that it has fluted legs with gold filigree cuffs."

"Klement so admires your father's work," said Willete. "Do you think your aunt would be willing to sell it?"

Klement put his hand on Willete's. She fell silent and shrunk into her chair.

"My dear," he said without a glance in her direction, "I sincerely doubt that either Lala or her aunt would willingly part with anything so beautiful."

Lala suddenly felt dizzy. Her ears buzzed and the people sitting at the table suddenly seemed far away. She inhaled...a horrible stench filled her nose....

"Do you smell something burning?" she asked Josef.

"No."

The others agreed.

A distant voice whispered in her ear...

"...*Go*...."

Lala stood. "I must go...look in on Amalie. If you'll excuse me."

A quizzical stare from Josef followed her out of the room. She checked the kitchen and saw nothing there to cause the sensation she experienced. Then she heard a faint sound coming from her daughter's room and rushed there.

Lala entered the room to find Amalie sitting up in her bed, crying. Lifting her up, Lala cradled the child into her arms. "What happened, love?"

"I had a bad dream," she mumbled between sniffles.

"Mama knew you did and came straightaway to make it better. Tell me what it was and Mama will make the bad things go away."

"The lion in Papa's painting came to eat me."

"That will never happen. Mama is going to take that bad lion, put him in a cage and lock the door so he'll never get out."

Amalie nuzzled into her mother as Lala rocked her, murmuring soothing words. Gradually the child's crying subsided and she finally fell back asleep. Lala laid her down in her bed, tucked her in and kissed her forehead.

She stood in the doorway, gazing at Amalie, thinking of how earlier at the dining table she'd been struck by images from her past. Of the day Cossacks attacked her shtetl and set it aflame, the stench of burning flesh, of finding charred remains in her home, of a single word issued by a dying man....

"Go."

Her visions began thereafter, offering guidance and solace, and sometimes a prediction of the future. But the grotesque images had nothing to do with Amalie's nightmare and everything to do with Lala's. Of what were they warning her?

CHAPTER EIGHT

Winter dug its claws into Prague. Sub-freezing days and snow flurries turned the streets treacherous. Lala and Amalie spent more time in the house. Finding activities to occupy her daughter proved challenging. Amalie disliked anything messy, like drawing with charcoal. In the morning Lala helped her practice grooming and getting dressed, then read to her before lunch, when her energy level fell. Lala also invented games that taught the child while playing and having fun. They would spend afternoons sorting a bag of buttons into different colors or sizes, or sit by the window and count the vehicles along the street. Sometimes Amalie would play along, but "no" had become her favorite word, and she used it often.

From the moment Amalie awoke she challenged nearly everything Lala said, from not wearing a fragile party dress at breakfast to putting away her color blocks. At one point Lala became so frustrated with Amalie's contrariness she raised her voice to scold the child, which culminated in a temper tantrum. Baffled and unsure of how to handle it, Lala felt too embarrassed to call her mother for help. She considered running downstairs to get Josef, then decided against disturbing him at work; she'd find a way to solve the problem herself. Lala finally put Amalie in her bedroom and closed the door, letting her scream and cry by herself until she settled down. Amalie remained sullen the rest of the day, even when Josef returned to the apartment.

Once Josef put Amalie to bed, Lala called him into the parlor. She'd poured two glasses of cognac and offered him one. "We need to talk about how to control Amalie's headstrong nature. I'm concerned that without proper discipline her behavior will grow worse."

He cradled the glass in his hand. "It's perfectly normal for a child to resist going to bed."

"But not everything her mother says." She relayed what had happened earlier. "I finally shut her in her room because I didn't know what else to do and frankly, I grew tired of her screaming over nothing."

She took a good swallow of cognac to calm down before continuing. "You are not here during the day. She constantly argues with me about what to wear, what to do, why she must."

"She's spirited and inquisitive."

"She's also demanding and bossy, and when you indulge your daughter by giving her whatever she wants, you make the situation worse."

He sipped his cognac. "I agree. She's now at an age when she must obey the rules. You take charge of her discipline. I promise I will stand by your decisions and not interfere in front of Amalie. If I disagree, we'll discuss it in private and come up with a solution."

"That sounds reasonable."

He set his glass on the table. "Spending too much time alone with each other is wearing on you both. Amalie has friends and so do you. Invite them to visit."

Zoe began to drop by with Charis about once a week. The women drank coffee and chatted about the art community while the girls played. Lala enjoyed having some adult company during the day as well as a vicarious connection to the artworld through Zoe's budding career, something she missed getting from Josef. It prodded Lala to resume drawing, at first sketching the children, and then the room. She retrieved the blueprints from the home remodel, and while Amalie napped Lala sketched new arrangements using pieces she'd seen in shops, photographs and Josef's gallery.

Although the visits had a congenial effect on Amalie's behavior, Charis had become timid around Amalie. When Lala mentioned it, Zoe shrugged it off as a phase. Perhaps Zoe was going through a phase as well; she appeared thinner each time she visited, and she never touched a bite of food Lala put out for them.

After a few visits, Zoe began asking Lala if she would mind her daughter "for a while, no more than an hour," while she took advantage of the light, or shadow, or fog, to get a photograph. Those "a whiles" grew in time and frequency. Lala had difficulty communicating with the child as her language skills had hardly progressed beyond a few words. Whenever she offered snacks to the girls, Charis would devour hers and then hide more in her clothing. Worse, Lala noticed how unkempt Charis appeared on most visits, her hands and face unwashed, her clothes soiled or so wrinkled she might have worn them for days. Zoe had weaned her daughter quite early from the breast, but Charis still wore diapers.

Lala had to say something to Zoe, even if it meant risking their friendship.

Zoe came to visit a week later with Charis. The child looked clean and happy to see Amalie. Lala suggested they sit in the parlor and let the children play together.

"I was about to make myself a cup of tea. Would you like some?" Lala asked Zoe.

"Thank you, yes." Zoe set the overloaded burlap tote she carried by her feet.

Lala wondered if it contained necessities for Charis alongside photography equipment, but didn't ask. She returned from the kitchen with two steaming cups.

"I'm so glad you're home today," Zoe said as Lala set her tea on the table. "I confess I had an ulterior motive for coming over."

Lala attempted a passive face as she awaited Zoe's usual plea.

"Do you remember the dual exhibitions in Paris a few months ago, where Vilem and I had our work displayed in separate galleries? Based on that showing I've sent out inquiries to eleven galleries, here in Prague and across Europe, and I've received positive responses from three, including Paul Rosenberg in Paris."

Lala clasped Zoe's shoulder. "Why Zoe, what exciting news. You must be so thrilled."

"I am. I've worked so hard to achieve recognition for my

work."

"What a shame photography doesn't get the same level of respect as other art forms."

"And let's be honest. Being a woman made it harder to break through."

"You deserve success, Zoe. Your photographs are as good as any I've seen."

"They're not only good, but unique, don't you think? No one does what I do, and it's finally catching the interest of the art community. Just imagine — Paul Rosenberg wants to display my work, again. No one bought Vilem's paintings when he exhibited in Paris, but Paul sold two of my photographs of children."

They chatted awhile about the galleries Zoe chose to contact, proper framing, and how best to display her art. Vibrant with joy, strands of hair tumbled from Zoe's makeshift bun down her cheeks as she spoke, enthusiasm echoing in her voice. Her commitment to her work had finally begun to pay off, Lala silently acknowledged as she swallowed envy with her tea.

From her bag Zoe removed proofs of her photographs and samples of frames. Lala was about to offer her opinion when she caught a whiff of soiled diaper. Amalie no longer required them, but Lala checked her daughter to be certain.

"Zoe, Charis needs a new diaper."

"I'll tend to it at home. These unembellished frames look modern to me. Do you agree the black one would complement my photos better than the silver?"

"What about your daughter?"

"Don't worry, she doesn't mind. Black frame, or silver? I value your opinion."

"My opinion? I think you're neglecting your daughter."

Zoe recoiled. "Just because I don't respond the second she needs something doesn't mean I'm neglectful." She stood and glared at Lala. "Or is this about that day when Vilem and I got our schedules mixed up?"

"It's more than one day. Charis is often unwashed when she visits and she's so far behind in her language skills she can barely communicate. You're her mother. That little girl lived inside of you for nine months. How can you treat her like an afterthought?"

Zoe cried out, "I'm desperate. We can't afford to hire someone to care for her. Vilem is busy and I don't have the time."

Lala saw Amalie flinch when Zoe raised her voice, but Charis didn't react. "You don't have time? Is your photography more important than your daughter?"

"You don't understand. I have to be the best, all the time. Did you know Zoe is Greek for 'life?' That's my life. My family expects me to be everything for them. But I can't." She began shuddering. "I just can't."

Lala helped her into a chair. "When was the last time you ate?"

"If I don't make it into this exhibit, my career will be over." Zoe bowed her head. The pencil holding her bun in place fell to the floor, spilling her black hair over her shoulders.

"No, it won't. It may be postponed, but in a few years Charis will begin school and you'll have more time to focus on your photography."

Zoe bolted to snatch Charis from the floor. "We have to go. If I don't get to the frame maker today, he won't be able to meet my deadline." She flung her bag over her shoulder and sprinted to the front door.

Amalie trailed after her friend. Waving, she called out, "Bye-bye Charis," as Zoe slammed the door behind them.

Yes, bye-bye, thought Lala. She picked up the pencil and threw it away.

CHAPTER NINE

Lala brought Amalie to the Hotel Europa to attend Pearl von Anhalt's birthday party. After greeting Mamie and Moritz, she excused herself and returned to the lobby to study the design layout. More than twenty years had passed since the hotel's remodeling. Its Art Nouveau style, while beautiful, felt dated.

On impulse she asked the desk clerk to speak with the manager. When he arrived she introduced herself as Mrs. Smetana.

"Mrs. Josef Smetana?" he asked, and she nodded.

His eyes grew eager. "How may I be of service?"

"I thought I might be of service to you, should you want to make any changes in the décor of your hotel. I have experience in both home and commercial settings, including hotels and inns." A slight exaggeration, though she felt the conversion of her parents' home and Paulina's should count.

The manager issued a polite smile as Lala offered him her calling card.

"We at the Hotel Europa are quite proud of our tradition of providing guests with the ultimate in service, luxury and comfort," he stated.

"As am I of my work, which includes the Excelsior Hotel."

Lala recognized the subtle change in his expression. She'd seen it before, in Josef, when he uncovered a rare antique priced by someone who had no idea of its value.

He took the card with thanks as she returned to the party.

The bellman on duty held the door open as Lala wheeled the stroller carrying Amalie out of the opulent hotel into Wenceslas Square. Although still chilly, with spring only weeks away, the sun whispered a promise of warmer days.

Lala hid the party favors, American candies Mamie had shipped in to give out to the little guests, in her coat pocket. She'd confiscated the bag filled with tiny foil-wrapped chocolates shaped like an oil can that were called "kisses," sticky pieces of salt-water taffy from Coney Island, and a chocolate, peanut and caramel confection called an "O'Henry" bar. Otherwise, with her daughter's penchant for sweets, the candy wouldn't last long but the tummy ache would.

Having promised her mother a visit, she guided the stroller toward the river. Being so close to Paulina's business, Lala considered stopping by first, but assumed her sister would be busy getting her new fashion line ready. Rather than disturb her at work, she'd call her tonight and find out what Jacub wanted for his upcoming birthday. Hard to believe her nephew would turn seven in two weeks. It seemed like yesterday when Paulina first brought him home. Even harder to believe Amalie would be three in a few months. Time flew by—

"Mama, I want a piano."

"You do? Why is that, love?"

"I saw one at the party," said Amalie. "A man played music on it and Pearl's mama sang songs." She immediately launched into one about a dog named Bingo.

Amalie had never sung before, so her melodious voice and perfect pitch surprised Lala. This was the first time she'd shown an interest in anything artistic. Amalie was too young to take lessons, but Lala could cultivate her daughter's budding interest in music by encouraging her to sing.

As she pushed the stroller over the Legion Bridge, Lala had second thoughts when Amalie repeated the song about the dog for what seemed like the hundredth time. Lala drifted...images of the hotel's interior danced in her mind, the splendid Arte Nouveau paneling and lighting, how she would refurnish it...until the repetitive melody distracted her.

She asked her daughter, "Did you learn any other songs, love?"

Amalie did, a rather grotesque one about three blind mice, which she proceeded to sing over and over. Lala wondered if the original English version sounded as gruesome as it did translated into German. She longed for a reprise of that Bingo dog by the time she reached her mother's building. She nodded to the four women sitting in the park across the way and they nodded back. Leaving the stroller in the entryway, she carried Amalie upstairs.

The irresistible aroma of cinnamon filled the hallway as Sarah opened the door to her apartment. "Come in, you're right on time." She lifted Amalie from Lala's arms and cuddled her. "Bubbie's been baking."

More sweets. Lala bit her tongue while her mother smothered her daughter with kisses.

Sarah carried Amalie into the kitchen, with Lala

following. Sarah's prized cinnamon cake sat cooling near the window. "It should be ready to eat soon. In the meantime, tell me all about the party."

Amalie talked a little about the decorations, food, and Pearl's gifts, but she spoke of the music in great detail. As she sang for them, she pantomimed playing the piano on the table.

"My, what a lovely singing voice you have, dear."

"I can sing more for you, Bubbie."

"All right, but maybe not about those horrible mice and their tails. How about the song with that pleasant dog, Bingo, was it?"

"Bingo was his name," she sang, then plunged into the next chorus.

While Amalie entertained Sarah, Lala went to the living room and stepped out onto the balcony. Laughter trickled up; she saw it came from the women across the street. One rocked a baby carriage while another relayed an incident that had the other women engaged. Then at four o'clock they all got up, wished each other a good rest of the day and went back to their respective apartments along the block.

"Lala, would you like some cake?" her mother called from the kitchen.

"A small piece." She returned to the kitchen and sat at the table. There was something comforting about her mother still serving her after all these years. It gave Lala a sense of continuity, reminding her that while she was a mother with a daughter, she was also a daughter with a mother.

Sarah's perception of small didn't match Lala's but she enjoyed every bite. She'd never asked for the recipe. The cake was so inextricably tied to her mother it wouldn't be the same without her.

"Lala, don't forget we have yahrzeit for your father coming up. He would have been sixty." She said it without that quiver in her voice. "I have memorial candles if you need them."

"Thanks, I'll take one with me." Lala set her cake plate and fork by the sink.

The telephone rang and Sarah answered it.

"Hello, Ivo. How are—oh no!"

Lala leapt up.

"Lala's with me. We'll meet you there." Sarah hung up, looking close to tears.

Lala's jaw clenched. "What is it, Mother?"

"Paulina. She's bleeding badly. Ivo's taking her to St. Francis Hospital." Sarah picked up Amalie. "We need to go there now."

They arrived to tragic news; Ivo told them Paulina had lost her baby, a little boy. Convinced her first miscarriage hadn't been caused by an infection or illness, Ivo arranged for an expert in obstetrics to examine her and ascertain why she miscarried a second time; the doctor was with her now. He left Jacub in the women's care and went upstairs to Paulina while Lala and Sarah sat on a bench in the lobby and waited. Amalie napped in her stroller. Sarah shared some of Amalie's candy with Jacub to ward off nervous hunger and dam the flood of tears that threatened.

Ivo returned; the doctor was examining Paulina. He stood facing the glass door at the entrance, staring into the distance, arms crossed over his chest, hands clasping his forearms like he was hugging himself. Jacub went to stand by his father's side.

Ludovik brought the automobile around shortly thereafter and met them in the lobby. His wife Elke offered to watch Jacub while the boy's parents remained in the hospital. Ivo felt he'd be more comfortable with Sarah. Lala thanked Ludovik for his offer. She asked him to take her mother and both children back to Sarah's apartment and then return for her.

While Ivo paced the hallways, Lala sat on the hard bench in the lobby and waited, hands passive in her lap. Idle. It reminded her of sitting shiva. Outside the hospital's windows, the shadows cast by trees along the riverfront lengthened as the afternoon wore on.

A commotion outside brought a nurse's aide rushing to open the door. In marched Mamie, followed by the von Anhalt's chauffeur carrying a copious arrangement of flowers. Mamie spotted Lala and hurried over.

"I stopped in the store and they told me she was brought here. How is she?"

"All we know is she lost the baby."

Mamie took Lala's hand. "I'm so sorry. That's awful, especially this far along." She turned to her chauffeur. "Have those flowers sent to her room."

Lala attempted a smile. "They're beautiful. How thoughtful of you, Mamie."

"I hoped to cheer her up with them, but a fat lot of good it will probably do under the circumstances. "

A fat lot? Some of Mamie's expressions bewildered Lala, but she caught the gist. "It will remind her that others care."

Mamie nodded. "I'd stay but we're off to Southampton, England to board the RMS Olympia for New York. Moritz has grown tired of all the demonstrations and shootings in Germany, not to mention the crazy talk he hears from his family in Bavaria. The final decision on Germany's War reparations is due any day, and it's not going to be pretty. Besides, my family wants to see Pearl before she grows up. And do give my best to Willete. Tell her I'm sorry to miss her son's baptism, although I have no idea why she invited me."

"Of course you do, Countess. And since Josef and I weren't invited, you'll have to tell her yourself. Safe travels. When will you return?"

"Late spring, in time for Amalie's birthday." She gave Lala's arm a squeeze. "Moritz is waiting in the limousine. Give my condolences to Paulina."

The von Anhalt contingent left the hospital and all fell quiet again.

The sky had begun to darken when a nurse summoned Ivo to Paulina's room. Sunset fell before he returned with a white-haired man, whom he introduced as Paulina's doctor.

"How is she, Doctor? Will she be all right?" Lala asked.

"Paulina is out of danger now. However, her baby came too early for us to save him."

"Was something wrong with the baby?" Lala asked him.

"Not at all. He was physically normal and healthy, other than being born too soon to survive. This is the second child Mrs. Chytry has lost midterm." He removed his glasses and rubbed his eyes. "My examination of her showed severe damage to her birth canal. She told me of the difficulties she had during the birth of her son seven years ago."

Although Jacub had been born a month early he weighed almost four kilos.

"There is an opening at the bottom of the birth canal," the doctor continued. "Normally it stays closed until a woman goes into labor. However, the damage caused by her first child's birth weakened the passage, causing it to dilate —

227

open up – once the baby she carried reached a certain size."

"How can you correct that so it won't happen again?" asked Lala.

Ivo placed his hand on her shoulder. "You can't."

Lala asked, "Does that mean...?"

The doctor nodded. "Paulina can't have any more children."

"Oh Ivo, I'm so sorry." She fought tears as she hugged him.

"Fortunately Paulina's all right." He appeared stoic. "We're grateful to have Jacub."

"We all are. May I see her now, Doctor?"

"Very briefly. She's weak and needs her rest."

"I'll take you to her room," said Ivo.

She saw Ludovik entering the hospital. "No, Ivo, you should be with Jacub now. I'll go to Paulina on my own. Have Ludovik drive you to my mother's to pick him up, then he can bring you home before returning for me."

"What about Amalie?"

"My mother can watch her tonight. None of us should be alone right now." She kissed his cheek. "Go, be with your son."

She waited until the men left before climbing the stairs and walking down seemingly endless corridors until she found Paulina's room.

A nurse checked Paulina's pulse before walking out. Paulina lay on the bed staring aimlessly at the dreary curtains covering the window. She turned as Lala entered the room and attempted a smile, tears brimming in her eyes.

Lala choked back a sob as she neared Paulina's bedside. Her mouth went dry and she couldn't speak, couldn't find the words. Paulina shook her head; no words were needed. She extended her hand toward Lala.

Lala clasped it and sat in the chair alongside the bed. There she sat, holding her sister's hand, neither uttering a word, until Paulina fell asleep.

Lala held back her tears as Ludovik drove her home. He parked in front of her home and opened the front door for her.

"Your mother asked me to give you this." He handed her a yahrzeit candle.

"...He would have been sixty...."

Her father didn't live long enough to see his daughter marry. Never got to hold his granddaughter....

As she climbed the steps to her apartment, she could no longer fight the urge to cry.

Josef met her at the door and held her as she sobbed, patting her back, stroking her hair, murmuring, "I'm heartbroken, too."

He took the memorial candle from her hands and left it on the console. Together they went into their bedroom, where Josef consoled Lala as he had in the past, the way he knew best.

CHAPTER TEN

By mid-May, Lala, Josef and Ruth deduced Lala was with child when each day began with her vomiting. Ruth treated her with more compassion than her previous housekeeper. Josef, though delighted by the news, spent more time at work to provide for his growing family.

Lala fretted over how to tell the Chytrys. Paulina's miscarriage two months earlier, coupled with the doctor's diagnosis had dampened spirits at Jacub's recent birthday party, salvaged only by Amalie's exuberance. She stood before the party-goers and entertained them with song after song.

Although Paulina kept saying she accepted the doctor's pronouncement, Lala worried her good news might upset her family. She needed her mother's advice.

"What a lovely surprise. Come in," Sarah exclaimed when Lala and Amalie arrived. Lala was about to tell her mother the real surprise when Amalie blurted, "Guess what, Bubbie. Mama's been sick in the morning."

Lala's mouth flew open in shock. "Amalie, why would

231

you say that to Bubbie?"

"Because she always says I should tell her if it happens."

"Mother!"

"What? I get the news much faster this way." Sarah embraced Lala. "I'm so happy for you, dear. And Josef, of course."

"Bubbie, why are you happy Mama gets sick?"

Sarah cupped her granddaughter's face. "Because it means you're going to have a brother or sister soon."

"What if I don't want one?"

"It's too late. You're getting one." To Lala she asked, "How bad it is this time?"

"About the same most mornings."

"When are you due?"

"December."

Sarah clapped her hands in delight. "What a marvelous Hanukah gift for me."

Lala recoiled. "You're not hoping I have eight children, are you? That's not a present, it's a punishment."

Sarah laughed. It softened the lines in her face. Her hair, now white, complemented her pale complexion. However, other signs of her aging – the dark spots on her face and hands, the stiffness in her movements – unsettled Lala.

Sarah patted her hand. "Come into the kitchen. I'll make us some tea."

"May I have a treat, Bubbie?" asked Amalie.

"Of course you may. All I have is cookies."

The girl beamed. "I love cookies."

"Then sit at the table and Bubbie will bring you...how many, Mama?"

***

The women drank tea while Amalie finished her cookies. She asked to go out on the balcony and when Lala consented, Sarah took her. Lala nibbled a cookie until her mother returned to the kitchen.

Lala said, "I've told no one about the baby other than you and Josef, so please don't say anything."

"For how long?"

"At least until I begin to show."

"Does that silence include Paulina?"

Lala sighed. "With her it's not as much when as how. Any advice?"

Sarah put her hand on Lala's. "I'm going to tell you something, but you must first promise never to repeat it to anyone."

She and her mother had long ago sworn off keeping secrets except when absolutely necessary to protect someone. Lala agreed.

"You know how much Paulina grieved after her two miscarriages. Then learning she won't be able to have any more children came as a blow." Sarah looked around as if fearful of being overheard. She leaned in closer. "Although your sister has never said this in so many words, I get the impression she's actually relieved her childbearing days are over."

"How so?"

"At first, I thought she'd buried herself in work to block out the pain of her loss, but she's thriving. If she'd had the baby, she'd have to stop working awhile, and I don't think she wanted that, especially now that she's gaining so much attention in the fashion world. She can still care for Jacub and Ivo without giving up her business."

"You don't think she'd feel saddened or envious by my

news?"

"When has Paulina ever been envious of anyone? No, she may feel a momentary twinge of sadness, but she'll be thrilled for you and Josef. Go tell her."

"That's a relief. I was beginning to feel like I had no one to share my good news with."

"What about your friends?"

"What friends? Not surprisingly, Zoe has shunned me since I accused her of neglecting her daughter."

Sarah waved her hand. "Good riddance to her, I say. What about that odd American woman, or the banker's wife?"

"Mamie travels so much she's rarely here, and Klement's a good client of Josef's but we rarely socialize with them." She took a sip of tea. "Although I admire Willete for taking on Klement's children we've nothing in common. In fact, ever since our dinner they've kept their distance despite my friendly overtures. I'm not sure why. That night Willete requested your goose recipe, which I had Ruth write out for her, but she deliberately left it behind."

"Which recipe? I'll wager it's the one I make for Hanukah, Jewish-style."

"Yes, that...are you implying the Chermaks rebuffed us because we're Jewish?"

"Did they know that before?"

"Willete's seen the Chytrys at church...so, perhaps not."

Sarah refilled the kettle. "More tea?"

"I still have some left, but if you're making more I'd like another cup."

Sarah set the kettle on the stove to heat. "If you recall, I suggested joining the other ladies in the park a while ago. Have you considered that?"

Steam rose from the kettle as Lala finished her tea. While Sarah brewed another pot, Lala went to check on Amalie.

Lala observed the four women socializing beneath the bare-limbed trees. By their conversation and laughter they must be enjoying each other's company. A dark-haired woman, the oldest of the group, sat beside a woman who resembled her; Lala assumed a younger sister. A plump, apple-cheeked redhead perched next to her, chattering as she knit. On an adjacent bench sat a slender young woman who listened as she rocked a baby carriage. Lala wondered what they talked about. Surely not subjects that interested her. Probably neighborhood gossip and mundane goings-on with their homes and children. Then again, what could Lala offer now beyond that?

"Time to come inside, Amalie."

"No." She held tight to the iron barrier.

A break from this, even for a short time, would be most welcome, Lala thought. After some cajoling, she ushered her daughter back to the kitchen, where Sarah had poured more tea.

"Mother, would you mind watching Amalie for a while?"

"Of course not. Have you something to do?"

Lala fetched her coat. "I'm going to introduce myself to the ladies outside."

"Good for you," said Sarah. "Just don't talk politics. They don't think like we do."

"How do you know if you don't discuss politics?"

"You can tell by what newspaper they read." Sarah gestured toward her copy of the Tagblatt. "The one married to a Communist gets the Lidu and the two hardline sisters buy the Zeitung."

***

As Lala approached the women, the older sister looked up and squinted as the sun beamed into her face. She appeared to be in her early forties, judging by the lines around her ice blue eyes. Dark curls framed her angular face.

"You're Mrs. Hafstein's daughter, yes? We wondered when you would introduce yourself."

"I thought I might be intruding."

"Not at all. I'm Dagmar." She motioned for Lala to sit.

"Hello, I'm Lala. Lala Smetana."

Dagmar gestured to the woman who resembled her. "This is my sister Ignacie."

Ignacie extended her hand. "Hello."

Before Dagmar could introduce the redhead, the animated woman set her knitting aside, stood and approached Lala. "I'm Terezka. I live in the apartment above your mother's. I've seen you come by with your little girl. May I say your daughter is lovely. What's her name?"

"Amalie."

"Such a pretty name, and so unusual."

The young mother had honey blonde hair framing a wide face with a squared jawline, anchored by an aquiline nose. She looked up. "It's French."

"That's Bente," said Dagmar. "Come sit with us."

An hour of passable conversation had elapsed when Sarah walked Amalie across the street, pushing the empty stroller. "She's ready to go home and see Papa."

Lala took her daughter's hand. "Did you have a good visit?"

"We did," Sarah interjected. "We had an interesting talk.

Amalie wanted to know if I had any children."

The women got a chuckle out of that.

Sarah continued, "She also wanted to know how you get a baby."

Lala responded, "And what did you tell her?"

"Why, you find them on the front doorstep."

The other women smiled and nodded their approval of Sarah's answer, but Lala took her mother aside and whispered. "Why did you tell her that?"

Sarah whispered back, "What did you expect me to say, the truth?"

"Of course not, but at least a gentle version of the truth, not some fabricated nonsense."

"But I didn't make it up. For me it was the truth. I first laid eyes on you standing in Naomi's doorway, and Paulina joined our family the night she showed up on our doorstep when the government confiscated her shop."

Lala threw up her hands. "I can't argue with that." She lifted Amalie and put her in the stroller. To the women she said, "I'll see you next week." She kissed her mother good-bye.

Sarah patted her arm. "Call your sister as soon as you get home."

"No, this should be done in person."

Lala wheeled Amalie's stroller into Paulina's shop. Miss Horáčková nodded a greeting to them as she wrapped up a purchase for a handsome woman who looked familiar, but Lala couldn't place her. Miss Horáčková then escorted the customer and her chauffeur to the door.

"Thank you again, Mrs. Masaryková. Good afternoon."

Miss Horáčková bowed to President Masaryk's wife as she left the shop. "Good afternoon, Mrs. Smetana. How may I be of assistance today?"

"Is my sister here?"

"She is upstairs in the factory. Would you like me to escort you there?"

"You needn't leave the shop unattended. If you'll point the way?"

Miss Horáčková bent to look at Amalie. She smiled. "Little Miss Smetana is fast asleep. Would you prefer to leave her here with me rather than disturb her nap?"

"I'd be grateful. I won't be long."

The clerk guided Lala to Paulina's office and through the rear door, where a stairway led to the next floor. As she climbed, Lala could hear the whir of sewing machines. She followed the noise until she entered a brightly lit room with half a dozen tables set up for cutting and another half-dozen where seamstresses assembled garments at those droning machines. Along two windowless walls Paulina had installed deep chute-like shelves to store rolls of fabric, organized by color and pattern with matching thread in attached baskets; the third wall contained storage for everything from scissors and pattern markers to ribbons and buttons. The room resembled the upholstery department in Josef's former factory, compact and efficient.

Lala spotted Paulina handing a roll of lace to a seamstress. Paulina looked up, smiled and after giving instructions to the woman at the machine, hurried to Lala.

After a buss on the cheek, Paulina said, "You haven't seen my factory yet. What do you think?"

"It's brilliant, Paulina. What a well-organized operation you have here. How many dresses can you produce now?"

"At least twelve a day, and this is just ready-to-wear. What brings you here?"

"I'm sorry to interrupt you at work, but I needed to talk to you. In person."

Paulina's brow furrowed. "I can't leave right now, but come with me to the storeroom where it will be quieter."

She escorted Lala out of the factory and across the hall to a smaller room with muted lighting. Dozens of completed garments hung from racks in one corner, with the rest of the space devoted to storage. Paulina shut the door, muffling the sounds of the machines.

A look of concern swept across Paulina's face as she took Lala's hands in hers. "I hope this isn't bad news."

Lala gave her a pained smile. "As do I." She found herself at a loss for words.

"Just tell me. Whatever it is, we'll get through it together."

I'm worrying her. "Paulina, I'm expecting another child."

Paulina's face lit with joy. "You are? How wonderful. Congratulations. " She hugged Lala tightly. Then she stood back, looking quizzical. "Why would you let me think otherwise?"

Lala let out the breath she'd been holding. "I didn't want to upset you."

"Oh my friend, how could you possibly think for one moment I'd be upset by such joyous news?"

Tears gathered in Lala's eyes as she hugged her sister once more. "Oh Paulina, I'm so lucky to have you."

CHAPTER ELEVEN

Lala returned to her mother's neighborhood a few days later to give the new social avenue another try. After taking Amalie up to Sarah's apartment she greeted the women in the park. Terezka moved her knitting bag aside to make room for Lala to sit.

"What are you making?" asked Lala.

"A sweater for my son. My mother taught me to start knitting for next winter in the spring so I'll have enough for him to wear by the time he needs it." She finished another row. "As I was saying, my sister wrote to me about this shocking book she'd read. It's called Women in Love. Have you heard of it?"

Lala had, courtesy of Mamie, who'd gotten a copy before the book was banned, but she kept that to herself.

Terezka's knitting needles flapped like bird wings. "I'd heard the book was quite racy, so naturally I was curious. I convinced my sister to mail it to me last month. I hid it in my nightstand where my husband and son wouldn't find it and read it a few pages at a time when they weren't home. I finally finished it this morning."

"What did you think?" asked Ignacie.

"Well, racy doesn't begin to describe it."

"Did you like it or not?" asked Dagmar.

Terezka shrugged. "I didn't really understand some of it. I'd say I liked the beginning a great deal but not so much how it ended...kind of like making a baby." Her eyes grew large. "Oh, my!" She blushed redder than her hair and giggled uncontrollably.

Lala held back until the others broke into laughter, which woke Bente's six-month-old son. When the laughter trickled off, Bente announced, "My husband wants me to have another baby."

The laughter having loosened her restraint, Lala exclaimed, "So soon?"

"Some women swear it's easier to have them close together," noted Ignacie, gesturing to Dagmar. "Our mother had us three years apart and bore one brother in between."

"But we were smarter than that," said Dagmar.

Bente rubbed her son's belly to quiet him. "I'd rather wait until Petr's at least two."

Terezka commiserated. "My husband tells me I must submit to him, like it says in the Bible."

Dagmar shook her head. "Leave it to men to get that passage wrong. The Apostle Paul said, 'Wives, be subject to your husbands,' not submissive."

Lala reflected these women might have more depth than she first considered.

Lala began bringing Amalie to her mother's apartment twice a week so Sarah could watch the child while Lala sat in the park with the ladies. Terezka, mother to a boy Jacub's age, always brought her knitting. Bente tended to little Petr while Dagmar and Ignacie steered the conversation to topics they deemed acceptable, which centered around families and homes, crafts like cooking and sewing, and the occasional bit of neighborhood gossip. Although Lala drifted off when the chatter turned inane or judgmental, she grew to enjoy the companionship and, like the others, the respite from childcare.

When Lala mentioned her daughter's interest in music, Dagmar recommended a neighbor who gave piano lessons to children. "It would be a kindness to her as well. She's a war widow and mother with no other means of support."

"But not like Mrs. Graz next door," noted Ignacie through pursed lips, which suggested there was more to the story.

"Does she give lessons as well?" Lala asked.

Dagmar snorted at that and crossed her arms. "Mrs. Graz claims to, but she only gives lessons when her husband's at work, and only to men."

Ignacie wagged her finger. "My husband would say she plays piano with one hand."

Dagmar, who rarely smiled, allowed herself one at that.

"What does she do with the other hand?" Terezka asked between purling.

The answer finally registered when Dagmar glared at her, adding, "All sorts of men parading in and out of her apartment. Absolutely shameful."

Lala chuckled in recognition. "My husband once had a neighbor like that, except she never bothered with a piano."

Dagmar shooed a bird away from the bench. "The very idea of a married woman working. Only spinsters, and poor unfortunate widows with young children who must, ought to

243

work."

"Or a bastard's mother," her sister added, and Terezka agreed.

Lala bristled, then took a calming breath. "What are you making for dinner tonight?"

Sarah asked to take Amalie to Petřín Hill for a picnic and a romp through the cherry orchards, now in full bloom. Lala kissed them goodbye, then took her usual seat on the park bench.

Terezka showed off the sweater she'd finished for her son that morning. When Lala reached over to look at it, she felt the seams in her dress straining against her growing middle. "This dress has gotten too tight on me, and it's the loosest one I own."

"I hated shopping for maternity dresses," Terezka observed, tugging a length of blue yarn from her knitting bag. "They're horrible. Nothing ever fits right or looks pretty, not that a woman can look pretty with a belly as big as a whale. And what a waste of money. You know what I did when I got too big to go outside? I took a few of my husband's worn shirts, cut down the sleeves and wore them around the house." Her knitting needles clacked as she cast off her first row. "My husband's a big fellow with a belly to match, thanks to my cooking."

"How come you didn't go outside?" asked Ignacie.

"I was afraid to walk the stairs when I couldn't see my feet."

Bente's son began to whimper in his sleep. "Lala, I still have my maternity dresses. You're welcome to take some of them."

"How kind of you to offer, Bente, but my sister made a few for me."

Bente rubbed Petr's back until he quieted down. "I didn't know you had a sister. Is she older or younger?"

Lala paused. Paulina's birthday fell five months before hers, but Lala's actual birthdate had to be six months earlier. "We're...unidentical twins."

"Is she married?" asked Ignacie.

"Yes, and has a seven year old boy."

"Why doesn't she come around? Does she live far away?"

"No, but she only visits on Sundays." Lala wondered if she should leave it at that. It would be safer, but dishonest. "She owns a dress shop across the river."

Dagmar raised her eyebrows but said nothing. Ignacie refrained from commenting as well.

Terezka, who rarely refrained from speaking, said, "You always dress so beautifully, that explains it. Where is her shop?"

"On Jinrisská Street."

"It must be near Paulina's, that high-class shop I read about in the society pages."

"Paulina is my sister."

"She is?" Terezka sounded star-struck. "I hear everyone from President Masaryk's wife to the Countess von Anhalt shops there. Have you met any of her famous clients?"

"A few."

"Imagine, wearing clothing from Paulina's all the time. Maybe you should give your hand-me-downs to Bente instead of the other way around." Terezka giggled as she began another row. "How does your sister manage with a husband, a child and a business? Does her husband work?"

"He's a professor at Charles University. Paulina has hired

staff to run her shop."

The conversation halted when Petr woke up, crying. Swaddling him in his blanket, Bente lifted him to her breast to nurse. "I used to work, before I married."

"What sort of work did you do?" asked Lala.

"Have you been to Bonne Fleur, that French lingerie shop across the river? Madame hired me as a store clerk. I'd bring the merchandise into the fitting room and take it out to fold away afterward."

Bente's eyes glazed and a faint smile appeared. "All those frilly chemises and petticoats. Never in your life could you imagine such beautiful things. My favorite part was taking whatever the ladies didn't buy from the changing room and folding it. Madame made me wear cotton gloves so my hands wouldn't snag the material. But sometimes, when she wasn't looking, I'd take my gloves off and run my fingers over the lace edges, the feathery silk, so soft...as delicate as tissue paper." She shrugged and her reverie fell away. "I dreamed of having something from that shop, but I could never afford it."

"And yet you enjoyed working there," Lala said. "Would you ever consider returning to the shop?"

"To buy something?"

"Or to work."

Bente didn't answer, but Lala saw the wistfulness reflected in the young woman's face.

"If you like folding clothes that much, Bente, you can come to my house and fold our laundry," Ignacie scoffed. "I've got plenty to keep you busy and you won't have to wear gloves."

Dagmar snickered.

"You do it for your family and you're a wife and mother,"

Ignacie added, wagging her finger at Bente. "You do it for someone else, you're a common maid. Am I right, Dagmar?"

"Absolutely. Some women do things for their husband, others do those same things for money."

Bente plucked her son from her breast and put him back in his carriage as if to protect him from the nastiness directed at her. "Are you comparing what I did to Mrs. Graz?"

"Of course not, but I can't understand why any married woman would want to work outside the home when she didn't have to."

Lala stood beside Bente. "Because some women prefer to do something beyond housework and child rearing, even if you don't understand why, Dagmar. Haven't you ever wanted to break away for a while to pursue a hobby, or nourish your spirit? Don't you tire being around children all day? Long for adult conversation?"

"Why do you think we sit outside like this during the week?" She and Ignacie laughed, and Terezka soon joined in.

Bente kept her head down, her face taut. "I suppose you're right. Why would I want to work when I have a husband and baby? Maybe I should have another child, like he wants."

"What do you want, Bente?" Lala asked.

Bente said nothing, but her open face bore the sadness of a life denied. She'd obey her husband's wish to have a child, obey the tenets of the women who gathered in the park. Her world had shrunk so small she couldn't fathom journeying to the other side of the river to browse in the shop where she once worked, or even to look in its windows.

Dagmar crossed her arms. "Lala, you shouldn't put such nonsense in her head. She's too young to understand the ways of the world."

Keeping her temper in check, Lala said, "The ways of the world change all the time." She checked her watch: nearly two o'clock. Her mother would have Amalie for two more hours. She ran her hand over her expanding belly. "If you'll excuse me I really must do some shopping."

Lala returned before four carrying a small oval box. She greeted the women, still sitting on the benches.

"Bente, I have something for you." Lala handed her the box.

Bente's eyes grew when she saw it, having recognized the packaging. She looked up at Lala with gratitude.

"What is it?" asked Ignacie.

Bente showed them the box with Bonne Fleur's nosegay logo stenciled on top. Terezka reached out to it but Bente pulled it away from her grasp.

"Aren't you going to open it?" asked Terezka.

Bente stared at the box she held with trembling hands. Finally she put it in the carriage. "No, I'll wait until I'm home."

"But we want to see it," insisted Terezka.

"I'm sorry, but I will not show this to anybody, not you, not my husband. This is for me and me alone." She stood and enfolded Lala in a hug, whispering, "You can't imagine what this means to me. Thank you."

Lala whispered back, "Trust your heart," before Bente ended the embrace.

Bente tucked the blanket around her son and pushed the baby carriage away from the benches. Lala saw her mother approaching a block away. She wished the women a pleasant evening and walked off to meet Sarah and Amalie.

CHAPTER TWELVE

A scorching August sun ascended over the city. By nine o'clock in the morning the pavement already simmered. Lala closed her bedroom windows to slow its advancement into the apartment. Sitting at her dressing table she dabbed lipstick over the sore she gave herself from biting her lower lip. She wiped away a smear with her finger, set the lipstick in her drawer, then with one deep breath for courage, went back to Amalie's bedroom to supervise her dressing.

Amalie had pushed aside the summery yellow and white striped jumper Lala put out for her and instead had chosen a long-sleeved knit dress, one of her favorites, from the bureau.

"Amalie...?"

Lala and Amalie remained quiet though dinner as Josef prattled on about his workday. After they put Amalie to bed, Lala tried to relax in the living room with Josef. She asked him to pour two cognacs for them.

Josef gestured toward her mouth. "What has Amalie done now?"

Lala touched her swollen lip as she described Amalie's

249

latest temper tantrum. "Then I said, 'Amalie, why are you holding that dress?'"

"What you should have said was simply, 'You shall not wear this dress today.'"

"I realize that now, Josef, but I couldn't think of an effective response on the spot. Besides, if I'd said that she'd have fought even harder."

"What did you say to her?"

"That she'd worn that dress as a two-year-old and now that she was three...."

"Very clever. At her age she'll avoid anything babyish."

Lala stood, hands on hips. "But it took ten minutes of arguing with her to get to that point. I might as well ask her to do something I don't want her to do. Then it's more likely she'll behave or do what she should. Your daughter is determined to fight me on everything."

"I know where she gets it from. You should see yourself, standing there ready to do battle."

She peered down at her aggressive stance and forced her body to relax. With a wave of her hand, a gesture she'd picked up from her mother, she said, "I'll make us tea."

"Determined," he repeated as Lala was leaving the room. "A good way to describe her."

Sarah laughed when Lala told her the story the next day. "He calls Amalie determined and you think he meant it as a compliment to you." Her mother had arrived early to help with dinner for the family.

Lala failed to get her mother to understand her crises with Amalie. Sarah, like Josef, spent much less time with the child. Free from the responsibility of constant caregiving, they could indulge Amalie, and they adored her, which she rewarded with obedience and geniality.

Lala repeated the incident from the day before. "And again today; she wanted to wear a dark red wool dress with long sleeves, utterly inappropriate for the season. I selected two lovely summer dresses for her to choose from and still she ranted. I don't know—"

Lala fell silent as Amalie came into the kitchen, dressed in a blue gingham bloomer dress, a gift Mamie sent from America. "Cookie, Bubbie."

Lala interjected, "No cookies before dinner, Amalie."

The child's mouth tightened into a pout. "But I want one now."

Lala clenched her jaw to refrain from biting her lip. She took a deep breath and let it out. "No. Cookies. Before. Dinner."

With hands on her hips and a look of ferocity, Amalie glared at her mother. "You won't let me do anything – no cookies, no red dress." Her voice reached a decibel level marginally below yelling.

Lala felt the quake of anger building inside her. "I said no cookies before dinner. And you are wearing what you wanted to wear."

"Only because you said I had to wear this dress or the yellow dress you like and I didn't want to wear that dress today! Papa would let me wear whatever I wanted!" And with one huff she stormed off, leaving Lala staring at her mother who'd borne witness to Amalie's tantrum.

"Now do you see what I must endure with her?"

Sarah nodded. "I know, dear. I know."

Although her mother and Josef assured her that family would shrug it off, it embarrassed Lala when Amalie

251

disobeyed her in front of them. Especially Paulina and Ivo, whose son always behaved well. "Sometimes it seems like every conversation with her ends in an argument, or worse," she grumbled.

"I know, dear. I know."

"Such outrageous behavior," Lala added to draw more sympathy from her mother.

"I know, dear," Sarah repeated. "I went through the same thing with my daughter."

It took a moment for that to register. Lala turned, shocked by Sarah's comment. "Come now, Mother. I never behaved like that."

"You don't remember having a fit over a dress in front of your aunt and uncle's important company?"

The Grossfleisches. As an impoverished child, they'd mocked her lack of social graces.

"You can't possibly compare standing up for what's right with what Amalie's doing?"

"You don't understand," Sarah insisted. "She knows yellow is her aunt's favorite color and yours is blue. You upset Amalie by making her choose between those two dresses. Worse, you forced her to wear something Paulina didn't make for her."

"I don't want her thinking she must wear couture clothes all the time."

"And she doesn't, but Paulina will be here tonight."

"Paulina won't care what her niece wears, but I care about Amalie's behavior—"

Sarah squeezed Lala's hand to silence her. "Dear, she may not always do 'what' she should, but if you listened to her you'd know she always does 'as' she should. Yes, she acts willfully and she's headstrong, like her mother. But she's also honest and fierce, someone who will fight for what she believes, whether it's showing respect for her aunt by wearing one of her dresses or fighting off a violent mob from thrashing a foreigner. Like her mother."

Sarah sat down and tapped the table with her fingertips. Lala sat beside her.

"When your father and I took you in, you talked a lot about your papa and mama, how you had his eyes but her nose and mouth...'No girl should have a pear nose like Papa's,' you used to say. Thankfully, you don't and neither does Amalie. But what about the baby you're carrying, or others you may have in the future? You vaguely remember what your Russian family looked like, but you were too young to know them other than as your mama and papa, or how much you may resemble them now, either physically or in character."

"I hadn't considered that."

Her mother continued, "Amalie and the baby you're carrying may be your only living blood relatives. There's a part of you in her that you may not see, or want to see. You're much more alike than you let on."

"It's a fair point, but I was never this fussy."

Sarah made an exaggerated roll of her eyes and said in falsetto, "Oh Mother, I don't want that Irish lace on my dress. It's so common. I must have Swiss lace and nothing else will do!"

Lala recoiled. "I never said that...not in that way...did I?" But her mother's laughter dispelled her assumption.

She sighed. "So this is 'Bubbie's revenge,' is it?"

"Just wait until she gets married and has a daughter. Then it will be your turn." Sarah patted Lala's hand. "I'll talk to her. Maybe she'll listen to me."

***

Sarah volunteered to take Amalie home with her for the night to give mother and daughter a much needed break from each other. Her mother promised she'd talk to the girl. Lala wondered if it would do any good, but there was always hope.

Lala waited in the living room for Josef to join her. She reflected on the conversation at dinner, centered on Germany's growing inflation. A friendly debate ensued over whether the War reparations imposed were punitive or justified. Lala said she thought both and Ivo agreed. He brought up the political violence that had been erupting in Berlin, which he blamed on anti-Communist sentiments and "other factors" beyond the plummeting value of the German mark.

She could see why so many Germans hated Marxist groups like the KDP, but felt the recent assassination of Foreign Minister Walter Rathenau, a respected industrialist, marked a new depth of depravity. Germany's war effort would have failed early on without his brilliant management of resources; even Vienna sought to emulate his success. His reward? Getting shot in the street like an animal by the same thugs Moritz's Bavarian family admired. Thugs whom she suspected received financial support from private sources as well as sympathetic banks.

Did the assassins target Rathenau solely for his connection to the despised Weimar Republic? Lala thought not. It bore one commonality with the killing of two KDP Party leaders a few years earlier, after their Spartacist uprising failed. Out of decorum, Ivo had sidestepped the issue of anti-Jewish sentiments rising in Germany, spearheaded by the militaristic Freikorps, but he'd implied it.

She wondered if Klement's bank had any involvement with the group...no, impossible. An art lover, a connoisseur of fine things, could never support violence or virulent anti-Semitism. Klement collected pieces by Jewish artists, including Lala's father. He'd even referred Lala to Willete's physician, one of the finest in Prague, when Lala told him she couldn't bear the thought of using the same doctor as had Paulina.

As Lala reached for the newspaper she felt a stirring within; a kick? She rubbed her belly and turned to the society column as Josef sat beside her. Time to put her dark thoughts aside.

He took the newspaper from her hands and grinning, tossed it aside.

"I was reading that," she protested.

"No you weren't." He sidled up to her and kissed her cheek. "You look lovely tonight."

"I won't for long." She snatched the newspaper from where Josef had tossed it and fanned herself with it. She couldn't wait for summer to end; the heat aggravated her hot flashes. She got up to open a window.

Josef followed her. "You always look beautiful to me. Beautiful, enticing...." His fingertips glanced along her arm, tantalizing as a seductive whisper.

She turned to face him. Her body melted into his as he drew her toward him.

He kissed her, gently at first and then more deeply as she responded in kind. She caressed his chest with her fingertips. His hands slid down her back and cupped her bottom, pressing her into his body, igniting her passion. Holding her by the waist he lifted her and sat her on the sideboard, his mouth still exploring hers. She felt him part her legs. The hem of her dress inched higher and higher as his hands roamed up her inner thighs, past the tops of her stockings until they touched her bare flesh. With a moan, she reached to open the buttons on his trousers and met every stroke of his fingers with one of her own.

"Take me to our bedroom," she begged, her arousal mounting.

Lala lay in bed next to Josef, breathless and happy. Their lovemaking had slowed in frequency and intensity since Amalie's birth, more perfunctory than passionate. Tonight felt like an erotic return to the early days of their marriage. It thrilled Lala that Josef still desired her and could satisfy her desires.

She rubbed her belly to quell another kick. "We need to start preparing for the baby's arrival. Four months will go by quickly. I found a crib I like, but we can use Amalie's carriage again. She'll have outgrown it by the time I give birth. We'll also need warmer blankets and clothes. Oh, and I'd like new curtains for the nursery. The ones we used before are quite feminine and something tells me I'm carrying a boy."

He kissed her. "Prepare the nursery any way you'd like, a perfect chore for an expectant mother."

CHAPTER THIRTEEN

Sarah came to fetch Amalie for an outing to Petřín Hill on what should have been a glorious April morning. By now the cherry trees would have exploded with pink blossoms, dappling sunshine in the park. Spring flowers would be blooming, their colorful heads dancing in the light breeze. Children would be playing....children.

Lala closed the draperies in the nursery that Ruth had opened when she arrived to clean. The sun had no right to shine so brightly. Trees shouldn't be leafing out, flowers ought not poke through the ground, enlivening the city with their profuse colors. Life had stopped for her; how could it go on outside?

"Why don't you come with us, Lala, get outside in the fresh air," her mother pleaded. "Sitting in the house by yourself will do you no good."

"Not today, Mother." She glanced away, toward the carpet. The four round indentations left behind by the crib's legs had finally disappeared. The crib went to charity, for some more fortunate mother.

She gave birth on the last day of December, with overcast

skies threatening snow. Her son, whom she'd named Jakob Daniel for her father and Josef's, survived mere minutes. He'd let out a hearty wail when he emerged but fell silent when the doctor whisked him away to be cleaned...

"This occurs sometimes in newborns...their lungs are too immature...they can't breathe...." the doctor had said. Josef, grief-stricken by the loss of another child, could not speak about it, but Ivo expressed surprise at the doctor's explanation.

"The condition, though fairly common in early births, is rare in full term infants," Ivo noted, though quickly added, "However, there is no reason to believe this could happen again."

Letters of condolence poured in from family and friends. Paulina spared Lala the agony of returning the layette and baby gifts, except one Lala wanted to keep – a stuffed bear from America. Josef had assumed it came from the von Anhalts; Lala didn't tell him Gershom and his new bride Louise sent it.

Cuddling the soft bear brought moments of respite from the overwhelming sorrow. Willete Klement vowed she'd think twice before using that doctor for her next pregnancy. Mamie simply grasped her in a hug and held her as she cried.

For months Lala felt bereft of life. Not only little Jakob's, but hers. She knew this could not continue; it would not continue, this weight in her heart and spirit. It would gradually begin to fade. One drop would fall away each morning until she could feel alive again.

Most days she managed to pull herself together and function, but sometimes a memory or a trace from the past – a piece of clothing, the indents in the rug – sent her tumbling into a pit of sorrow deeper than any grave. She sensed Josef's patience with her had begun to ebb but she couldn't bring herself to put her grief aside and get on with life. Grief was all she had left.

"Amalie, let's get you dressed," said Sarah. Lala glanced at her daughter, who was still in her pajamas. Lala felt shame wash over her for being so neglectful of Amalie and she left the room, closing the door behind her. She heard amiable chatter through the door as she walked away, striving to find the words to express gratitude to her mother for her help with Amalie, and to ask forgiveness from her daughter for being inattentive. None came.

Lala waited by the front door to say goodbye. Ruth brought out a basket with a picnic lunch.

Sarah asked, "Would you put it in Amalie's stroller?"

"No, I won't go in the stroller anymore," insisted Amalie. "I'm a big girl now."

"Yes you are, but you're also too big for Bubbie to carry. What if you get too tired to walk home?"

"Please, Bubbie, I can do it, I'm almost four."

Lala stifled back a gasp. Her mother's words returned to her...

"...You're much more alike than you let on..."

...as did familiar words from even longer ago. Lala couldn't tell if she wanted to cry or laugh. Maybe both.

"I'll carry you, Amalie," she said as she picked up her daughter and cradled her.

"Are you coming with us, Mama?"

"I am."

"Will Papa come, too?"

Lala smiled. "He might. Let's ask him."

Ruth took the picnic basket from Sarah. "Then I ought to make more food."

CHAPTER FOURTEEN

Ivo's thesis on the Italian Renaissance was nearing publication when Paulina announced she would discontinue her ready-to-wear line to concentrate on her thriving couture business. Their milestones deserved celebrating, as did Lala's emergence from her cocoon of sorrow. Lala invited the family to dinner, along with the von Anhalts.

She heard the front door open as Josef came upstairs with Paulina, Ivo and Jacub.

"Congratulations to you both." Lala bussed them both before hugging Jacub. Ivo's gait seemed more rigid than usual. Lala asked him about it as he set aside his walking stick.

"My leg stiffens when I sit too long. Unfortunately, between my research and writing my book, it's unavoidable."

Lala admired the gown Paulina wore, yellow with touches of jet beading along black lace panels that stretched down her sleeves and around the dropped waist. Exquisite. Tailored for her sister's figure, as Lala's flowing blue crepe dress was to hers, yet so different. Paulina's talent had evolved over the years. She seemed to have endless creativity and skill, advancing her artistry every season. Lala wondered what she'd have accomplished had she pursued designing interiors – would her ideas have stayed fresh and original like Paulina's?

The doorbell announced the von Anhalts' arrival with four-year-old Pearl. They exchanged greetings, and after bringing the children into the breakfast room with Amalie and Ruth, the adults settled into the living room.

"Josef will pour whatever you would like while I check on the dinner preparations and the children." Lala went to the breakfast room to find the children eating their dinner and Ruth getting the first course ready to serve. "Everything looks splendid, Ruth."

"Thank you, Missus."

Lala stopped by the children's table. "Are you enjoying your dinner?"

"It's delicious, Antila." Jacub gobbled a forkful of noodles to prove his point, which spattered the table with butter. Lala took the washrag from the sink and as she wiped the table, Amalie gazed up at her. "Mama, isn't Bubbie your mama?"

"Yes she is, love."

"Then why do you call her Mother and not Mama?"

The question caught Lala by surprise.

Fortunately, Jacub spoke up. "That's because everyone has their own special name for her. I call her Grandmama, you call her Bubbie, my mother calls her Mama Sarah and Antila calls her Mother."

It was as good an explanation as any for her daughter. Some day when she was older she would hear the true story about her mother's origins.

"If my brother didn't die, what would he call her?" Amalie asked.

Lala stiffened.

Jacub said, "What about Babička? That's what I call my

262

other grandmother."

"You have two grandmothers?" Amalie scowled. "Mama, how come he has two and I only have one?"

Lala threw the washrag into the sink. "Papa will explain that to you later."

Over dinner Ivo divulged that Paulina's shop had become a popular destination for the wives of ambassadors visiting the nation's capital.

"She's entertained more dignitaries than our president," he joked. "I'm so proud of her."

"As am I," added Lala. Paulina remained unassuming as compliments fluttered around her like butterflies. Lala wondered if her own expression matched her words; the envy she felt toward her successful sister embarrassed her.

"I finished Amalie's birthday present. I'll bring it next week for her party," said Paulina. "Lala, you must be needing new clothes by now. I've set aside some of my finest pieces. Come in next week for a fitting."

"I should as well," said Mamie. "We're traveling soon."

"Where to?" asked Paulina.

"We haven't decided. Moritz wants to avoid Germany."

"Too dangerous, between the hyperinflation and the political discord," he explained. "I fear for Mamie's safety."

"The rich American," she said with a shrug, drawing a chuckle from all except Moritz.

"My dear, you were the rich American a few years ago when the exchange rate was four marks to the dollar. Now it's one million marks."

"Then we should spend our money there. If I buy something for a dollar, it will still be worth one dollar next month, unlike their currency."

"Unfortunately, Mamie, that only applies to Germans who have something of value to sell," said Ivo. "Strikes, demonstrations and discord are as unchecked as inflation. I'm concerned the next step will be more violence like the Kapp Putsch three years ago."

"At least that coup failed, which forced the Freikorps to disband," Lala observed.

"Moritz heard they're now part of the group that was behind Rathanau's assassination," said Mamie.

Moritz nodded. "Many of their followers hid out in Bavaria and joined Hermann Ehrhardt's Marinebrigades. They call themselves the Organisation Consul now, an officious name for a group dedicated to overthrowing the government."

"Your relatives probably helped them," said Mamie. "We hear the same rhetoric from his family in Bavaria. You can't have a civil conversation with them anymore. A few years ago they took Moritz to the Munich Hofbrauhaus to hear some windbag spouting off, a failed artist no less, who called Jewish people a race instead of a religion. It reminded me of the way some in my family talk about the Negroes. Anyway, you'd think they'd lock him up in a loony bin. Nope. They made him the head of the Nazi Party – and many Germans agree with him."

Ivo asked, "What about vacationing in Italy?"

Moritz shook his head. "With all the violence going on? Their fascist government has ruined the country. They've practically sanctioned the militia, running around in their black shirts like, like..."

"Like the Organisation Consul in Germany?" Mamie suggested.

"Germany never sanctioned the Organisation Consul like Mussolini has the Camicie Neri," noted Ivo as Ruth refilled his wine glass.

Moritz glared into the distance. "Not as tacitly."

After their guests left and Amalie was in bed, Lala went to her bedroom to undress while Josef returned to his office to work on his month end closing. Tomorrow he'd take Amalie to Prague Castle. Lala would have most of the day to herself to...she'd find something to do. She felt movement within her, the phantom kicks some women experience after birth, and rubbed her belly until the sensation quieted. Her mood dipped as a pang of longing rose in her. Sadness for her son, created in a moment of sadness. She would recover from the tragic loss, as she had in the past. As had Paulina. It took Paulina a while to accept her condition. Heartbreaking as it was, it left her free to develop her business, her artistry. Unlike Lala, who gave up her dream of designing rooms to....

Stop that! she admonished herself. She had to focus on her grieving family – her daughter, her husband and her home. Next week Amalie would turn four.

Paulina had to bide her time due to the War, but she finally opened her shop. Jacub had been nearly five. Like Paulina, Lala would prepare for that day.

CHAPTER FIFTEEN

While accepting her role as solely wife and mother for the present, Lala spent much of her free time sharpening her skills. She repeatedly drew basic shapes – circles, squares, and straight lines – until she perfected them in freehand, and measured every room in the house and every piece of furniture to assess the proportions until she could visually estimate length, width and depth within a few centimeters. She practiced until she could accurately sketch a room in little time. She read all she could and kept a clip file of ideas or potential sources she found in magazines and the newspaper.

Amalie accompanied Lala everywhere she went. During their long walks through the city, Amalie would sing softly to herself or chat about whatever she saw. Some days she would read aloud all the numbers from street addresses or the letters in street signs. Other times Amalie would point out species of birds.

Lala looked for inspiration some days; on others she sought a diversion from her routine. A few times she saw the president's automobile drive by, and one afternoon she thought she spotted Conrad Veigt in a café having a lunch meeting with Klement Chermak, but then realized the man only looked like the German actor.

As Amalie matured she became more confident in her physical abilities, and her push for greater independence seemed reasonable as she gained new skills. Amalie could be trusted to complete certain tasks on her own, such as undressing and grooming, although not always in a timely manner. Lala rarely needed to rush anywhere and so let her daughter proceed at her own pace. Lala's resolve had a calming effect on herself, which transferred to her daughter, and the girl's combative behavior settled. Having turned four, although still demanding and bossy, she no longer challenged Lala constantly.

A few times a month Lala brought Amalie to museums, in part as a way to progress to a musical performance. Like her cousin Jacub, being around adults had advanced her vocabulary, which aided Lala in teaching her to express her frustration and anger with words.

Lala continued to encourage Amalie to sing, and taught her new songs. Josef agreed she'd be old enough to begin piano lessons after her fifth birthday next June. At age six she would begin school, freeing Lala up for several hours during the day.

Ruth had already set the table when mother and daughter returned from window shopping in the Old Town. Lala sat Amalie at the table and had just served her dinner when a knock at the door startled her.

"Who could that be at this hour?" asked Ruth as she went to the door.

A breathless Ludovik entered. "Ma'am, Mr. Smetana just

called. He said you and Miss Amalie should join him for dinner at a fine restaurant to celebrate."

"Celebrate what?"

"He didn't say, but he's with your sister, Ma'am, so it must have something to do with her." He tipped his hat. "I'll wait in the car."

Ruth closed the door. "I'll get the child into her best dress. You go and get ready." As she ushered off Amalie, she muttered, "Wonder what it could be?"

Lala had the same thought as she slid into her gold evening dress, a loose unfitted style that Paulina had experimented with. The design had been inspired by the discovery of Tutankhamen's tomb, though Paulina sought to translate the imagery in a contemporary way. Lala had liked the geometric ornamentation, reminiscent of modern architectural flourishes currently in vogue.

She checked her appearance in her mirror, dressed in one of her sister's designs. Naturally, what else would she wear? She fought off the knot in her gut. The celebration would likely be for some milestone her sister had reached, and why not? Pauline deserved every bit of success she'd earned, and as her partner, so did Josef. Lala fixed her hair, applied lipstick and checked her reflection one more time. Yes, she did love the dress.

The automobile stopped in front of the Hotel Europa.

Lala held Amalie's hand as they walked through the lobby to the restaurant. Lala sensed eyes on her; men's meant one thing, but the women's glances were for the dress she wore.

The maître d' escorted them to a table where Josef, Paulina and Jakub waited. Once they were seated, Josef beckoned the waiter.

"Another glass of champagne, for my wife – no, bring the bottle, and a glass of whatever concoction you served the boy for my daughter."

The waiter bowed and left.

"Is Ivo coming? And Mother?" Lala asked.

Josef kissed Amalie's cheek, which made her giggle. He took Lala's hand and kissed it as well. "Unfortunately, Ivo had to work and couldn't join us for dinner, though he promised to stop by if he finished before too late."

"And Mother said she was too tired to come out tonight." Paulina looked resigned. She, like Lala, had mentioned the signs of aging in their mother.

The waiter returned with a small glass filled with a pale red beverage, which he set before Amalie, a coupe, and a bottle of champagne, which he poured for Lala.

Amalie tasted her drink and declared, "It's fizzy."

Paulina explained, "It's bubbly water added to fruit juice."

Josef lifted his coupe and the women followed suit.

"What are we celebrating?"

Josef glanced at Paulina. "An ending and a new beginning."

"And family," Paulina added.

"And family," repeated Josef, "For that is what we will be from now on."

"I still don't understand," said Lala.

"Josef, tell her," urged Paulina.

"For the last eight years I have served as Paulina's silent partner in her business. Together we have made it a success, and a profitable one at that. So much so that Paulina no longer needs my backing. She's ready to be independent and run the company on her own."

"I can never thank you enough for what you've done to help me create my business into what it is today, or repay you—"

"Nonsense," Josef laughed. "You've repaid me every koruna I've invested, and more."

"I mean beyond money, Josef. You taught me how to run a business, how to set up a factory, balance the manufacturing side and the retail operation." Tears sprang into her eyes. "And Lala, you were there from the very beginning, getting me the backing I needed to launch my business, helping me with my first store, inspiring me as a designer. I will always be grateful for the faith you had in me, for how you helped bring me to this point, but most of all, I'm grateful that you're my family."

Josef clinked his glass to Paulina's and then Lala's. "To us."

Paulina added, "To all of us."

"And to your success." Lala took a sip and set the glass down when she felt tears coming on. Were they of joy or jealousy? She couldn't tell.

Patience did not come easily to her, but she would have to bear the frustration of doing what needed to be done now, without crying, without withering. With or without Josef's backing, financial or otherwise.

Her time would come.

PART THREE

MALA STRANA, PRAGUE
August, 1924

CHAPTER ONE

"What do you think?" Mamie asked as she marched into the Smetanas' apartment and spun, showing off her short bob hairstyle. "It's the latest in Hollywood."

"Very au courant, and flattering," noted Lala as Moritz entered. When the Chytrys arrived, Paulina would approve of Mamie's cut as well as her gown, undoubtedly one of Paulina's designs. Lala started to close the door when she heard footsteps and the plunk of Ivo's cane on the stairs.

Following greetings all around, Josef encouraged Mamie to mix a batch of a cocktail she called "The Bee's Knees."

"It's all the rage in America," she explained. "With Prohibition, all you find is dreadful grain alcohol. The honey and lemon mask the roughness, but when mixed with good whiskey, it's like a spiked lemonade."

Lala tasted it. She added water to dilute the sweetness as Mamie recounted the couple's brush with danger at a speakeasy during their last trip to America, leaving minutes before police raided the secret drinking parlor.

The three couples continued their post-cocktails chat in the dining room as Ruth ladled consommé into bowls. At

Josef's urging, Ivo talked about his continuing research of Italy's Renaissance.

"My book has now been translated into four languages. I'm flattered to say several universities in Europe, including Oxford in England, have added it to their curriculum. I'm working on a new volume, which will explore the connection between art, politics and religion in the post-Renaissance era."

"A thrill a minute," quipped Mamie, which made Ivo chuckle.

"No, I don't suppose Agatha Christie need worry about me. But enough about my boring project. Josef, you haven't said a word about your gallery."

Josef wiped the corners of his mouth with a napkin. "No shop-talk at the table."

Lala thought that a strange thing to say as he'd just asked Ivo about his research, but Josef preferred to let their guests talk about their lives.

As Ruth cleared away the soup bowls, Josef steered the conversation toward the Olympics in Paris. "Did you attend any games while you were there, Moritz?"

Mamie responded, "We went on July seventh to see my distant cousin, Harold Osborn compete. And wouldn't you know, he won the gold medal for high jump. And if that wasn't exciting enough, a few days later he won another gold medal for Decathlon, the only athlete to do ever that. If you ask me he should have won ten medals."

Lala said, "I must confess, I didn't follow the Olympics." She asked Moritz, "How did Germany fare?"

"The organizing committee did not invite Germany to participate this year. Frankly, I can't blame them."

Josef said, "I don't understand, Moritz, why you're still angry with your countrymen, just because of a few bad eggs."

Moritz offered a rueful grin. "You don't hear the way they talk like I do. Pure venom. They hate the nations that defeated them – particularly the Russians, as well as the Communists, the..." He paused. "...Anyone they consider disloyal to Germany."

"And that list is growing," noted Ivo as Ruth set a plate of trout before him.

"A period of adjustment," noted Paulina. "That's what Klement Chermak says, according to his wife."

"I didn't know you two had become close," Lala said, modulating the accusatory tone in her voice.

Before Paulina could respond, Mamie interjected, her eyes flaring. "Lala, you're not the only woman in town who patronizes Paulina's shop."

Lala recoiled in embarrassment.

Paulina deftly separated a trout fillet from the bone. "Willete parrots whatever her husband says."

Lala saw Moritz stiffen at that.

Mamie gave his hand a squeeze as if to say, "stop that," and said, "Her husband must be doing quite well if she can afford your clothing, Paulina."

Josef interjected, "Getting back to Germany, they will have to come to terms with the Armistice conditions eventually."

Ivo nodded. "First they must curb their growing hyperinflation, if they're to recover, which will be difficult until they settle their reparations. Then the different parties need to find common ground." He turned to Moritz. "If they could get past their—"

"They won't," Moritz stated with a head shake.

"Another reason why he wants nothing to do with his family in Bavaria," said Mamie. "Remember us telling you about that firebrand Nazi at the Munich Hofbrauhaus? That's the same man who went on trial for treason after the putsch in Bavaria."

"We followed it in the Tagblatt," said Josef. "The court found him guilty."

"Unfortunately, the trial brought him and his views into prominence," said Lala.

"They sentenced him to five years in prison," said Josef. "He may be a celebrity now, but rest assured, by the time he gets out he'll be forgotten."

"Moritz found out some of his family participated in the putsch," said Mamie. "They bragged about bursting into the beer hall, then someone shouted and fired a gun. At that the security ushered all the politicians speaking that night into a back room. Then the rioters moved their protest to the Feldherrnhalle monument. Can you blame Moritz for not wanting to associate with dangerous people like that?"

"Give them some time," said Josef. "Germany's trying to become a democratic nation, like us, and like us they're experiencing growing pains. Eventually they'll sort out the fractious politics, inflation and territorial disputes. After all, we've had problems with our ruling coalition."

"Czechoslovakia's emergence as a democratic nation is a rare success story in Eastern Europe," Ivo noted. "But Josef, you seem to believe Germany will follow in our political footsteps, while I worry it will be the other way around."

Lala wondered why the usually vivacious Count had become so pessimistic. "Moritz, what did you mean when you said, 'They won't?'"

"They won't curb their inflation as long as they're under the thumb of the Versailles Treaty. It's destroying their economy, their industry, and their spirit. How many have lost their life savings now that the mark is worth nothing? How many are starving because they can't afford to buy food, or freezing because coal is too expensive? It's left Germany ripe for radical parties and mercenary groups, because when you're desperate you'll reach out for whatever salvation you find. You'll believe whoever assures you it's not your fault. You were wronged. Betrayed."

The others at the table exchanged glances, seemingly as curious as Lala to hear more.

Moritz continued, "There's always a grain of truth in what they say, which makes the lies easier to believe, the reason why these groups grow stronger each day. I predict once organizations like them take control, Germany will become increasingly aggressive as they challenge the Armistice bonds that tether them." He reached for his wine glass. "And when I say aggressive, I'm being optimistic. They're ruthless."

"How can you be so certain?" Lala asked. The others leaned in to hear his answer.

"The Weimar Government is weak," Moritz said. "They tolerated extremists to do their dirty work, such as putting down the Socialist rebellion a few years ago, but their tenuous partnership didn't last. Whether the Nazi's putsch in Munich or political assassinations carried out by the Organisation Consul, their goal remains to take over the Government. Having never accepted defeat in the Great War, they're determined to replay it with renewed vigor, and they will, thanks to outside support and funding. They'll gather strength by spreading their lies and goading more disciples into their fold. Then about twenty years after they'll make their move in November, around Armistice Day."

Mamie issued a mirthless chuckle. "Do you have a crystal ball somewhere, Moritz?"

"It's logical."

Josef declined Ruth's offer of more dilled carrots. "I can see the significance of Armistice Day, but what makes you so certain Germany will break its bonds on its twentieth anniversary?"

Moritz replied, "Have you noticed how many children have been born since the Great War ended? And even more in Germany. The men came home defeated, angry and humiliated. They reunited with their wives, married their sweethearts, and started families. Birth rates rose sharply in the post-war period. And all those children will begin reaching their eighteenth birthday in 1937." He gripped his silverware so tightly his knuckles turned white. "Out of the ashes of the Great War, they've created a new generation ready to fight once more."

Mamie dabbed her mouth with her napkin. "Somehow, Moritz, I don't think any nation wants to fight another war, especially one as destructive as the last."

His eyes grew darker, his gaze returned to the table. "They're counting on that, as they count on fanning hatred of any group they perceive as anti-German or inferior to them."

Lala was about to change the subject when Josef did it for her. "Speaking of Germany, I've been planning a business trip to Berlin. Klement's been buying up fabulous pieces of art and antiques for next to nothing." With a lighthearted chuckle he added, "I think he's trying to beat the Americans to the punch."

Moritz laid his silverware on the table. "Josef, I consider you a friend, so let me give you some friendly advice. Exercise caution around Klement Chermak. For all his posturing, he's not someone to be trusted, especially by you and your family."

A startled silence fell around the table. Lala suspected Klement's work with the German government lay behind Moritz's warning. Josef turned ashen at Moritz's pronouncement. He signaled Ruth to refill everyone's wine glasses.

Small talk gradually commenced, but Lala sat quietly, hearing little beyond a slight buzzing in her ears.

She recalled the sensation happened when she read the Chermaks' condolence note: "...*I will think twice before I use that doctor again....*"

And it had happened one other time, though she couldn't recall when, or what had triggered the sensation.

After their guests had left, Lala felt a headache coming on, likely from overindulging in wine. She stretched her fingers in discomfort; drinking too much caused her hands to swell and the tight band of her engagement ring hurt. With a wince she twisted it off and placed it on her dresser as she massaged the swollen finger. After putting away her evening clothes she donned a dressing gown and lounged in bed with the newspaper. She flipped through the pages, scanning each article whether it interested her or not, until an advertisement in the classified section caught her attention. A house offered for sale, at quite a steep price, but something about the address rang familiar. Finally she knew why – the striking Renaissance-style mansion at the tip of Tržiště Street she had first seen on her honeymoon. She'd stood awhile and admired its graceful architecture. It would have made a charming home for her family. For anyone. It still would....

"...*You're my wife and a mother... isn't that enough?*"

No, she thought. It no longer was.

CHAPTER TWO

Lala's headache lingered into the morning. She forewent getting dressed and reclined in the living room wearing her robe and slippers. Her housekeeper cleaned the bedrooms while Lala indulged in a pot of tea and summoned her courage to arrange for a tour of the mansion for sale. If the condition inside matched the exterior, it would make a lovely home and a superb project to renew her creative spirit.

After viewing the property she would fetch Amalie from her sleepover at Bubbie's, granting time to calculate how best to broach the purchase with Josef when he eventually got home. He'd been working long hours recently, his way of grieving.

Ruth entered the room with her cleaning supplies in hand. "It's getting hot outside. I've taken the liberty of closing the windows in the bedrooms. Shall I shut these as well?"

"Yes, please do." Lala stood. "I should get dressed. I'll leave you to your work."

She headed to her bedroom, anticipating the day ahead. Beads of sweat dimpled her hairline. A tepid water bath would feel soothing.

***

Lala buttoned a lightweight housedress over her camisole and knickers. She reached down for her shoes and observed five naked fingers on her right hand. She'd taken off her engagement ring last night. Lala went to fetch it from her dresser.

It wasn't there.

Dread raced through her as she searched the dresser top, the floor, and then each of the drawers. She repeated her search, yanking garments from neatly folded stacks and flinging them aside, to no avail. A murmur from the past, hunting for her missing bundle of possessions in the Zedek house, began to haunt her; the dread intensified as her spirits sank.

"Ruth, please come here," she called out.

Ruth rushed into the room, worry etched into her face. "Missus, is something amiss?"

"I can't find my gold ring with the pearl and diamonds. I left it on the dresser last night and now it's not here."

"I didn't see it when I cleaned the room, Missus, but I hurried through." Her look of concern deepened. "It could have fallen on the floor." She got down on her hands and knees and searched the room, including under the bed.

"Perhaps it got caught in your cleaning rags," Lala suggested. Ruth hurried out to fetch her basket of supplies, but it wasn't there.

Lala paced to quell the panic. That ring had sentimental value beyond its price. She had to find it.

"We'll search the trash," Lala said, worry mounting. "Where did you put it?"

Ruth grimaced. "I've already taken it outside, since

today..."

"...Is when the trash is picked up."

The women rushed down the stairs and raced out of the building. The trash bin sat beside the curb. Ruth lifted the cover. Empty; the trash had already been carted away.

Lala fought back tears, as did Ruth.

"Oh, Missus let's look upstairs again. I don't think the ring got tossed into the trash."

"We'll never know, will we?"

Ruth winced. Lala placed her hand on Ruth's shoulder. "Don't blame yourself."

Lala suddenly felt spent. Unable to summon the strength to walk up the stairs to her apartment, she entered Josef's shop. A tinkling bell summoned Josef from the back of the store.

"Why aren't you dressed—Lala, what's wrong?"

She burst into tears and buried her face in his chest. She told him what had happened, her voice quivering as she sobbed.

Josef held her tightly, comforting her in his embrace as he stroked her hair. "Don't cry, love. We'll get it back and if not, I'll buy you another ring, the finest, most beautiful ring you can imagine."

"No, Josef, don't. It was the ring your father gave your mother, that Armin gave me. It became a symbol of our love. Nothing can replace it."

He choked back a sob when he said, "Please, let me try."

CHAPTER THREE

Josef volunteered to bring Amalie home from her overnight stay. Either Sarah or Josef must have cautioned the child, for when she arrived home, Lala noted she behaved more cooperatively, hardly fussing or arguing.

Ruth and Lala kept searching, for naught. Lala and Josef had to convince Ruth not to blame herself. Without knowing what happened, blame couldn't be assigned. Nevertheless the loss upset the housekeeper, who set about her work without her cheery demeanor.

The next day Lala remained in bed until noon, lacking the fortitude to get up and dress beyond her robe. Amalie brought a book into the bedroom and curled up with Mama. Lala read it aloud and afterward the child kissed her and left her in peace. Josef remained positive, often saying the ring would surely turn up, and likely in the oddest place.

After a week had passed Lala knew the ring would never be found, no matter what Josef said. It took Josef a few days longer to agree. The finality crushed her; she languished in bed, shutting out the world as she had when she learned of the villagers' curse. Could the loss of her ring...? No, she'd promised herself not to let that poison her thoughts. No one could put a curse on another person; their words came from anger at their own loss and pain, but their anger held no magical power.

And yet, every time she sought to launch her design career, something tragic had happened. Her sister's two miscarriages. Her son's death. And now the most precious family heirloom gone. Was it truly coincidence?

That night the heat kept Lala awake for hours. The next morning she slept until the parlor clock chimed ten times. As she lay in bed, she heard footsteps approach.

Josef pushed open the door, carrying a bed tray with a cup of tea, a bread basket, a plate of cheese and a jar of her mother's cherry jam. Surprised to see him home on a Monday morning, Lala sat up. "Josef, why aren't you making your appointed rounds at the dealers?"

"You have me worried. Please eat something, love." He placed the tray at the foot of the bed. "Would you like to sit at the table or stay where you are?"

She scooted back against her pillows and he placed the tray over her hips. "How thoughtful," she said, unfolding her napkin. "This is what I ate for breakfast the first morning I stayed with my aunt and uncle—"

"No sad talk, love. Forget about the past. Let's focus on the future now."

She nodded. Josef's solicitousness touched her. She didn't feel hungry, but spread jam on a slice of bread and took one bite to please him after making such a grand effort. "Are you going to watch me eat?"

"I'll do whatever you want. I can't bear to see you like this."

She reached over and stroked his cheek. "Who could understand how much that ring meant to me better than you?"

Josef stiffened and looked ready to cry. That ring meant a great deal to him as well, yet he refused to blame her for her carelessness. Only she did that.

The sound of a truck parking in the street distracted them. Josef turned toward the window. "I must return to the shop for now, but I'll be back soon." He took her hand and kissed it. "I love you more than you can ever imagine."

He opened the bedroom door as Ruth approached.

"Mr. Smetana, Mr. Cerveny called to—"

"I know what it's about. Thank you, Ruth." To Lala he said, "I'll be home early for dinner. We'll put Amalie to bed and enjoy a quiet supper, just the two of us."

"That sounds lovely," she said.

She sipped her tea and waited until Josef left the apartment to push away the tray of food. "Ruth, please take this back to the kitchen," she said as she got up.

Ruth entered the room, worry creasing her face. "Won't you eat something, Missus?"

Lala donned her robe. "Perhaps later."

Ruth took the tray from the room.

Lala sensed someone near; Amalie stood in the doorway.

"Come in, love."

Amalie took tentative steps into the bedroom, a forlorn look on her face. "Papa said you lost your ring."

"Yes, love, I did." Lala sat in the velvet chair at her dressing table and brushed her hair into place.

"Is that why you're sad now?"

Lala twisted her brown locks into a bun and pinned it up. "Yes, I am very sad about it now, but I promise I won't always be sad."

Amalie moved closer to Lala. Her finger stroked the plush fabric of the chair. Lala picked the girl up and placed her on her lap. She planted a kiss on the top of Amalie's head and cuddled her, the image reflecting in the dressing table mirror – mother and daughter.

"Mama, who is Armin?"

Josef must have told the child how her mother first received the ring. "Many years ago, long before you were born, Papa had a son and his name was Armin. He grew up to be an artist, the one who painted the picture of me when I was a young girl."

"Is he dead?"

"Yes. He died during the Great War."

"I heard Uncle Ivo talking about him. He said Armin was his friend."

"They were good friends. I was his friend, too. Papa and I loved him very much. That's why we named you after him."

"Uncle Ivo said a bad man hurt Armin and that's why he died."

"Unfortunately, bad people do bad things, love."

"Why did he want to hurt Armin?"

"He didn't, he thought Armin was someone else."

"A bad person?"

"No, just another man who looked like Armin."

"What happened to the bad man?"

"The police locked him up in a place far away, where he can't hurt anyone again."

Amalie nestled into her mother. "If you find the ring, will it bring Armin back?"

"Unfortunately, no. But he lives on in Papa's heart, and in mine."

That evening, after Josef put Amalie to bed, he and Lala sat down to a light supper in the dining room. Throughout he would glance at her and then direct his gaze elsewhere. Josef seemed full of anticipation. Midway through the meal she caught him suppressing a grin. She knew that look; he meant to surprise her.

"Josef, you look like you swallowed a canary."

"Do I?" His face went blank.

Ruth came in to clear the dinner dishes. Josef raised his finger to have her stop.

"Ruth, would you stay a while longer tonight? I want to take my wife somewhere this evening. We should be back in half an hour."

Ruth brightened. "Of course, Mr. Smetana." She smiled at Lala.

"Where are we going?"

Josef stood. "You'll know when we get there." He helped Lala from the table.

Where could he be taking me, she wondered as he escorted her downstairs to the street, where Ludovik was waiting by the automobile. Whatever the surprise was—*oh! Could it be?*

The beautiful house on Tržiště Street. She'd forgotten about it in the aftermath of losing her ring. Had he discovered it was up for sale and remembered how much she'd admired the mansion? He'd surprised her before, by purchasing their current house. A thrill coursed through her at the possibility, though she reminded herself that the surprise might be very different. Still, as they drove along

Tržiště Street her heart beat a little faster.

The car passed the mansion and kept going.

Ludovik stopped the automobile in front of an antiques store. Josef helped Lala from the vehicle and led her into the shop. She glanced around at the display of silver pieces on shelves and cabinets to the left, and cases of antique jewelry along the right side.

The proprietor greeted them by name. "I have your piece ready, Mr. Smetana."

Lala could see the anticipation on Josef's face. He'd bought her something, ostensibly to cheer her up. Perhaps he found another ring similar to the one she lost. If so, she would thank him for the gesture. In time the new piece might hold as much meaning for her as the first.

The dealer emerged from the back with a small leather box and handed it to Josef.

"Love, I know how much my mother's ring meant to you, but as you recall Armin gave it to you. I decided to buy you a new ring, not to replace what is gone, but to present you with something from me to show you how much you mean to me. How fortunate I am to have won your love. How much I love you."

She felt herself welling up.

Josef held the box before her, and opened it.

Inside sat an antique gold navette ring. The diamond-shaped base looked to be almost three centimeters from top to bottom point, fitted with at least two dozen diamonds, with a large round ruby popping from a braided gold encasement in the center. Never in her life could she have imagined Josef would give her a ring so large. So extravagant. So gaudy.

The dealer asked her, "Would you like to try it on?"

Josef removed the navette from its box and slipped it on her right ring finger. It felt heavy; the bottom point nearly grazed her knuckle.

Flabbergasted, Lala turned to Josef with a thousand questions in her eyes.

"I believe you've stunned Mrs. Smetana," the dealer said, looking almost smug. "You were right when you said, 'That ring will be perfect for my wife.'"

Lala stopped herself from saying what crossed her mind.

Which wife?

CHAPTER FOUR

Ruth offered to mind Amalie while Lala ran her errands. Lala went downstairs to meet the automobile. She peered into the shop and noticed many bare spots; Josef had sold quite a bit of merchandise recently.

On her way to Paulina's, Lala asked Ludovik to drive past the house on Tržiště Street. The For Sale sign remained in the window, with instructions to inquire within.

"Would you please stop here?" she asked.

As she stepped out of the vehicle, a man's hand poked through the damask draperies behind the window. The fabric shimmied as his fingers latched onto the sign and pulled it away. She stood there, watching in dismay, until the draperies stopped moving.

Ludovik parked the automobile in front of Paulina's shop. As she stepped out Lala noticed the new placard suspended from the entrance advertising the shop, a literal sign of Paulina's success. Two mannequins in the front window displayed a day and evening sample of her couture work. Lala felt pleased the semi-sheer draperies she'd selected remained, which allowed in daylight while providing privacy for the clientele.

A posh millenary shop had relocated to the street; several high end boutiques and restaurants were under construction or had opened nearby, replacing many of the more pedestrian businesses on the block. The workman's bar across the street, where struggling artists like Vilem Vesely lingered over their beer steins, was now an elegant café. Soigné women sat at tables draped in linen to drink tea and nibble on flat wedges of streusel-topped frgále or cream-filled rolls of puff pastry called kremole. Paulina's success gentrified the area into a tony shopping and dining destination.

"Good morning Mrs. Smetana." Miss Horáčková's greeting rang out as she opened the door. "Madame is fitting a customer. I will inform her that you're here."

Inside, some of Paulina's custom designs adorned dressmaker molds. With few garment racks remaining, the shop looked streamlined, the emphasis on viewing rather than browsing.

Miss Horáčková returned. "Madam Paulina and the Countess asked that you join them. May I bring you coffee?"

"Yes, thank you." Lala stopped briefly to admire a chic black dinner dress on display near the door to Paulina's quarters. At another time she might have snapped it up, but she'd grown averse to wearing black, of what it had come to represent.

Paulina pinned adjustments to Mamie's gown while Lala sipped her coffee. She half-listened to the women's conversation, which focused on Mamie's travel and local gossip. When Lala set her cup on the table, Mamie's eyes flared as she asked, "What's that on your finger?"

Lala extended her right hand. "A gift from Josef."

Paulina eyes widened. "Oh my, you weren't exaggerating when you described it. That's, um, quite a ring."

"I'm surprised you can lift your delicate hand with that rock weighing it down." Mamie wiggled her fingers. "Even sausages like mine would have trouble wearing that."

"He thought this would make a suitable replacement for the ring I lost."

Mamie snickered. "Nonsense. What did he do? It must have been something bad."

"I don't understand."

"Come now, Lala. A man wouldn't buy that ring unless he did something he's sorry for."

Surprised at that, she blurted, "He's sorry that I lost my ring."

"Sure, you can believe that if you want, but—"

Paulina interrupted, "Shall we change the subject? Lala's had enough sorrow of late."

Lala flinched. "Do you believe Josef did something he regrets as well?"

Paulina set down her pin cushion. "That ring doesn't suit you and he would know that, but I won't speculate as to why Josef bought such a flamboyant piece for you."

Mamie scowled. "Sorry, girls, but he's a man and men all think the same way."

Paulina quickly interjected, "That's not fair, Mamie. Josef could have chosen it to symbolize his success rather than Lala's taste. I presume his business is doing well...." Her voice trailed off as she returned to pinning Mamie's gown and the room fell silent.

The choice had bothered Lala, too, but she attributed it to

a lapse of judgement. It had taken her months to emerge from her shell of grief over the loss of their son, leaving her vulnerable and unable to cope with another loss. Josef had been grieving as well, burying himself in work, gone for hours late into the night....

She'd kept her first thought, that it would more befit Romy, to herself. It never occurred to her that the ring could be anything other than his attempt to placate her, but the more she thought about it, the more Mamie's comment sounded plausible.

The situation had been puzzling, and a piece of that puzzle was missing. She said her goodbyes and left.

Ludovik held the automobile door open for her as she got into the vehicle. "Where to, Mrs. Smetana?"

She exhaled audibly. "Take me back to Tržiště Street."

The property manager assured her the building had been sold. Lala insisted he keep her calling card in the event the sale fell through. Outside she crossed the street to get a better view of the building. Why did it hold her attraction, more than other properties? Although quite beautiful it wasn't as if that was unique in Prague. But something about it had captivated her since the first time she saw it while on her honeymoon, the same day Cerveny presented the will in which Lala inherited Romy's fortune. Josef had even chuckled about it...she recalled his words...

"You may be wealthier than I am now."

She'd been thinking about Romy ever since Josef had given her the navette ring...

"Nonsense. What did he do?"

After the reading of Romy's will she'd wondered why

Josef remained in his cheap apartment when he could have lived elsewhere. She found out why — Xenie, his mistress during the dark days of his grief over Armin's death and Romy's betrayal. She believed him when he'd sworn that relationship ended the day she showed up at his doorstep and he'd given her no reason to doubt his faithfulness.

"Sure, you can believe that if you want, but—"

Did she truly want to know? And what would she do if Mamie was right?

Lala dearly loved Josef, but she'd never seriously considered what she'd do if he'd been unfaithful. Wives stayed in marriages for one of two reasons — they wanted to, or they had to.

She returned to the automobile.

"Shall I take you home now, Mrs. Smetana?"

"No, Ludovik, I want to go to Letenská Street first."

She entered an arcaded building and climbed two flights of stairs to the office she sought. Inside the young man she'd encountered on her honeymoon looked up from his paperwork, his face partially obscured by a prosthetic mask of tin. He greeted her by name.

She affected a cordial smile to mask the trembling inside her. "Good afternoon, Tomas. I would like to see Mr. Cerveny."

CHAPTER FIVE

Lala reviewed the paperwork from Cerveny in the dining room. It took a few read-throughs to comprehend it all, but the money in her name was adequate for her family to live comfortably into old age. The sense of freedom, of exhilaration that gave her nearly took her breath away. She did not have to depend on anyone financially. What a rare privilege.

She heard the front door open; Josef had come home earlier than she expected. She refolded the paperwork into its envelope, which she snuck inside the chest that held their best silverware, and listened.

His footsteps trailed off as he went into the living room, then the clink of glass; he'd poured himself a drink. She heard him leave the apartment and followed behind as he went downstairs to his office and closed the door.

She waited a moment before knocking. She heard papers rustling and a drawer closing before he said, "Come in."

She affected a smile. "You're home early."

"Just briefly to find some paperwork." He stood and kissed her cheek. "I will be home very late. Don't wait up for me."

His smile looked as disingenuous as hers felt.

Lala saw to Amalie's dinner, read her a story and put her to bed before sitting down in the dining room for her own meal. She retrieved the paperwork from the silverware chest and looked at the numbers again. All that money – what should she do with it? What could she do with it?

What do I want to do with it?

Days ago, the answer would have been to purchase the house on Tržiště Street outright if it were in good condition. She'd furnish it to create a beautiful home, either for her family if Josef agreed, or if not, then as a demonstration of her skill at designing. As with the showrooms she once sought to design, clients would see her ideas brought to fruition. Having been locked out of Josef's business for several years, she had only her clip file as reference for the cost of furnishings, but if she studied Josef's invoices to get a sense of pricing—

The ring of their telephone startled Lala.

"Mrs. Smetana?"

She tried to place the man's voice.

"I understand you enquired about the property at Tržiště Street."

Her heart quickened. Was the house available? "Yes, and I am still very interested in purchasing it if the last offer fell through."

She heard a chuckle on the other end of the line. "It did not, Mrs. Smetana. I just bought the building."

"And you're calling to inform me the property is off the market. Thank you," she said, though she couldn't keep the disappointment out of her voice.

"That is not why I am calling. I wondered if you would consider submitting a proposal to convert the mansion into the finest luxury inn to be found in Europe, like you did at the Hotel Excelsior. If I like your concept I would provide you with a substantial budget."

"To whom am I speaking?"

She heard him chuckle again. "Why Mrs. Smetana, I'm surprised you don't remember me. I'm the current owner of the Excelsior Inn, Otokar Zahradnik."

Lala brought Amalie to her mother's. Sarah offered to watch her granddaughter while Lala met a "friend" for lunch.

"Good," said Sarah. "You ought to get away and socialize with other mothers, share your experiences."

Lala kissed her mother goodbye. "I'll return before two."

Her mother understood; Lala wanted to avoid seeing the women in the park.

Lala arrived at the mansion ten minutes early, remembering Zahradnik's fondness for punctuality. At precisely noon a new Rolls Royce stopped in front of the building. Lala couldn't resist smiling when Smolak stepped from the driver's side to assist Zahradnik out of the automobile. The ostentatious uniform looked ridiculous on the tall stocky man, but she respected Zahradnik, who'd kept his promise to retain Josef's household staff; he must be a reasonable employer for Smolak to have stayed on. A good sign.

Zahradnik had grown stouter; as he waddled over to her he employed his ivory adorned cane. She accepted his outstretched hand.

"Mrs. Smetana, you haven't aged a day, unlike me. Shall we take a look at the building?"

The property manager rushed out to greet Zahradnik and escort them inside. Even stripped of furniture, the rooms were as beautiful as Lala expected, with high ceilings, arched windows and marble columns adding support to the upper level. The ground floor interior showed signs of wear but not damage. The parquet floors needed refinishing, wall and ceiling molding were cracked in places. Electric chandeliers hung in the living room, dining room, and what must have been the master bedroom, and one antique chandelier dangled from a large room toward the back. Droplets of wax clung to several crystals.

They climbed the stairs to inspect the rooms on the upper level. Lala found four large bedrooms, a large linen closet, a toilette, and one bath. Plumbing had been installed some time ago, but it worked. Lala pointed out some water damage near the windows on the upper floor to Zahradnik.

"I noticed that as well," he said. "I had the roof inspected and it does not leak, nor do the windows. This was caused by a window left open during a rainstorm."

Once they'd finished inspecting the interior, she retraced her steps, peering into each room, imagining how the space would look with furniture suited for guests. Zahradnik remained silent. He followed behind as she progressed through each room, taking mental notes.

"What do you think about my offer, Mrs. Smetana?"

"I'm interested, Mr. Zahradnik. My only concern would be the size of the property. You couldn't host many guests here."

"One of the reasons why it shall be so exclusive."

"How do you intend to make it profitable?"

"By charging a great deal to stay. That's where you come in. Anyone can fill rooms with expensive furniture and fixtures in precious metals. Staff can be trained to cater to a guest's every whim. Yet I've never been to a luxury hotel that was as comfortable and relaxing as the Excelsior. You have a knack, Mrs. Smetana, to provide more than luxury. You can create an oasis, where people will want to be, and will pay good money to do so.

"I made an offer to the owner of the building contiguous with this one. If he accepts, we could break through the dividing wall and conjoin the two properties, expanding the inn by seventy percent. I estimate that will take a year if all goes well, which it never does. Someone familiar with reconstructing properties would be needed to consult with us—"

"I oversaw a complete renovation of the building my family now lives in, so I'm familiar with the process."

"How fortuitous." He seemed pleased. "Now that you've seen the building, what do you think?"

"About the offer?"

"About what can be done? How do you see this after its conversion?"

She knew exactly what he was asking and had her answer prepared. "A jewel box, Mr. Zahradnik, holding precious things, each superb in its own right. Nothing should dominate or outshine the others. It all must fit together to create one beautiful vision."

He mused over that. "And how do you intend to accomplish that?"

"You haven't offered me a position yet, nor have I agreed to help you beyond this meeting."

"I admire your shrewdness. Very well. If you can come up with a new concept as appealing and profitable as you did for the Excelsior, the job is yours, if you choose to take charge of the operation." He handed her a business card with a figure written on the back. A substantial figure. "That is my budget for the project. It will double if my offer to purchase the building next door is accepted. And if you can get the work done to my satisfaction on or below budget..."

She waited for him to finish his thought.

He pounded his cane on the floor for emphasis. "...I'll pay you ten percent of the amount."

Lala hoped he didn't hear her gasp.

CHAPTER SIX

With an hour remaining before she had to pick up Amalie, Lala tucked the blueprints for the building under her arm and crossed over to Old Town to search for inspiration by window-shopping the galleries and antiques stores dotting the streets between Old Town Square and Wenceslas Square. She stopped before an art gallery near the bridge. A notice in the window, featuring Zoe Vesely's work, advertised a photography exhibit in early October. *How wonderful for her.* Despite their falling out, Lala respected Zoe's art.

A rear door inside the gallery opened and out stepped Zoe, looking gaunt, with a man Lala presumed owned the business. Following closely behind them was a young woman holding the hand of Charis. Zoe and Vilem had managed to hire a nanny for their daughter, a positive compromise as well as a sign of their growing success. Unlike her mother, the once scrawny child had filled out and appeared well cared for. Zoe spoke briefly to the nanny, then she and the man disappeared through the rear door as the nanny escorted Charis from the shop.

Lala greeted them as they approached. "Hello Charis, do you remember me?"

The child looked up at Lala and shook her head.

"No, I suppose you were too young." Lala extended her hand to the nanny. "I'm Mrs. Smetana. Charis used to come by with her mother to play with my daughter Amalie."

The nanny shook Lala's hand. "Oh, yes. Vilem has mentioned you and your husband many times. We're so grateful for all you've done to further his career."

She's being rather familiar. Lala thought it inappropriate for the nanny to call her employer by his given name, much less speak about him in such a personal manner, but kept it to herself. "Amalie's visiting her grandmother," she said. "I'm on my way to fetch her. If you have time, would you like to join me so the girls can be reacquainted?"

"What a lovely idea. I wish we could—oh, forgive me, I'm Mrs. Vesely."

A family member. That would explain the familiarity. "How are you related to Vilem?"

The woman lifted Charis in her arms. "I'm his wife."

Vilem had obtained a divorce six months earlier at Zoe's insistence when her career began to flourish, the new Mrs. Vesely explained. Frantiska had met Vilem at a rally and fell in love with both him and Charis.

She apologized, "This all happened suddenly. We weren't sure how to announce this outside of our circle. And I wish we could join you today. It would be lovely for us to get acquainted, but I must keep a strict schedule with Charis. Unfortunately, her unruly life has led to some behaviors which I'm working to correct."

Lala, satisfied that the child finally had the nurturing she needed, wished them well. After making a vague promise to see each other soon, they parted ways. She crossed the Charles Bridge and went to pick up Amalie. Invigorated by her new assignment, Lala couldn't wait to review the building's blueprints, start sketching the rooms and planning layouts. Her mind reeled with all she would have to do, including making a workspace for herself, one that Josef would not recognize as such. She did not want to tell him of her assignment just yet. She would also need to ask her mother for more child-care help. How to manage everything without Josef finding out? That would be the real challenge.

She reached her mother's street shortly before two and found Amalie tossing bread to the ducks along the river bank while Sarah watched from the park bench.

"Oy, you're finally back!" Sarah exclaimed as she beckoned Lala over. "I need to rest here a few minutes."

Lala laid her palm over her mother's forehead. "Are you unwell?"

"No, just tired. Now I know why God made parents young."

Lala bent to kiss her mother's cheek. When had she become old? Little changes, like her hair turning white and her face wrinkling, happened gradually. However, Lala hadn't noticed, or didn't want to notice, other signs of aging, nor had she foreseen a problem with her mother providing child care.

Sarah pressed her hands against the bench slats to push herself up. "I should start dinner before I'm too tired to cook."

"Would you like me to come upstairs and help you?"

Sarah waved her off. "No, dear. You take Amalie home and have dinner with your husband. I'll manage just fine, like I always do." Sarah reached up to pat Lala's cheek.

"Amalie, come say goodbye to Bubbie."

Amalie scurried over and kissed her grandmother.

Lala took Amalie's hand. Despite the warmth of the mid afternoon sun, she detected a slight chill in the air, which always seemed to begin on September first. Lala buttoned up her daughter's coat as she watched her mother slowly cross the street. The stoop in her posture, the hesitance in her step, the stiffness in her swelling joints unsettled Lala. She couldn't imagine losing her mother, not any time soon.

Asking Sarah to watch Amalie more than once a week would impose upon her. As Lala walked with her daughter along Janáckovo, the enormity of the project she sought became clear as she mentally ran through all the aspects. She now had yet another consideration before taking on Zahradnik's project. She would not be able to do this on her own.

Amalie had been singing softly to herself, or perhaps to the birds perched in the trees.

"What's that you're singing, love?"

"A song about a farmer. Bubbie taught it to me. She likes when I sing."

"I do, too...Amalie, would you still like to learn how to play the piano?"

"Could I, Mama?" She sounded quite excited.

"Let's find out."

Lala headed back to Janáckovo. Setting up Amalie's piano lessons with the teacher in her mother's building would take care of one day a week as well as relieve her mother. Sarah could spend time with her granddaughter before and after lessons, which would free her of the burden of watching Amalie all day. Another possibility occurred to her.

Ahead she saw Dagmar and Ignacie holding court on their bench. Terezka sat nearby, knitting, with Bente beside her, but not her son, who would be two now. Each acknowledged Lala as she approached. Only Bente stood and smiled.

"Well, well. I'm surprised to see you, Lala," Dagmar said dryly.

"No more surprised than I am to be here, but I'd like to arrange for my daughter to take piano lessons. I remember you mentioned a good teacher." She emphasized the word "good".

Dagmar said, "That would be Mrs. Suková, the war widow. Your mother knows her."

"Thank you."

Bente reached out to Lala. "We heard about your son...how heartbreaking. I'm so sorry for your loss."

"You're very kind." Lala cleared her throat to keep from choking up. "And what about you? Did you decide to have another child, like your husband wanted?"

A tiny smile escaped from Bente as she shook her head. She placed her palm across her chest and mouthed, "I'm wearing it."

Now Lala smiled. "Bente, if you have a moment, I'd like to talk to you privately about an idea I had, which may interest you."

"I ought to pick up my son from my neighbor down the street. If you walk with me, we can talk along the way."

Lala waited as Bente folded her blanket. Two hands shorter than Lala, Bente had a delicate figure that belied her physical strength. She registered every emotion with a subtle gesture, a raised brow or narrowing of her eyes, which changed from blue to gray. She bid good day to the women and Lala did the same.

Lala explained the opportunity offered to her. "It's something I would dearly love to pursue, but I'll need help managing the project, including child care. Since you told me how much you enjoyed working, particularly with fabrics, I thought of you."

"I must admit it sounds tempting. What sort of schedule were you thinking of, since I would not want my husband to find out. I doubt he'd approve."

"We share that in common. For now, I would only need you a few hours a week, midday, while our husbands are at work. After the construction phase begins, and if we're both satisfied with the arrangement, we could increase it to twenty hours a week."

She discussed salary and duties in the initial stage of the project. "This will be a high-end venture, with a clientele similar to the customers you catered to at Bonne Fleur."

They stopped in front of a building at the end of the street.

"Little Petr is upstairs."

"Why don't you take a day or two to think about my offer," Lala said.

"Actually, I've made up my mind." She offered her hand. "When do we start?"

CHAPTER SEVEN

Lala paced the parlor. *Where could I work privately from Josef?* An area large enough to spread out. Blueprints, full-size renderings, fabric swatches – *would Paulina...?*

No, she didn't want to put her sister into the middle of this. Josef was family as well as Paulina's former business partner. And Paulina was allergic to dishonesty. It had to be somewhere else.

The ground floor contained Josef's antique shop and gallery. The first floor held his office and storeroom – *could I...? No, he'd find it there.* Could she construct a place? Tell Josef she wanted to redo the apartment? Ruefully she acknowledged she'd converted every square meter of the building into usable space for Josef's business and their living quarters without planning a work space for herself...

Except....

Lala called out, "Ruth, would you listen for Amalie while I run an errand?"

"Where is she, Missus?"

"Napping in her bedroom. I'll be quick as wings."

313

Lala fetched the master set of house keys before leaving the apartment. She climbed to the top landing to the place Lala sought. She tried a few keys until she found the one that unlocked that door.

She brushed away cobwebs as she stepped into the attic. Fortuitously, she'd added electricity and replaced the dormer window during the remodel. The room would be adequate for setting up a worktable, a small easel, and a chest to hold supplies. Natural light from the window and a skylight kept the space from feeling oppressive.

This will do.

After putting Amalie to bed, Lala dined alone, as she had many nights lately. Josef professed to have evening appointments to seek merchandise in sellers' homes. Whatever kept him out late gave her time to work on her project in secrecy. She set up a rudimentary studio in the attic, where she kept the future hotel's blueprints. Each day she copied the dimensions of a room in her sketchpad and made preliminary drawings in preparation for her next meeting with Zahradnik at the end of October.

Lala had told Josef she would occasionally invite a friend with a young child over to visit, which Josef thought would keep both mother and daughter amused. Lala merely smiled and let him assume that. Lala, who hadn't seen Bente's son Petr since he was an infant, wasn't sure how Amalie would get along with a boy three years her junior. Any discord could derail her plans. She would see to it that they got along. She had to, or else her plan would fail. Lala would not entertain the thought of failure. She couldn't.

In the lamplight of the parlor, Lala studied her latest sketch, of the large foyer that would become the hotel's lobby. She compared it to the notes she took while touring the building, adding details like the flooring and light fixtures to the sketch. She set her pencil down to contemplate a nook on the left side of the space, how best to utilize it.

She closed her sketchbook at the sound of the front door opening and Josef dropping his keys on the console. She glanced at the mantle clock – half past eight.

"I'm in the parlor," she called out softly to avoid waking Amalie.

Josef entered looking tired, or perhaps crestfallen if unsuccessful in finding anything worth purchasing. He kissed her forehead and sat down beside her.

"Sketching, I see." He reached across for the pad, but she pulled it aside. "You don't want me to see them?"

"Not until they're finished."

"I'm glad you found a pastime that you enjoy."

Pretending to ignore him, she suppressed a smile.

He noticed.

"I didn't expect you home this early," she said, turning to face him.

His fingers glanced across the side of her face. "I missed you."

Her smile escaped. "Then I'm even more delighted you're home."

He leaned over and kissed her cheek before moving his lips along the side of her neck. His hands slid down her back as he coaxed her closer.

Her lips parted, her breath became rushed as his hands continued their exploration of her body. She pushed her sketchpad aside as his lips sought hers.

***

Bente arrived on time the next morning.

"What a lovely home you have Lala, but I expected it to be so," said Bente as she entered the apartment, Petr in her arms. The toddler hid his face in his mother's neck, so all Lala could see was his platinum hair.

"I'm afraid he's rather shy now. I do hope he'll outgrow it."

"He's darling, Bente. Please don't give it a thought."

"Who's darling, Mama?" Amalie approached.

"Love, do you remember Mrs. Cerna, the lady who lives near Bubbie?"

Amalie studied Bente's face, then shook her head.

"But I remember you, Amalie. My, you're such a big girl now."

Amalie smiled and curtsied.

"Petr, say hello." Bente urged, but the toddler stayed nestled against her.

"Hello Petr, I'm Amalie. Would you like to play with me?"

At the sound of her voice, he turned. When he saw Amalie, he squirmed until his mother put him down. Amalie reached out her hand and he grabbed it.

"Mama, may Petr and I play in my room?"

"Yes, love, but leave the door open. Mrs. Cerna and I will be in the parlor."

"Come on, Petr."

Still clutching Amalie's hand, the boy followed her down the hall without a glance back at his mother.

Bente looked bemused. "Your daughter seems to have charmed my son."

"She has that effect on men – her father, her cousin, her uncle...." Anything in pants, even short ones.

"I don't envy you that when she gets older," Bente commiserated both in tone and expression. Her open face spoke volumes. Lala had always been able to tell during their gatherings when Bente held her tongue. The most subtle movements of her eyes or mouth conveyed more than words, and while she spoke cautiously when they socialized with the women, Lala had never known her to lie.

"It solves the problem of them playing together. Let me get my sketches."

They settled in the parlor, where the children's patter could be heard. Lala opened her sketchpad and showed the drawings she'd made to Bente. "These should give you a sense of what the project will involve. We've already discussed some aspects. You might find other areas you'd like to work on once you've reviewed the sketches. Then we'll create your position based not just on what I'll require, but your interests and skills."

"That's grand, Lala. No one's ever asked me what I wanted to do." Bente's finger traced along the drawing, pausing at the nook that had stymied Lala. "What is this supposed to be?"

"I haven't decided yet. It could be a shop, or a niche for more private conversation."

"Private," Bente repeated. "We enclosed a niche in our apartment to make a room for Petr. Could this space be enclosed to create a separate room for private meetings?"

"That's a brilliant suggestion. I'll let you look over the rest of the sketches while I check on the children. Then shall I make us some coffee?"

"Thank you, yes."

Bente was studying a sketch of the lobby when Lala returned with the coffee service. She poured a cup for Bente and passed it to her. "Your boy looks so much like you."

Bente added cream into her cup and stirred. "He has my hair and eyes, but his father's nose and build."

"What does your husband do for a living?" Lala asked as she poured a cup for herself.

"Petr's a painter."

Surprised, Lala exclaimed, "How marvelous, how did I not know that? Oils? Watercolors?"

Bente giggled. "Houses. He also hangs wallpaper."

"Oh, I really must expand my horizons. How silly of me to assume—"

"It's not silly. I like that you think that way. It's one of the reasons why I chose to work for you."

Any doubts Lala might have held about hiring Bente eased with that.

"Your husband would make a good resource for tradesmen, or he might want to bid on the project, that is, if you don't object to him finding out about your involvement."

"He may be old-fashioned, but by the time we reach the point where we'd have to hire finishing workers like Petr I will tell him what I'm doing." Bente held up the sketch of the lobby. "Did you take measurements of all the rooms?" Bente asked.

"No, I worked directly from the blueprints."

"Could I see them?"

"They're in the attic, where I've set up a small private workspace. I'd take you there but I don't want to leave the children alone."

"What if I came back tomorrow?"

"My housekeeper will be here. She won't mind watching

the children for a few minutes while we review the plans upstairs."

Bente finished her coffee. "Then until tomorrow...boss."

They both laughed at that, but Lala liked the sound of it. Very much.

CHAPTER EIGHT

The sound of the front door closing and approaching footsteps woke Lala. She glanced at the bedroom clock on the mantlepiece; half past eleven. The temptation to ask him why he was coming home so late passed quickly. She rolled over and pretended to be asleep.

He entered the room and Lala could hear him undressing. He made no sound other than a stifled yawn. Then he crawled into bed and fell asleep almost immediately. She detected no alcohol on his breath, no unfitting odors on him. Whatever kept him out so late made him so exhausted he overslept the next morning.

Bente and Petr returned at ten. Lala introduced them to Ruth as her friend and Amalie's playmate. Ruth agreed to watch the children while Lala gave Bente a tour of the building.

"You're fortunate to have household help," Bente said as they climbed the steps to the attic.

"I am truly fortunate for a great deal. I try not to take it for granted."

"If I could afford help, I'd have it. Hmm, I can use my salary to hire someone — no, it will be put toward a radio."

Lala fished the key from her pocket. "My husband wants to wait until they air more than one hour of programming daily. Imagine, turning a dial and hearing music." She unlocked the door and let Bente enter. "I've heard from friends that the BBC in England broadcast a sporting event."

"How wonderful it would be to hear other voices besides mine and Petr's when we're home." Bente turned in a slow circle.

"Tight quarters." Lala noted.

"We'll manage."

Bente was indefatigable, Lala decided as she rolled out the blueprints. "This is the main floor."

Two slender creases formed between Bente's brow as she perused the drawings. "What are these lighter lines here?" she asked, pointing to one side.

"That indicates a break in the wall, in this instance a window." Lala ran her index finger to a swinging line on the drawing. "This shows a door and the direction in which it opens."

"I can see this almost as if it were in three dimensions."

"That's a rare skill, which will be useful to our project," said Lala. "I'm so glad you accepted my offer."

"And I'm very grateful you thought of me." Bente's face turned sober. "I can't begin to tell you how much I missed you when you stopped coming around."

"Part of me craved the companionship, the feeling of belonging the group offered, but I couldn't stand by and listen to the sisters spout their prejudices with Terezka parroting them. I went on the offensive and unfortunately, you became the casualty. I'm sorry."

"I understand. I'm sorry as well, for never thanking you for what you did for me."

"I recall you did."

Bente shook her head. "Not properly, because your gift changed me. It made me see how unhappy I was gossiping with those women. We had little in common, but somehow I thought if I spent time with them I'd come to appreciate my life as it was. Accept my role as wife and mother, and be satisfied with it. I believed it until the day you brought up working."

"I joined the group for the same reason as you," Lala acknowledged. "But that day, I could see the longing in your face when you talked about Bonne Fleur."

"I never appreciated how much I missed working there." Bente blew out air as if to extinguish a burning memory. "All my life I had to do what I'd been told, by my father, by my husband. When I worked for Madame, I had to as well, and yet I never resented it."

Lala understood. "I suspect that weekly envelope of koruny was part of the reason."

Bente agreed with a nod. "It gave me a sense of value, that something I did was worth koruny. That's why Dagmar and Ignace's comments hurt me. Being entrusted with the merchandise made me feel important, even if I couldn't afford anything I touched. I could enjoy having them before me, knowing they exist. I imagine it's like seeing masterpieces in museums."

"I know what you mean," Lala responded. "My sister hired me to design her first shop. When she handed me my first wages, I felt so proud and excited." She remembered the feeling of empowerment that came with her earnings.

"Why is it husbands can understand that for themselves

but not their wives?"

Lala shrugged. "Because men make the rules?"

Bente considered that. "I was taught in life, we all have roles we must play, and if we don't, we're bad, or strange. But something changed the day you gave me that gift from Bonne Fleur. I brought it home and tried it on, and as if by magic I suddenly felt strong." Her fingers curled into her palms. "Powerful. Capable of doing housework, raising my son, being a good wife...and much more. It almost scared me into taking it off, but I didn't. And the best part?" She laughed. "Nothing bad happened. I still cooked, cleaned and cared for my husband and son. The world didn't shift off its axis."

"No," said Lala. "But you did."

Bente's eyes welled, but she held her head erect. "Something soft and delicate made me feel like I wore armor, shielding me from opinions and attitudes that grind away a woman's spirit. Always being told what to do, how to do it, and how it isn't good enough. It got me through many afternoons on that park bench, and a few arguments with my husband as well."

She paused for a breath. "I meant to ask your mother for your address so I could come to see you, tell you all of this, and then there you were, offering me this wonderful opportunity." She clasped her hands. "Offering me salvation."

Lala, unsure if her urge to hug Bente should be acted upon, wept. Bente settled it by hugging Lala.

Bente wiped away her tears. "I'm so glad to have met someone who understands."

"We have much to discuss. Amalie loves to romp in the cherry orchard on Petřín Hill. Shall we take the children there? They can play together while we talk."

***

Bente nestled Petr in his stroller and tucked a blanket around him to ward off the autumn chill. Amalie walked alongside him, keeping the boy entertained with her chatter and songs.

"What a lovely voice you have, Amalie," noted Bente.

"Yes, I do," she said matter-of-factly, and the women chuckled.

"I'll sign her up on Wednesday for a weekly lesson with the piano teacher near your apartment," said Lala. "My mother promised to watch her for a few hours afterward. I won't have to worry about child care for that day, and when I'm further along in the project, I can bring work for you to do at home if it won't interfere with your routine."

"How far have you gotten?"

"Those room sketches you saw with the layout of furniture, but I need to decide on what furnishings to select. The final designs must attract the type of clientele the hotel will want. When I designed the Excelsior—"

Bente gasped. "You did that? My word, your family is so accomplished, what with your sister running the most successful dress shop east of Paris and you creating the most successful hotel...I'm speechless, and a little intimidated."

Her comment surprised Lala. "I'm flattered you consider my work on a par with Paulina's."

Bente gave her a curious look. "Don't you? You should."

Lala never considered her work equivalent with Paulina's, but Bente truly meant it.

"I had designed the Excelsior as a home. I'd considered guests staying there, but not paying guests."

"What did you do to convert the rooms into a hotel?"

"Nothing. The current owner cited the design as the main reason he bought the mansion." As Lala said that, it occurred to her what an accomplishment that had been, echoed by the look of awe on Bente's face. "When he offered me this position, he told me, 'Create an oasis where people want to be, to stay, and will pay good money to do so.'"

"Obviously they will need a great deal of money to spend on lavish accommodations." Bente's voice went flat.

"You can't build something grand and not expect it to be expensive," Lala noted.

Bente attempted a cheery look. "Fortunately for the hotel's owner there's no shortage of wealthy people."

Lala recalled her mother's advice..."*Don't talk politics. They don't think like we do.*"

"Bente, are you concerned I'll find out you sympathize with the Bolsheviks?"

Bente's eyes darkened to gray but she said nothing.

They crossed over to the park. Amalie let go of the stroller and skipped ahead in the direction of the cherry orchard, their leaves hinting at the golden hue they'd soon turn. Amalie had never skipped that smoothly, or for that long before, mused Lala. Another milestone in her daughter's development. When they reached their destination, Amalie scooted off to gather fallen leaves between the gray trees. Finding none, she brought back a piece of bark.

"Those are cherry trees, Petr." She held up the bark for him to see the lenticels. "You can tell by these marks on their trunks that look like they were cut, but they weren't. In spring they have the prettiest flowers. Soon their leaves will turn red and gold and then they'll fall down."

Lala indicated toward an unoccupied park bench. "Shall we sit there?"

Bente pushed the stroller to the bench and sat. "Petr needs to take his nap."

Lala buttoned Amalie's sweater. "Amalie, will you play quietly by yourself for a while?"

She nodded. "I'll be quiet as a mouse, Mama."

Bente rocked the stroller in a gentle back and forth motion to soothe her son to sleep. "You designed the property that eventually became the Excelsior. How did that come about?"

"Pure luck." She wondered how much to tell Bente about her past. "Long before I married, I was engaged to a young man whose family owned the mansion that became the hotel. He was killed, and his mother, who died not long after, left her home to me in her will. By then I'd married Josef, and he had no interest in living there."

"That's understandable. What man would want to live in his wife's old beaux's family home, one more luxurious than he could provide."

Lala continued, "I wasn't sure I could sell it with the Great War still raging. I absolutely refused to sell to a war profiteer, but the man who contacted me made his fortune honestly."

"Will you recreate the atmosphere of the Excelsior or do something different?"

"A bit of both. The intimacy, yes. However, the Excelsior is a country inn where visitors go to escape the city, enjoy nature. I want to translate what appealed to guests there into an environment more suitable for a city hotel."

Bente, seeing Petr had fallen asleep, stopped rocking the stroller. "I think you're working this backward, Lala, designing the hotel to attract a certain type of guest. Instead, you first ought to identify the type of guest you want to

327

attract. Not how to promote it, but to whom." Bente's face registered a range of emotions. "And at the risk of being called a Communist, based on what you told me about selling the Excelsior, wealth can't be the only criteria. We have to consider character as well. What led you to think I'm aligned with the Communists?"

"One, because I understand your objections to what we're doing. You believe it's unfair to segregate people by wealth and station. I agree in principle, but after what I've lived though I no longer believe life can be fair or equitable. And two," Lala added, "you're married to a Communist."

"How could you know that?"

"Let's just say my mother told me."

Bente glanced at Petr. "What did he say to her?"

"It wasn't anything he said. He reads the Lidu."

"Your mother's a perceptive woman. However, I don't read the Lidu. I prefer the Ceske Slovo because I'm anti-Marxist, one of the reasons I argue with my husband."

"I have no issue with your socialist viewpoint as long as it won't affect your work on this project."

"I understand what is needed. I can separate the two."

"Then we should have no problem."

CHAPTER NINE

Lala bid goodbye to Bente in the park and returned home with Amalie for lunch. Before entering the building she paused on the ground floor landing. The gallery seemed even more empty than a week ago. She lifted Amalie in her arms and opened the door to the shop.

Hanus sat behind the reception table, engaged in a book. He slammed it shut and leapt up as she entered.

"Afternoon, Mrs. Smetana. Miss Amalie. If you're looking for Mr. Smetana, he isn't here, but I expect him back before closing time."

"Rather quiet here."

"Yes, ma'am." He pushed the book aside.

"Then again, I don't see much merchandise to entice customers."

"Mr. Smetana has been selling a lot lately." He nodded with more enthusiasm than seemed necessary.

"But not replacing it with new merchandise?"

He glanced around. "I don't know about that, ma'am. He asks me to receive new shipments, but I haven't seen any come in recently."

Lala forced a smile. "I'll let you return to your duties."

She brought Amalie to the apartment, where Ruth had lunch waiting.

"Ruth, I forgot something downstairs. I'll only be a minute."

Ruth poured a glass of milk for Amalie. "I'll keep an eye on her."

Lala fetched the housekeys and went to the first floor. She unlocked the door to the storeroom, curious to see if anything there could be brought down to the shop.

Inside she found no antiques or furniture of any kind, nor objets d'art. Only row upon row of paintings, at least a hundred if not more, stacked upright in crates and propped against the walls. All featured images of the Great War, grotesque scenes of death and destruction. Men charging into battle, corpses strung on barb wire, rifles with blood dripping from their bayonets. The convulsive force of bombs exploding, debris flying. Smoke-filled skies and gouged landscapes. She riffled through a crate of pen and ink drawings, bleak satirical works showing politicians feasting and toasting each other while sitting upon mounds of dead bodies, women and children frantic to hide from an approaching onslaught. She held up a caricature of Kaiser Wilhelm gnawing on a globe.

Some of the work seemed journalistic, meant to capture a slice of history on canvas. Others subjected the viewer to the horrors of war in a more expressive way, with bold strokes and nauseating colors. The imagery was surely meant to disturb. From an artistic point many were magnificently rendered, but who would want this hanging in their home? It seemed more appropriate for an art history class or museum exhibit, and well into the future at that.

What had possessed Josef to buy all of these works?

Lala locked up the storeroom before returning to the apartment. Upon opening the door she could hear Amalie singing "Alle Meine Entchen." Lala tiptoed toward her daughter's bedroom, where she saw Ruth watching the girl act out the lyrics of the song as she sang.

"All my ducklings,
swimming in the lake,
swimming in the lake,"

Amalie sang as she turned in a circle.

"Heads in the water,
tails up in the air."

With that, she put her hands on the floor and pointed her bottom at the ceiling.

Ruth applauded. "Well done, Miss. One more verse and then I must return to work."

Amalie took a deep breath.

"All my little doves,
sitting on the roof...."

Lala waited until Amalie clap-clapped to send the doves flying over the roof. "Lovely, Amalie, but it's time for your nap."

The child beamed at the compliment. She bade goodbye to Ruth and followed her mother into her bedroom.

As the girl undressed, she asked, "Do I have to take a nap?"

Lala reminded her, "You need to get your rest, love. Tomorrow you begin piano lessons."

"Will I learn how to play 'Alle meine Entchen?'"

"I'm sure that can be arranged. Did you have fun playing with Petr today?"

Amalie laid her dress on the chair. "I like him. He does whatever I ask."

Lala refrained from chuckling. "He likes you. You're a big girl and he feels honored that you'll play with him." She pulled back the covers. "Since you are a big girl you will have to look out for him."

Amalie hopped into the bed and laid down. "I do. I remember what you and Papa told me about being a big sister for the baby, but he didn't live, so now I can be Petr's big sister."

Lala felt a catch in the back of her throat as she tucked the blanket around her daughter. "He would like that, too."

Amalie fell asleep right away. The walk to and from the park tired her out. Being around Petr seemed to have a calming effect on the little girl. The relationship might suppress some of the quarreling between mother and daughter as well, as long as Amalie's bossy nature didn't get out of control.

Ruth popped her head into the parlor. "Missus, I'm off to the market. I'll see if they have those Spanish oranges you like."

"Thank you."

Lala sat in the parlor, pencil and note pad in hand, and read through the notes she'd taken the day she met with

Zahradnik at the building. Certain words kept cropping up – luxury, exclusive, comfort...

"...As comfortable and relaxing as the Excelsior...."

Yet different. A country inn takes advantage of nature, a city inn, culture. She'd described her vision to Zahradnik as a jewel box, beautiful in its own right, without any element dominating another.

She roughed out a few sketches, but none of them felt right. Something was missing....

"...Not how to promote it, but to whom."

She jotted ideas for identifying the customer the hotel wanted to appeal to. Wealthy for sure. People who could appreciate quality over quantity. People who sought more than luxury, more than comfort. An oasis.

Lala spread the sketches out across the sofa table and studied them, looking for a clue, for inspiration. For her it had always come from great art. She took a few art books from the shelf and thumbed through them, studying each illustration and reproduction, assessing what made it such a fine example of its school of work.

A few ideas bubbled up, but no inspiration.

After sketching for another hour without a breakthrough, she balled up her drawings and put them in the trash bin, next to a table with a stack of papers. The corner of what appeared to be an illustration poked out.

She eased it from the pile with a few gentle tugs and examined the charcoal sketch of a couple at the Moulin Rouge; quite good. The signatory monogram shocked her – the artist's initials T L within a red circle, with a horizontal bar between the vertical lines to form an H for Henri. A Toulouse-Lautrec. But Josef would never treat it so carelessly if it were. She carried it downstairs to the gallery.

Her entrance interrupted Hanus assisting Josef in moving a chest of drawers to partially fill an empty space. She held up the sketch, determined to keep her tongue mellow no matter what. "Dear, is there some reason you left this lying about?"

"Don't be concerned. It's a forgery."

She looked at the sketch again. "Are you sure?"

He exhaled loudly, his annoyance apparent. "The paper has a watermark from a company that didn't exist during the artist's lifetime."

She nodded. "How clever of you to have noticed." She turned to leave, but changed her mind. "Are you planning to make changes to your shop and gallery?"

"Why? It works well as is."

"I wondered, since your inventory is so low, I thought you were clearing out the space to do some work on the interior."

Josef said nothing, but his face had reddened.

"Business must be very good, then."

He offered a smile as fraudulent as the Toulouse-Lautrec sketch.

CHAPTER TEN

When Lala brought up the subject of piano lessons for Amalie, Josef ruled she could not begin studying until she turned six, almost a year away. Not shouldn't, couldn't. Lala pressed for a reason, but Josef would not discuss it. Even Amalie's tears of disappointment wouldn't change his mind.

She tried on several occasions to get him to confide in her, but he always maintained nothing was wrong. Lala found it hard to believe. She recognized the signs of preoccupation; he'd become distant, as if he'd erected a wall between them, though Lala could not fathom why.

Every day Josef worked in his shop or went out seeking clients. Evenings he would return to their apartment for dinner and some playtime with Amalie before going back to work. Some nights, after Amalie fell asleep, Lala coaxed him into making love, but although he enjoyed it as much as she, afterward his pleasurable mood would vanish and he'd close himself off. Then he would leave to meet more potential clients, or go to his business office to pore over the profit and loss reports for his month-end closing, working late into the night.

Lala would be in bed, either asleep or pretending to be, when he came home. Rumors of mistresses abounded during Josef's marriage to Romy; she'd met one herself. He'd never given her any cause to believe that practice continued in their marriage, but Mamie's observation made her wary...

...*"What did he do? It must have been something bad...."*

Occasionally she'd catch a whiff of tobacco smoke in his hair or a hint of whiskey on his breath but she didn't detect any telltale signs of infidelity or other licentious behavior. She doubted either caused Josef's sudden remoteness. He'd been adept at keeping his affairs private for decades. Even Xenie. This had to be something so foreign it left him flummoxed.

Lala took advantage of Josef's absences. Once they put Amalie to bed and he returned to his business, she could work undisturbed on her project until she went to bed. It should have left ample time to finish her proposal for the hotel, but she could not decide how she wanted to proceed. It frustrated her to think that, when she finally had her chance to chase her dream, her creative ability had deserted her.

How much had her designs contributed to the reputation of the Excelsior? Zahradnik credited her with much of its success, as did Bente...

"Don't you? You should."

Yes, I should, Lala thought. As she did, she reflected on how quickly Bente had become an asset. More than an asset. An ally. Lala might have found more inspiration or culled advice from her, but little Petr and then her husband Petr had caught a cold and Bente asked to take the rest of the week off to tend to them. Then Zahradnik contacted her; he'd procured the adjacent building. Her budget doubled, along with her workload.

Her mother called and asked to see her and Amalie. It gave Lala a valid excuse to shelve the project awhile.

She arrived with Amalie after lunch for their visit. Following hugs and kisses, Sarah brought them into the kitchen, redolent of butter, sugar and cinnamon.

"It's good to finally see you both. I missed you." She put the kettle on the stove to boil.

Amalie sniffed the air and beamed. "I missed you, too, Bubbie. I love you so much. May I please have a cookie?"

"If Mama says yes."

"Mama says yes," Lala said. "I want one, too."

Amalie piped in, "And I want one two three four."

Sarah took a cookie from a platter on the counter and handed it to Lala. "Here's your cookie, Mama." To Amalie she said, "Only two."

"Four," countered Amalie as Sarah plated a few more cookies.

Lala took a bite of hers, still warm and crispy around the edges. "I'll leave it to Bubbie and Amalie to sort out."

"Ahem – 'mama', if you're going to eat that, please sit at the table and use a plate," Sarah admonished Lala, which drew a giggle from Amalie.

"May I eat my cookies on the balcony, Bubbie? Then the birds can have the crumbs that fall down."

"All right, dear, but bring them out on a plate, and if you can manage not to break it I'll be grateful."

Amalie took her treat to the balcony.

Pressing her hands on the table, Sarah eased into the chair

next to Lala with a loud grunt. "Now that you've eaten your cookie, tell me what's eating you?"

Lala shrugged. "Nothing. I'm fine."

"Don't lie to your mother, dear."

Lala should have known better. "There's a project I'm attempting in my spare time, but I can't seem to find the inspiration to even begin."

"Is this something you want to do or have to do."

"The former."

Sarah chuckled. "That explains it. When you would like to do something, there's no urgency to get it done like when you must do something." She took a cookie and nibbled on it.

"As simple as that?" Lala asked. But what her mother said made sense. In the past, doing whatever she had to do had dominated Lala's life. Now she had no compelling need to motivate her into action. Josef took charge of the business with Hanus. He supported the family financially, so she didn't have to earn money. Ruth took care of the housework. And Amalie was old enough to manage basics like eating and dressing.

"Mother, would you mind watching Amalie while I run an errand? It won't take long."

"Go. Leave her to me," said Sarah as the tea kettle began to boil.

In the building next door, Lala found Bente's apartment number on the residents listing, went upstairs and knocked.

"Lala, what a surprise. I'd invite you in but with my two men sick—"

"No bother, I was visiting my mother and thought I'd stop by to ask if you needed anything."

Bente stepped into the hallway, leaving the door ajar. "How kind. Thanks, that won't be necessary. What about you? Is there something I can help you with? I feel badly that I left you in the lurch this week."

Lala's emotional dam of frustration broke in Bente's presence, flooding her with doubts. "Honestly, there's nothing for you to do as I'm not making any progress. I'm completely devoid of ideas or direction on this project. What made me think I could do this?"

Bente looked puzzled. "Lala, why do you always underestimate your accomplishments? You talk about your sister, your husband, the Excelsior, their success. Don't you see that you're at the heart of it all?"

Lala shook her head. "You flatter me, but I played a marginal role in each of their businesses."

"Rubbish. After you mentioned your sister was the dressmaker to society, I became curious. Her popularity grew with the patronage of Countess von Anhult. Didn't you introduce them?"

"I see where this is going, but Paulina built her clientele on her own," said Lala. "She convinced Mamie – the Countess – to come to her shop."

"Which you designed." Bente crossed her arms. "The articles written about her always mention the eye-catching display of clothing as much as their style. But you don't think that contributed to your sister's success." She paused to let that sink in. "How could she afford to open her first shop?"

"A silent partner invested in the business."

"Did you have anything to do with that?"

"Again, I made the introduction, but it was Paulina—"

"Lala, don't you see that you're the real reason Paulina has become successful?"

"I would never say that again," Lala asserted.

Bente's eyes widened. "Ah, so you've talked about this."

Lala exhaled loudly. "Long ago, I brought up having introduced her to her benefactor. She became upset, and rightly so. It led to a fight and we didn't speak to each other for weeks."

"You hurt her feelings, but it doesn't make it any less true, does it?"

"Granted, it was a factor."

Bente exclaimed, "Why, isn't that also true of the man who owns the Excelsior? You did all the important work, designing the interiors the society pages rave about, before he stepped in with a check and took over. And you helped your husband by giving him the best pieces from the home you inherited to launch his business." She placed her hand on Lala's shoulder. "Don't underestimate your abilities, Lala. It's what's holding you back."

CHAPTER ELEVEN

Day after day Lala stared at her sketches of empty rooms, with every wall, door, window and chandelier in place, but no furnishings. Not even a cohesive concept. She would take Amalie on walks and search for ideas in shop windows, restaurants, even peer through windows into people's apartments. One day she'd see a 19th century antique that appealed to her, only to spot a more modern piece later on that made her reconsider. Why was she having so much trouble coming up with a design?

"... When you would like to do something, there's no pressure to get it done like when you must do something."

Then how had she managed to make such a success with the Excelsior?

"...Don't underestimate your abilities, Lala. It's what's holding you back."

While Amalie napped, Lala paced the parlor, recalling how she came upon her idea for the mansion. She'd gone from room to room, pondering how she could use the existing furnishings to make each space more inviting, more welcoming. Lala tried revamping one bedroom. It didn't change her mind that something was missing, though what that something might be evaded her. Then Mrs. Havlik entered, and Lala sought her opinion...

"Mrs. Havlik, what do you think this room lacks?"

The woman thought for a moment. "I would have to say it's what all the rooms in this house lack. People. A room is just a place to store things unless it's occupied."

Mrs. Havlik's astute comment inspired Lala back then. What would it take now?

"Mama, help me with this."

Amalie interrupted Lala's pacing. She'd put on the same pink dress she'd worn that morning, which she'd buttoned all by herself, its untied sash trailing behind her. She held out the ends of the wide sash for Lala to tie into a fluffy bow.

Amalie had always held strong opinions about her likes and dislikes and conveyed them, sometimes forcefully, sometimes manipulatively, even before she could speak. She resolved never to wear certain colors. Yellow belonged to her Aunt Paulina, blue to her Mama. Amalie disliked most greens and anything remotely orange. Red, pink, and violet dominated her wardrobe.

Lala inspected the hem, which her mother had let down a few months earlier after Amalie's growth spurt.

"This dress is too small for you now."

"It fits better than my other dresses, except my favorite." She grinned. "I can wear that."

"That" being a costume Paulina had made for Amalie as a birthday present. Adapted from a French couture gown, it featured a slim top with a drop waist and longer flared skirt. Paulina added glitzy beading, something she'd seen in

Mamie's Hollywood magazines. Paulina had explained to Amalie that the ensemble, which included a feather-trimmed capelet and turban, should only be worn at home when she played dress-up.

"We must buy some new clothing for you."

"Can't we ask Aunt Paulina to make me a few dresses?"

Lala paused to consider the consequences before answering. Amalie had a better command of language now, which eased some of her frustration in expressing her opinions, and she'd matured enough to display more patience as well as rational thought. However, sometimes she reverted to temper tantrums when she didn't get her way.

"She may not have time to do that, as she's busy with her dressmaking for grown-ups. Instead, if we go to the store, we can buy a few dresses right away, instead of having to wait for Aunt Paulina's staff to make them."

Amalie scowled. "I don't like going to the store."

"Why not?"

"They have so many dresses to choose from, it's hard to decide what I want."

Out of the mouths of babes. Lala scooped her daughter up, gave her a big hug and kissed her cheeks before putting her down. "You, love, have given me a great idea."

CHAPTER TWELVE

Miss Horáčková greeted them at the shop's door with an apology; Paulina wasn't in that day. After exchanging some pleasantries and an explanation for their visit, Lala took Amalie's hand and they left.

"We need to buy you at least one dress today. Since you don't like going to the store, would you like me to select something for you – no green, yellow, blue or orange, of course."

"No, I want to pick out my own dress."

"I thought you—" Lala stopped before Amalie's change of mind led to an argument. She'd learned to pick her battles carefully. "Very well, we'll go to the shop around the corner."

With only a dozen choices in Amalie's size and acceptable colors, shopping went quickly. They left the store, Lala laden with packages. As they approached the Charles Bridge they passed the gallery where Lala had spotted Zoe last month; it now held a showing of her photographs. A sign in the window advertised an exhibit by Zoe Assisi. She'd used her

345

father's home town as a surname, likely to avoid a connection with her ex-husband, whose political activities had eclipsed his reputation as an artist.

Lala gestured toward the window. "See those pictures inside?" she asked Amalie. "Those were taken by the same lady who took the photograph of you on your second birthday."

"The one you have on the mantle in the living room? I like that picture. May we go in to see the others?"

Lala brought Amalie into the gallery and set her purchases on a table by the door. The owner acknowledged her with an indifferent nod as he shadowed a well-dressed couple examining the photographs.

"Mama, pick me up so I can see them better," whispered Amalie, mindful of the others in the gallery, a benefit of earlier trips to museums.

Lala lifted the child in her arms and stood before the first photo of a woman and a young girl walking along a street away from the camera, their hands clasped and heads tilted toward each other as if in conversation.

"Even from the back they look happy, like they belong together." Amalie observed. "It must be a mama and her daughter."

"It does look like that," Lala conceded, but knew it wasn't. She recognized the child as Charis and the woman as Frantiska, Charis's stepmother and the current Mrs. Vilem Vesely.

They continued to browse the exhibit while the owner explained each photograph to the couple. They offered no opinions or preferences. Amalie, however, expressed her opinion of every photograph they looked at. She amazed Lala with her astute observations about the poses, the exposures and especially the expressions on the subjects' faces.

"Have you any questions about Zoe?" the gallery owner asked the couple, to Lala's surprise; she'd never heard any professional refer to an artist by their first name.

"Does the photographer always work with children?" the woman asked.

"Primarily, a specialty of the artist."

Lala smiled inwardly when the woman said, "I've never seen anything so unique, which is why I suggested to my husband to come in. We've discussed adding some photographs to our art collection, but we want something...significant." Lala assumed she meant something that would impress others.

"Who has he apprenticed with? Any of the more famous photographers?" her husband asked.

The owner paused before answering. "The artist is self-trained and has exhibited throughout Europe, including Paris."

"Hmmm...Paris, you say?" the woman commented as she snuck a pair of round rimmed glasses from her purse. She put them on to gaze at the display card next to a large format photo, printed with the picture's title and cost, then slid them back into her purse.

"An emerging talent, reflected in the current prices," acknowledged the owner. "Another reason to admire the work." The owner avoided referring to Zoe by gender, allowing the husband's assumption that Zoe was a man to stand.

"What do you think?" she asked her husband.

"What kind of name is Zoe anyway?"

The gallery owner cleared his throat. "I believe it's Greek."

The man chortled. "Well, that certainly explains a lot. Sounds awfully feminine, like these pictures. But you know what they say about those Greeks—"

His wife put her hand on his arm and he harrumphed.

"These photographs are beautiful, but perhaps not right for us." She thanked the owner for the information, and the couple departed.

The gallery owner gave Lala no more than a glance before sitting at his desk in the rear of the gallery. After she and Amalie finished looking at the photos, ignored and unaided, Lala set Amalie down and gathered her packages; her daughter's presence stopped her from chastising him. She took hold of Amalie's hand and continued to the bridge and home. Her annoyance prodded her into a brisk pace.

"Mama, what do they say about the Greeks?"

"That they taught the rest of the world a great deal about how to live and think."

The truth appeased her.

"Mama, is Zoe the name of the lady who took those pictures?"

"Yes, love."

"And Zoe is a girl's name, so why did the man think the pictures were taken by a man?"

"Because the owner of the gallery never told him that Zoe was a woman."

"Why not?"

Lala took a deep breath to subdue her annoyance. "Because he thought if the man knew that, he wouldn't buy any pictures."

"But he didn't buy any, so why would it matter if Zoe was a man or a woman?"

"A very good question, Amalie." She pondered how to

proceed in an honest but age appropriate way. "Some—no, many people believe that ladies can't, or shouldn't, do certain things that are considered men's work."

"That's what Bubbie says, men do some things and women do other things, and that way everything gets done. I asked Papa if that's true and he said yes..."

That came as no surprise to Lala. "Amalie, you can carry your new shoes." Lala handed the girl a small package while she shifted the rest she carried to her other arm.

"...But," Amalie continued, "Papa also said it's not fair."

"Papa is right." She'd bear that in mind when telling him of her employment offer.

Amalie switched the conversation to her new clothes as they walked home, distracting Lala from window shopping for her project. The last thing she needed was more ideas to juggle; her packages were enough.

They reached home shortly before four o'clock, Lala with hopes of convincing Amalie to nap again so she could sketch before Josef returned for dinner. Her daughter's earlier comment sparked an idea and she wanted to explore it while still fresh.

Amalie scooted up the stairs with her package as soon as Lala opened the front door to the building. Lala glanced into the shop. Josef wasn't there. She also observed that no merchandise had been sold, or added.

She caught up with Amalie on the landing and opened the door to their apartment. Lala spotted the day's newspaper on the console; Josef must have brought it up while she and Amalie were out. She trailed Amalie to her bedroom with her purchases. As they passed the parlor she saw Josef in his chair, clutching his decanter of cognac. His body slumped as though weighted, his face haggard, though whether from exhaustion or melancholy she could not tell.

Before Lala said anything, Amalie cried out, "Papa, what's wrong?" and ran to him.

He offered her a weak smile and sat her on his lap. "I'm fine, Amalie, and very happy to see you." He kissed her cheek.

"You look sad, Papa. Why are you sad?"

Lala entered the room and laid the packages on the sofa. "Amalie, Papa's tired and needs to rest, and so do you. Please go to your room and get ready for your nap while I talk to Papa, then we'll both come to tuck you in."

"No, I don't want to nap, I want to stay with Papa."

In a gravelly voice, Josef told the girl, "Do what your mother says, Amalie."

She pouted at that, but obeyed.

When Amalie had gone into her room, Lala went to Josef's side. She took the decanter from him and placed it on the side table. "Will you finally tell me what's troubling you?"

"I'm tired, that's all."

"I can't say I'm surprised, considering the hours you've kept for the last few months. But you're not in bed, or napping on the sofa. So forgive me, but I don't believe you. What is going on with your gallery and shop? You've hardly any merchandise left, nothing new coming in and nothing being sold." She stopped herself before mentioning his trove of War art. "Does this have anything to do with that Toulouse-Lautrec forgery?"

With a grimace he muttered, "What a stupid mistake I made with that."

"A mistake, perhaps, but it's not going to bankrupt us, is it? Put it aside and move on. You've acquired many fine pieces over decades. Why are you obsessing over this one?"

His grimace deepened, but he said nothing.

CHAPTER THIRTEEN

Amalie was thrilled when Josef came to tuck her in for her nap, and more thrilled when he said he'd join her. He sat on the edge of the bed and took off his shoes, jacket and tie while Amalie undressed. Together they laid down in her bed and cuddled as Lala tucked them in.

"When you both awake from your naps, Amalie will model her new clothes for Papa, and then we'll have dinner."

Amalie smiled and nestled against her father's chest. Josef wrapped his arm around the girl and closed his eyes. His face relaxed and he appeared calmer. Lala closed the draperies and after kissing them both on the forehead, left the room.

Lala suspected Josef's troubles went beyond buying the forgery. She and Josef had arranged to talk further that evening after Amalie fell asleep. Nothing would be solved until then, so she forced herself to put everything but her project out of her thoughts.

Lala fetched her sketchpad before going upstairs to her attic workroom. She tacked the blueprints for the hotel across the wall and studied them. A fresh approach germinated from what her daughter had said earlier. It wasn't that Amalie didn't enjoy shopping for new clothes, but too many choices overwhelmed her. Lala faced the same quandary and sensed the answer lay in limiting the choices by narrowing the concept and making it more concrete in her mind.

She mulled what she'd pitched to Zahradnik...an oasis...a jewel...a perfect jewel.

Lala trusted she'd find the answer by studying artwork. Her books, like the stores, offered too many choices, whereas the gallery now offered too few. Josef saved the pieces they liked best for their personal collection.

Returning to the apartment she went from room to room, studying the many canvases hanging on the walls of their home. She lingered on the Claude Monet painting of Chartres in the morning, admiring the mood evoked by the muted colors. As a child she deemed it blurry, but pleasant. She stopped briefly before the Ludwig Meidner pre-War Berlin street scene, which impressed Lala so much Josef bought it, but its frenzied imagery wouldn't translate into a calming environment. The Canaletto, the Corot. All fine works of art. But fine wasn't good enough. She needed to study a masterpiece. Fortunately, she and Josef owned one.

It had been years since she last stood before her portrait. She'd been Armin's muse, inspiring this master work. It took a moment to accept the young woman gazing back was she; ironically the name of the work. Lala forced herself to be objective about the painting and ignore the youthfulness she no longer possessed. Instead she focused on how Armin chose to portray her, how he brought a liveliness to her figure. His use of two-point perspective created the illusion of depth and spaciousness behind her. The pose appeared natural, relaxed and at the same time active, as if she would step forward any moment. Her face looked engaged and thoughtful, almost curious, filled with unasked questions.

She recalled he'd sketched her sitting in his room, but in the painting he portrayed her standing barefoot on a snow leopard skin. A setting of refined elegance grounded in wildness, she'd thought the first time she saw it. Her eyes moved from her pose to the other elements, only a swath of ivory brocade draped across an antique high-back chair, the rest as bare as her feet. Armin had used a swirling brush stroke for the background, blending analogous neutral shades slightly darker than the foreground.

Something Bente said sprang to mind...

"Wealth can't be the only criteria. We have to consider character as well..."

As well as Amalie's observation...

"I don't like going to the store...they have too many dresses there. It's hard to find what I want."

Wealth and character. Simplicity.

And balance. She'd concerned herself with what to put into the hotel, but not what to leave out. Positive and negative space. In décor as in artwork, the negative space held equal importance to the positive, which created a warm, welcoming and relaxing environment.

A setting of refined elegance grounded in wildness. And innocence contrasted with sensuality, she acknowledged now, in a girl on the brink of womanhood. The tension generated by the disparity made the painting exciting.

The hotel would be distinctive – luxurious and cozy, like the Excelsior, but more intimate. And no playroom or nannies; it would cater to an adult clientele – businessmen, couples, newlyweds, lovers – with a staff dedicated to making their stay balanced between relaxing and stimulating.

Every space, from the lobby to the guest rooms, would provide comfort and ease for guests, for what could be more extravagant than that? Many hotels boasted crystal chandeliers and silk rugs, rooms filled with ornate antiques and gilded fixtures. But a room where the furnishings faded into the background and served a functional purpose rather than decorative? Where a bed floated like a raft in a sea of calm, surrounded by sensual surfaces and soft muted colors, like her Monet? That would be a unique experience.

Why had she tried to do this project on her own, when no one's success was achieved without help, either financial or inspirational? She'd often laid the groundwork for that success, as she had with Paulina, and with Josef's business, as well as the Excelsior.

"Don't you see that you're at the heart of it all?"

After searching through shops and restaurants, studying art, poring over blueprints and sketches of the project, inspiration finally came, and from within her inner circle. Listening to her daughter and Bente provided the kindling, but Armin's portrait lit the spark.

Lala had found her muse.

CHAPTER FOURTEEN

Lala and Josef preserved a cheerful countenance in Amalie's presence. The child modeled her new dresses for Papa, earning compliments for each, while Lala made supper. At the table, Amalie recounted her day to Josef, of the plants and birds and litter she spotted walking to the Old Town, the colors and buttons and lace on the dresses she'd tried on, the poses and facial expressions of the people in the photography exhibit; all the minutiae an adult would ignore but had captivated her. He encouraged her with questions, his attention unflagging, his curiosity genuine.

After they ate, Lala asked Josef to read Amalie a story and put her to bed while she cleaned up the kitchen. She finished quickly and sat in the parlor, waiting for Josef, dozing on and off until he joined her.

"She's finally asleep. Shopping does excite the girl."

"She seemed more fascinated by Zoe's exhibit."

Josef put the decanter back on the bar table before joining Lala on the sofa. "I'm surprised you'd want to see her work after your falling out."

"Why not? She's talented, and she saw to her child's

wellbeing. I may not agree with what she did, but I understand how circumstances forced her into making a difficult choice."

"When will I get the bill for Amalie's new clothing?"

"Likely by the end of the week." Josef had sometimes questioned her about household expenses before, but Lala detected a subtle tone of anxiety tonight. "What happened to put you in such a dispirited mood."

He squirmed in his seat and turned away from her. "Don't concern yourself with this, this minor setback which I'll correct soon. Very soon."

"No, I insist you tell me. Purchasing one fraudulent drawing wouldn't put you in a state of despair, so don't insult me by saying whatever problem you're facing is minor."

"I can fix it," he countered in a raised voice, his fists clenched.

"Fix what?"

"I made a bad deal. It happens sometimes, but I—"

"Start from the beginning."

He turned to face her. She kept her expression neutral, hoping to draw the story from him. "Please," she implored.

"I put a deposit on several antiques with a new dealer, who instead sent me reproductions. I refused delivery and demanded my money back, but he refused to return my deposit. When I threatened to sue, he said, 'Go ahead, it will cost you far more in legal fees than it's worth.' I checked with Cerveny and he agreed. Cerveny also warned me this dealer has cheated other buyers."

He continued, "To make up for that loss I invested in a collection of excellent paintings inspired by the Great War. I remembered the powerful work of pre-war artists in Berlin and thought I could corner the market by buying them early on. I hadn't counted on how much people want to forget the war and the horrors of battle, but I'd committed to purchasing the works and if I backed out I would have lost the deposit I put on them—"

"And admitted you'd made a bad judgement."

"I knew they'd sell eventually," he insisted. "I promised to make the final payment at the end of August. Then an artwork a client had sought for over a year became available at the same time."

"The forged Toulouse-Lautrec?"

He nodded. "He understandably backed out, which left me with a negative cash flow. "

"So what did you do?"

"I—" His hand went to his mouth as if to stop the words from coming out. "I asked Cerveny to intervene and work out a deal for me to pay out the amount I owed in installments. The previous payment nearly depleted my account and I have one more to make at the end of this month, provided I can raise enough capital. I sold everything I could in the store and stockroom, regardless of price, in some cases for less than what I'd paid for them to make the first three payments."

"You should have told me sooner," she cried. "Why didn't you? Why, you could have asked me for the money."

His volume rose with hers. "I should be responsible for my own debts, just as I should be responsible for supporting my family, not you. What kind of man am I if I can't do that?"

Lala saw an opening, if she could convince him to let her work. "Why must you take on the burden by yourself, when I'm capable of helping you?"

"You already help me by taking care of Amalie and our

home. That's your job. Mine is earning a living."

"Love, some women want nothing more than to marry, tend house and raise children, and find satisfaction in doing so. However, you married a woman who can do that, and more."

Grimacing, he shook his head. "Not that again. Married women shouldn't work if they have husbands—"

"No, they should cook and clean and raise children, or if they have the means, hire someone else to cook and clean and raise their children," she hollered back.

"Sarcasm doesn't acquit you well."

"I did what you asked. Cared for our daughter, stopped working in your business, even joined a group of other married women who sat in the park near Mother's apartment, discussing laundry, knitting, recipes. Listening to their malicious gossip. I tried that, Josef, and I couldn't stand it. But perhaps you should gather with those women, for they agree with you – married women shouldn't work, 'Only spinsters, and poor unfortunate widows with young children who must, ought to work – or a bastard's mother.'"

"Lala, mind your language!"

Her voice rose with her anger. "When Amalie asked you about men and women's work, you agreed with my mother, but also added you thought it wasn't fair. You said the same thing to me when you shut me out of your business. And yet you still insist I can't work, that I'll be taken advantage of, or somehow hurt your reputation."

"I agree it isn't fair—"

"Mama, Papa, don't fight." Amalie cowered in the doorway, clutching her old stuffed panda and near tears.

"Oh, love, come to Mama." Lala opened her arms, beckoning Amalie to cuddle. The child fell into her mother's embrace and rested her head against her breast while Josef reached across to stroke her cheek.

"Why were you shouting?" she asked.

"We were talking very loud. Papa and I are sorry that we woke you."

Sniffling, she nestled against Lala, her breath audible. Her eyes slowly closed and blinked back open a few times. Lala could feel her daughter's body relax, her breathing slowed. She carried Amalie back to her bed and tucked her in with a soft kiss on her forehead. She then tiptoed back to Josef in the parlor, where he'd poured them both a small glass of cognac.

"I thought we needed this," he acknowledged.

She indulged in a good swallow before setting the glass down. "In Berlin, when you learned I worked for Paulina, you said to me, 'If you're intelligent, artistically gifted and very determined, then why let those talents go to waste.' Why should it be different now that we're married?"

"Because I can't control the world. I can't even control what happens to me all the time, and I'm a man."

"But you can control how you react to it. You don't have to follow what's always been done if it's wrong. So many wrongs continue because people become accustomed to it. How many sellers won't deal with you because you're Jewish?"

"Anti-Semitism is very different than women competing with men in the workplace."

"Not so. There's a difference between choosing not to work and being told you can't, you must marry and raise a family. You scorn those who don't fit your vision of how people ought to live, as so many have scorned our ancestors, and worse," she argued. "If you'd been born four hundred

361

years ago you wouldn't have been allowed to work in a gallery, let alone own one. You'd be driven into an evil necessity like money lending, then damned for being a usurer. That's like forcing someone to eat human flesh and then accusing them of cannibalism."

"I don't see your point."

"You may think you're saying I can't work because of society's rules, but you're endorsing the notion that I can't because of how I was born. You decry anti-Semitism – all prejudice based on religion, nationality, or political beliefs. What is the difference between ignoring or cheating a customer because of her sex and doing the same because of her religion?"

He didn't respond.

Lala would keep her project a secret from him, for Josef wouldn't accept the idea of her working even if it would bring in extra income. Even if it made her happy to earn her place in the world.

She studied his face. The creases on his forehead had deepened, accented by the white hair along his brow that graduated to gray. How much was due to age, how much from worry?

Her first priority had to be her family. "Josef, let's put this discussion aside and return to your debt. If you'd told me sooner, I could have helped by cutting back on expenses."

"That won't make a difference," he muttered.

Concerned by that, she asked, "Do you owe that much?"

After a long silence he admitted, "More than I'm comfortable with, but as I said, I'll take care of it."

"I'm sure there's more that we can do if we work together. What about some of our artwork, or jewelry – why, you could sell that navette ring you bought me, which couldn't have helped your financial problem."

"Absolutely not. You're keeping that ring."

That ring meant more to him than to her. "There must be some pieces in the apartment we can sell—"

He flared, "I'm not selling any more of our personal property to cover this!"

"Shhh, lower your voice – what do you mean, 'any more?' There's nothing missing from the house that I've noticed. What have you sold without telling me?" She tried to think of something she hadn't seen in a while, but his face paled so suddenly it worried her.

"Come now, Lala. A man doesn't buy a ring like that unless he did something he's sorry for."

A wave of queasiness hit her. "Josef, what happened to my ring?"

CHAPTER FIFTEEN

Josef grew paler. Lala emptied her glass of cognac into his before handing it to him. He drank it down as if desperate for it, as a starving man would bolt food. He set the glass on the table. Lala flinched at the sound of it impacting the wood, then the room fell silent save for the mantle clock ticking away the seconds until Josef spoke.

"I needed money quickly to make up for the shortfall. When I saw your ring on the dresser, I thought if I pawned it I could settle my accounts and then buy it back. Unfortunately, the pawnbroker sold the ring before I could return for it." He let out a long breath of air. "I'm sorry, so sorry."

Lala tried to absorb the shock of it, but couldn't fathom Josef doing something so devious. How desperate had he become? "So instead of telling me right away, you kept it a secret all this time, and worse, went deeper in debt buying that gaudy ring. And to think I blamed Ruth—"

"I misled you – deliberately. There, I've said it." He threw up his hands. "I admit it."

"How could you have done something so awful? And for

what? Money? Why didn't you ask me for help?"

"It was foolish and I regret it," he sputtered. "I should never have taken your ring without asking. But more than that, I should never have even considered getting you involved in my financial problem."

"But you're missing the point. Why not, Josef? Why shouldn't you come to me if you have a temporary shortfall? Even if it wasn't temporary."

His expression soured. "Because, for the hundredth time, I'm supposed to take care of my family financially, not you."

"Oh Josef, you've said that over and over, but that's not what marriage—"

Josef's face turned bright red as his voice rose. "Can you hear yourself? No matter what I do—"

She shushed him, begging him not to wake Amalie again.

He leapt up and paced the room like a caged animal. He looked angry enough to pick up something and throw it. His hands flailed as he growled, "When I keep things to myself you never fail to remind me that's not right, and when I'm honest and tell you, then you don't believe me or disregard what I say. No matter what I do I'm always wrong."

Lala took a moment to absorb the sting of his anger. "I can see you saying that...."

"Except...?" he snapped back.

"No excepts. What you said is true, much as I hate to admit it. I'm sorry for treating you that way. There, I've said it as well." She bit her lip. "I haven't been fair with you, either."

He nodded. His color returned to normal.

She cleared the table, giving them both a moment to calm down. "Let's return to the problem at hand, paying off this debt you hold. I promise to refrain from recriminations and listen to what you have to say, and then we'll work together to find a solution. Agreed?"

He nodded again.

"How much do you owe, and to whom?"

"I have all the files in my desk in the bedroom. I'll check on Amalie, then bring the paperwork for us to review."

"I'll make tea."

He rose from the couch. "Better make it coffee. This may take a while."

Lala's recent private meeting with Cerveny refreshed her understanding of finances so she could follow the figures Josef presented to her. Still, after an hour of reviewing his payment agreement, business ledgers, accounting log and receipts, Lala's head spun. The coffee kept her alert but contributed to a growing headache.

"I think I understand this now, Josef. You overextended yourself with the purchase of war art from several dealers, but I agree that much of it will eventually sell. We should also consider museums, as they might take the entire collection rather than try to sell it piece by piece. Mamie mentioned one in London, dedicated to the Great War. You ought to contact them to see if they're interested, and there may be others."

"I like that idea."

"Good. Now what about that forgery. Do you have any recourse with the seller?"

He slumped.

"Who sold it to you?"

"Klement." His pained expression coupled with his posture screamed humiliation.

"When you said, 'What a stupid mistake I made with that,' did you mean mistaking the fake Toulouse-Lautrec as real, or for trusting Klement? Because the forgery was quite good; it's no surprise you thought it was legitimate." Lala poured herself another cup of coffee. "Did Klement sell it to you in good faith, or did he pass it along to you deliberately?"

"I...I can't be sure, except...he referred me to that shady antiques dealer. He also offered to waive half the debt in exchange for your father's desk, to which I said no."

Lala saw through Klement's plan. Taking what he coveted wasn't enough; he wanted to ruin Josef. "Do I know the buyer who urged you to get the drawing?"

"No. I didn't know him either, until he walked into the shop to ask me if I could get it for him." He offered a pained smile. "At the time, I thought he was someone famous, that actor from a movie we saw a few years ago, The Cabinet of Dr. Caligari, but it wasn't him...."

Lala's temper rose. Josef wasn't alone in being made into a fool....

A buzzing in her ears drowned out the sound of Josef's voice, a buzzing so loud it made her nauseated. But she clearly remembered seeing a man who resembled the star of that film, Conrad Veidt, in a café with Klement a year earlier.

Moritz had been right when he warned them not to trust the man. Lala suspected Klement's work with the German government lay behind Moritz's advice, but shortly after she experienced a buzzing sensation that drowned out talk at the dinner table. That sensation occurred when she'd read Willete's condolence letter, and before that, when she and Josef hosted the Chermaks. She'd adored Klement in part because he admired her father's handcrafted furniture so much.

It began during dinner...they'd been talking about her father's masterpiece when something Klement said triggered a vision...

"I sincerely doubt that either Lala or her aunt would willingly part with anything so beautiful."

...Taking her back to her childhood village the day of the pogrom, wandering through ravaged streets, surrounded by death.

Lala swallowed hard. Thinking back to that night, what Klement meant by what he said...

"... would willingly part with anything so beautiful...."

No, she decided. It went beyond his words and his gesture. The mismatched look on his face, with a warm beaming smile and an icy, faraway glaze in his eyes, like storm clouds turning a bright green ocean into the color of cold steel. As a child she'd say his face smiled but his eyes didn't, a sure sign of lying. This went beyond lying, though. Willete referred Lala to her doctor. When Lala gave birth to Jakob he cried out, a good, hearty wail, but fell silent when the doctor whisked him away to be cleaned...Willete did whatever Klement said....

In that instant Lala could see it. This man was pure evil.

Josef yawned. "I can't focus on this anymore."

She left the coffee service on the table. "Ruth can clean up tomorrow. Let's go to bed."

He followed her to the bedroom. The buzz subsided as memories flooded Lala's thoughts. As a child, when she'd given up all hope, Sarah, the woman who became her mother, taught her the best way to repel that evil....

"If you go back, you'll surely die, and they will win. But if you live, then they'll fail, and if you live a long and happy life, then they will fail miserably."

Living well, succeeding despite everything the Chermaks had tried to do – a good first step, but it wasn't enough. Lala didn't know how, or when, but she would make him pay for all the misery he'd brought to her family.

Make him pay dearly.

CHAPTER SIXTEEN

Exhausted from the previous night, Lala and Josef both slept in until the morning sun streamed through the gap in their bedroom window draperies. She left Josef to sleep longer as she rose from their bed and donned her robe.

Ruth had fed Amalie and saw to getting her dressed in one of her new frocks. Lala thanked the woman as she poured herself a cup of fresh coffee.

"Where is Papa?" asked Amalie as she pushed her breakfast plate aside.

Lala stifled a yawn. "He's still asleep, so let's be quiet this morning." They still had much to discuss. "Amalie, would you like to visit Bubbie today?"

The child nodded.

"Ruth, would you be able to take her to my mother's?"

"When would you like me to bring her back? Or will you send the car for her later?"

"We'll bring her home," Lala said as she placed the call to Sarah.

***

With Amalie out of the apartment, Lala and Josef felt free to speak frankly, which despite their pact gradually led to louder voices as he rejected every suggestion she made to settle his debt.

"Why do you have to be so stubborn?" she cried.

"Why do you have to be so dismissive of my judgement?"

"Because you're being stubborn—"

"As are you," he challenged back.

He'd vetoed selling their personal art, furniture, or jewelry. He fought her on scaling back their staff, even temporarily. Nor would he allow Lala to cut household or personal expenses beyond anything frivolous.

Lala had one resource she'd kept in reserve. The time had come to play that advantage.

"I may have a solution. I'll share it with you if you promise to keep an open mind."

"Which makes me think I won't like it."

"An open mind, love."

He leaned back and crossed his arms over his chest. "I'll listen."

"I've no doubt you acted in good faith, but were deliberately deceived by Klement."

"I can't prove it, though."

"That doesn't matter. Our goal is closing this account so we can be rid of that monstrous man. I want us to use my inheritance to pay off the debt."

He couldn't have looked more shocked if she had struck him. "Absolutely not!"

She held up her hand. "You promised to listen, so hear me out. First, as I've long said, it's not my money, it's ours. For better or worse, we share the debt as we share everything, including the inheritance Romy left me. Tainted money at that. What better way to settle an equally despoiled account? Poison to poison."

"I'll never take your money, not under any circumstance." His voice had risen.

She matched it decibel for decibel. "If you could put your stubbornness and your pride aside for one moment—"

He shouted back, "You think my refusal to use your inheritance comes from pride? Are you that naïve?" His voice cracked and he gasped for air. "Lala, thanks to my blunders, I have no money to speak of anymore. We own the house, the shop and the gallery, our possessions, but I'm practically bankrupt."

Startled to see tears filling his eyes, Lala felt helpless. The only time she'd seen him this upset was upon learning of Armin's murder.

"I am an old man with a young wife and child. If anything were to happen to me, I no longer have the resources to leave you and Amalie to live on in comfort. That's more unbearable than being duped." He blinked, sending tears streaming down his face. "You must not touch your inheritance. It may be all you have in the future."

She took him into her arms and cradled him against her, wondering how she could have been so blind. "We'll figure something out, love, something amenable to both of us." She held him close, stroked his back to calm him. "Please don't worry about me, Amalie, or any of this."

When his tears subsided, Lala drew him to her and kissed him. He responded with an urgency that went beyond passion, beyond lust. She lay back on the sofa and pulled him to her. He followed her lead as they tore at each other's clothing to accelerate their frenzied lovemaking. He purged his anger and pain with every thrust, like an animal marking its territory, and she took it. Carried away by the ferocity, she gave herself over to the raw pleasure. When it ended, he lay exhausted atop her, his breath heaving, their bodies soaked in sweat. She thought back to their first kiss in Berlin as they hid from a vicious mob, how it had begun as a comforting gesture to soothe the pain and fear brought on by violence and turned into something very different. She fell in love with Josef at that moment.

More than ten years had passed since then. It seemed like a lifetime ago. Their lives had changed so much, except she remained deeply, passionately in love with Josef. She knew he'd do anything for her and their family. She'd do anything for them as well.

After they dressed, Josef said he needed time to think.

"A walk would do you wonders. Could you go to Mother's and bring Amalie home?"

"What will you do?"

She smiled playfully. "Fluff up the pillows on the parlor sofa before Ruth returns."

He wrapped his arms around her waist and kissed her. "What would I do without you?"

"As long as you can offer more of what we enjoyed earlier, you'll never find out," she teased. That pried a grin out of him.

After he left, Lala straightened up the parlor, then went to the kitchen. Ruth had filled a bowl with apples. As Lala bit into one, the telephone rang. Chewing it quickly, she rushed to answer.

"Lala, it's Paulina." Silence, then, "I need to see you as soon as possible. Can you come to my shop at two today?"

"Can't you tell me now?"

"This needs to be done in person."

Privacy could never be assured over the telephone.

Lala told her, "I'll be there by two o'clock."

Paulina sounded hesitant, but calm, so it couldn't be anything too serious, Lala thought as she hung up.

Lala checked the clock in the parlor; almost ten-thirty. Enough time to make one stop before meeting Paulina. She fetched the box holding her navette ring and dropped it in her purse before going to Josef's shop.

Hanus stood when she entered. "Good morning, Mrs. Smetana. May I be of service to you?"

"Do you have the name and address of the jeweler who appraises the pieces Josef buys?"

"I'm not sure who he is using now, as his former appraiser passed away earlier this year. I believe he's someone recommended to Mr. Smetana by a client."

"Do you know which client?"

"A banker, as I recall."

"Thank you."

She left the shop intent on finding a trustworthy jeweler to appraise the ring, settling on one Mamie favored. She entered the shop and asked the clerk to see the owner.

A middle-aged man with thinning brown hair and a kindly face emerged from the back room. "May I help you?"

"I would like to have a ring appraised. It's old, and I'm curious to know its current value."

"I would be happy to look at it and give you an estimate," he said with a wan smile. The fee he quoted was modest, so she accepted and handed him the opened box.

The jeweler stepped behind a glass-top counter filled with extravagant bracelets. From his pocket he plucked a glass loupe and placed it to his eye as he held the ring beneath it. He didn't take more than a few seconds before repocketing the loupe and returning the ring to Lala.

"What can you tell me about this ring?"

He gave her a sympathetic look. "It's paste."

"Meaning?"

"It looks authentic to the naked eye, but the stones aren't real, and the gold is plated, not solid."

He then wrote down a figure on a business card and handed it to her. She stared at the amount in disbelief, but deep down she knew the estimate, unlike the ring, was real.

So much for selling it to pay down Josef's debt. It would hardly cover the week's groceries.

Lala arrived at Paulina's on time. After a cordial greeting, Miss Horáčková whisked Lala into Paulina's back room where another guest awaited Lala's arrival.

"What a surprise, Mamie. I didn't know you were back in Prague. Are we gathering together for a celebration — I didn't forget your birthday, did I?"

Paulina poured a glass of sherry and offered it to Lala, who declined, until Paulina said, "We asked you to come here today to tell you something...Mamie, you found out. Lala should hear it from you."

Lala sat without thinking and took the proffered glass from Paulina.

"I know what happened to the ring you lost."

Lala put the glass down. "So do I. Josef told me he took the ring and sold it."

Paulina and Mamie turned to each other with stunned looks.

"He sold your ring?" Mamie blurted. "Why would he do that?"

"He had some—excuse me. You said you knew. What did you think happened to it?"

Mamie hesitated, her face tightened as she calculated the situation.

"Mamie, coyness isn't your strong suit. Out with it," insisted Lala.

"I had no idea how the ring got sold, I only know it was found because I saw someone wearing it."

"Are you sure it was my ring?"

"Absolutely, especially considering who I saw wearing it."

"Who?"

"Tell her," urged Paulina.

Lala focused her gaze on Mamie, who stared back with a hard look.

"It was Willete."

CHAPTER SEVENTEEN

"Willete had my ring on?" repeated Lala. "Where could she—"

"I don't know. I only noticed it by accident," said Mamie. "I saw her and Klement last week at some swanky party at the Nocni Klub – by the way, she's expecting again – dining with a German couple, a pair of Bavarian skunks according to Moritz. I wanted to avoid her and Moritz wanted to avoid the Bavarians, but as we ducked out I saw her showing the ring to the skunks, flashing it in their faces and acting like it was the crown jewels."

Paulina refilled the sherry glasses and took a seat across from Mamie. They sipped as Lala told them how Chermak had targeted her family, skimming over how close he'd left Josef to financial ruin.

Paulina nearly spilled her drink when Lala mentioned her theory behind the death of her son. "Ivo expressed his doubts about the doctor's explanation but he never suggested it happened deliberately. Do you really believe they could have planned something so heinous?"

Before Lala could respond, Mamie blurted, "I do" with a

firmness that left no doubt that Lala's theory was plausible.

Mamie continued, "Chermak makes no secret that he hates Communists, but he hates Jewish people more."

"A sham based on an irrelevant coincidence," said Paulina. "Many of the founders of Communism were Jewish,"

Mamie agreed. "That, and he, like many Germans, blames the Jews for losing the War."

"Yes, the current trope that Jews refused to fight and forced surrender," noted Lala.

"But that isn't true," Paulina said. "Ivo told me Jews fought on the side of Germany and the Empire, and in greater numbers than their population. Germany's failures in the field led to their loss."

"The tide turned when our American boys joined the War," Mamie added.

"And then losing her allies one by one in the months leading up to Armistice Day," Paulina said. "Including us."

"When did truth ever matter to hateful people," Lala declared.

"Skip the history lesson, girls," said Mamie. "How are we going to get Lala's ring back?"

"If Josef pawned it and Klement bought it, the transaction was legal," said Paulina.

Mamie snorted, "So what? I don't care, and I doubt Lala cares about that. We have to figure a way to get it back."

"The thought of that disgusting woman wearing my ring makes me sick, but Paulina's right – I have no legal recourse." She glanced around the room. Normally she'd find dozens of dresses waiting for Mamie to try on, or a rack of purchases waiting to be boxed for her. Now the only hint of fashion in the room came from an open storage cabinet filled with evening accessories. This wasn't a shopping excursion. These women were here to help her.

Lala's mind began to plot. "I couldn't do anything transparently illegal or I'd be as awful as them."

"Then what can you do?" wondered Paulina. "If you think she'd be willing to trade it for one of my dresses...?"

"As much as I want the ring back, I can't bring myself to reward her."

Mamie offered, "Maybe we can trick her into returning it to Lala."

Yes, Lala thought, some poetic justice, after Klement tricked Josef. "I may have an idea, but I need more time to work it out. Can I rely on your help?"

"What would you need us to do?" Paulina asked without hesitation.

Lala wasn't sure how she would make this work. Willete's greatest passion was her children, but Lala would never demean herself to use them in a scheme. Willete worshipped her husband and would do anything for him. Lala would build the exchange there. The pieces were almost in place, but she needed one more element to reel Willete in, and she knew how to bait the trap. "Paulina, I may want to borrow one of your dresses."

"Consider it done."

"What about me?" asked Mamie.

"I may need you to drop a bit of gossip to Willete."

"That I can do. Anything else? Go on, ask. I'd love to knock that little chippy down a peg or two."

Paulina let out an embarrassed laugh. "Mamie, you do have a way with words."

But Lala had moved beyond what Mamie had said to how the missing element suddenly materialized. It needed to hinge on Mamie, her circle, and Willete, thought Lala.

Mamie pressed, "So what can I do?"

Lala strode to Paulina's storage cabinet filled with decorative accessories. Glancing through the open shelves, she spotted what she'd hoped to find. She lifted up a sparkling jeweled tiara and held it out toward the women.

"Practice your bowing and curtsying."

Mamie laughed. "You're going to sting her, huh?"

"Mamie, I usually can get the gist of what you say, but that one I can't figure out."

"Sting," she repeated. "Do a con on her."

Baffled, Lala turned to Paulina.

"I believe she means pulling the wool over Willete's eyes."

"Yes, I intend to trick her by taking advantage of her adulation of royalty."

Paulina added, "I can certainly—" A knock at the door interrupted her. "Yes?"

Miss Horáčková entered. "Sorry to disturb you, Madam, but your mother is on the telephone. She says it's important."

"I'll take it in here." Paulina picked up the receiver. "Mama Sarah?...as a matter of fact she's here...." Paulina listened quietly, but her eyes widened and she turned pale. "I'll tell her."

"Paulina, is Mother all right?"

"She's fine, but Josef came to pick up Amalie...she said to tell you he's having trouble breathing."

CHAPTER EIGHTEEN

Mamie instructed her chauffeur to drive Lala to her mother's apartment. Sarah had called the doctor as soon as Josef's breathing became labored. He examined Josef and was preparing to leave as Lala arrived.

"Not to worry, Mrs. Smetana, his heart and lungs are sound. Your husband experienced an attack of nerves brought on by anxiety. I've given him something to calm him, which will cause drowsiness." He closed his medical bag. "He can return to moderate physical activity once the medication wears off, but he must avoid anything stressful for a while, at least a month until his nerves settle down."

"Thank you, Doctor. May I see him now?" she asked as her mother entered the room.

"He's in the guestroom."

"And he's doing fine, just fine, dear. Go see for yourself," Sarah said. "Thank you, Doctor, for coming so quickly." She escorted him to the door.

Lala waited until her mother saw the doctor out to ask, "Where's Amalie?"

"She wanted to be with her papa. You should as well."

383

Lala placed her hand on her chest; she could feel her heart pounding. "Would you take Amalie back to our apartment? Mamie's chauffeur is waiting downstairs, he'll drive you. Then ask Ludovik to pick us up."

"Why didn't Ludovik bring you?"

"That's a story for another time." Lala left it to her mother to surmise a connection to Josef's condition. "Please call Paulina, let her know Josef's feeling better so she won't worry."

"I already have. Should I pack an overnight bag in case you need me to stay?"

"Why not? I'll have Amalie help you," Lala said as she opened the door to the guestroom.

Her eyes meandered across the room. Josef's jacket and tie draped over the back of a chair, his Oxfords sat beside the nightstand, their laces askew. Josef lay motionless on the bed, his shirt half-unbuttoned, his eyes half-closed, his arm around Amalie cuddled against him. Her eyes were red from crying, her breathing more fitful than his.

She sprang up and ran to Lala. "Mama, Papa got sick," she cried softly as Lala picked her up. They clung to each other as Lala observed Josef, his head lolling side to side in response to their voices.

"I heard, love, so I came right away. The doctor said you made Papa feel much better," Lala whispered as she set Amalie down. "Now let me talk to him, while you help Bubbie pack a bag for a visit." The girl hesitated, reluctant to leave. Lala stroked Amalie's cheek. "I'll watch Papa. You go help Bubbie," she added, fighting back her own tears. "She needs you."

Lala's battle for composure faltered as soon as Amalie left the room. She sat on the edge of the bed, taking Josef's hand in hers, and sobbed. Memories of her father's final hours haunted her, the shock of his sudden death...

"*...I am an old man, with a young wife and child. If anything were to happen to me...*"

"Lala, why are you crying?"

She looked to Josef, her eyes stinging with tears. "I'm not ready to lose you."

"You won't, not yet. I promise," he said, his voice as weak as his smile.

She squeezed his hand. Her tears stopped and her resolve strengthened. She said, "You made it very clear how you wish to run our lives, but this episode demonstrates it isn't possible. We have to find another way to solve our financial dilemma and that will take both of us."

He attempted to sit up, but Lala ordered, "Don't. I spent the last two days hearing what you had to say and now you will listen to me. There is only one thing in the world that's precious to me, and that is my family. What's most precious to you, Josef?"

"You and Amalie, of course."

"You'd do anything to care for us, keep us safe and well protected."

"I'd give my life for you both."

"I would prefer you didn't need to."

He attempted a chuckle. "It wouldn't be my first choice."

"And you trust me with raising Amalie?"

The question confused him. "Of course, you're her mother."

"We both know that doesn't always assure the best care for a child. You've entrusted me with raising her, not because I'm her mother or your wife, but because you know I'm capable of doing it. You even agreed not to interfere with my decisions."

"Yes, and you're a wonderful mother."

She released his hand. "But then you have a long history of entrusting me with what's most precious to you, beginning with my engagement to Armin. And again, during the Great War. You asked me to take charge of your factory despite my being an inexperienced woman barely past childhood."

"You didn't have to do it alone, you had—"

"Gershom to help, yes. Another novice with no experience running a factory. But you tasked me with overseeing the conversion to an entirely new product line. Me, a young woman whose sole qualification was her engagement to the owner's son. Yet I did it, successfully."

"I loved you then, Lala, and I still do, more than words could ever express."

She stood and faced him. "Then don't express them with words, but with actions."

"What can I do to prove it to you?"

"Trust me once again. Trust me to take charge of this problem and fix it. You know I can do it, if you stop fighting me."

"Lala, you can't use your inheritance—"

"You've made that clear, and I respect that. I have another option."

"Which is?"

"I can work and earn the money. I want to do this. Please let me—no, I'm no longer a girl and you are not my mother. I'm not asking anymore, I'm telling you I am going to do this. I've been invited to apply for a position."

"I appreciate what you're trying to do, but working in Paulina's shop will not bring in enough to pay the household expenses, let alone what I owe."

"But this will." Opening her purse, she took out Otokar Zahradnik's business card and passed it to Josef.

Josef perused the printed information on the front. "Is this the man who bought the mansion from you?"

"Turn it over," she told him.

He stared at the adjusted figure. "What is this?"

"My budget for a project. He wants me to conjoin two buildings and design the interiors of a new hotel in Prague, a few blocks from our apartment. He'll pay me ten percent of that figure in salary."

Josef's eyes widened. "That would be—"

"A great deal of money, sufficient to pay off our debts with enough left over to keep us solvent. Having seen how much the rooms I'd designed in the mansion contributed to the success of the Excelsior, he contacted me to work on this new venture."

She put the card back in her purse. "A shrewd businessman like him considered me to design and oversee the transformation of a pair of buildings into a successful luxury inn. He'll trust me, a married woman with a child, to handle the project. Will you?"

CHAPTER NINETEEN

Josef tried to sit up again; this time she helped him. His face registered confusion, in part from the sedative the doctor had given him. Lala believed it would make him more acquiescent, though she didn't want him accusing her of taking advantage of him in a drugged state. She'd have to choose her words carefully.

"Josef, I'm saying this now because the medication will keep you calm. I know you don't want to hear this, but you cannot work right now, it's too stressful for you. Your health is more important. Amalie and I need you to get well. Hanus can manage the shop."

"And you propose going to work while I stay home...and what? Sit in the house all day and watch Ruth clean? I can't do that. And who will take care of Amalie? Your mother's no longer able to, not for more than a few hours. Have you thought about that?"

"I have, and the answer is obvious."

"Not to me, it isn't."

"You've always said your children will never be cared for by a nanny."

"And I will not budge on that." Josef swung his legs over the edge of the bed.

"Nor will I." Lala sat beside him, watching for signs of dizziness.

He attempted to stand, then reconsidered. "A child needs a mother—"

"A parent," she corrected him as she picked up his shoes from the floor.

He looked to her, puzzled. "A mother is a parent."

"So is a father."

He still did not grasp what she was proposing.

"Then who will take care of Amalie while you're working?"

Lala handed him his shoes to put on. "You, love."

With Lala's help, Josef finished dressing. He finally felt able to stand and walk around Sarah's apartment to get his footing. Lala led him to the balcony; fresh air would revive him as they waited for Ludovik. Across the way Lala spotted the women sitting on the benches.

Josef breathed in the chilly air. "Everything is topsy-turvy."

"The doctor sedated you, love. You're feeling woozy, but it will pass."

"No, this idea of yours, you going to work and me taking charge of Amalie."

"What has you concerned? What others might think, or if you're up to the task? Because I don't care a whit about the former and I trust you completely with the latter."

"You truly believe I can take care of Amalie as well as you?"

"Better. You have more patience than I do. You have enough common sense not to allow her to do anything dangerous, harmful, or destructive. She adores you and will obey you more and challenge you less than she does me. And you adore her. Imagine spending every day together, going for long walks in the city, or to the park, just the two of you. You can teach her things only a father can teach her."

"But what do I know of dressing her, fixing her hair, or countless other female ablutions?"

"Love, she can comb her own hair and she mostly dresses herself. You know how to open and close buttons, put on shoes, tie her sashes."

"Sashes?"

"It's no different than tying your bowtie. And Ruth won't mind helping with little things like braiding and bows in her hair. As for 'ablutions', she's only five. Just keep Amalie away from my evening clothes. She likes to play dress-up."

"But what about—"

"She'll tell you what she needs help with, and I trust you to figure out the rest. You managed to take care of yourself when you lived alone in Prague. Besides, I'm not going away. We'll still share in parenting her, except you'll take on the primary role."

Lala let him mull on that. She saw Dagmar, Ignace and Terezka gather their knitting and blankets to leave the park.

"Are those the women you used to meet with?" Josef asked.

"Yes, except for Bente, who left the group. She's working for me now; it includes child care on some days. Occasionally she'll bring her two-year-old son to play with Amalie."

"You expect me to mind not only our daughter, but another child?"

"We can reconsider that arrangement. But little Petr's a darling boy. He's thoroughly smitten with Amalie and will do whatever she says." She caressed Josef's cheek. "You might as well get used to that now, love."

Ludovik drove up and parked the automobile in front of Sarah's building. The women froze mid-street and stared at the luxurious vehicle.

"We should leave right now." Josef said as he guided Lala back into the parlor.

"No rush, love. You need to take care going down the stairs. Ludovik can wait."

"Yes, but I want to see the look on those ladies' faces when you enter the automobile with me."

Lala laughed. "You are feeling better."

CHAPTER TWENTY

On the way home in the car, Josef drifted in and out. He'd doze briefly, then pepper Lala with questions, which alternated between her plans for the household to curiosity about Zahradnik's offer. In a coherent moment he asked about the project. She explained her concept.

"How do you envision bringing it about?"

"I've been researching Walter Gropius's philosophy on modern architecture. I'm looking to create a similar sensibility in the interior design of the hotel."

"The architect who designed my factory was influenced by the work of Gropius. But the building you'll be designing is Neo-Renaissance. How can you reconcile both styles?"

"By following a thread inspired by Ivo's research on the Renaissance. I believe we're entering a new period of artistic revitalization amidst political, social and religious upheaval."

"I'll be curious to see how you interpret that into hotel rooms." He stifled a yawn, which Lala attributed to exhaustion rather than the topic.

"I anticipate seeking your advice from time to time."

"I'd like that."

His voice drifted off as he closed his eyes. They rode the rest of the way in silence.

Ludovik parked the car. Josef stumbled getting out, so Ludovik helped Lala escort him into the building and up the stairs. When he entered, Amalie rushed to greet him, which brought out a glow in Josef's face.

Sarah emerged from the kitchen wearing an apron. "You're looking much better, Josef," she said. "Are you hungry, or would you rather rest awhile?"

"I'm ravenous."

"Good," said Sarah. "The food's ready and the table is set. Let's eat."

Sarah had sent Ruth home early and prepared the evening meal herself. The four had dinner together, with Sarah helping Amalie at the table. Josef watched Sarah as she cut Amalie's meat and dumplings into small pieces before setting the plate before the girl. Lala could practically see him taking mental notes.

The food perked up Josef. After they finished eating, Sarah offered to read to Amalie before bedtime.

"But then I want Papa to read me a story," she announced.

"Bubbie goes first, then Papa," Josef said.

"That's right," said Sarah. "Or as my mother always said, age before beauty. Come, dear." She followed Amalie to her room.

Lala linked her arm in Josef's. "You ought to get to bed early tonight."

"Tempting, but perhaps I've had enough excitement for one day."

"Love, I meant to rest," she caressed his cheek. "But I like how you're thinking. Shall we wait in the living room until Mother has finished reading to Amalie?"

Josef sat in his favorite chair, facing Lala's Monet painting. Lala offered him a drink, which he declined. She straightened the grouping of photographs on the mantle, including the picture of Amalie taken on her second birthday by Zoe.

She'd taken many that day; all had been good, but this one, in half profile, looking away from the camera, illustrated her daughter's spirit. Little Charis, off-camera, had grabbed a stuffed rabbit and made it dance, eliciting a marvelous response from Amalie. Zoe took full advantage of the parlor's windows, two sources of natural light that backlit and shone on Amalie's face. Her eyes wide and curious, her mouth half smiling and partially open as if speaking, her sitting position engaged with her surroundings. Similar to the way Armin painted Lala over a decade earlier.

Josef interrupted her thoughts with another question. "Lala, will you be doing all your work at the hotel? You'll need an office there."

"I haven't gotten that far, but I might. Meanwhile, I've set up a small office here."

He looked around. "Wherever you put it, you hid it well."

She extended her hand. "Come, I'll show you."

He seemed surprised when she guided him out of the apartment, more so when she led him up the stairs. She unlocked the door to the attic room and pulled the cord to turn on the light.

"When did you create this?" he asked.

"It took over a month, working a half hour here and there, when Amalie napped or visited my mother.

Occasionally Ruth would watch her for a few minutes if I had to run upstairs for something, and you've seen me sketching in the parlor or the breakfast room."

"And you kept it a secret from me all this time."

She sat on the edge of the desk. "Are you being rhetorical? For us to make this plan work—"

"No accusations," he said, the truth evident in his tone.

"Although we'll reverse roles for a time, we still need to work closely together, even more so considering how Jakob's death tore us apart. During shiva for my father I remember my Aunt Naomi saying, 'Why does it have to take a tragedy to bring people together?' If we'd grown closer after our loss, all this might have been avoided." She lowered her head. "I'm sorry, we said no recriminations."

"You grieved in the same way I grieved after losing Armin. We're more alike than you think. We both lost our first family to violence, and we lost baby Jakob, but we tried to deal with our grief independently instead of depending on each other for strength and comfort."

"No Josef, I remember you tried to help me, but I pushed you away, and everyone else."

"I didn't try enough."

"You did, but I'd been so unprepared for what happened, I couldn't accept it." She would wait until Josef's health improved to tell him her theory about Jakob's death.

He studied the blueprints for the building Lala had pinned up on the walls. "This is quite an undertaking."

"It's larger than our building, but I saw to that with little problem."

"As I recall, several of the workmen would only respond to me."

"If I decide to hire any of them again, I will remind them

of that, and let them know if their attitude doesn't change, I'll dismiss them on the spot."

Josef spun around. "When did you become so formidable?"

"You forget, love. I raised an obstinate and defiant daughter, who's probably wondering why her papa isn't there to read her a story as promised. Go downstairs and I'll join you in about an hour. I have some work to do."

"If I can help you—"

"Not with this problem, love."

He went downstairs and as soon as she heard him close their apartment door she sat at her desk, intent on writing a plan to get her ring back. Picking up a pencil, she pondered ideas. A sting, Mamie had called it. How apt. Lala wanted Willete to get stung, make that woman suffer; her husband as well. Visions of revenge rolled around in her mind.

She put her pencil down.

With all the responsibilities she had to assume, she couldn't concern herself with Willete. Instead she would do what she'd always done – concentrate on taking care of her family as well as ridding their lives of every mark of the Chermaks' betrayal. And she would make changes to the house to accommodate their new living arrangement, as she had during the Great War. Aside from her attic office, she'd convert the dining room into a workspace for Bente and her, near enough to watch Petr when Josef and Amalie took their walks.

Tomorrow, Lala thought, I'll contact Paulina and Mamie to thank them for watching out for me. Josef and I will explain to Amalie how and why our parenting roles will change.

Miko Johnston

After that, she would begin the hard work of converting a Renaissance-revival mansion and the adjacent building into a 20th century masterpiece. Tonight, she'd tuck in her daughter, kiss her mother goodnight and cradle her husband in bed until he fell asleep.

CHAPTER TWENTY-ONE

When Bente arrived with Petr, Lala made introductions and explained the new arrangement. After Josef and Amalie left for a morning stroll and Bente had put Petr down for his nap, the women adjourned to the dining room.

Bente listened as Lala explained her concept of borrowing from the classical style and reinterpreting it into something modern, yet compatible with the period features of the building. "I'm not sure what you're aiming for, Lala," she said. "I understand the words but I can't visualize the concept from them."

"I haven't worked out all the details yet in terms of execution. You could help me with that. What part of my explanation wasn't clear?"

"About paralleling the artistic creativity of the Renaissance with the current era. It sounds very complicated, and it shouldn't."

"What do you suggest?" Lala asked.

"If you want to convince Mr. Zahradnik, try to explain your concept in simpler terms," Bente suggested. "Then once you've gotten his interest, go into more detail. My husband says people react more to catchy slogans than to drawn out intellectual discourse."

"Good advice. What about this – I want to convert a Renaissance revival mansion into a modern luxury hotel that blends the artistry of both the Renaissance and the current era."

"Much better. Now let's see what you've planned."

Lala spread out some of the drawings she'd made. "The ground level will have a restaurant, a grand salon for galas and a few smaller rooms for intimate gatherings, which will attract locals and visitors to the city. This allows the hotel to promote itself as a place to gather as well as to stay, thus creating another source of income. In keeping with the modern ethic only natural material will be used, and a color palette inspired by nature."

"What about the upper floor?'"

"Currently there are eight chambers, including two larger rooms above the original building's entrance. The other six are generously sized. They could be combined to make three suites, but five rooms might be insufficient. I'm leaning toward conjoining two smaller rooms in the back into a suite. That will give us seven."

"Seven is a lucky number," Bente said.

"Seven chambers. I like the sound of that. And I'll carry out a homogeneous design plan in each with slight variations once we come up with a theme."

Bente asked, "By that do you mean a style or design element each room will have in common?"

"Yes. I'd like your help with that. Have you any ideas?

"I'd have to think about it."

"I find going by instinct promotes creativity," Lala told her. "Say whatever comes to mind and I'll jot everything down. They won't all be worthwhile, but I find the more you leave your mind open to ideas the better they flow."

"Perhaps something unique to the city. Prague has so much culture – the opera, the symphony—"

"Theater." Lala scribbled notes as they took turns spouting possibilities. After the first few suggestions the ideas came at a more rapid pace.

"What about nature?" Bente suggested. "Flowers, for example, or trees."

"Art."

"History."

"The seasons."

Ideas kept pouring out. Lala turned the page and wrote until they could think of nothing more. Lala read the list out loud. Each suggestion was met with a tepid reaction or dismissed.

Bente held up one of Lala's sketches. "I feel we're missing the obvious here. How do we describe the vision you're after?"

They heard Petr stirring. Bente went to get him while Lala looked over her sketches.

Seven chambers. Seven. A prime number. A lucky number. What else did seven mean?

Bente returned with Petr in her arms. The boy rubbed the sleep from his eyes and asked, "Where Amalie?"

"She'll be back soon," Bente told him.

Lala noticed the boy peering down at the drawings on the table. "What do you see, Petr?" she asked.

He pointed to a sketch of one of the chambers and his finger mimicked the arch of the window. "Circle," he said, then with his finger drew the rectangle of the bed. "Square."

Lala looked to Bente, who nodded and said, "It certainly captures the spirit."

"And the simplicity. Circle and Square. I like it."

Bente hoisted Petr up on her hip. "I'll let you work while I take him into the parlor."

"Why don't I join you and we'll wait there for Josef and Amalie to return."

"How did you convince him to take charge of your daughter while you work?" Bente asked. "Not long ago you didn't want him to know about your project."

"Things change."

Following Lala's schedule, Bente arrived in the morning and put Petr down for a nap in the guestroom while Josef took Amalie out until lunch. Bente and Lala worked together in the dining room until Petr awoke, then Bente would mind him while Lala kept working. When Josef and Amalie returned, they gave the children lunch and let them play before naptime while the adults ate. Josef cataloged his war art and the women resumed working until the children woke from their nap. Bente took Petr home afterward and Lala continued until dinner while Josef minded Amalie. It took a few days to adjust, but by the end of the week, their routines had settled into an easier rhythm.

Josef's spirits improved; he slept well and suffered no serious anxiety, which helped Lala make steady progress.

On Sunday, they agreed to take a well-earned break and bring Amalie to her grandmother's for an overnight visit. By nightfall, an evening of passionate lovemaking left them both gasping. They curled up together and caught their breath.

Lala caught Josef smiling. "I'm glad I can still make you happy," she said.

He leaned over and kissed her forehead. "This week has

been a most pleasant surprise, caring for Amalie, more than I would have thought. She's full of opinions about everything, and has such a delightful way of looking at the world. She takes it all in, asks questions and soaks up knowledge. Her curiosity knows no bounds, it seems. We spent a morning wandering Petřín Hill and she astounded me with her knowledge of the trees, plants and birds, even insects." His smile broadened at the memory. "I find myself rediscovering so much through her eyes and her thoughts. It's...."

"Refreshing?"

"Yes, that's the word. Refreshing."

"Remember that, love. The day will come when all that exuberance and curiosity will feel exhausting."

"I doubt that."

Lala smiled but said nothing. Better he discover that himself.

"I especially enjoy our outings. At first I worried people would think it odd to see a father taking care of his young child, but they probably assume I'm enjoying the company of my granddaughter." He chuckled at that, but his smile faded into a grim line. "Sometimes I think that, had life turned out differently, instead of raising a young child, I would be spending afternoons with my grandchild."

"As much as I loved and adored Armin, we could never have made a marriage work."

They lay next to each other in a loose embrace. Several minutes passed in silence.

Josef propped himself on his elbow. "I don't know why, but being with Amalie makes me think not only of her future, but of the past, yours and mine. There's always been a piece of you missing because of what happened to your first family. I never understood it, until I recognized I, too, had a piece

403

missing. I didn't have a chance to make amends with Armin before his death, let him know I much I loved him. All the more painful because the circumstances that led to his murder made me see I could have accepted his inclination toward men and still loved him, but sadly that realization came too late.

"Losing our son brought back that sense of loss," he said with sadness evident in his voice, "but when I saw how much you suffered, and how nothing I could say or do would change that, it tore me up inside. It also clouded my judgement, for I don't believe I would have taken so many missteps, nor fallen so far into Klement's trap, had my reasoning been sounder." He shook his head. "I never would have taken your ring."

She hadn't told him who'd bought it, or how worthless its replacement turned out to be, for fear of upsetting him.

"And now I've made you suffer more," he continued. "I don't deserve you."

"Don't ever say that. You saved my life. You made my life. I would never have become the person I am without you."

He kissed her. "I promise I will spend the rest of my life, whatever time that may be, making you happy."

"You already do, love."

"Not enough, not yet. But I will. I absolutely will."

CHAPTER TWENTY-TWO

With Josef caring for Amalie, Lala could utilize Bente more for her project. Lala sent her to search out sources for materials and labor. Josef occasionally included Petr in his outings and after both children had their afternoon naps, he would read to them.

When she worked alone, Lala shifted to her attic office. Being in a separate environment purposed for work helped her focus. With winter approaching it had turned cold, so she put on one of Josef's old sweaters, wrapped a wool scarf around her neck and continued refining her sketches. The circle and square concept defined the geometric nature of her designs. It fit beautifully in the restaurant with its round tables and square-backed chairs. The grand salon featured semi-circular banquettes with tables surrounding most of the perimeter like a ring of horseshoes, with a series of square lighting fixtures hanging over the dance floor in the center of the room. Having celebrated her seventh wedding anniversary that year, she added a touch of anniversary symbols to each of the seven chambers – a paper lampshade in number one, a leather chair in room three. With that complete she set about

405

making the final versions in pen and ink renderings.

Beds built into low L-shaped units of chests and shelves. A bed with a free-standing wall headboard that rotated so guests could sleep facing the windows, or reverse it to block sunlight. A mattress, floating on an island of wood in the center of a room, surrounded by shallow bookcases and cabinets close enough to reach a book or robe while in bed.

And her finale – chamber seven, which spanned the width of the building. A bi-level suite with a sitting area in the lower portion and along the windowless back wall a platform, three-quarters of a meter high and over two meters deep, containing a built-in chest of drawers and a desktop below. Four steps led to the upper level where a bed would be placed on the platform, centered below a coved ceiling. Certainly no other hotel in the world would feature rooms as unique as hers.

Too unique?

Doubts crept in. The calendar added to her frustration; she had less than a week before making her presentation to Zahradnik. What if he didn't like what she created? Her family's future hinged on this job and the money it would bring in. She pushed her qualms away and set about making her final renderings. Josef had said he'd wait until they were done before offering his opinion.

Ink drawings in hand, Lala returned to the apartment to call Paulina. The time had some to tell her sister about her project. She trusted Paulina's judgement and taste, and who better to know what would appeal to Lala's prospective clients – affluent modernists.

She went to the kitchen to find an empty pot sitting on the stove, a water-filled basin in the sink and no food on the counter or work table.

Ruth entered with an armful of potatoes, looking flustered. "Missus, I'm glad you're here. Will this be enough for dinner?"

Lala glanced at the five potatoes Ruth set in the sink. "It would depend on what you're making with it."

"But that's just it. This is all Mr. Smetana wanted me to make. Potatoes, boiled whole in their jackets, served with soured cream and salt. No meat, no fish. Just potatoes."

Lala attempted a smile. "He probably has some special treat planned, Ruth. Cook the potatoes as he asked. How long will it take?"

"About an hour." Ruth took the pot from the stove and filled it with water.

"Perfect. I've an errand to run. I should be back by then. Before you start the potatoes, would you call my sister and tell her I'm on my way?"

Lala strode briskly, prodded by worry. Josef asked for a peasant meal. Was he being overly cautious or had their finances deteriorated that badly? He'd apprised her of their savings and spending, so she assumed the former, but it still disturbed her. And she lied to Ruth, too ashamed to admit the family was struggling. Potatoes for dinner. They hadn't eaten so meagerly since they'd had to do so during the Great War. The idea unnerved her, for there was no reason to subject Amalie to their financial dilemma unnecessarily, should it be unnecessary. Her rapid pace and fretting left her out of breath as she reached Paulina's shop.

"She'll join you shortly." Miss Horáčková said as she brought Lala into Paulina's quarters to wait. Lala glanced at the dresses on the mannequins, dresses that not long ago she could have ordered for herself without a thought. A few weeks of eating potatoes and I won't fit into any of those gowns, she thought with perverse humor.

Miss Horáčková brought Lala a cup of tea. "Madam should be down any minute. She's finishing up with the head seamstress in the factory."

"This is a personal matter and she's busy. Perhaps I should wait until she's home."

"That won't be necessary, Mrs. Smetana. She asked me to make you comfortable while you wait. May I bring you something, perhaps some pastries with your tea?"

The offer tempted her, but she said, "Thank you, no. I must watch my figure."

Miss Horáčková smiled and nodded in understanding. "Then I won't intrude any longer." She closed the door behind her.

Lala went to look more closely at an evening dress that appealed to her, a long-sleeved sheath in plum velvet. Unlike most fashionable dresses that hung in a straight column, this one nipped in at the waist. Gathered fabric waterfalled from a beaded band above each hip, adding a bit of flounce and ease of movement to the skirt.

"I knew you'd like that one," she heard Paulina say from behind her. "I had you in mind when I designed it. Remember that dress with the hobble skirt that I made for you, with the hidden trousers underneath?"

"How could I forget? It's what caught the attention of—" Lala fell silent.

"Romy Smetana, the day you introduced us," Paulina finished her sentence.

"You needed a little help from me then. Now I'm here to ask you for help." Lala detailed her new venture to Paulina.

"With Josef having to rest, this is the perfect opportunity for me to launch my business. Would you look at my designs and give me your opinion?"

Lala spread the drawings across the table. She explained the basic concept, using the catchy phrases she and Bente formulated.

"Do you think the designs are too unconventional?" Lala asked.

Paulina mulled that as she held two chamber sketches up, side by side. "If you were designing a hotel with dozens of rooms, then perhaps. But with seven rooms, no." She laid the drawings on the table. "I began my business selling mass appeal clothing. Now I cater to a select clientele. My clothes have to appeal to them, and often to a single client. That is how I see your rooms. Different, and yet approachable and intuitive. They're ingenious. You've stripped away the fussiness and what's left is practical and intriguing, like the clothing I design if you don't mind my saying so."

"Mind? I can think of no higher compliment." Lala exhaled. "What a relief. Thank you, Paulina. I'd been having doubts, but your encouraging words knocked them away."

"Then you should celebrate your new project with a new dress." She unbuttoned the gown on the mannequin.

Lala stood and gathered up her drawings. "I didn't come to shop today, only for advice."

"Can't you do both?" She held up the dress to make her point.

"Perhaps another time, but now I must focus on making this project a success."

"I'm certain it will happen for you. I hope you're not as worried as you sound." Paulina returned the dress to the mannequin. "Lala, don't think you have to be a success immediately. Look how long it took me to build my business. You're putting far too much pressure on yourself. Naturally you want to succeed in this venture, but you've time to build your success."

Lala began to tremble. "I must go. Ruth will have supper on the table—" She tried to leave but Paulina grabbed her by the wrist.

Paulina's eyes grew dark and frown lines creased her face. "What is going on with you?"

Lala felt her knees weaken. She sat down and buried her face in her hands.

"You're scaring me, Lala. You're acting as if your life depends on this project."

Lala couldn't bear to look at her when she responded, "It may."

CHAPTER TWENTY-THREE

With tears blinding her eyes, Lala told Paulina the truth about her family's financial situation. "Before, I wanted to take Zahradnik's offer to prove to myself I could work and raise a family. But when Mother called about Josef's health scare, everything changed. I feared Josef would die. I knew I had to take the job and make it a success."

Paulina listened without comment. "I'm so sorry about your predicament." She handed Lala a handkerchief.

Lala touched it to her eyes. "You were right, our future does depend on this project."

"Right as well about being scared by your behavior, and frankly, hurt that you didn't ask for help. Why do you always think you're the only one who can take on problems in the family? You did the same during the Great War, working in Josef's factory and running two households."

"Mother couldn't do it, and you were with child. What choice did I have, then or now? Josef must rest and avoid any undue stress, and he won't touch my inheritance, with good reason."

Paulina walked to her desk, opened a drawer and pulled

411

out a folder bulging with papers. "Miss Horáčková?"

Her assistant entered. "Is there something you need, Madam?"

Paulina handed her the folder. "Would you please total these invoices for me?"

Miss Horáčková disappeared with the folder.

Lala put the handkerchief on the table. "I ought to go now. And thank you for not insulting me by offering me money."

"You're not leaving yet. We have one more issue to settle."

"Which is?"

"You won't get paid until you submit your designs and Zahradnik approves them. Can you manage until then?"

Lala hadn't mentioned the potato dinner. "We haven't had to lay off any of our staff."

"Do you have enough money for food?"

Lala looked away. "Nothing extravagant, but we won't starve."

Miss Horáčková returned with the folder and a piece of paper. Paulina took them and thanked the woman before she left.

"Please give me a moment." Paulina sat at her desk with the paper and a pencil. Lala saw numbers written on the paper. Paulina appeared to be doing a calculation.

"What is that all about?" asked Lala.

"This – " Paulina rested her hand on the folder – "is a record of every purchase made by Mamie. And this – " she held up the paper – "is a total of those purchases." She opened another desk drawer and brought out a check ledger. "I'm writing you a check for ten percent of her purchases, a commission payment which you earned and deserve, minus twenty-one koruny."

"Don't do that, Paulina. I won't accept it."

"You will accept it." She wrote the check and handed it to Lala. "Take it."

Lala refused again.

"Then explain to me why you'd take a commission from Zahradnik for your work but not from me."

"Because I didn't work for you."

Paulina cried, "Really? Who designed my shop? Found financial backing for my business? Brought in the client that propelled my success? For that matter, who took me in when I lost my home and shop in the Great War, helped raise my son, sacrificed food from her plate to feed Jacub and me? You say you don't deserve it, but who does more than you?"

Lala acknowledged Paulina had said exactly what Bente had told her. "All right, but ten percent is too high. Make it five percent, for Amalie's age. Perhaps it will bring me luck."

"I'll make it seven percent, for seven rooms and seven years of marriage. And seven is a lucky number." She tore up the first check and wrote out another. "Seven percent, minus twenty-one koruny." She opened her purse and took out twenty koruny. "You'll need some money on hand until you can cash that check."

"What's the last koruna for?"

"I may be partly to blame for your troubles. Buying out Josef from my business left him flush with cash while he was still grieving the loss of your son, which could have contributed to his financial blunders. I'm reinstating him as my business partner, and the cost to buy back in is one koruna." Paulina put the check register back in the drawer and closed it with a bang. "Use some of that cash for marketing on your way home. Buy meat, or that fish you like.

Otherwise, knowing you, you'll eat nothing but potatoes for a week."

Lala rushed through the front door into the kitchen. "Ruth, I'm sorry to be so late." Lala handed her the package with the fish she'd bought. "I asked the fishmonger to fillet this, so fry it simply and we'll eat when it's done."

Amalie was very talkative throughout dinner. When Josef had been working late hours Lala and Amalie often dined alone. Now that she spent her days with her father, she recounted their time together at the table to Lala.

"...and then Papa put our picnic lunch in a basket and we walked along the river and crossed the bridge to Strelecky Island, but it was too cold to sit on the grass so we wrapped ourselves in blankets and had our picnic on a bench and watched the swans and I tossed them bits of my lunch and you know what? Swans like bread but they won't eat pickles. And then...."

Lala smiled as she listened. At times she missed being with Amalie as she embarked on new adventures, but hearing her daughter's experiences with Josef, the excitement in her voice, the adorable way she described it all was something Lala would never have experienced if she'd been the one taking Amalie to those places. Josef also chose activities Lala would not have thought of, so it expanded their daughter's experiences in a positive way.

"Did Papa tell you that he and I picnicked in Strelecky Park many years ago, before you were born? And we ate the same thing."

"I'd forgotten about that," Josef said.

"Did you enjoy your fish, love?" she asked him.

He set his fork down. "It was quite a surprise."

"I surprised someone today, too, Mama," Amalie interjected. "We saw a man standing on the street near St. Nicholas Church playing music on a, an..." her lips moved silently as she tried to parse out the word. "An accordion." She said it slowly, enunciating each syllable. "And he had a plate with hellers and koruny in it and when people passed by, they put more money in his plate. Papa wanted to keep walking but the man played a song I knew so I sang it for him and you know what? He said people should give me koruny for singing." She paused to take a breath. "When I grow up I want to stand in the street and sing for koruny. I enjoyed the fish, too, Mama. I could eat fish for dinner every night."

Lala glanced at Josef when she said, "Then Papa will ask Ruth to buy more tomorrow."

After they put Amalie to bed, Lala and Josef sat together in the parlor, where she told Josef the source of their entrée.

"I wish you hadn't told Paulina about our financial situation. It's embarrassing. And you can tell her I will not take any more money from her, and neither will—"

Lala held up her hand. "You may turn down her offer if you want, but please don't make decisions for me. The commission I earned from Mamie's business will keep us afloat until after I meet with Zahradnik, and with any luck we won't need anyone else's money after that. Besides, I didn't visit Paulina to tattle, I sought her opinion of my concept for the hotel."

"Is it completed?"

"Would you like to see it?"

"Very much."

"Let's go into the dining room."

She brought in her drawings and laid them across the table as she briefly explained her concept. He studied each one, taking his time.

She wondered when he would say something. She valued his opinion as much as Paulina's. If he criticized her work, or found fault with it, would she crumble? No, she decided. She'd listen and evaluate his comments for merit, then separate any personal animus he might hold for having to rely on her as the current breadwinner.

He picked up the drawing of Suite Seven.

"I have a suggestion."

Keeping her voice neutral, she said, "I'm listening."

"I think you should move out of the attic and into my office. You'll be much more comfortable there during the winter months when you'll be working on the next phase of your project." He placed the drawing back on the table.

"There will only be a next phase if he agrees with my concept," she reminded him.

"I recall Zahradnik as a shrewd businessman with an instinct for what his clients want," Josef said. "He proved that with the Excelsior. I expect he has the foresight to recognize the brilliance of the work you've done here."

"Brilliance?"

"The way you adapted components of modern architecture to create furnishings, and on top of that blended them seamlessly into a building in a more traditional style. It's fresh, exciting and very original."

"Then you believe Zahradnik will accept this?"

"He'd be a fool not to."

His opinion stirred more than her confidence. She took him by the hand. "Let's go to bed."

CHAPTER TWENTY-FOUR

Standing before her open closet, Lala pulled dresses, suits, whatever she thought would be appropriate to wear on this, the most important day in her working life. The day her family's fortunes would be saved or destroyed...

"Mrs. Havlik, what do you think this room lacks?"

The woman thought for a moment. "I would have to say it's what all the rooms in this house lack. People. A room is just a place to store things unless it's occupied."

"Whatever made me think of that?" she asked her reflection in the mirror. A good reminder, though.

Lala held the first of two final choices against her, a pared-down morning dress, tres chic in Copen blue. Next she posed with a skirt and matching jacket in a subdued charcoal. The dress embodied her creative side, the gray, paired with a white blouse, imparted a businesslike aura. Which would be better? Luckier? Whatever she wore would forever be entwined with Zahradnik's decision.

Her confidence surged with the soft aqua ensemble. She returned the gray suit to her closet and dressed. She pinned her hair into a conservative knot, fastened the buckles on her most comfortable shoes, and forewent jewelry. She decided not to wear her ladylike cloche, instead choosing her pewter rolled brim hat with a pleated band, which resembled a man's pork pie hat. Her ensemble combined modern chic with classic style, echoing the designs she created for the hotel. She checked her reflection in the mirror once more; a smartly dressed woman looked back.

"Mama?" Amalie called through the door.

"Come in, love."

Amalie stared in silence as Lala gathered her purse, gloves and portfolio.

"How does Mama look today?"

The child's head moved from side to side as she considered the question. "You look like a painting."

"I do? What kind of painting?"

"A pretty one."

"Thank you, love. Will you go tell Papa I'm about to leave?"

"Papa isn't here."

Lala's gloves fell from her grasp. "He left?"

"Someone very important called him on the telephone before breakfast."

"Who was it?"

Amalie shrugged. "I don't know."

"Then how do you know it was someone important?"

"Because Papa called him 'sir'. Papa never calls anyone 'sir' except the knights in my storybook. He said he had to go somewhere, but he would be back before you had to leave."

She wondered if Moritz had arranged some business transaction with one of his royal relatives. She could understand him dashing out for that. But she had to leave now. She couldn't risk arriving late to the eleven o'clock meeting.

Her hand flew to her brow. *No, no, no!* Had her rapid breathing caused her fretting, or the other way around?

This is too much pressure, she thought. From the moment Zahradnik considered her to design his next hotel until the painting of her youthful self had inspired the project's concept, the feeling of weight on her shoulders didn't go unnoticed by Bente or Paulina. Mamie said it best – "Good pressure kicks you in the drawers, and bad pressure knocks you down."

Fretting wouldn't steady her nerves, only paralyze her thinking. *Balance.*

It was ten-thirty, enough time to make the fifteen minute walk to the site. Where was Ruth? She hadn't arrived yet, and it would take too long to bring Amalie to her mother's or Bente's. How could Josef—

She heard the front door slam and footsteps rushing down the hallway.

"Lala? I'm back."

Josef.

"Where's Ruth?"

"She needed the week off." He kissed her cheek. "I'm sorry I had to rush off like that, but Cerveny called about an urgent matter."

Cerveny – the "sir" Amalie referred to. Lala put on her coat. "Was it worth almost shattering my nerves today of all days?"

Josef's face brightened and his eyes practically glowed. "I believe it will be."

Lala willed herself to be calm, to stand in place without tapping her toe or nervously pacing, to relax her stiffened posture as she waited in front of the Tržiště Street mansion. Arriving ten minutes early helped, but once she got there time slowed and each minute that passed felt like an hour. Memories cropped up of waiting in the lobby of the Hotel Grande in Berlin days after the Great War began, until her family could flee the city and return home.

Eleven o'clock came and went. Lala, more nervous than before, wondered if she'd made a mistake about the time, or the date – no, he scheduled their meeting for today at eleven. She forced herself to remain calm.

At eleven-twenty the limousine parked in front of the mansion. Smolak exited, looking very grave, and opened the door for Zahradnik.

"My apologies, Mrs. Smetana. An unforeseen dilemma caused our delay."

Smolak lowered his head.

Zahradnik continued, "I have some rather unpleasant news, Mrs. Smetana."

Lala braced herself.

"It is my sad duty to inform you that my cook, Mrs. Havlik, collapsed this morning and passed away. A heart attack, apparently."

"I'm very sorry, Mr. Zahradnik. What a loss. She was a fine woman, so kind to my family during some difficult times. Please send my condolences to your staff and her family."

He nodded. "I will."

"Strange, she came to mind earlier...." *Don't think about that now.*

"You're intuitive, a good quality to have." He took a ring of keys from his pocket and opened the front door leading to the mansion's tiled foyer. "Shall we proceed?"

Lala had organized her renderings in the order of their

walk-though, beginning with the lobby. She explained her basic concept in the mansion's foyer as he unlocked the second door. As they entered each room she gave Zahradnik the accompanying rendering with a brief explanation of her plans for the space.

He liked her idea of placing a cocktail bar in the lobby. "And that adjacent alcove?" he asked, referring to the niche that had troubled her earlier.

"Three private rooms for business meetings or intimate gatherings."

As they entered the next space he looked at the rendering and asked, "Why is the dining room twice the size we'd need for our clientele?"

"It's meant to be a restaurant, so residents and visitors alike can dine and enjoy the ambiance." She added, "It will provide another stream of income, as well as build word-of-mouth enthusiasm."

He continued through the main floor, glancing at the renderings as he inspected the space, until they reached the future ballroom. "You don't intend to keep the gold-plated fixtures, crystal chandeliers, or antique furnishings?"

"The idea is to redefine luxury in more modern terms."

He looked around the space again, then shuffled the renderings to the back of his stack. "Let's see the chambers upstairs."

They went from room to room, in order. He had many questions about the designs, which she responded to with her reasoning for the choices. Lala tried to determine whether he didn't understand or disagreed with her concept. Remembering what Paulina advised, she addressed his concerns by showing him how despite the uniqueness of the designs, the chambers would function in the same way as a standard hotel.

"All of the rooms are spacious. However, while some people like expansiveness, others prefer a room that's cozy and secure. I've provided both," she explained as he studied two renderings.

"And this movable section?" he asked, indicating the free-standing wall headboard.

"The windows in this chamber face east, and not everyone likes morning sun."

They ended the walk-through with the two smaller rooms in the rear of the landing. "I intend to combine them into one large suite." She opened both doors so he could get a sense of the space. "Each room has limited windows, which is why I took advantage of the wall space and created the platform. It functions as an elevated bedroom, giving the sense of two rooms without walls. It will appear more spacious than it really is."

"The platform also serves as the top of the dresser and the desk?"

"Yes, blending storage, work and sleeping into one seamless stretch."

He shuffled through her drawings one by one, his expression unreadable, and upon reviewing them all, returned them to the portfolio for Smolak to carry. "I can say with absolute certainty I've never seen rooms like these before. They are quite...distinctive; one could say radical. The question is will customers be intrigued enough to stay in them."

"Enough to fill seven chambers. I agree, not everyone may want to stay here, but most couldn't afford to. However, with a hotel of this size, access will be limited, like all things exclusive. Do you spend much time in Prague anymore, Mr.

Zahradnik?"

"Not since the Great War ended."

"It's changed. We're compared to Paris now as a lively and progressive city. Prague has become a haven for artists, architects, writers and photographers. Why do they flock here? For the creative atmosphere. People are open to new ideas, much like Italy during the Renaissance."

"But will our guests understand?"

He needed more assurance. "The rooms puzzle you because at first glance they do not look like what you expect, but they will be crafted from high quality materials and introduce designs appropriate for their purpose. They have drama, which will entice customers out of curiosity. But to appeal to guests, to draw them back again and again takes more than familiarity. They must function in an appropriate and obvious way."

He still looked unsure.

She tried another approach. "I'd like you to look at each room and imagine yourself checking into it with your luggage and briefcase. Where would you unpack and store your clothing? Prepare for a business meeting, or a night out? Read the morning paper? Sleep? My designs require no explanation. I've planned out every detail, from placement of the light switches to seating for guests regardless of their size. You enter any of these chambers and intuitively know where to stow your belongings. Where to sit and where to sleep. When you're in a foreign location, what can be more comforting, more relaxing...more luxurious than that?"

Zahradnik rubbed his chin. "I understand what you're saying but I'm not convinced yet. I need time to consider if I want to risk going with your design or choose something more traditional." He gestured to Smolak, who presented him with his hat. "Give me a few days to make up my mind. I will contact you before the end of the week."

A lump formed in her throat she couldn't swallow down. She forced a smile, shook his hand, and walked out.

CHAPTER TWENTY-FIVE

Too agitated to face anyone, Lala fled toward Old Town. Changing her mind at the Charles Bridge, she wended through streets leading to the promenade along the river. Her pace turned brisk, the purse she clasped swung aimlessly back and forth, along with her arms. Mid-autumn sun filtered through the few leaves left on the maple trees, its light pale and cold. Had she pushed her ideas too much? Was her concept too extreme? Was he unsure or unimpressed?

She stopped at a corner to allow traffic to pass, then glanced around.

Where am I? Peering over her shoulder she saw Strelecky Island and the Legion Bridge far behind her. She'd lost track of time and place, her mind overrun with what was at stake, how much lay in the hands of a businessman for whom creativity had to be a means to fill his wallet.

She rested on a bench and stared at the river through a break in a hedgerow of trees. Stared at her family's future. Josef couldn't work and Amalie was due for another growth spurt. If Zahradnik rejected her concept, everyone would learn of her family's travails. Lala would have to cope with family and friends eyeing her with pity, patting her shoulder and feigning smiles that lied as unconvincingly as their words of encouragement. She pictured her mother bringing food, Paulina stuffing a few koruny in her coat pocket, Mamie passing along Pearl's hand-me-downs; she could hear the excuses accompanying their acts of compassion.

Lala felt tears advancing. Even her parents in the shtetl, as poor as they were, wouldn't take charity. How could she, who had so much, accept it? She felt herself slipping into that dark space..."*that crazy curse you believe hangs over you,*"...and fought back against her demons.

She rose from the cold bench to finish the long walk home. A fluttering startled her; a kestrel had perched on a tree branch, a mouse in one of its talons. Rare to see the small falcons this late in the season; most would have migrated by now. As long as it could feed itself....

Lala reached the block where her mother and Bente lived. Her assistant would want to know how the meeting went. Instead she entered her mother's building. Lala hadn't mentioned the job, knowing how Sarah felt about her wanting to work. Now she could give her mother the chance to say, "I told you so."

Sarah offered her cheek to Lala for a kiss. "Come in, dear. What brings you here?"

"I heard Mrs. Havlik passed away today."

"Oh, what sad news. Such a kind woman. I'll my send condolences." She patted Lala's hand. "Come into the kitchen, dear. My kolace should be cool by now." Sitting on the kitchen table was a platter with a dozen round sweet rolls, the dimples in their center filled with dark fruit. "Would you like one with poppy seeds or prunes?"

"They look delicious, but I don't want to spoil my appetite this close to dinner."

"Then take some home." She put six kolace in a napkin and tied the ends together.

"No, Mother, I'm not taking food home," Lala cried, more forcefully than she'd intended.

Sarah remained calm. "Would you like to borrow my handkerchief instead? You wouldn't be this upset over Mrs. Havlik's passing, so what is it – Josef's not ill again?"

Her tears returned. "He'll be fine as long as he avoids any undue stress. Unfortunately, I'm not sure I can protect him from that." Lala explained her situation.

Sarah shook her head. "Oh Lala, Lala, Lala, after all these years you still haven't learned."

"If you're going to give me an argument about working–"

"Dear, if Josef can't work and you can, then so be it. But why do you always think the world rests on your shoulders? You still believe you have to solve every problem, take care of everyone. You and you alone, like you took it upon yourself to care for me during wartime—"

"Not this again," groused Lala, but Sarah continued.

"And Berlin, when you chased a vicious mob away and saved an innocent man from a beating. Did you first announce your indignation and ask for our help? No, you rushed into the street singlehandedly. And countless other times before that, including when you stood up to bullies who taunted Paulina after her father died. You could never accept help, even when you were young. It was always, 'Let me do it, I can do it, for if I have nothing to do, I have nothing'. You'd lost your family and your home, yet you refused to let your father and me take you in. And why? Because you misunderstood what that meant. Charity, you called it. But it's not charity to help someone you love who needs help. It's just love."

Lala fell into her mother's arms, sobbing. Sarah held her as she cried. When Lala calmed, she sat up and dried her eyes with Sarah's handkerchief. "I feel better now."

"Of course you do. Such a burden to carry alone. I was afraid you'd start believing in that meshugenah curse business again."

"I should have told you sooner."

"Yes, but I understand why you didn't. You thought I would criticize you for wanting to work. But this goes beyond your desire to be a creative type, or a modern woman."

"If I don't get this job, we'll be ruined financially, for despite your pep talk about accepting help, no one has the kind of money we'll need to pay off our debts."

Sarah waved her hand. "Don't worry, you'll get the job."

"And how do you know this?"

"I can't tell you. You'll be angry."

"How can I possibly be angry with my brilliant mother—what did you do?"

"I..." she looked away. "I went to a very reliable person for information."

"What sort of information."

"About our family's fortunes."

"You met with a banker?"

Sarah shook her head.

"A financial agent? An accountant? A stockbroker?"

Each met with a head shake.

"Then who?"

Sarah thrust out her chin and announced, "A fortune-teller."

Of all the answers Lala could have conceived, that one never made the list. "How could you waste your money on a charlatan?"

Her mother gave her The Eye, the withering stare she used to put people in their place. "She can't be a charlatan, she's Hungarian. They're the best."

"Of all the foolish—"

Sarah crossed her arms in defiance. "All the women in the neighborhood swear by her. She's never wrong, and you're proof. I asked about Josef's health and she said he'd find a new occupation that would make him live longer. And," Sarah added, "She said a man close to you would do something to free you from a great burden."

Her mother must have assumed Zahradnik was that man and the burden was her family's debt. "I don't believe a word of it, but I'm so desperate now that if she's right, I'll pay for your visits myself."

"I also asked her if I would get any more grandchildren and she said not yet, but I'd live long enough to enjoy one more." Sarah handed Lala the wrapped kolace. "Now go home and have dinner with your family. And stop fretting so much. It makes you look older."

CHAPTER TWENTY-SIX

Lala staggered into her apartment on aching feet, tucked the shoes she'd taken off before climbing the stairs underneath the console and dropped her purse upon it. Had she time to shower before starting dinner? Had she the strength?

The sound of growling mixed with giggles and shrieks rang out from the parlor. There she found Josef crawling on the floor, chasing Petr and Amalie around two back to back chairs set a half-meter apart, a blanket tented over the chairbacks.

She watched in amusement as the children scooted underneath the blanket while Josef called out, "Where are you?" More giggling erupted from inside the "tent." Josef crawled over and lifted the corner, revealing their hiding place, and they shrieked again and ran off.

Josef acknowledged Lala standing in the doorway. "You're back. Amalie, Mama's home."

Amalie looked up, her face aglow and her eyes bright with laughter. "Mama," she cried as she ran to Lala, arms outstretched. Petr stayed back to see how the game would change. Josef grabbed him around the waist and tossed him in the air as the boy emitted squeals of delight.

"Well, hello. What a fine greeting this is." Lala scooped up Amalie and waved to Petr. "What are you up to?"

"We're playing a game Petr taught us, Mama."

"Where Mama?" he asked.

"I don't know, Petr. Josef, do you?"

"She came with him to await news of your meeting. When you didn't return I offered to mind him while she went to the site to find you. I'm surprised you didn't cross paths."

"My meeting ended hours ago. I took a walk to see Mother."

Amalie nuzzled against Lala. "Mama, tell us what happened."

Lala brushed a strand of hair back from Amalie' face. "Love, there's nothing to tell...yet."

Josef's brow furrowed.

Lala heard a knock at the door. She put Amalie down. "That must be your mama, Petr."

As soon as Lala opened the door, Bente clutched her chest and heaved a sigh of relief.

"Lala, I looked all over for you. I couldn't stand the suspense of not knowing so I went searching...never mind that. How did it go? What did he say?"

She waited until Bente entered the apartment to answer, "I don't know yet." She tried to appear cheerful.

"When do you think you will?"

"He wants a few days to decide." Lala put on her best optimistic face as she shrugged out of her coat.

Bente saw through her. She laid her hand on Lala's shoulder. "He'll say yes. I know it."

Petr, hearing his mother's voice, ran to her. She picked

him up and smoothed his tousled hair. "Look at you, all rumpled and smiling."

Josef stood, placed his hands behind his waist and arched his back. "He had his nap and a snack, then a story and some playtime."

Bente dressed Petr in his coat and hat. "I should take him home now, but I'll return tomorrow. I expect by then we'll have something to celebrate."

From your lips to God's ears, Lala thought as she hung up her coat. She closed the door after they left. Josef and Amalie eyed her from the hallway.

"Josef, should you be roughhousing with the children?"

Amalie answered for him. "Yes!"

Lala rustled up stuffed cabbage for dinner. She whipped a few eggs with milk, soaked bread in it, then mixed in a tin of fish. As she stuffed each cabbage leaf, she reflected that if Zahradnik rejected her design she could no longer afford a housekeeper. She'd miss Ruth, always so kind and cheerful, respectful and competent. Then again, not working would leave time to cook and clean and sew, do the marketing and laundry. She set the table and called Josef and Amalie in for dinner.

Amalie took one bite of her meal and set her fork down. "I don't like this."

"It's fish, love. You said you could eat fish every night."

"Not this fish. It doesn't taste good."

Lala was prepared to answer, but she'd ceded disciplining to Josef. "Papa?"

"If you don't want to eat your dinner, you don't have to."

Lala got up to slice some bread for Amalie, but Josef

signaled her to wait with a downward sweep of his hand. "But you won't get anything else to eat."

His strictness surprised Lala. He'd always been so lenient with Amalie, but he seemed to take his caregiver role seriously.

"Then what will I have for dinner?" Amalie pleaded.

"Surely there's some part you like. What about the cabbage?"

"I don't mind cabbage."

"Then eat that and leave the rest."

"What if I'm hungry?"

"Then eat the filling."

Pouting, she slammed back in her chair with a snort, arms crossed. Josef continued eating, as did Lala. They ignored Amalie when she returned her attention to her plate. With her fork she pulled the filling from the cabbage leaves and poked through it, scraping the fish off nuggets of bread. After finishing that she ate the cabbage.

"That's my good girl," Josef told her. "Now you may have a few slices of apple, if you say...?"

"Please. Papa, can Mama read me the story about King Arthur?"

"Not tonight, love. You have to go to bed early, remember?"

The pout returned. "Whyyyyy?"

"Because you argued with me about naptime, and what did Papa say? Every time you do that you must go to bed fifteen minutes earlier. How many numbers does the big hand on the clock move every fifteen minutes?"

"If I give you the right answer can I stay up later?"

Josef threw his head back. "Five years versus – how many weeks? Lala, you have no idea how much I love and admire you right now."

Amalie chose to sulk in her bedroom alone. Lala volunteered to help her wash and put on her pajamas, reminding her daughter she could play by herself until bedtime, when she and Josef would return to tuck her in.

"No, Mama, I want you to do it."

"All right, love. I'll come back when it's bedtime."

Amalie pointed to the clock on her mantle. "When the big hand is on the twelve and the little hand is on the eight."

"But not tonight, love. Bedtime will be when the big hand is on the nine and the little hand is on the seven. Until then." She kissed her daughter. Leaving the door to her room ajar, she joined Josef in the living room, where he'd dozed off. He'd set out two crystal champagne coupes on the table. She stroked his cheek until he opened his eyes.

"Oh, there you are." He yawned. "Sorry, I got tired after minding those two all afternoon. If it wasn't for our naptimes—"

"Our?"

"I've taken to putting them down in our bed and sitting in the chair nearby. Once they fall asleep, so do I, and when they get up it wakes me." He yawned again. "Still, I'm exhausted. Even when there's only Amalie, the constant questions, the challenges. Sometimes it seems like every conversation with her ends in an argument, or worse."

Lala recalled saying the same to her mother once. Sarah's answer fit. "I know, love. I went through the same thing with my daughter."

"I see. When you had to deal with her she was 'my daughter,' but now that I have the responsibility for her she's yours."

At least he hadn't lost his sense of humor. She asked, "What are those glasses for?"

"I chilled a bottle of champagne to celebrate."

"That might be premature."

"So I gather." He patted the cushion next to him on the sofa.

She sat beside him and relayed the details of the meeting. "He promised to make up his mind by the end of the week, which also is the day your final payment is due."

"Did you get a sense of how he'll decide?"

She shook her head. "I made the best arguments I could. Everyone, including Zahradnik, agreed the designs were strong and functional, but also quite avant-garde. I knew the risk going in...."

"But you had to be true to your vision."

"I believed that is what he wanted from me, but I may have been wrong." No tears came at that; instead she gathered strength from knowing what had to be done. "We must consider how we'll cope if Zahradnik says no. And that, love, will begin with cutting our expenses, starting with our employees."

He slumped. "I've never done that. Even during the Great War, when I lived in that hovel of an apartment, I kept on the household staff and paid all of the hospital bills."

"And you had every right to make that sacrifice for yourself, and even for me, but not for Amalie. You saw how she reacted to dinner tonight. I made it for convenience rather than economy this evening, but what good is a home filled with art, antiques and fine jewelry if we can't afford groceries. Love, we have to face the possibility of needing a loan."

"We'll still be in debt, because of my stupidity." He lowered his head, covering his face with his hands.

"Don't say that. You weren't stupid, you were cheated. And yes, we may still owe, but better to family, or the bank, than to Chermak. We can cope with the payments without that deadline looming over us."

She lifted his face and took his hands in hers. "Once he's paid, we have options for raising money to pay back the loan. We can sell some of our possessions without pressure. We can close the gallery or the shop, or both, and rent them out. Then once we move what's left in the storeroom to the attic, I can convert it back into an apartment, your office as well if necessary. As a last resort we'll let go of our staff, with excellent references."

She paused to allow him to absorb that before continuing. "You ought to reconsider Paulina's offer to renew your partnership. She may be ready to open a second shop, which I can help with. You could as well, particularly if she chooses a location in another city."

"I will speak with Paulina, but only if I can contribute to the business." His posture straightened. "I can also contact the factory. They might value an experienced representative in Prague, one with the same surname as the company."

Heartened by his contributions, she pushed further. "First we will rid ourselves of all obligations to Chermak. Then, we must protect Amalie and keep ourselves in the black, whether than means we share working, homemaking and child rearing, or split those responsibilities. All this is predicated on a worst case scenario. Zahradnik could phone any moment to say he wants to go ahead with my plan. And even if he doesn't hire me, that doesn't mean another entrepreneur wouldn't."

Lines of worry etched his face. How could she have convinced Zahradnik if she couldn't convince her own husband?

"I know this sounds frightening, but I don't want you to worry. No matter what happens in the next few days, or months, or years, as long as you stay alive and healthy, and Amalie happy and growing, we will be all right. Nothing will come between us. And remember that all the people you've helped to succeed over the years are more than happy to return the favor. Not out of obligation, but out of love." She kissed him. "Think about that while I put Amalie to bed. Then I'm coming back for you."

He sighed. "I'm tuckered out, love, but I'll try my best."

CHAPTER TWENTY-SEVEN

An upset stomach awoke Lala in the middle of the night. Josef lay asleep, as did Amalie when Lala checked. Slipping on her robe to ward off the night's chill, she padded into the kitchen to make a pot of mint tea, which always soothed her stomach. She blamed the strain of waiting rather than her cobbled dinner for the burning in her gut.

Lala carried the tea in to the dining room, pushed aside her sketches and drawings, and set the pot on the table which had been her work desk of late. Time to return it to its true purpose. She moved the lamp back to the library, gathered her paperwork into a pile to stow away and returned her drawing implements to their drawer. A quick dusting of the tabletop, then she poured a cup of tea. If Zahradnik approved the project, she'd set up her workspace in Josef's office downstairs. If not, she would need more than the mint tea she sipped to quell her stomach.

She set her cup on the window sill and parted the draperies. The faint light of streetlamps traced the outline of rooftops against the night sky. No other lights glowed in the windows; was she the only person unable to sleep? She searched for the moon, as she had done since childhood on difficult nights. Despite a cloudless sky she saw nothing but stars dotting the black void above.

"As wide awake as me, I gather."

She turned to see Josef standing in the doorway.

"Searching for the moon?" he asked. "You won't see it; it's new tonight. What is it you often say — 'a nearly full moon is a sign of change.'"

"It always has been for me." She offered him some tea, which he declined.

He gazed at her with a quizzical expression, half-smiling. "Do you want to return to bed?"

Her mind churned as much as her stomach. "I doubt I can get back to sleep now."

"Who said anything about sleeping?"

Afterward they lay together, legs entwined, Josef caressing her back. She ran her fingers over his chest, damp with sweat.

"Much better than mint tea," she declared as she laid her head on his arm.

He brushed the hair from her face. "I'm happy I can still please you, at my age."

"Don't say that, love. All that boisterous play with the children left you exhausted last night." She kissed him. "You more than made up for it now."

"But do I make you happy? That you married me?"

She sat up. "Where is this coming from? Have I ever given you cause to worry about that? Because if I did—"

"No, love. I can't help myself from wondering about it, after all the mistakes I've made."

"You were cheated, Josef."

"It's more than that. I tried to do what was best for us — for you — because I thought I knew better. I never understood how difficult it was for you early in our marriage, having to care for Amalie, our home, your family, and all the while denying you the opportunity to do something for yourself, like I had with my new business."

She nestled into him. "And now that you've had a chance to live my life for a while, so to speak, you do. How does Mamie put it? 'Walk a mile in my shoes.' That's what you've done. Now you understand me a little better."

"Better than you think."

"Why are you looking at me like that?"

He feigned indifference. "How do you mean?"

"Like the character in Amalie's book about Alice. You're grinning like the Cheshire Cat." The last time he looked at her like that he gave her the navette ring. "You never explained why you had to see Cerveny."

His fingers stroked the length of her back with the gentlest of touch. "Remember the first time I did this? You swooned and I had to carry you into my office."

"How could I forget. That memory sustained me through three years of the War."

"Memories," he repeated.

"You can't fool me, love. What have you done?"

"I picked something up from Cerveny yesterday morning."

"Yes, when you dashed out without a word and left me worrying—"

He placed a finger on her lips to silence her. "And I told you it would be worth it. I planned to wait until you found out about your contract before giving it to you. Now I think it best to give it to you now, not as a celebration, or a

441

consolation, but a good omen."

She sat with her back against the headboard. "What is it?"

He reached over to his nightstand, turned on the light and opened the drawer. "Close your eyes."

She complied.

He took her hand and placed a small square object that weighed practically nothing, thin as a piece of paper, on her palm.

"Open them," he said.

She looked down at a photograph, quite old, showing a young couple at what appeared to be their wedding. Puzzled, she turned to Josef.

"Look closer."

She held the photo under the lamplight and studied the two people depicted. They looked familiar, she though, though she could not place them. The man stood straight and proud, one hand on his chest, the other on the chairback where his bride sat. Strong hands, the hands of a laborer or craftsman. His nose, tapered at the bridge, widened at the nostrils, like a pear. His grin radiated joy; she could see it in his eyes. The woman, elegant and pretty, dark hair pinned up. Even seated Lala could see she had a shapely figure, slender and tall, taller than most women. She held a small clutch of flowers tied with ribbon...delicate hands with curled thumbs, like Amalie's....Josef's parents? No, they would have married long before....

Memories rose from deep within a place in her heart, locked up long ago...voices from the past returned...it couldn't be. How was it possible...?

"Josef, is this...are they...?"

"Your parents, that is, your original parents from Russia. This is their wedding photograph."

"But how...where...I...."

He stroked her arm. "I've had Cerveny continue to keep track of the survivors for your protection, especially after one woman was murdered, and to learn what he could about your past. The widow of the Rabbi passed away recently. She had this in her bible."

"How do you know who they are?"

"Turn the photograph over," he said.

She read the notation printed on the back.

Rozina and Jonah Groissman
Five October, eighteen-ninety

Below that someone had written:

Luba Chaya Groissman:
Twenty August 1891 – Twenty August 1891
Luska Shana Groissman:
Twenty August 1891

It all meant nothing and yet it meant everything. Images floated to the surface and popped open like bubbles in water, more than Lala could follow. They paled against what she now saw, what she never knew. "Dear God, I had a twin sister? I don't know what to say."

"She must have been sickly at birth. They named her Chaya, for life. You they named Shana, for your beauty."

"What am I to make of this?"

"It proves what you've been told since the beginning, what I've always known. You were meant to go on, to survive. More than survive, thrive. You lived when your sister didn't. All you went through – the pogrom, the Great War,

443

the loss of our son. Yet you're here, stronger than ever. As I first told you in Berlin, when you love someone deeply you have strength. I've drawn on your strength, the strength that comes from my love for you, Amalie and our family."

His arm encircled her and drew her head to his chest. "It takes more than strength to get though life. It also takes courage, which comes from being loved. I see that every day in my time with Amalie, and with you, who stood by me no matter what. I had to find a truly meaningful way to show you how much I love you, always and still, so you could stay strong in your love for me and find the courage to face whatever happens in our lives."

She studied every line and shadow of the photograph. Slowly their faces grew more familiar...Mama's smile that brightened her face, Papa's big brown eyes that danced when he laughed...his laugh...Mama's worrying...Papa's carving....

Shards of memory.

She stared at the photograph until it blurred and let her vision grow soft. Suddenly she was Luska, in Sarah's mother's apartment in Russia, staring at the only thing she found in the wreckage of her home. Her Bohemian crystal goblet. It was meant to be her beacon, but she'd given it to Gershom when he had to flee the country.

The photograph came into focus again, but she saw them as she remembered them. Their final words came back to her...

"You'll know, Luska. It may be something he says, or does, that means something special to you, but you'll know...trust your heart, for that is where we will be...."

Trust. Her new beacon.

She gave the photograph back to Josef. "We must put this away somewhere where Amalie won't find it. I'm not ready to tell her about my past."

"I agree; she's too young. I'll lock it in our safe tomorrow."

She burrowed under the covers. "Tragic to think someone survived the pogrom only to be murdered later. Do you remember her name?"

"Radova, I believe."

"I recall a widow referred to as Mrs. Radovich."

"A sarcastic reference to her position and wealth."

"I remember her son Lev teasing me..." Memories flowed. "She paid Mr. Chelmsky's butcher bill with so much cheese he gave me some to eat the morning I went to the river. My last meal before the pogrom."

"Cheese? How odd." He pulled the covers up and spooned with Lala.

Lying together, she recalled what the fortune-teller had told her mother...

"*... a man close to you would do something to free you from a great burden....*"

"Josef, you truly believe this is a good omen?"

"I had Ivo ask an astronomy professor at the University to research lunar cycles in the last century." He nuzzled his cheek against her neck. "You, Lala Hafstein Smetana, formerly known as Luska Shana Groissman, were born under a nearly full moon."

CHAPTER TWENTY-EIGHT

Bente arrived around ten o'clock, carrying a napkin-covered basket and her son. She put Petr down and he immediately ran to Josef, who picked up and swung him around.

"He's grown very fond of your husband," Bente said. "He spent half the evening talking about Amalie's papa."

"We'll have to come up with a better name for him to use. I hope your husband doesn't mind."

"Not at all. Petr's a good man but he's more distant with young children. My father was the same with my brothers and me, but that changed as we got older." She proffered the basket. "I saw your mother in the street this morning. She asked me to bring this for us and the children." She lifted the napkin to reveal the rest of the kolace Sarah had baked.

"They'll make a perfect snack." Lala put the basket in the kitchen.

"Any news yet?" Bente asked.

"Nothing. You're welcome to stay but there's no guarantee he'll decide today. Or tomorrow. Or Thursday."

"Your mother said she spoke to someone who said you'd

447

hear today."

"I wouldn't count on her source." She filled the kettle. "Coffee, or tea?"

Each took turns watching the children while the other two passed the time with busywork or small talk. Josef kept Amalie home so he'd be present if Zahradnik called. Bente volunteered to take both children for a walk, but Josef recommended she stay, ready to celebrate when they got the news. Lala loved his optimism, but when they were alone he confessed the real reason – Bente might be too distracted by what was at stake.

After lunch, Josef put Amalie and Petr down for their nap. Once the children fell asleep, the adults relaxed in the parlor, interspersing stories from their lives with stretches of quiet.

Bente ended a length of silence with a loud sigh. "I'm so nervous. I wish there was something we could do to speed up the process."

Lala agreed.

"This must be what Petr went through waiting for me to give birth to little Petr. Josef, does this remind you of waiting for your children to be born?"

"More like waiting for a train home when the Great War began."

"Where were you?" she asked.

"Berlin. Lala and I, along with our families and some friends, had come to the city for my late son's art exhibit." He proceeded to tell Bente how they sat in the lobby of the Hotel Grande, waiting for the hotel manager to secure transportation back to Prague. Bente listened, rapt, when

Josef described how Lala ran into the street to save an Englishman from a beating.

"I'm shocked but not surprised. Lala's the bravest woman I've ever met. But Josef, you must have been terrified for her."

"To say the least. Her father and I rushed out to bring her back. By the time we got outside and through the crowd, she had the situation well in hand."

"Again, I'm not surprised. What was the worst part of being stranded in Berlin?"

"The waiting," Josef acknowledged. "The interminable waiting."

"Every minute felt like an hour, every hour like a day," Lala said. "At several points I believed time had stopped."

"Or moved backward," added Josef.

"I don't suppose you have any pleasant memories of that time."

Lala turned to Josef. "Oh, one or two. Although our situations were, shall we say different back then, it was when we first acknowledged having feelings for each other."

Bente widened eyes probed for details. "That sounds very romantic, Lala."

"But mostly we sat around waiting, waiting, waiting for something to happen. Wondering when it would happen. If it would happen."

Josef glanced at his watch. "And so it begins again."

They sat for a while without talking, the silence marked by the ticking of the mantle clock.

Tick, tick, tick.

Josef leaned forward. "I do recall the manager bringing us some fine cognac that evening, after I demanded a bottle." He looked to Lala. "It isn't evening yet, but perhaps we can make an exception? One glass? With your mother's kolace?"

"As my friend Mamie would say, 'It's five o'clock somewhere.'"

A pleasant warmth coursed through Lala after finishing her cognac. She'd observed Bente mimicking Josef as he swirled the amber liquid in his glass before taking a sip.

"My, this tastes smooth," she exclaimed before taking the last bite of her kolac.

"Who'd have thought it would pair well with pastry." Lala gathered the empty glasses and plates. "The children should be getting up soon. I'll make us some coffee and cut up one kolac for them to share, then you can take the last two home for you and your husband."

"I'll let you know how well they pair with beer."

The phone rang. Lala almost dropped the plates.

"Leave that for now," said Josef. "Go answer it."

She went into the kitchen and lifted the receiver. "Hello?"

It was Sarah. "Did you hear back?" she asked.

Lala exhaled. "No, Mother, not yet."

"Then I won't keep you in case he's trying to call, but you call me as soon as you hear, no matter what. And call your sister. And Mamie. But call me first."

Lala heard stirring from her bedroom; the telephone must have wakened the children.

Bente offered to watch Amalie and Petr while Lala and Josef waited in the parlor for the phone to ring. The coffee offset the effects of the cognac, leaving Lala alert but calm. Josef reread the Tagblatt. She selected a book but put it back;

she couldn't focus.

The telephone rang again. Lala jumped up, smoothed her skirt and went back to the kitchen to answer it.

Paulina on the other end asked, "Have you heard anything?"

"Not yet."

"I won't keep you. Good luck. Let me know as soon as you find out. Mother, too. And Mamie as well; we're on pins and needles."

Lala hung up. She thought she should start dinner until she noticed the time — two thirty-five. Barely an hour and a half since they finished lunch.

This was Berlin all over again.

Tick, tick, tick.

Outside the shadows lengthened as the sun dipped below the rooftops to the west. Lala rewrapped the last two kolace. "You ought to take Petr home and start dinner," she said as she handed the basket to Bente. "I doubt we'll hear anything today."

"May I return tomorrow? On my own, of course, not to work."

Lala fetched Bente's coat and scarf from the front closet. "You're always welcome to visit, Petr as well."

CHAPTER TWENTY-NINE

Lala searched through the pantry and ice box for something to make for dinner. An idea eluded her. She asked Josef for his opinion.

"Make whatever you like. It doesn't matter to me."

"I can't decide." She heard weariness in her voice.

"You're anxious, love." He kissed her forehead. "Zahradnik's delay in responding may be a good sign. He's giving your concept a great deal of thought. What you must remember is he didn't dismiss your ideas out of hand, so don't assume the worst because he hasn't called yet. Patience is not your forte, but you have no choice but to wait until he makes his decision."

"You're being so reasonable, and all I want to do is throw something."

"Then throw something into a pot for dinner. Have we any leftovers?"

"Not enough for the three of us."

"Then do what I did in my bachelor days, chop them and add a few eggs."

"Brilliant, but will Amalie fuss?"

"Call it an omelet. She's developed a fascination with all things French, thanks to Paulina. Chop everything fine, a good way to expend some of your nervous energy. I'll watch Amalie while you prepare dinner."

As he left the kitchen the phone rang.

Josef stopped and returned, grinning in anticipation.

Lala waved her hand. "It's not him, it's probably Mamie this time." She reached for the phone. "Either that or Mother's Hungarian fortune-teller."

"Is this a good time to talk, Mrs. Smetana?"

Her nerves jolted. "Yes, Mr. Zahradnik. Have you come to a decision?"

Josef shook his finger and mouthed, "Patience."

She could hear Zahradnik inhale.

"You certainly don't beat around the bush, do you?"

Lala clutched her chest. "I apologize if I—"

He chuckled. "No, no, I like that about you. Frankly, I'm the same way, but I didn't call to compare dispositions with you. I have been reviewing your concept since we met yesterday, going over it again and again."

"And what have you concluded?" Her teeth clamped over her lower lip as she waited for his response.

"I've studied the designs and can see how they would function well. Your point about the rooms being – what's the word – intuitive? I see that as well. They answer all the questions, they tick off all the boxes, and yet... I still don't understand it."

"What can I clarify for you?"

"There is nothing to clarify. I look at each rendering and think how different they look compared to anything I've seen before. How will my customers react to it? Will they be able to appreciate your vision, or will they think it too...?"

"Avant-garde?"

"Yes, that is the word. Avant-garde."

Lala felt her opportunity slipping away, along with her confidence.

"I like the uniqueness of the ground level spaces," he continued. "I can visualize your reception space in the lobby, tables and chairs in the restaurant, a dais and dance floor in the grand salon. I can understand that. But the chambers upstairs seem very unconventional."

What could she say to convince him? Should she state that they could be changed, made to resemble a more familiar hotel chamber? It might salvage the deal, guarantee he would hire her. What was stopping her?

"Trust your heart...."

She looked to Josef, standing in the doorway, watching her, and gazed into his dark eyes to seek guidance. His beautiful eyes that radiated concern and curiosity. Even as a child she observed a warmth to them, more so when she fell in love with him.

She responded, "They are unconventional, deliberately so."

"As you explained to me at our meeting yesterday. A way to merge the traditional architecture of the building with a more modern look. It's striking to be sure, which is why it's taking me so long to make up my mind."

"If you need more time, Mr. Zahradnik—"

"I could look at these drawings for the next twenty years and still wonder. No, Mrs. Smetana. This has nothing to do with time. It has everything to do with confidence. My instincts led me to purchase your mansion to create the Excelsior, and to make you an offer to do the same in my new hotel."

"I beg to differ, Mr. Zahradnik, for if you truly wanted the same, you would have asked someone to copy what I'd already done. Instead you sought me out for something comparable, yet different."

"A fair point. I found what you presented to be very different, but my hesitancy comes from whether it is comparable. I realized my decision has to rest, not on whether I understand it or even like it, but on whether I have enough confidence in your vision, enough trust in you, to go forward with this project. So to answer your original question, yes. I have come to a conclusion regarding the project."

"Would you care to share it with me?"

Zahradnik let out a hearty laugh. "Mrs. Smetana, I'm a businessman. I'm very good at what I do because I've learned I don't have to know everything if I can surround myself with talented people who know what I don't. I had the vision to buy the mansion you designed and turn it into the successful inn it is today, but it took your skill and talent to bring it to fruition. I'm betting on you to do it once more."

"Does that mean....?"

"Mrs. Smetana, the position is yours."

CHAPTER THIRTY

The news didn't fully penetrate at first. She hung up, dazed and unable to speak.

"What did he say?" asked Josef.

"He said...yes."

Josef let out a whoop of joy. "I knew you would win him over!" When he extended his arms to her, the reality of what happened finally burrowed through her brain fog and she ran to him. He lifted her up and swung her around in a circle, both of them laughing and shouting in glee. Lala became aware of Amalie staring at them, looking utterly confused; the poor child couldn't tell if their hollering came from anger or happiness.

Josef set Lala down. "Amalie, Mama just got some very good news."

"Then you're happy?" she looked unsure, but hopeful.

"Very happy," Lala told her.

Amalie clapped her hands and shouted, "I'm happy, too!" Then she looked confused again. "Why are we happy?"

"Papa will take you to the parlor and tell you all about it while I call Bubbie and Aunt Paulina."

457

"Then may we have dinner? I'm hungry."

A good reminder. Soon Lala would undertake the year-long conversion of two mansions into an exclusive hotel, but first she had to feed her hungry child.

Lala called her mother first, as promised, and asked her to tell Bente the good news. Josef returned to the kitchen and offered to make dinner. While Amalie watched him chop up leftovers, Lala phoned Paulina and finally Mamie. All expressed their congratulations and delight. Each offered to host a party to celebrate, but Lala asked them to wait; she had much to do and needed to get started immediately. One looming problem remained to be resolved.

As Lala set the dining room table she heard a loud pop. Smiling, she fetched two champagne glasses to add to the setting as he brought the bottle to her.

Amalie entered and took her seat. Josef followed with a basket of bread and the egg concoction he'd made, set out on a serving platter. He'd rolled the eggs around the filling to make it look appetizing.

"What is that?" asked Amalie.

"A classic French omelet, like you would find in Paris." He cut the roll into three pieces and served it before pouring two glasses of champagne.

Amalie took a tentative bite of her serving. "Papa, now that Mama is going to work, does that mean you will be cooking dinner every night?"

Lala answered, "Probably not, love. Ruth will be back next week."

Her daughter peeled back the rolled egg. "I miss her," she exclaimed as she scraped away the filling.

***

The excitement delayed Amalie's bedtime. She wasn't keen on going to sleep, but the good news coupled with the champagne left Lala and Josef feeling randy. They negotiated one extra bedtime story, but she resisted.

"We're having so much fun. Why must I go to bed now?"

Lala had tried coercion, bargaining, and firmness, to no avail. She decided to try honesty.

"Because Mama and Papa want to go to bed and dream about tomorrow."

"Well, why didn't you say so? I can do that, too." She got into her bed without further argument. Lala tucked her in and kissed her goodnight. She turned off the light and went to meet Josef in their bedroom.

He'd already gotten under the covers. She unbuttoned her housedress, sensing his eyes on her as she did. It pleased her that after bearing two children Josef still enjoyed watching her undress. Two children...the fortune-teller told her mother something...

"...I asked her if I would get any more grandchildren..."

"Josef, remember when we first married, I wanted to wait to have children?"

"Because of the shortages, and I agreed."

"Yes, it allowed us to postpone having Amalie until the Great War ended. We ought to revert to that approach until I finish my project. I can't risk finding myself..." *Why am I being coy with him?* "I don't want to get pregnant right now."

He drew a deep breath. Would he lecture her or react harshly?

"If I understand you correctly, you do not want to have another child until this project has been completed. I take it to mean what you asked for on our honeymoon – a temporary postponement. I will agree to that."

"I'm relieved you understand."

"You can thank our daughter. Since I took on primary caregiving for her I've learned I must listen closely to what she asks. Otherwise I may not understand what she really wants."

She finished undressing. Foregoing her nightgown she stood before him, naked, feeling the heat from his gaze. "Thanks to your tutelage I know some delightful ways to enjoy ourselves without risk."

He pulled back the covers.

Josef's naked body spooned against her back, his arm draped over her breasts. Sated, Lala drifted deeper into the netherworld of sleep. As the pleasure of their encounter subsided, the topic she'd avoided awakened like a hungry baby, howling for attention.

Her twilight state disturbed, she addressed the weight of their debt, beyond the capability to pay it off. Convinced its origins lay within an evil plot to destroy her family, she could not bear to remain obligated to that devil. For years she fought off the belief that the pogrom's victims, as well as the survivors, had damned her for being the peddler's daughter. She would not allow Klement Chermak to replace the curse with his own, or worse, add to it.

She would accompany Josef to Mr. Cerveny's office tomorrow morning where she would withdraw the balance of their debt from her inheritance. When Josef balked, she'd explain how once she deducted their living expenses from each paycheck, the remainder would go to pay herself back.

"There won't be enough," he would say, and she'd remind him the budget she'd submitted included child care. He'd now earn that fee instead of Bente. Lala could foresee situations where Josef might be helpful in her project, which would allow him to earn even more. Some or all of that money could be put toward replenishing her inheritance.

Lala felt Josef stir; he rolled over and pressed his back against hers. She would not wake him to tell him of her plan; better to wait until morning. She savored the feel of his skin against hers and willed her mind to let go for now, let her drift off to sleep.

CHAPTER THIRTY-ONE

As Lala anticipated, Josef balked at her idea, but her reasoning persuaded him to agree. She observed him throughout each step, reassuring him when his breathing quickened and urging him on when he faltered. With their debt discharged a palpable calm fell over them both. Josef surprised Lala in another way; he cleaned out his office in preparation for her to move in, complete with a telephone, which he had transferred from his shop.

"You'll be more comfortable here, and the children won't disturb you."

"How thoughtful. I'll go fetch my—"

"If there's anything you need help with, just ask."

Josef waited in the doorway. For a second he reminded her of Vostok, the Zedeks' white-haired butler she'd met as a child, anticipating an order. She almost bit her lip at the memory. Josef looked so expectant, as if he couldn't move unless she responded otherwise.

Lala had envisaged separation anxiety from Amalie, not Josef. That might be all it was. Still, for this arrangement to succeed long-term, she and Josef would have to establish a mutually satisfying work agreement. Just as Lala had chafed when she'd been limited to household and child care duties, she could understand Josef feeling similarly. How much smoother their lives would be if they could interchange roles and responsibilities as needed, for them as well as Amalie.

"Since you asked, I need a storage space to warehouse deliveries for the project until the interior renovation is completed. I'll be working here, so a location close by would be advantageous. You did a superb job of handling that for Paulina. Could you search for a place while you're out with Amalie?"

"I will start this afternoon, but first I'll see to lunch. Shall I tell Ruth you'll be joining us?"

"I wish I could, but I'll be too busy." Would that trigger his anxiety? Would he bring her lunch out of thoughtfulness, or neediness, or not think to do it and leave her without food?

"I'll have her bring a plate of food down for you."

A practical solution.

Blueprints. Charts with all stages of the project marked and cross-referenced with a calendar. Time-frame estimates. An open accounts file cabinet with separators for each letter of the alphabet. Lists of all the vendors, craftsmen, construction workers, miscellaneous suppliers of everything from meals and washroom products to lightbulbs and stationery. Pens, pencils, charcoal; pads for drawing and writing. And finally, her renderings, pinned along the fabric-covered wall of his office. She'd first tested the idea in his former office when she ran his factory and found it useful, one of many skills she honed while working there.

Thrown into management and forced to learn as she did

— like a child thrown into a lake learns to swim, or else — the lessons stuck with her. The position required organization, long-term planning, discipline, and most of all, the ability to get men, often many years her senior, to listen when she spoke, do what she asked, and help her learn by sharing their knowledge and experience with her.

No longer needing Bente for child care, Lala offered her the option of cutting her hours or taking on more project work and seeking her own child care for Petr. Bente preferred the latter; she suggested Josef watch Petr while she worked, while she could take over child care duties on occasion. She offered to pay Josef. That pleased Lala; she left them to set up a schedule on their own and returned to her office.

Buried deep in work, the ring of the telephone startled her.

"Good morning, Mrs. Smetana. How is work progressing."

She chuckled. "Quite well the entire time; which has been two days, Mr. Zahradnik."

"I've an additional task for you — I want you to design the sign that will hang over the entryway, with the name of the hotel. Show me a few drafts and I'll pick the one I prefer."

"You've decided on the name, then."

"I did, and if I must say so, it's perfect."

"What is it?"

"The Moderni."

Ruth brought down a tea tray. Lala had her set it on the table near the window.

"Mrs. Cerna took Amalie and her boy to the park, and Mr. Smetana's in his shop." Ruth poured a cup of tea for

Lala. "You got a stack of letters and cards delivered, Missus, and all of it from America. You almost never get mail from America, and today you get four pieces. Funny, that." She chuckled to underscore her point.

After a brief tea break, Lala fetched the correspondences from America.

The envelope on top had a New York address she didn't recognize. Inside was a letter from Karel, who'd recently taken ownership of the Greenwich Village gallery where he worked after his boss passed away. Although he wrote with pleasure about his new situation, the tone of the letter implied the deceased was more to him than his employer. She would send him a note of congratulations and condolences.

The second was a postcard of snow-covered mountains in Colorado, where Mamie and Moritz were traveling. She turned it over to read the message:

> Moritz and I finally will have a home in America. We broke ground on our forty acre lot in Glenwood Springs, Colorado, a half-day's drive west of Denver. The area is a mile (1.2 km) above sea level, so we're taking it easy until we adjust. Prohibition keeps us from drinking too much alcohol, so it's just as well. My folks are thrilled to spend more time with Pearl. We'll call on you next time we're in Prague.

The third correspondence felt thicker than the others, but she recognized the Brooklyn address on the back. She unsealed the square envelope and pulled out an engraved announcement decorated with a stork wearing a hand-painted blue bow.

Gershom and his wife Louise had a little boy whom

they'd named Henry Jack after Gershom's father Hershel and Louise's brother Jacob, killed in the Great War. She opened the card to find a photograph of the couple, the new mother holding her infant son in her right arm. When Gershom wrote of his marriage, he'd mentioned Louise had contracted polio as a child, which left her left arm withered. He'd lost one leg in youth and made a joke about how they two would not become one, but one and a half. She had a pleasant face. He'd grown stouter, but looked very happy.

She moved the photo aside, which revealed a note written on the card in Gershom's hand:

Can you believe it? I have everything. May you as well. Gershom

p s 'Jack' is for your father, too.

Gershom often confessed his fondness for Lala's father, but the naming gesture touched her. A congratulatory note and gift was in order.

The fourth letter, on engraved stationery of a quality she rarely saw, came from a Mr. William Robertson of Pittsburgh, Pennsylvania.

She didn't know him, or anyone in Pennsylvania. She opened the letter and as she read, her vision clouded as tears formed. She didn't know whether to laugh or cry over what she held in her hand.

A fortune-teller had predicted... *a man close to you would do something to free you from a great burden.* At first she thought it meant Zahradnik, until Josef surprised her with the wedding photograph of her mama and papa. Now she knew better. Judging by the letter, behind the man who would free her stood a mediating woman.

467

Lala had promised to pay for her mother's visits to the gypsy woman if the information proved true. It would cost her The Eye and an "I told you so," in addition to the visitation fees, but it would be worth it.

CHAPTER THIRTY-TWO

She heard a knock at the door; Josef opened it with one of his cat-ate-the-canary grins. "I have good news for you, love."

She took a deep breath. "I do as well."

"Let me tell you my news first. I assure you it's better than yours."

Lala laughed inwardly. "I doubt that, but go ahead."

"I found the ideal location for your storage. I want you to see it, right now."

"Love, I'm wearing house clothes. I must change first."

"I assure you the owner won't mind. Come." He extended his hand to beckon her.

"All right, but I still haven't told you—"

"See my surprise first and then tell me yours."

He led her downstairs. She peered into his shop and saw it almost filled. "Oh my, you have merchandise to sell again."

"That's not the surprise." He unlocked the door to his gallery, which had paper covering the glass door. With a push the door swung open to reveal the place stripped empty, its windows covered like the door.

He gestured her to come inside. "I moved the remaining

artwork into the shop to free up this space for you. Large enough to hold whatever you'll need to store, and as asked, close to home – you can come here in your robe and slippers if you want. I've papered the windows for privacy, but you ought to add signs facing out, advertising the hotel."

"I'll put my sketches up."

"It's too soon for anyone to see what you've done. You want to build curiosity and interest. Just advertise, Coming Soon: The Moderni. Use the logo you've designed, but nothing else. You don't want anyone stealing your ideas."

"I wouldn't have thought of that. Brilliant."

"And the best part?" He flashed a self-congratulatory look. "As I will be the landlord, you can deposit the rent check into your inheritance account. Now that's brilliant, yes?"

She agreed. "You've outdone yourself, love."

"Then it's settled. Now tell me your news."

"I have another project for you. Do you have a complete inventory of the Great War art in your storeroom, with their value?"

"I could assemble one in no time. Why?"

"Because a man in Pittsburg Pennsylvania would like to buy the entire collection."

It took a moment for her words to register with Josef. He couldn't have looked more beatific if angels danced before him.

They clung together, laughing in each other's arms, then crying. They hugged and kissed, and between the laughter and tears she told him of receiving the inquiry in the mail.

"Let's go back to your office," he said with urgency in his voice.

"You want to read the letter for yourself," she acknowledged. It would make it more real.

"That too," he said as his fingers ran down the length of her back. "Do you remember the first time we let Amalie stay overnight at your mother's?"

"I recall we took full advantage of the privacy. One particularly memorable activity stands out."

"Shall we try that at your desk? It would be more comfortable than this floor." His hands slid to caress her bottom.

"Our desk," she cooed as he led her out.

They dressed quickly afterward. Bente would return soon with Amalie.

"I never did read the letter," Josef noted as he buttoned his trousers.

She handed it to him. "He wants the entire collection for a war museum he's building, dedicated to his son killed in the Great War. He must be very wealthy to do that."

"Pittsburgh is the center of America's steel industry," Josef said as he read. "I wonder why he addressed the letter to you. For that matter, how did he know about my collection?"

"Keep reading, love."

His eyes darted across the page, then lifted toward her in wide-eyed amazement. "Zoe?"

"He apparently met her in Pittsburgh and she convinced him to make the offer."

Josef's puzzlement remained. "For my collection? I discussed a few pieces individually, but only you knew the extent of my purchases. You had suggested a museum for the collection. Did you make inquiries?"

She shook her head. "She is in the art business, perhaps she heard...?" She wouldn't put it past Chermak to spread the news, but that possibility hadn't occurred to Josef. "Does it matter? You have in your hand nothing less than a miracle."

"This will put us right again. You can replenish your inheritance and we can return to life as before." He folded the letter and returned it to its envelope. "It truly is a miracle."

Josef prepared a complete inventory of his collection and asking price. Lala drafted a letter to Mr. Robertson, which Josef advised her to telegraph rather than mail, and another to Zoe to express her thanks. The men finalized their deal within a week. Josef assigned Hanus to handle crating and shipping. At Josef's request, Robertson arranged to have payment sent from a European bank to quicken the process.

When the check arrived, Josef insisted on depositing it into Lala's inheritance account. Lala then withdrew the amount that exceeded the original account balance. It would more than sustain them until Lala's next paycheck; it allowed for a splurge. Josef set aside a sum to buy winter clothes and shoes for Amalie. Lala had a similar thought for herself.

Miss Horáčková escorted Lala into the back room, where Paulina greeted her with a glass of champagne and a hug. "To your success. I'm so proud of you, my friend."

"I couldn't have done it without you, Paulina. You gave me the courage to fight for my concept." Lala spotted the same Toulouse-Lautrec sketch as Josef's forgery in a frame, hanging on the wall behind her desk. Was Paulina's the original? "When did you get that piece?"

"Josef gave it to me." Paulina said with a sly grin. "It's a fake, but customers won't know."

"No harm in that. Now I'm ready to celebrate with one of your stunning dresses."

Paulina opened her wardrobe and pulled out the plum velvet gown Lala had admired. "I saved this for you. Would you like to try it on?"

Lala slipped into the dress and stood on a platform while Paulina made adjustments to the sleeves and hem.

"You still do your own tailoring?"

"I have several excellent seamstresses, but I prefer working with my favorite clients. Besides, I hardly ever see you anymore, unless it's for a fitting." Paulina tapered the sleeves with pins. "With us both so busy that won't change anytime soon."

"We'll find time, I promise."

"There, done."

The pinning completed, Lala took off the dress.

Paulina intervened before Lala could put on her street clothes. "You'll need to take more than that gown."

"We may not be in debt anymore but I can't be extravagant. One is enough."

"I don't want to be indebted either. Josef agreed to return as my partner, but he refused to take payment in cash, only merchandise for you." She brought out a lavender silk housedress and a daywear ensemble in dark red.

"They're beautiful. Please pick one, I can't decide which I like best."

"What do you mean, 'pick?' I owe you both."

Miko Johnston

Lala considered what to do with her windfall. Something meaningful. A glance at her naked right hand sparked the answer. She wrote a note with instructions, sealed it with the money inside an envelope and sent it to the one person she could trust with her request – Smolak.

CHAPTER THIRTY-THREE

With work at the hotel underway, Lala hired an ambitious worker from her crew for a second job, returning Josef's empty storeroom back to its original state – a small apartment. She planned to create a second work area for Bente and Josef; the old bedroom would become his office, the dining room an office for Bente, and the living room a playroom for the children under the watchful eye of their parents. To make a desk for Bente, Lala had the worker sand the top of the kitchen's work table. With it out of the kitchen, she found room for a small table, perfect for the children's lunch and snacks.

Lala asked Ludovik if he would supervise the moving and placement of the furniture, working from a floor plan; if he handled it well she'd propose he join the hotel crew. He accepted her offer with enthusiasm. Josef contributed a few pieces languishing in his shop; Lala filled in the rest from the apartment and her old attic office.

After a trial run, both Josef and Bente begged for more storage. While Josef took Amalie to buy Christmas presents on Bente's day off, Lala tackled the apartment revamping.

She stood on the third step down from the landing, safely

out of the way, as two workmen maneuvered a cabinet through the entryway. As she watched, stemming the urge to intone, "Be careful," she heard the door to the building open below.

Zoe entered, carrying a leather tote. She had gained some weight and while still thin she no longer looked gaunt. Lala greeted her and professed her gratitude.

"My pleasure. I owe you and Josef so much for your support early on in my career. When I learned how Klement Chermak took advantage of your grieving husband, and why, I couldn't stand by and do nothing. I exhibit throughout the world now, so I made inquiries at every gallery and reception."

"How did you find out?" Lala asked.

"Word gets around in this business. I've met collectors and dealers who harbor all sorts of bigotries. It's not uncommon, or fair. I've had to fight for everything I've accomplished as a photographer because I'm a woman – and I fight harder than any man would, if he had to."

"And you accomplished so much," Lala said. "I took my daughter to see your recent exhibit. She absolutely adored your work."

"I'm flattered. I wasn't sure you'd want to see it, after our last parting."

"I always admired your talent, Zoe, but I couldn't stay silent."

"Please know I never resented you for saying what you did. I knew you were right. It helped me face up to my limitations as a mother."

"I met Vilem's wife last fall and she explained your situation. You saw to it that your daughter has the love and care she deserves, now from three parents instead of two."

Zoe turned rueful. "No, unfortunately. Vilem gave up a promising future as a painter for political haranguing. He'd rather complain about the wrongs in life than work toward changing them. Or work, period. Frantiska and Charis have moved into my home. Frantiska is a better mother than I could ever be, but I'm a better father than Vilem." She reached into her tote. "I brought some photographs taken at your daughter's second birthday."

Lala scrolled through them, several of the children playing, and a few of the families gathered in the parlor, evoking memories of happy times.

"I'll understand if you want to cut out the Chermaks from the photograph," Zoe said. "It still shocks me how many people say awful things about others, but I worry about the silent ones like Chermak more, the greedy hypocrite. He works to stabilize Germany's government while privately undermining it for his own profit. You know, Chermak took out a two million mark loan from Germany prior to reparations. Since the devaluation of their currency, his payments amount to nothing compared to the koruna."

Lala invited Zoe to see the apartment in mid-progress. Zoe immediately noticed her photograph of Charis, the first Lala had bought, hanging in the playroom. She commented how useful the room would be for the children.

"I should return home," Zoe said as Lala finished the tour. "Charis likes me to be there when she wakes from her nap."

"I know the feeling. Once we're set up here, why don't you bring her by?"

***

Winter danced in with holiday cheer. By mid-January the festive decorations vanished, leaving no diversion from the short days and cold weather. Brisk winds rippled the river's water and shook the naked branches of trees while gray skies hovered for days like a bad omen.

Lala had avoided serious problems in the early stages of her project; she knew that luck wouldn't last, and it didn't. A section of the upper floor flooded when a water pipe burst, which caused an exterior wall to partially collapse. That would set back completion of the hotel from next Christmas to spring 1926.

Lala walked to the hotel to see the extent of the damage. Wood barriers surrounded a stretch of rubble. The foreman had cordoned off a section of the street near the collapse. She looked up at the gaping hole in the side of the second building. The wall had fallen on a quiet side street without damaging the main structure. It could have been worse. Lala set aside her schedule and switched her focus toward whatever could get done.

Her plans changed again when the project foreman showed up at her office.

"Ma'am, the repair is not going as well as we had expected. The water has gotten into crevasses in the walls. It freezes at night and thaws during the day, further weakening the structure."

"Will the wall collapse even more?"

He looked grim. "Can't say for sure, but it might."

"I have deliveries to that address scheduled all week."

"I'd advise you to find another place for them."

She leaned back in her chair and mulled the problem. "Has this sidelined any of your workers?"

"A few, ma'am"

"Send them here. They can move the smaller items from the ground floor storage room into the attic or next door to free up more space." She gave him the key to the small apartment. "See how much you can stow in the rooms across the way to free up space downstairs. I'll have Bente contact the vendors to postpone shipments if possible."

As winter gave way to spring, one critical decision remained – choosing craftsmen to build the furnishings. She reviewed the bids, all higher than anticipated. Weighing the need for quality over cost, she searched through a file of clippings from newspapers and journals that spoke of the modernist movement. In an interview with Walter Gropius, architect-director of the Bauhaus School of Design in Germany, he endorsed the use of machinery to create items as beautiful as they are functional. Could luxury and mass production co-exist?

Lala brought the subject up during dinner.

"Why not?" said Josef. "They did in the factory. We turned out beautiful, well-made pieces at a fraction of the price of handcrafted furniture."

"I ought to contact the managers and invite them to submit a bid."

"Mama, is that the factory where you and Papa used to work?"

"It is, love," said Lala. "Why?"

"I want to go there and see it."

"I wish I could, but I'll be too busy—"

"Why don't I go in your place?" volunteered Josef.

"What about Amalie?"

"I'll take her with me."

***

Josef left on the morning train with Amalie. Bente had the day off, so Lala returned to inspect the progress on the hotel. Iron flanges had been installed to stabilize the wall, now half repaired. The rubble had been cleared. Anyone walking along Tržiště Street might not see—

Ahead, Lala spotted Willete crossing the street, dressed to the nines, heading in the direction of Old Town. Lala waited until she'd passed before returning home.

A bad omen.

CHAPTER THIRTY-FOUR

"...and when the train left the station everything outside started moving, faster and faster, and all I saw were buildings, but then the buildings were farther apart and soon there were hardly any, just trees and fields and farms until we reached the station, and...."

Lala listened as Amalie described the day she spent with Josef in the town where Lala's parents had brought her as a girl not much older than her daughter. She saw it anew through Amalie's eyes as she remembered feeling the same sensation during her first time on a train.

"Much has changed," noted Josef. "They're enlarging the station. The shops nearby have reopened, but twice as many have been added along the street past the market. And two new factories have opened up, including a weapons manufacturing plant owned by your employer."

"And the Smetana Factory?"

"Strahov passed away so Hajek manages it now. He thought of changing the name, but he's holding off until you complete your project."

"Did he say why?"

"He felt it would add prestige to the company as he expects to be a part of its success." Josef gestured toward Amalie.

"Tell me tonight, love. Amalie, what did you think of Papa's factory?"

"It was big."

Josef said, "Hajek gave us a tour, which Amalie enjoyed, didn't you?"

"Yes, I did. I saw the big office where Papa used to work, and you, too, Mama, and the rooms where they cut the wood and make furniture, and then Papa and I walked down a long, long hall to the room where Grandpa Jakob used to make furniture."

She took a bite of potato. "Everybody was very nice to Papa and me. And they all said nice things about you, Mama. Mr. Hajek said you saved everyone during the Great War."

"I wouldn't go so far as that but it's lovely to hear."

"He said you and Papa are like family, and he'll give you a good deal."

"A good deal of what, love?" asked Lala.

Josef chuckled. "She means a good price on the bid. I doubt you'll do better." He finished his wine. "Afterward I asked Smolak to drive us to your former house. That nearby section of woods had been cleared and a road put in for new homes. The current homeowners invited us in and let us wander the property. We walked to the hill that overlooked my former home, though you could barely see it now through the trees, then we visited your father's grave."

"Papa and I put four pebbles on the gravestone, two for us and two for you and Bubbie."

She cupped Amalie's chin. "Thank you, love." She presumed Josef didn't take Amalie to the mansion.

"I showed her the bushes you had planted after you met Armin," said Josef. "Amalie asked so many questions, about you and me and him."

Ruth entered the dining room to clear away the dishes. "Miss Amalie, do you want to finish your potato before I take your plate?"

"Yes, please."

Lala added, "After you're finished, go play in your bedroom while Papa and I talk awhile, then I'll come in and read you a story from any book you choose."

Amalie rose from the table. "No book. I want you to tell me a story about Armin."

She looked to Josef. "I will, Amalie."

Lala and Josef left Ruth to clean up while they returned to the parlor. Josef gave her the bid to peruse as he poured two glasses of cognac.

"I can't thank you enough, love," said Lala. "This will compensate for some of the overruns due to the collapse, which means I'll retain more of my commission. How did you get the bid so low?"

He swirled his glass and took a sip. "I prepared a convincing speech, but it turned out to be unnecessary. Hajek expressed gratitude toward us both, and wasn't surprised to learn you were handling the hotel project. I felt proud, and yet ashamed."

"Ashamed? Of what?"

"Myself. My thinking. I knew the factory thrived under your tenure, but my distaste for the products blinded me to your successes. I never associated it with your input, nor credited you with the skills you developed there and brought to subsequent projects."

"You never saw it for yourself, having been forced out."

She set her snifter on the table. "Was it strange being back there after all this time?"

"More pleasant than strange. Unlike before, no one recognized me."

"You're not the only one Smolak drives around in that automobile anymore."

"Join us next time we travel back."

"I'd like that."

"We'll stay overnight – at the Excelsior. Then we can see the plaque you had Smolak mount in the garden."

"I wondered if he'd told you." After writing her request to him, the chauffeur saw to having the bronze plaque made, cast with the inscription:

Dedicated to Armin Smetana
Beloved son, friend and artist
1890 – 1914

The casting included a dragonfly above his name and a bumblebee added to the lower left corner. She considered installing the plaque by the bushes where as a child he'd stashed his drawings of the naked stableman, and later had hidden Karel's love letters. Ultimately she decided it should rest in a happier place and chose the rose garden.

"Zahradnik would allow us to enter the garden without checking in. Are you sure you want to stay there?"

"I'm ready, if you and Amalie stand by my side."

CHAPTER THIRTY-FIVE

With the wall secured and the plumbing repaired, work on the hotel's interiors continued. Hajek sent his best workers to build the furniture onsite and supervise the installation. Bente's husband Petr applied for a painting position. The foreman, impressed with his skill, hired him on. Bente found out when Petr boasted how he earned the job on his own merit. Back on schedule, Lala was about to leave for a site inspection when the telephone rang.

"Lala? Would you mind stopping by to pick up your dresses?" Paulina asked.

Ah, Josef's "salary", she thought, until she heard Mamie in the background say, "Don't tell her that. Say it's for Amalie." Paulina shushed Mamie before saying to Lala, "Please come over."

What were those two scheming? "I must stop at the hotel first. Give me an hour."

Lala met with the foreman, who assured her all was proceeding on schedule. She went from room to room, checking the work. In the ballroom she spotted Petr on a ladder, painting an arch between columns. Nearby she watched Petr's assistant slide his metal drywall knife over a cracked wall, slowly and methodically, filling the cracks and smoothing the surface. For a moment it reminded her of Josef, of his hands running over her body with the same deftness and skill. Josef's talent in the bedroom plastered over many a small fissure in their marriage.

Upstairs she found three workmen finishing the platform in the freshly painted suite, the table and chairs safely ensconced beneath a drop cloth. She lifted the cloth from a chair to inspect the upholstery; precisely as ordered.

"How much longer will it take to complete this suite?" she asked the workers.

The head carpenter removed his hat and wiped his brow. "Another day at least, maybe two. Then we'll start on the three odd-numbered rooms from the side that collapsed."

The carpenter and his assistant took a freshly sawed board from a workman to install. The workman tossed the extra piece onto a pile of wood cuttings.

"What will you be doing with those scraps?" she asked the carpenter.

"We'll salvage as much as possible."

She picked up the cut piece and asked, "What about this piece?"

"It's too small, Ma'am."

"Then I'd like it cut it into blocks for a little boy, some made into squares and some into circles. Sanded, but left unvarnished so I can paint them."

"I'll have my apprentice do it," he said, then wiped his brow again.

Next she inspected the repairs. Petr's crew had worked their magic on it; no one could tell the wall had collapsed. Satisfied, she left for her next appointment.

A brisk fifteen minute walk brought her to Paulina's. Miss Horáčková greeted her and brought her into Paulina's back room. Mamie's presence didn't surprise her, but Josef's did.

"What have you done?" she asked, suspecting whatever it was would be pleasant.

Paulina and Mamie huddled together behind Paulina's desk. Lala noticed the forged artwork was missing.

Josef stepped forward. "Thanks to these ladies, I have something for you, something I've neglected to give you before now. Something from me to express how much you mean to me, now and always."

"Love, you already gave me that navette ring."

He rolled his eyes. "That gaudy hunk of metal? That was fake."

Her mouth flew open. "You knew?"

"Not when I bought it, but Mamie told me—"

Lala glared at her. "Mamie!"

"Let him have his say."

Lala returned her attention to Josef.

He reached into his pocket and retrieved a small box. Then he got down on one knee.

She giggled. "Are you proposing?"

Mamie and Paulina shushed her in unison. Chastened, and curious, she raised her hands in surrender and waited.

Josef opened the box and turned it toward her to see.

Inside sat a ring that looked exactly like the one she lost.

Josef took it out of the box and showed it to her before he slipped in on her finger. The markings, the inscription, the C-shaped scratch on the pearl...

This was not a copy. This was the real thing.

"Josef, how on earth did you...?"

"You can thank these ladies."

Paulina wore the biggest grin and Mamie looked ready to burst open like an overbaked potato. She nudged Paulina. "Tell her the whole story, and don't leave anything out."

"Lala, you gave us the idea to use Willete's fascination with royalty to trick her. We knew the bait had to be special, not just someone titled, but an actual royal. We chose Princess Cecilie, Kaiser Wilhelm's daughter-in-law. Mamie got her lady's maid to play the part."

"But isn't the princess tall and dark-haired, the opposite of that young French girl?"

"You mean Veronique? I scared her off years ago," said Mamie. "My current maid, Gretel, is German. Her mother was a house maid but her father was a duke, if you get my drift, so she understood what was needed. As soon as Willete saw me bowing in front of 'Cecilie' she was convinced. She begged me to introduce her, but I kept saying it wouldn't be proper."

Paulina continued, "We lured her for months; she'd come here hoping for a glimpse of the princess. Finally Mamie set the trap by allowing Willete to join her entourage and offering to present her when the princess arrived for a fitting. Gretel played her role brilliantly. While everyone fawned over her royal highness, Gretel extended her hand and as Willete bowed, she caught sight of your navette ring, which Josef kindly lent us."

"Kindly? He was more than happy to, after I blabbed it was fake," said Mamie. "Willete gushed over it as I expected. Gretel let it slip the 'prince' gave it to her after she caught him philandering with the wife of a duke. Then Gretel admired Willete's ring, saying how elegant it was. That flattered Willete, but when the princess offered to trade, Willete said no; her ring meant so much to her. I thought we missed our chance, but Paulina salvaged it brilliantly."

Paulina continued, "I believed the ring's real value to her came from taking it from you. Willete had expressed curiosity about the Toulouse-Lautrec hanging on my wall. I could see it appealed to her. I explained I took it as collateral for a loan, without naming names. She wasn't aware it was a forgery but obviously knew it belonged to Josef. When she turned down the exchange, I thanked her. 'Lala would be devastated if the ring were truly gone,' I said."

Mamie shook her finger "That did the trick. Willete made an offer to Gretel – if the princess bought the Toulouse-Lautrec from Paulina, Willete would exchange the artwork for her ring. The princess 'demanded' to buy the painting. Paulina cried, 'Now Lala has lost her ring forever,' but as the princess was willing to part with her navette, would she sell it to Paulina to give it to Lala? She made an offer, Willete countered and eventually outbid her. When she left to get money to pay for it, we laughed so hard you could have heard us in Berlin."

"But that wasn't the end of it," said Paulina. "The next day Willete returned to demand her ring back from the princess; she found out from Klement the art was a forgery. I expressed shock, for I knew the person who asked for a loan had no idea as he bought it from reputable source. Willete couldn't argue that, otherwise she'd admit her husband deliberately cheated Josef. She stormed out, bragging that at least she got a good price on her ring. You should have heard what she called me when she found out it was as fake as the drawing."

"I'm stunned. I can't believe you did this all for me."

Mamie waved her hand. "Aw, honey, you would have done it if you weren't so busy. We just stepped in. Besides, I loved taking that sow down a couple of pegs."

"I can't thank you all enough. This ring means more to me now than it did before." She kissed Josef's cheek, whispering in his ear she'd thank him properly at home. "Mamie, where is this Gretel?"

"It's best you don't meet now."

"But I must thank her."

"Don't bother. You'd be amazed what a woman will do for the price of a navette ring and a gorgeous dress."

CHAPTER THIRTY-SIX

THE HOTEL MODERNI
GRAND OPENING RECEPTION
SATURDAY, THE TWELFTH OF JUNE
NINETEEN TWENTY-SIX
AT TWENTY O'CLOCK

Lala fanned herself with the engraved invitation announcing the event. Newspaper reporters, photographers and critics gathered outside the Neo-Renaissance mansion on Tržiště Street underneath the new awning that extended to the curb. Lala peered at them from the window in Chamber One.

A reporter, his writing pad at the ready, kept moving his jaw up and down. Chewing gum. Lala figured him to be American, the well-dressed man behind him as well. Someone from Architectural Record, with any luck. A good review from the prestigious journal and clients would follow.

A few guests arrived early and mingled with the crowd. Lala spotted Hajek with his wife and their daughter Marie, who was engaged to be married. Hajek had booked the wedding reception in the hotel's ballroom.

Lala backed away from the window and checked the mantle clock – only thirty minutes left before the grand opening. Underneath her gown she wore the pin her father had bought for her wedding, hanging from a chain, for luck. She touched it through the material, felt it press against her heart. Time to go downstairs for a final check, then join the reception line. But first, so as not to forget in the excitement of the evening, Lala jotted an invaluable memo – find out how best to remove chewing gum from surfaces.

In the ballroom a jazz quartet set up their instruments on the dais. Lala hired them to perform their version of popular songs, believing the interpretive nature of both music and décor would fit together. She gazed around the room as they warmed up, the melody sounding familiar, yet different – exactly as she meant her interiors to function.

Lala passed through the ground floor areas for a final look and proceeded to the lobby before the appointed time.

Zahradnik sat in a chair, Smolak and cane in waiting, his face tight. Most might think this expressed impatience, but Lala, who'd worked with him for almost two years, knew he was nervous, and nothing but a successful launch would ease that.

Bente had made her own gown to pacify her husband, though she did accept some advice on constructing it from Paulina. When they arrived, Lala overheard Petr complain to his wife about having to dress up in a bourgeois suit, but four-year-old Petr looked blissful in his father's arms. Bente confessed to Lala that the boy's affection for Josef nudged his father to give the child more attention.

Paulina stood far back from the entrance, Ivo by her side, holding her hand, and Jacub between them, holding the small camera Lala and Josef had given him for his birthday in March. Jacub had turned eleven... *look how tall he's grown since then.* Mid-chest to his mother.

Her sister's acclaimed spring collection had finally earned her an invitation to show her fashions in Paris. Tonight she wore an exquisite but subtle gown, as Lala knew she would. She wanted Lala to be the star of the evening. The same reason why Mamie opted to arrive late to keep the focus of the guests on the hotel and Lala's work.

Nearby sat her mother, a walking cane propped by her side. She'd aged markedly; her joints had stiffened and she'd shrunk two centimeters in height, but her mind remained sharp. She groused about her looks, but Lala found every crease and line in her face beautiful.

Amalie sauntered by. Last August, Lala and Josef took their child to her first day of school. Amalie cried before going in, Josef and she cried going home. *Now look at her, poised and confident. Hard to believe she's turning seven.*

As her daughter neared Bubbie, Sarah grabbed her to smooch her cheeks, but Amalie pulled away.

"No, Bubbie."

"What do you mean, no?"

"I'm too big for that. No more kissing."

"All right, big girl, then no more cookies."

Lala knew her mother meant it. Would her daughter?

With an eyeroll Amalie offered her cheek and said, "Just two."

When her grandmother released her, Amalie danced away. Her eyes sparkled as much out of excitement as for the red dress her aunt had created for her. After Lala wore her lavender day dress, Amalie crossed that color off her list and declared she would only wear pink or red from here on, or as she put it, the color of cherries. Paulina complied; she appliquéd cherries on the white collar and ordered shoes and gloves that resembled the bark of cherry trees.

Lala and Josef promised Amalie she could stay until half past eight, then Ruth would bring her home, along with Petr. Ruth gladly accepted the overtime, which also allowed her to be present for the opening celebration.

Amalie danced by again. Lala watched her as she fluttered her hands like wings and spun around to make her skirt billow out... *like a bumblebee.* Her heart soared as she peered through the front window at the night sky and whispered, "I miss you, dragonfly."

"What did you say, love?" asked Josef, but she shook her head. He looked resplendent in his new tuxedo coat, more modern than his cutaway tailcoat and top hat. And handsome. He still preferred to comb his hair straight back instead of parting it, as many younger men favored, but it suited him. Lala assumed he did it to show off how thick his hair remained, even as it had turned white. He reached out to pluck a piece of lint from her gown and she thanked him with a smile. The little thrill she felt whenever she looked at him had returned, and in many ways, had intensified.

At two minutes before eight, the hotel staff gathered in the lobby to greet the incoming guests with trays of champagne.

Josef extended his hand to her.

She took it, held tight, and waited for the lobby clock to strike eight.

CHAPTER THIRTY-SEVEN

Lala had vaguely recollected she was born in August; notations on the back of mama and papa Groissman's photograph revealed her actual birth date fell on the twentieth. She kept it a secret. She would continue to celebrate her birthday on the twelfth of July to honor her mother Sarah and father Jakob, who raised her. They had given her the new date to fit her new identity. That included a new year of birth, as their marriage necessitated Lala to be a year younger, something she could finally appreciate. No one other than Josef, Sarah, Paulina and Mr. Cerveny knew she would turn thirty-five that summer.

Josef and Paulina had had the foresight to reserve the ballroom of the Moderni for Lala's birthday celebration, otherwise it wouldn't have been available. Every chamber had been booked through September. Locals and visitors alike flocked to the restaurant to glimpse the new hotel, and the public rooms for rent had only scattered availability. The success of the hotel, while not universal, was unequivocal amongst its growing legions of fans.

The Slovo praised the Moderni's unbiased hiring

practices, safety protections and the fair wages paid its workers, but rebuked its elite status. The Lidu made similar observations, admiring the project's vision but criticizing its decadence. The Bohemia and the Listi held the opposite view; both condemned the radical design but praised its exclusivity. The Tagblatt wrote two articles; the front page carried a column touting the facility as a world-class addition to the city, while the society page focused on the guest list, describing their denizens mingling with the upper echelons of art, architecture, and politics.

Lala's assumptions about the two American journalists proved correct. The gum chewer worked for the Associated Press, an organization that covered international news for several American newspapers. Congratulatory letters arrived from Karel, Gershom, and Mr. Robertson. The dapper man, who introduced himself that evening, had published a flattering article in Architectural Record.

She spotted Paulina, Ivo, and Jacub entering the ballroom and rushed over to greet them with a kiss. Lala turned in a circle before Paulina, knowing she would want to see how well the gown she'd designed for Lala fit.

Paulina nodded her approval.

"Happy birthday, Antila." Jacub handed her a small package.

"Thank you, Jacub."

"I made that for you."

"May I open it now?" With his assent she unwrapped the gift, a framed photograph of her, taken at the grand opening.

"I took that picture with the camera you gave me."

"It's very good, Jacub," She kissed his cheek. "You have a talent for photography."

Ivo said, "He's been assisting Zoe on weekends, carrying

her bags and helping her set up equipment, and in return she's teaching him how to use the camera."

"Mother and Father introduced me," Jacub noted.

"Mother and Father?" Lala turned to his parents.

Paulina looked back wistfully. "He's decided he's too old to call us Mama and Papa anymore."

"I'm so glad you're here. This may be the last time we see each other for a while."

The band grew loud, so Paulina leaned in. "Why don't you and Josef come to Paris next month when I present my fashions? I can get you tickets to the event. If it's successful—"

"It will be, Paulina."

"Then you and Josef can help me find a location to open a second boutique there."

"Wouldn't that be marvelous?" Lala sighed. "A new project is in development, so I may not be able to travel then."

"What is it?"

"It's too soon to say anything, but I'll keep you apprised. She asked Ivo, "What will you and Jacub be doing?"

"We'll join Paulina in Paris until September. Then I begin a whirlwind tour of European universities; I've been invited to lecture on my research. Jacub will come along."

A waiter offered the adults champagne. They toasted each other as Josef swooped in and greeted the Chytrys. "May I steal my wife away for a few minutes?"

Ivo nudged his son. "Let's go say hello to Grandmama." To Lala he added, "We'll take her home tonight."

Paulina wiped lipstick from Lala's cheek. "You go mingle and we'll talk later."

Josef led Lala out of the ballroom toward the lobby.

Miko Johnston

"Where are we going, Josef?"

"You'll see." He brought her into one of the private meeting rooms. Waiting inside was Mr. Cerveny and his assistant, Tomas. Both stood when she entered.

She set her champagne glass on the table. "What a delightful surprise. Josef, thank you for inviting them, but why aren't you in the ballroom with the others?" It was then she noticed a folder holding papers. A business transaction at her party?

Cerveny offered his hand; she shook it.

"Mrs. Smetana, let me first wish you a happy birthday. I do not want to take you away from your celebration any longer than necessary so I'll get straight to the point. I am retiring, and Tomas will be handling your affairs from here on, along with Mr. Smetana's." He paused and looked to Josef. "Your husband wanted me to secure something to present to you as a gift, however I asked him to allow me that privilege. I've known you as long as he has, and while our relationship has been professional, I have, and always shall, hold you in high regard. Please allow me, as my final act as your executor, to present you with this." He handed her the folder.

"Is this a document I need to sign?"

She sensed Josef becoming emotional. A glance revealed him smiling but his eyes brimmed with tears.

"No," he said, "Not to sign. To treasure."

"Open it," urged Cerveny, also smiling.

Inside was a police report from the town of Kharkiv in the Soviet Republic of Ukraine.

"Why does this town sound familiar?"

498

"The pogrom survivors from your shtetl split into two groups. The ones that assimilated settled in that town," said Cerveny.

"It's where that Radova woman was murdered," added Josef.

As she read another name cropped up. Mr. Vichenko, the farrier. "He confessed to her murder." Confused, she looked to Cerveny. "Is there some reason you're showing me this?"

"You told your husband something that made him suspicious — in the days leading up to the pogrom, Radova began paying her bills with cheese."

"I remember the butcher telling me that."

"Mr. Smetana wondered why a woman of means would pay her bills with cheese, and the answer finally occurred to him—"

"Cheese is perishable," Josef finished Cerveny's point.

Cerveny flipped to the second page of the document. "In a deathbed confession, Vichenko told police the two had been drinking heavily on the anniversary of the attack when Radova revealed she took a bribe from two Cossacks who wanted to punish the man who invented the cart latch. She prepared to escape with her son and as much as she could carry off before they struck, which is why she'd been paying her bills with cheese. The Cossacks surprised her by attacking hours earlier and razing the shtetl. Her son ran back to the village to save Vichenko's daughter, and they both perished. When Vichenko learned the truth, he killed her."

As the reality of the news sunk in, Lala felt faint.

Josef helped her into a chair. "All the years you felt guilt for what happened because of your papa. It was never true; he wasn't responsible for the pogrom. The person who was, has been avenged."

"Josef, you arranged all this for me?"

"Love, I've always told you I know you better than you think."

She finally understood the prediction of her mother's fortune teller, *"A man close to you would do something to free you from a great burden."*

Lala thanked the men and wished them well. The news, coupled with the happy occasion, left her giddy and elated. She took Josef's arm and returned to the ballroom.

A waiter approached, drawing a crowd. While Josef greeted a client, she put her champagne glass on his tray and asked him to bring her a cup of mint tea and a few bread canapes without toppings.

A familiar tinkling came from the piano. Amalie played a tune she'd learned and sang along. Many guests tittered when she began, but soon quieted and listened as her euphonious voice rang out. She sat still until they applauded, then curtsied and walked back to Ruth, ready to take her home. Lala heard many guests complimenting Amalie's singing and poise, especially for a girl so young. No one applauded louder or longer than Sarah.

Lala asked Ruth to leave the folder on her desk when she brought Amalie home, then joined her mother.

"Wasn't she grand?" gushed Sarah, still applauding. She smiled, and her face lit up like the sun, the love for her granddaughter apparent. "So what did Josef give you for your birthday, besides the party?"

"The greatest gift of all." Lala leaned down and whispered in her mother's ear, "Tell your fortune teller she was right."

"What about?"

"Everything," she said as she headed back to Josef, standing at a cocktail table with Moritz and Mamie. The men must be in deep political conversation, Lala thought, judging by how far Mamie's eyes had rolled back in her head.

"I came to rescue you," joked Lala, and Mamie rewarded her with a hug.

"And not a moment too soon. These two are still fighting over Germany's destiny." Mamie signaled a waiter carrying glasses of champagne. "Over here, if you don't mind." She took a coupe and offered one to Lala, who declined.

"Is your new home finished?" Lala asked.

"Almost, that's partly why we're here, waiting for it to be completed. We'll be living there half the year and when we're not traveling we'll be in Paris or here. We gave up our suite in that stuffy hotel in Wenceslas Square. I found a place I like better."

"Where," asked Lala, before it occurred to her they intended to stay at the Moderni.

Their husbands overheard and joined their conversation. Josef asked Moritz, "When are you going to return to Germany?"

"Not for the foreseeable future, Josef. I have no desire to go back, something you should understand."

"If you mean staying at the Excelsior, I finally have. Lala, Amalie and I took two rooms a few months back, had a lovely time. Finally saw my son's memorial plaque."

Lala couldn't tell if Josef hadn't grasped what Moritz implied, or if the time he spent with Amalie had given him a more optimistic view on the world.

Moritz grimaced. "The Nazis held their annual rally in Nuremburg last week, their biggest turnout yet. They're clever, I'll give them that. They've abandoned taking the government by coup d'état and switched to the ballot box. If conditions in Germany don't improve, they could succeed."

"You're too pessimistic, Moritz. You overlook all the good that has happened. Your foreign minister and Aristide Briand just brokered the Locarno Pact together. Imagine, less than ten years after the Great War, a Frenchman and a German negotiated a peace agreement." He patted Moritz on the shoulder. "There's hope. There is always hope."

Mamie took her husband's arm. "Come, let's get a real drink at the bar while we still can."

Alone again, Josef took Lala in his arms. "Would you like to dance?"

"Perhaps later."

"What about a glass of champagne?"

"What I'd really like is some mint tea."

"I have it here, Madam," said the waiter who'd taken her order. "And your bread," he added as he placed both on the cocktail table.

Josef thanked the waiter. "Your stomach bothering you? You didn't have any trouble last month at the grand opening celebration."

"Different problem, love, and different cause." She gestured toward her mother struggling with her cane to stand. Two busboys immediately materialized, taking her by the arm and escorting her to the Chytrys.

Josef slipped his arm around Lala's shoulder. "Your mother will need more help from here on."

"I'd like to move her closer to us. What if we turned the vacant shop downstairs into an office, along with our office above, and convert the small apartment into a place for her to live?"

"Why not bring her to our apartment?"

"Oh love, that's sweet but it wouldn't work now."

Josef nodded in understanding. "Too many stairs for her

to climb."

"That too."

Josef looked quizzically at her.

"We won't have enough space for my mother to move in with us."

"Why can't she take the guest room?"

"We're going to need it." Lala set down her mint tea. She nibbled a piece of plain bread as she turned to him and smiled.

Life had taken her to unexpected places, the journey equally tragic and miraculous. Horror and sorrow could give way to contentment, even joy, through the gift of love. No matter what, there's hope, she acknowledged as she ran her palm over her belly. There is always hope.

ACKNOWLEDGEMENTS

This book could not have been written without the help, support and encouragement of many people. I'm especially indebted to Heather Ames and Bonnie Schroeder of the Pacific Online Writers Group, who worked with me chapter by chapter. Many members of the Whidbey Writers Group, Sequels Group and Tommys Group helped with earlier incarnations of this novel, and I'll add a shout-out for The Writers in Residence, my long-time blogging group.

Special thanks go out to my beta readers: Renee Le Verrier, Sue van Vonno, Betsy Fleetwood, and Jill Amadio, as well as Audrey Mackaman, who designed the cover and interior for this book. Unending gratitude to Kitty Kladstrup, who edited the manuscript, Dot Read for the final polish, and to Mike McNeff, who saw to getting it published. And last but certainly not least, my husband Allan.

AUTHOR BIO

Miko Johnston first contemplated a writing career as a poet at age six. That notion ended four years later when she found no "Help Wanted" ads for poets in the classified section, but her desire to write persisted. After graduating from New York University, she headed west to pursue a career as a television and print journalist until deciding she preferred the more believable realm of fiction. Johnston lives in Washington (the big one) with her rocket scientist husband.

www.ingramcontent.com/pod-product-compliance
Lightning Source LLC
Chambersburg PA
CBHW030237030726
47493CB00022B/84